Pathlighter

Book One of the Pathlighter Trilogy

Rob Leigh

Praise for Pathlighter

"Non-stop action, compelling characters, intriguing villains, and expansive worldbuilding." —Quinn Giguiere, *Silverstones Blog*

"Leigh manages to create a really spectacular story, mixing themes such as grief, loss, and found family with the tension of having to combat against demons while not knowing if you can trust in those on your side." —Jamedi, *Jam Reviews*

"A page turner that really leaves you hanging for more at the end." —Joshua Walker, Author of *An Exile of Water and Gold*

"If you enjoy deities, mythology, and religion in your books, here is a must-read for you." —Beard of Darkness Book Reviews

"Darkly original with a plot that hooks you instantly." —Scott Palmer, Author of *A Memory of Song*

PATHLIGHTER

LEIGH BOOKS

Contents

Acknowledgement

I am proud to present to you *Pathlighter*, a novel that has been in the works for over a decade. It has been an incredible, transformative experience to see this story start from a small variation on Greek Myths and evolve into the novel you hold in your hands. Getting this book off the ground has been in no small part thanks to all of the people listed here.

Firstly, some of the earliest readers and providers of feedback for my work include former teachers Jenae Green, Staci Laird, Professor James Colburn, and Professor Shannon Olson. Their critique and encouragement gave me the confidence to continue working on personal projects like this one.

As writing this book became more and more of a reality, I had several people pushing me creatively. Among them, Caleb Asay got me into the juggernaut that is Sanderson and reinvigorated my passion for telling fantasy stories on the page during the pandemic. Nick Guerrier, the best DM to sit behind the screen, also has constantly pushed creativity for characters both on and off the gaming table. While you both may not see your influence in the everyday, I hope you see the results in this story.

Getting this book written was a time-consuming process, but getting it to resemble something readable took nearly as long. For that, I have three people chiefly to thank. Annie Laird received this story in its earliest form and gave feedback that took this novel in the right direction. Claire Ashgrove provided chief developmental editing on this story, and I can't thank her enough for her measured and insightful expertise in the process. I also had an exceptional copy editor in Jason Letts, whose experience and services are impossible to understate.

Others to thank regarding the publishing, marketing, and writing process include Professor Kevin Clouther, Leigha Atkisson, Matt Daniel, Megan Bormann, Matt Hebert, Marilyn Deal, and Daly Chochon. Your support, contributions, advice, and insight have meant so much throughout this process, and I don't think any amount of thanks will fully express my gratitude.

The cover art of this book was illustrated by Felix Ortiz, an incredible talent who brought my characters to life and showed excitement for this project right from the start.

Lastly and most importantly, I would like to thank my parents, Scott and Krista. You have both been my biggest supporters throughout this whole process from the time I first started forming the idea for this novel. You are the ones who took me to the library from an early age, turned out the light when I fell asleep reading, and are still weathering the results of showing your seven-year-old *Lord of the Rings* almost twenty years ago. This book would not exist without you, and the support you have given me means the world.

Because of all of these people, *Pathlighter* is now a reality. I hope you enjoy the novel.

Part I

The Chosen of Iarus

An Observant Speech

J ames stepped carefully around the huddling, sick townspeople crowding the ragged stone paths.

There were more than yesterday, he noted. They didn't seem to pay him much mind. Even so, he kept a hand on the hilt of his sword as he trekked through the dusty alleys, a cloth covering his mouth and nose. This illness was starting to spread at a worrisome rate, and there had been no indication that it would die out.

The waning sun cast a blue haze over the bleak, bleached stone buildings, and a weak breeze deposited a thin layer of sand onto any uncovered surface. James could feel the grainy sediment grinding against his foot in his right boot. There was no use emptying it. He squinted above the rooftops toward the sun and its gradual lean toward the west. He would have to hurry if he was going to make it to the Pathlighter's Outpost on time. James's attention snapped toward the square as he recognized the sound of voices, many voices. It was odd to hear conversation at all anymore. Most of the people were sick, and those who were healthy hardly left their homes. He approached the square as another feeble wind blew particles of sand at him.

He came to the square to see a few hundred people huddled together. The wide, rectangular plaza was packed with the sick and healthy alike. *This is unusual.* He frowned. Maroon and Gray banners hung all over the courtyard, the sigils of Boane. It was said that these were the holiest of colors. However, James assumed the flag was like this because they were two of the easiest dyes to get ahold of in the desert.

The blue warmth of the day had taken a toll on the crowd. Everyone was covered in sweat but didn't dare remove any of their heavy layers and expose their skin to the blowing sand. People fanned themselves with their hands or any items that could catch the air. There was a dour mood pervading the gathering. The sickness overtaking everyone had made the people of Boane more desperate than ever. Some praying to the gods, some begging the consul, for all the good it did. Some had just resigned themselves to whatever fate came. Looking to its leader for answers, the sprawling city-state had been answered with silence. Clerics from the Temple of Iarus were taking advantage of the resulting unrest to push their holy doctrine on the desperate people.

James stepped into the square at the edge of the crowd. He didn't want to draw too much attention to himself. He was the only person in a full cloak under the sun. The heat of the day never really bothered him. On the contrary, the sun's rays felt refreshing the hotter they grew.

At the center of the square were three wells that had been boarded up and sealed. The water had been infected with the sickness everyone had been calling the Mangler. There was a man with a hooked nose in rusted armor pacing between the springs, apparently giving a speech. Judging by the man's rigid posture, James guessed that it was not a cheerful one. Hook Nose looked to be part of the Garrison, the consul's own city watchmen and soldiers. James pondered what he could be doing out in the square.

"My brothers and sisters, these days reflect dark times!" the soldier bellowed. "I see those among me who are sick, who are dying. I see those who cannot eat or clothe themselves."

Well, this one is observant. James shook his head. *Looks like the Garrison is making trouble.* What was the palace's own guard trying to stir up?

Not much for him to be concerned about. He wasn't consul, and it was looking more and more like good luck that he wasn't. Deciding he was no longer interested in Hook Nose's observant speech, he began to weave through the crowd. His head down, he pushed against the growing throng of tired and overheated onlookers as the speaker continued.

"Our people are mauled by disease, stripped of sustenance and dignity. Why did this happen? This is punishment by the gods!" The nostrils on the man's spear-like nose flared as he glared at the onlookers. "This punishment is for the greed and ignorance of the consul! Iarus condemns this greed, and we share the Pathlighter's disapproval!"

James rolled his eyes in skepticism of this theory. Most days, he wasn't paying attention, but when he was, the religious fervor pushed his patience.

Hook Nose continued. "The consul has stood by as his people suffered and perished, but this suffering has not reached him. The suffering has thrust upon us a call to action!" The soldier's face was dark red as he lost coherence.

The crowd around him murmured in consensus.

"We must punish the consul and all who serve him, as the gods have willed! They have demanded his sacrifice so that we may survive. The Temple has heard this decree from the gods!" Hook Nose's eyes bulged, his raw screams echoed by the enraged gathering.

So that was the play. The Temple was using the Garrison to slowly turn Boane against the palace. Good thing James was leaving town for the port before this got much worse. He brushed past an old man with wispy hair. His hand collided with the cane the man was carrying, which clattered to the stone cobbling. James knelt and plucked the staff from the ground, placing it into the hands of the elder. He made sure that he didn't touch the old man. Many said the sickness could spread at the slightest touch.

The man's wrinkled face broke into a small smile as he clutched the cane with his spotted hands. His sightless eyes looked blankly in James's direction. "The Pathlighter bless you, boy."

James sighed and nodded at the old man. "If you say so," he said irritably. He turned and continued through the crowd out of the square.

The sun was getting lower in the sky, and the cobalt hue that blanketed the city became much deeper. He hurried to the outpost for the lamplighters, lowering his maroon facecloth as he left the more populous area of the city-state. The waning sun cast an elongated shadow from his form despite his average height. As he walked briskly to the outpost, his boots kicked up wispy amounts of sand. Scorching stuff was everywhere.

James's stern green eyes settled on the outpost, where Igard would be waiting. Dusk brought a cool gust of wind that blew through the alleyways. James shook the sand out of his stringy black hair and continued onward. The waning sun felt extremely warm against his tan skin, but it would be gone soon. After nightfall, the gusts of wind that came through the city would chill through the flesh.

Many of the houses that he walked past had been abandoned. Since the plague had swept through the city, many had fled northwest to the port city of Epot Detharn or tried to cross the sea. Some had no doubt unknowingly taken the plague with them. It was hard to find a ship that would take passengers in when sickness was spreading freely through the area, but some may have been able to convince a smuggler or destitute sailor to take them in. Refugees already didn't have much choice in where to go. The Dunes of Knost stretched beyond the eye's reach to the south, and short, craggy mountains jutted above the horizon toward the far west. James could never remember the names of the mountains. Boane was an immense settlement, but almost a third of its people had left in the wake of the plague, or possibly died. James didn't know which.

James noticed a man lying still in the street ahead of him. His gray skin was covered in tiny crimson lacerations, a sign of the plague. There was a reason that the common folk had named it the Mangler. Some said it attacked inner organs and split them apart as well as producing shallow cuts on the outer skin. Victims often never knew they had contracted it until they were vomiting blood or bleeding from the eyes.

The poor man lay on his back, sightless eyes that were already covered with a film of fine sand staring up at the sky. His collar glinted in the fading sunlight. James peered closer to see that the corpse was wearing a pendant. The talisman around his swollen neck was a pure blue gem engraved with an eagle flying through a storm, the symbol of Etah the Breathgiver. The man's dried, mutilated fingers still clutched the totem of the Wind Goddess.

James turned his head away in disgust and marched toward the Pathlighter's Outpost. If he was late again, Igard would dock his pay. "Scorch me," he swore.

The sky had turned a dark indigo as he finally trudged up the steps of the Outpost, a squat stone building that barely went above two stories.

His shadow rippled up the stairs, a blast of smoky air hitting his face as he strode through the ancient doorway. The low ceiling of the outpost flickered with firelight, and the stone block walls were covered with blackened, unlit lanterns hung from hooks. The center of the entry chamber held a massive bronze brazier. Even from the door, the domesticated heat from the fire soothed James's frustrations. Lamplighters in gray cloaks similar to his stood around the fire, some praying audibly to the gods, some silently mouthing the words. Many of the lamplighters had taken oaths of silence to escape the Temple's wrath. Thieves, heretics, dissenters. Crimes were forgiven if they vowed never to speak again and to serve the palace.

Igard, an older man with a forked beard, looked up at James as he came in. His bushy eyebrows knit together in irritation, forming a scratchy caterpillar above his face. "You're late again," Igard called across the chamber.

The other lamplighters stopped and turned around to look at James silhouetted in the doorway. Some smirked at him and went back to their prayer.

James hurried to the brazier and squeezed into the circle. One of the others, a girl named Lenia, glanced at him as he stepped up to the flames. He pretended not to notice and bowed his head as Igard continued the prayer.

"Acknowledge our faith, Iarus, so that the light of our flames may never die out. For we will provide the sacred light from the Pathlighter to those who live in darkness. Acknowledge our faith, Etah, so...."

James stared silently into the flames. He had heard this prayer thousands of times before, and he and Gemmi had *said* this prayer a thousand times before.

Igard continued, "We ask that you grant safety to those of us who serve your will. Protect those who deserve your grace. Protect us from evils, whether they be demon, Altujan, or man."

Igard ended the prayer and glanced at the cloaked lackeys around him, expectant of their adoration for a well-rehearsed prayer. "Off you go."

For most of the time since he had joined the palace's lamplighters around thirteen months ago, James had cursed the profession, only staying around for the money. He could never understand why Iarus could scorching care whether they lit giant torches through town at night. A trivial thing for a god to want. The Temple's stories of great heroes, Champions of Iarus and such, never detailed them wasting their time with lighting sticks in the night.

The lamplighters turned from the brazier and shuffled to the hanging lamps on the walls. James felt a hand on his shoulder when he stepped toward the wall to retrieve a lantern. The hand was of course connected to Igard, glaring.

"What's your excuse this time?" Igard grumbled.

James shrugged. "I was held up."

"You expect me to just go with that?"

"I'd expect that you'll use any excuse to dock my pay, so it doesn't really matter, does it? The Garrison was gathering people in the market."

Igard's eyes narrowed. "Why would they do that?"

James shook his head. "They didn't have many nice things to say about the consul. Seems that they blame him for the city's problems." The Garrison wasn't exactly wrong. Stories of the ruler's decadent life rivaled the grand tales of the gods that the Temple espoused, but there was tangible proof to the stories about the consul. Meanwhile, the city-state of Boane was dying.

The older lamplighter stroked one side of his beard thoughtfully. Old was perhaps a bit of an exaggeration, but a man in his forty-eighth year was considered aged in this part of the world. There was barely any gray in his beard. He pondered, "The consul's own guard?"

Igard turned to the rest of the group. "Travel in pairs tonight. We're under the employ of the palace, and the palace isn't very popular right now, but the Pathlighter's word still dictates that we do our jobs and spread his light. Don't forget why we're here." The beard whipped through the air as Igard snapped his gaze back to James, who was trying to sneak over to his lantern and leave. "You were late again. I have to dock your pay."

James threw his hands out in exasperation. "I told you I was held up."

"Were you held up the other times?" Igard retorted. "You're wasting the palace and the Pathlighter's time by being late. The penalty is half your usual pay. Spreading the light of Iarus is not a task for drifters."

"I can't buy enough to eat with that," James scoffed. "Prices have gone up six times since last week." More importantly, he couldn't save enough to charter a ship after his business in the port, and he would need to be gone after business was completed.

Igard tossed him a small pouch. The meager coins in the sack rattled as James caught it. The pouch had a considerable amount of air in it. James opened it and peered inside. Seven bronze bits occupied a narrow corner of the bag. He scowled at Igard and pocketed the purse before stomping to his lantern. He didn't intend to let this go. Gemmi wouldn't have let this go either.

Plucking the lantern from the hook, he took up the lighting staff resting against the wall next to it and plunged it into the fiery brazier. With the staff ignited, he lit the lantern and carried it out of the chamber.

The air outside was much colder now, and the sun had fully submerged behind the horizon. Only a faint aqua hue appeared in the westward sky. James sighed and began to plunk down the stone steps of the outpost. As he got to the bottom and plunged his boot into ankle-high sand, a voice came from behind him.

"It looks like we're the only two left," Lenia said.

James looked back up the steps and saw the girl standing expectantly up at the entrance to the tower. She grinned and briskly descended the stairs toward him. Her curly dark hair bounced with each step.

James held his lamp aloft. "Igard held me up. I thought I was the last one out."

She grinned again. "I waited."

He returned a smile and motioned in the direction of the city. The two of them strolled off toward the nearest alley. Their gray cloaks rustled in the chilled wind. Her hair smelled faintly of cinnamon. The smell wafted over to him as he looked upward. The stars were strangely absent, keeping the night dark other than the moon's scarlet glow. There weren't any clouds out when he had gone to the outpost, but he gave only minimal thought to this before pushing the thought from his mind.

Lenia held her lantern steady at shoulder height. "I never see you at the Temple." She looked down at her feet. "You're actually a pretty hard person to find. I don't see you inside the city either."

"I live in the Collar," he said nonchalantly. The seedy outskirts of Boane. He didn't like to have many people around, especially people who maintained the Temple of the Pathlighter. He had no reason to. The plague had only reinforced that notion. Although Lenia's company did seem to make the argument less sound.

They came to the first post. Each pole featured a dish at the top that was filled with oil. These posts were spread throughout the city every three blocks.

James and Lenia had taken the southwestern edge of the city near an uninhabited building he had sheltered in for a short time. He had been moving from dump to dump for the last few years now. At nineteen, he was now quite good at settling and moving on when needed. Since Gemmi had died, he preferred it this way.

"I'll take the one down the way and meet you near the square," Lenia said, her teeth peeking from behind her lips again.

James half smirked as she walked away. He watched her for a moment before setting to work. Stepping on the foothold toward the base of the post, he hoisted himself up and brandished the lighting staff. The little flame on the end of the pole flickered as he swung it around to the basin. He slowed his motion and stared at the tiny pinprick of light.

The flame grew a little. James felt a tugging sensation in his stomach as the flame expanded and billowed with a loud, rippling whoosh. James's wide green eyes were illuminated by the orange glow of the flames—he could look at them forever—as he held the staff.

For him, it was a simple thought. *Grow.* Like raising a hand or blinking. He felt calm around the heat, tranquil, and fire seemed to have the same comfort around him. It was ridiculous of course, but he often found himself thinking *at* the flames, the flickering spectacle. Without Gemmi, he really didn't have anyone else to talk to. Igard said that speaking into the flames was speaking to Iarus himself, but James wasn't sure. Iarus didn't seem like the listening type.

James plunged the torch into the thin layer of oil in the basin. The top of the post ignited and cast a warm glimmer over the alleyway. There were hundreds of these lamps all over the city. He would do this several dozen times throughout the night. James was about to climb down when a movement at the edge of his vision caught his gaze. He swept his eyes over the stone and peered through the flames in front of him toward the west.

Movement fluttered at the end of the alley again, and James saw a man in a black cloak peeking at him from behind a building. He couldn't make out the man's features. The bottom half of his face was covered by a cloth, and his hood was pulled low enough that his eyes were hidden. There was a dangerous readiness to him, a tension that was maintained with the expectation of a fight. He was decidedly foreign, as very few people wore black in Boane. Usual day-time temperatures would make black clothing intolerable. James noticed the slight shimmer of a polished blade at the stranger's side. Whoever this person was, he was a person who at least was ready for a fight.

Deciding he'd rather not meet this man, James slid down the post to the sand and stone below. He swore as a thick splinter in the wood split the skin on his right palm. He landed, clutching his hand. The wound was not deep but would keep bleeding until he took the sliver of wood out.

He glanced at the spot where he had seen the figure. The man was gone.

James breathed deeply, dispelling the unease from his system. He and Lenia were already behind, and he didn't intend to give Igard another reason to dock his pay. Bitterness swam through his mind as he remembered the seven measly bronze bits in his pouch. That wouldn't be enough to even buy stale bread, much less charter a ship, even with his saved coin. His stomach gurgled. It would barely be enough to keep him from starving.

He continued toward the north, shivering a bit in the now-present cold. The blue haze of the sun had been replaced by that of the moon. A sliver of the crimson shape gleamed above him and lengthened the shadows around him. He sometimes imagined the monsters of his favorite childhood stories lurking within them. The Temple always had the best stories, recounting the deeds of gods and monsters, demons, and cannibals. His favorite had been about the great annihilation of Bo'Shk. The island was descended upon by a hulking beast. He shook his head as he remembered the clerics acting out the monster's roars.

He remembered how the clerics' voices grew small and afraid as they pretended to be the island villagers, praying for salvation from the gods. He remembered how he, Gemmi, and the rest of the children cheered as one of them stood tall and demanded that the monster leave the people alone, pretending to be the sturdy and powerful oceanic god Dathos the Wanderer. Astus and Iarus followed. The children had shrieked in delight despite hearing the story a few dozen times a week. The last two clerics, young women, had then pranced to the front and stoically declared themselves to be the feisty Etah and the gentle goddess Raslena the Builder.

Their Temple mentors had thrown everything into their performance of the battle. James's childhood memories were intermixed with his vivid young imagination of the tale. The suffering in Boane and the nearby port wasn't a story, but the clerics put much more work into a bedtime fable.

And that was why James was going to kill them.

Planning the deed had been relatively straightforward. The clerics all slept at the Temple in one place. Simply push over a brazier and block the Watchtower doors from the outside. Maybe even get the flames to grow a bit. Escaping would be the trick, for killing a cleric was one of the highest crimes possible on this side of the world. His vengeance would bring a manhunt down on him, one that couldn't be escaped unless he left the continent. It would be worth it to bring down the Temple and everything that his childhood caretakers stood for. First here in Boane, then in the port city. Both needed to go.

He was on his way to the next post before he saw the firelight above the rooftops. His heart stumbled as he realized that this light was far too bright to be from the light posts. There was something wrong.

The spires of the modest palace to the north were eerily lit with an orange hue, and shadows jerkily passed over the stonework like insects. James dashed to the bridge that led to the center of the city. He stood at the edge of the bridge and scanned the ominous glow. It was spreading. Firelight trickled across the skyline of the stone city. Smoke and flames continued throughout most of the eastern district then the agricultural district.

"I don't think your fire trick will work," said a calm voice behind him.

James ripped the chipped short sword from his scabbard and whirled around to face the origin of the voice. His eyes landed upon the man from earlier, not eight feet from him. The man's black, rough-spun cloak blew slightly as another gust of wind and sand sifted through the relatively open bridgeway. The hood on his cloak had been drawn back, revealing shaggy black hair atop the man's head. Most of his pale face was covered by a gray wool cloth. James could just see hardened blue-green eyes. A thin scar ran vertically through his left eye, tearing a bright pink groove through his face and giving him a permanently suspicious squint.

Pointing his sword at the man, James nodded toward the growing light of the flames across the way. "Was that you?"

The man shook his head slightly. His blue-green eyes stayed on James. Both eyes sized him up quickly yet indifferently, but the tension that James had seen before was still there.

James narrowed his eyes at the stranger. "What do you want?"

"I want to help you," the man in black replied. He pulled down the facecloth to reveal a straight nose, a hard, narrow mouth, and close-trimmed stubble, a face that was the essence of solemnity.

James realized that this man was only two or three years older than him. The scar had made him look close to ancient, and his expression didn't change as he continued speaking smoothly.

"It's going to get much worse here, and the farther away we are the better. Come with me and I'll explain." The foreigner's accent was flowing and rhythmic.

The Temple's influence reached far, and the language of the upper continent was used primarily here, but James supposed that strange accents would bloom despite the assimilation efforts. James couldn't place the stranger's attire. He wore a dark fencing shirt underneath the cloak, made of a tough, hewn material that looked unfamiliar. His pants were made of a lighter version of the same material, tucked into extremely worn travel boots.

The stranger postured and waited for James to respond. They stood for a moment on the bridge, studying the other, waiting for the other to make the wrong choice. The foreigner's arms were at his sides, idle. However, James knew by his stance that he was prepared for a fight if necessary. He could see a saber strapped tightly to the man's hip. James studied the foreigner through narrowed eyes. That couldn't be what this person really wanted. Things were always bad in Boane. A fire through the city had happened before once when a novice lamp-lighter had accidentally set a crop silo alight, not implausible. Was this the Garrison's work?

The stranger continued, "The gods are no longer with us here. We must leave."

Scowling, James looked back to the flames in the distance. When would these fools realize that the gods had never *been* there? The protection and grace they sought from these gods wasn't *real*, never had been. All the gods offered was cold indifference in exchange for fervent worship.

James took a step away from the man, "I'll be fine, thanks."

He pivoted and started across the bridge toward the lights. The stranger was right about one thing. If the Garrison was making trouble, he had to put his plans on hold and slip away into the night until chaos had cooled. He could at least carry out his vengeance in the port city. And when he left, it wouldn't be with some ass who gave him veiled threats.

He glanced over his shoulder and saw the man in black in the distance. The cloaked stranger drew his hood and moved into the dark of the streets.

The hunched ill were scattered through the alley, all lying in their own sick as James crept by the market toward the bridge that would lead him to his shelter. They paid no mind to the thickening smoke that hung in the air. It wasn't like he could help any of them. He had already left his lantern behind, preferring to keep his whereabouts unadvertised.

It was as he came to the edge of the market that he started to hear the screams. They rose above the distant sound of flames crackling and swords clashing. These sounds stabbed his eardrums, bringing his thoughts back to the raving speech that Hook Nose and the rest of the soldiers had given earlier that day. This was what the Garrison had been screaming about in the square that afternoon? This was their idea of a divine crusade, the massacre of sick, helpless people.

James's head buzzed with anger as he grew closer to the cries for help. This was the sacred task that the gods had ordered? The Garrison had just used the Temple as an excuse and as a shield, or perhaps the other way around. Were the clerics happy now?

He searched across the marketplace for soldiers, remembering that he had the palace symbol, a flaming moon, stitched onto his lamplighter cloak. Judging by the speech he had witnessed earlier that day, he would not be greeted with any amount of grace by the rioters if found.

The cobbled street was glistening with a viscous dark liquid. Slain innocents slumped in the puddles, killed indiscriminately by the Garrison, one of them with noticeably curly black hair. *Lenia*.

James's blood pumped with an enraged heat as he heard the voices of more killers coming closer. He quickly dashed behind a crumbling wall to conceal himself, cursing silently when he leaned against it and dislodged a flurry of dust and pebbles from the partition. The infrastructure of the city had been deteriorating for years. Another one of the consul's many blunders.

Torchlight flickered against the sun-bleached exteriors of the structures they strolled by. James swept his hair out of his eyes and quietly slid the sword out of his scabbard. The jeers of the murderers drew nearer. Sweat carved its way down his face as he held his breath.

The first of the men strutted right by James, missing him completely. The soldier was holding a low-burning torch, lightly swinging it back and forth as he walked. Light danced over his face, revealing Hook Nose himself. Here was the man who had used the Temple's divine prophecy to stir everyone into a frenzy, convinced them to overthrow the palace, and then killed the sick.

James's mouth drew into a hard grimace. This man *would* die. Any desire to just slip away unnoticed was squelched by a heavy, familiar desire for vengeance. Concentrating on the flame that was in front of him, James felt the pull in his stomach. He strained his eyes as he focused on the embers and directed a thought at the torch. The licking, ghostly blue, feeble flames bobbed, listening.

Grow.

There was a flash of yellow and orange as the dying sputter of torchlight exploded into a flare of white-hot light.

The Garrison men shrieked in surprise as their eyes were briefly overwhelmed by the sudden roaring flame that engulfed the torch. The leading soldier cast the shaft from his grip in complete terror, sending the crackling wooden handle spinning into a puddle of blood in the street.

Using this opportunity, James sprung forward and clubbed one of the men in the back of the head with his sword. The trooper shuddered and crashed to the street, his armor scraping against the worn bricks that made up the walkway.

The heads of the other men whipped up to stare at James, and he realized that there were no less than eight men, twice as many as he had thought and at least four times as many as he could handle. The Garrison soldiers started to creep toward him, their hands going to their weapons. Hook Nose rubbed his eyes and put a hand on his sword.

James didn't wait for them to continue. He immediately bolted back the way he came, sprinting through the alley. He weaved through the terrified afflicted who huddled together between the buildings. The guardsmen rumbled behind him, shoving the forsaken out of their way as they loudly pursued him. Their corroded armor clanged and crashed. The sound was maddening.

James's pulse threatened to burst his eardrums. He knew these streets well, but the Garrison had been patrolling them for as long as he had been alive. There was no way that he could lose them by means of misdirection.

They followed him through the next alley as he ducked past makeshift clothes-lines and spun to avoid more plague-stricken urchins. His lungs could barely hold any more air. His little stunt with the torch had sapped a large portion of his energy. He skidded in the sand as he tried to change direction before tearing down the narrow backstreet to his left. His eyes widened, finding himself barreling toward someone standing in the middle of the path. It was the black-cloaked foreigner.

"Duck," his smooth voice called.

James dropped and slid across the sandy stone as the man stepped forward and hurled a large knife at the pursuers. The blade shimmered as it twirled through the air before striking handle-first into the forehead of the first soldier, Hook Nose. Had the soldier been wearing his helmet, he would have felt nothing, but he had thrown his helmet down while chasing James through the streets.

The blow took Hook Nose off his feet and sent him crashing to the ground, pinned by his armor and dazed. The remaining murderers hesitated for only a moment before charging the man in black.

The stranger drew his saber, striking a peculiar stance that James had never seen before, standing laterally. Swinging his blade in a circular arc, he held the saber out toward the oncoming attackers.

As the Garrison men charged the stranger, another cloaked figure, this one in brown, leapt from the rooftops above and landed behind them, rolling as their feet touched down and crouching in a ready stance. This second mysterious person drew a sword and charged the incredulous soldiers.

James struggled to regain his breath as he watched the two cloaked combatants fluidly engage the Garrison. Sounds of shuffling feet and the screech of sword on stone and metal rang throughout the streets.

The brawl quickly turned in favor of the strangers, and the soldiers stumbled over one another, trampling themselves as their opponents moved in. One fighter flopped backward as the black-cloaked man kicked him in the center of his breastplate and shoved him away. His momentum carried him into his fellow soldiers, knocking a few to the ground. The second figure efficiently pummeled another soldier with the longsword hilt and plunged the blade through his exposed armpit.

One after another, the Garrison fell until they rested in a heap, some still groaning. James gaped, still sitting a few feet away. The once explosive din of the fight had now given away to complete, traumatic silence. He shuddered as he glanced at the surprised and horrified faces of the Garrison men as they gawked blankly at nothing.

The second stranger still held the steel longsword. The red-stained blade was engraved with runes from religious texts. Holding the hand-and-a-half hilt with ease in one hand, the stranger stepped around the defeated soldiers and looked in the direction of the man in black. "I thought we were going to stay *hidden*, Roy."

James could hear that it was a woman's sharp voice underneath the cowl. He could also hear a fair bit of annoyance in her tone, like an overactive whip.

The man in black spoke calmly, "That wasn't an option anymore." He sheathed his saber and paced to where James sat before crouching in front of him. The turquoise eyes gleamed from underneath his messy black hair. "What's your name?" He waited for an answer, expressionless.

James had to work up enough saliva in his mouth to be able to speak again. "James," he croaked. Roy nodded and held out his hand.

James took the hand warily and was heaved upward with ease. He attempted to thank the man, but his eyes were drawn to Roy's scar. Roy noticed, and a scowl darkened his face. The woman stepped forward, sheathing her sword, and dropped the hood of her cloak.

A single braid of black hair draped over her shoulder. She was a bit taller and a few years older than James and Roy. Her smooth, dark skin wrinkled as she narrowed her watchful amber eyes at him. Her polished white earrings shimmered in the growing firelight. "Why did we get involved in this mess for this one?"

Roy glanced at her and looked intently at James's face. He crossed his arms, working his mouth up like he might spit. "Because we just found the last one of us, Samira. We found Iarus's Chosen."

Samira stared incredulously at James for a moment. Her braided hair whipped behind her as she turned and looked excitedly at Roy. Her eyes shone with exhilaration. "You can't be serious! You're saying that we just *happened* across the last one?"

"Well, I did," Roy said, dryly. "You were elsewhere."

She shook her head and smirked briefly, "Well done, ass."

James looked between the both of them, irritation creeping into his cheeks. "I'm sorry, but what are you two *scorching* going on about?"

Samira's face lit up in a grin, and she stepped eagerly toward James, a hand outstretched. "Call me Sam," she said, her teeth glinting in the fading moonlight, "the Daughter of Astus."

The Devil on the Roof

Vayne favored his walking stick as he navigated his way through the burning central streets of Boane. The heat from the flames should have been excruciating, but he trudged through them noticeably unhurt. Just how old he was didn't matter. After a few centuries, numbers stopped mattering. His sagging, kindly eyes could see nothing, but he sensed that something was amiss. He didn't know how, but he knew that they were here, the Chosen.

The elderly man led two others through the blazing square toward the palace, flames crackling and popping nicely. The afflicted had removed and killed the consul hours ago, and now the once quiet and somber city was roaring with flames. He heard the others, Rhaiga and Dhorh, stop in the center of the square. The cool sand against his feet and the climbing temperature of the air bothered him not. Smoke and ash billowed around him unnoticed. Vayne took a few steps closer to the palace. He hunched and stared in the direction of the blaze, his blind eyes unblinking, cooking in their sockets from the heat.

Dhorh, sighing in the voice of his ten year-old host, moved around Vayne, sounding as if he was kicking sand from boredom. "I know how much you love not to look at things, but is there a reason why we're still here?"

Vayne smiled thinly, his lips stretching across his teeth in a way that was slightly inhuman. "All too often, having a sacred task can make you forget the beauty of your work. The plague worked better than I had hoped. And now we witness the glory of our labor."

"It wasn't that hard," the boy mumbled. "I barely had to convince the soldiers to attack the rest of the city. Their Temple did most of the work in getting them riled up at the consul." Indeed, after their consul was dead, the Garrison had to be convinced of a new target. It was good that the boy had picked up this new modern language from the humans. It would have been a hindrance to learn himself.

"They are weak-willed," Rhaiga said dispassionately, "They never take much convincing."

Vayne's ears perked up at the veil over her face fluttering in the scorching air, the blood dripping persistently, noisily, from her hands onto the stone.

He turned toward the woman's voice, his face hardening. "It's your turn now. The humans can't be allowed to rebuild hope. Deal with them."

The woman's joints cracked. "They chose the path, and I'll see them through," she said. Already, Vayne could hear her skin unknitting and rebinding itself as she took her true, ancient appearance. He felt her eyes, all three of them, watching him.

The old man nodded and swiveled his wrinkled face in the direction of the blaze as the palace roof collapsed with a satisfyingly loud rumble. The old man's sightless eyes rested on the origin of the noise. Though he couldn't see it, he knew that this was a monument of the enemy, countless faceless humans who stood in their way, and those meddlesome Chosen.

He waved the others away. "Go now. These flames must spread to the corners of the city. Kill anyone who tries to put them out." Vayne didn't hear Rhaiga and

Dhorh leave. He didn't need to. He knew they would end this city. They would end this entire wretched civilization and then rebuild the world they once had ruled.

***

James struggled to maintain the pace that Samira and Roy had set. His shaky breaths rattled in his throat as they tore through the smoky paths between buildings and ducked behind walls. The hood of his gray cloak flapped while he ran and made it difficult to see, but Samira had insisted that he have it up to keep the chances of being seen to a minimum. He couldn't argue with that. They stopped by one of the few wells that had not been boarded up due to the plague. The bucket appeared to have been taken by a fleeing refugee. James rested his hands on his knees, panting. "I don't...understand. How are you Astus's daughter?"

Samira inhaled deeply through her nose, standing with her hands behind her head. She appeared to be Kostran. Across the sea, Kostra was one of the largest kingdoms in the Collisun Empire, the home of the Shale Watchtower. Their typical amber eyes and dark skin were as well-known as their devotion to intelligence.

She regarded him. "I'm not actually his daughter. I was chosen to be his instrument. My real father lives across the sea, but Astus chose me to follow his guidance." Her Kostran accent was very loose, only chopping off the very end of her words. She inhaled through her nose again and let her hands drop to her side. "Just as Iarus has chosen you."

He shook his head, coughing. "That can't be right." The gods didn't care about him. If they had, then Gemmi would still be alive. Why in the world would Iarus choose a Temple deserter like him? He wasn't even sure he wanted whatever he'd supposedly been chosen for.

"I saw you manipulate that fire," Roy said, a few feet away. He craned over the well. "I've never seen anyone else do that." He took out an empty water skin and peered into the reservoir below.

James watched Roy hold the flask over the well. "The pail is gone," he snapped. "We'll have to try a different one."

Roy rolled his eyes dismissively and motioned with his hand as if he were pulling a thread from a piece of cloth. An echo of splashing water reverberated from the bottom of the well. James blinked in disbelief as a stream of water rose from the cavernous pit and flowed into the water skin like a liquid serpent. The leather sides of the skin expanded until they halted, bloated with the contents.

Roy corked the skin and tossed it to James. The remaining water, having been released, splashed back to the depths of the well. James nearly dropped the skin, watching Roy stroll past him toward a fork in the alley. Samira grinned—her high cheekbones made her look especially joyous and clapped James on the shoulder briskly. The force of her arm resembled a crack of thunder that sent him wobbling.

"Champion of Dathos," she said, jerking her thumb in Roy's direction, "drink up. We need to leave soon."

He stood for a moment and tried to comprehend what he had seen before gulping down the water greedily. Fresh and pure. The grimy swill that he had stashed away in his now surely torched shelter had been all he had known for the better part of a month.

Lowering the water skin, he ran his fingers through his stringy hair. This couldn't be real. The Temple had never mentioned anything about the gods choosing champions, not that the Temple had been very interested in the truth in any capacity. His memory strained to recall lessons and readings that he had tried to forget, the hours he and Gemmi had wasted poring over scrolls. The clerics had always taught that the gods were to be feared and respected, but they never said anything about champions or granting power to mortals. Were they just trying to trick him? She had walked further down the path toward where Roy waited.

"Samira, I don't understand any of this," he called after her. "The gods don't choose champions. And why would *I* be one?"

She turned around, a knowing look on her face. The shadows of her hood gave her eyes the eerie appearance that they were glowing, "I've heard stories of the clerics who settled here, outside the empire and across the sea. That they believed the gods left things to us entirely, that they didn't care about interfering in the lives of mortal men and women. I know that you must have a lot of questions, James, but we aren't safe. I can explain everything later." She shuffled through the sand over to Roy. "And I told you to call me Sam," she said over her shoulder.

James and Samira walked up behind Roy. He stood, contemplating at a fork in the alleyway. Smoke obscured both paths and made it difficult to see.

Samira placed a hand on her companion's shoulder. "I'm sorry, Roy. We were too late to find any answers."

Roy didn't turn around. He faced the smoky wall in front of him, shaking his head. "No. There's still time." His voice took a hard edge. "I know we need to get James out of here, but you promised me, Sam."

She grimaced, relented after a moment, and turned to James. "Which way takes us northwest?"

James pondered her question. They would have to be toward the west center of the city by now, the Faith District. If they left from the northwest wall near the Watchtower, it would put them a couple days' journey from the port city, Epot Detharn. "You mean to go to the port?"

Roy turned. "The Watchtower first, but the chaos here will hit Epot Detharn next. We need to get there and find a ship after I find my answers here. We have some coin left. It'll have to be enough."

James gestured with a determined hand toward the leftward path. This could work to his plans, armed escorts to the port and toward vengeance against the Temple. Vengeance for Gemmi. James wasn't sure what their intentions were at the Watchtower however. Best to wait on retribution until he found out what these two were really after. They obviously hadn't been expecting to find him out here. "This way leads us north. We can get to the Sandstone Watchtower if we cut through the alleys then the bridge."

Samira and Roy nodded before the three of them lurched into the smoke. The rumbling of the flames and collapsing buildings in the distance grew louder.

They ran for what felt like hours to James. The smoke grew thicker as they ventured farther north through the city. He felt the temperature of the air rising, especially in the direction of the city's center. His feet thudded against the cobbled walkways and slid in the odd pileup of sand. The screams of the people had mostly subsided. He shuddered when he thought of the brutal end that some of them had no doubt faced at the hands of the Garrison, a fate that he had narrowly avoided. Poor Lenia had gone right toward the center of the city where the fires started. She didn't deserve that.

Samira coughed and hacked as they made a short rest near the bridge to the upper territory of Boane. All three of them sprinkled ash and soot from the steadily creeping blaze. Ash caked into James's hair. He didn't dare move his head too much, lest he risk showering more dust over his companions.

Roy took a ginger sip from his water skin and passed it to Samira. She took a massive gulp before passing it to James. It took all of his restraint not to drink it all immediately. The water washed away the grime and dust on his tongue and replaced it with clean bliss. He drank sparingly before corking the skin. It may be a while before they were able to find water again.

James gestured to the water skin in Roy's hand. "Can't you fill it with water again? As the Champion of Dathos and whatnot?" He shook it derisively.

Roy shook his head. A faint plume of dust shook free from his thick hair. "Dathos is the god of the ocean. I could create water using my own energy and power, but it would be sea water."

"As the Chosen of a god, you can create the element of their domain through your own energy. You are the human embodiment of their will," Samira added.

"You mean to say that I could create a fire without using any materials?" James's eyes widened.

Samira nodded, her head spilling ash to the ground. "But it takes practice." Her eyes flicked upward as a building in the distance crumbled with a booming shamble. "We need to go."

James and Roy groaned and stood, their already tired legs aching.

"We should just be able to make it to the tower if we cross this bridge," James said.

Roy grunted and began to cross the stone bridge. Like the bridge toward the southwest side of the city, it was carved into stone over the only other source of fresh water in Boane, the Caltog River. The river cut vertically through the city-state. In recent years, the near constant heat had caused it to dry. The river was barely a trickle now. That trickle was now stained black by the ash from above.

James began to follow Roy over the bridge. He was halfway across before he noticed that Samira had not followed them. He looked back to see her alert, looking up toward the rooftops to the east. Her dark eyes searched the skyline of Boane for something that James couldn't see. Her right hand firmly grasped the hilt of her sword. She had seen something, and it was still there. He called out to her softly, "Sam?"

She gave the slightest shake of her head, warning him not to speak. She slowly pointed to her right ear. James stood at the center of the bridge and listened, holding his breath. The sound of the crackling blaze drifted closer. Black smoke billowed overhead and expanded into the sky, blocking out the moonlight. He strained his ears and focused on tuning out the inferno. The world stopped, and he could hear nothing. His head twitched as he finally heard what Samira must have heard. A faint scrabbling was coming from the tall stone building behind her.

The sound made the hair on the back of his neck stand immediately. There was something about the noise that didn't strike him as human.

Samira was already looking upward toward the edge of the roof. She drew her longsword and slowly started backing away toward the bridge, stepping in the ash that fell soundlessly like black snow.

Roy had crept to where James was standing. Holding a finger to his lips, he gave James a quizzical look. James shrugged and glanced back to see that Samira was on the bridge. Her eyes were still firmly trained on the roof of the building, boots silent in the sand and ash that now covered the surface of the bridge. A buzz of fear ran through the back of James's skull as two glowing eyes came into focus through the blowing smoke. The eyes gleamed through the smog. They rose from the roof impossibly slowly until whatever owned them was standing at full height. Whatever those eyes belonged to must have been extremely tall.

A third glowing eye opened above the other two, a sickly, dull sheen. The three eyes blinked in unison. He saw the passing shape of this new horror through a gap in the smoke. It was a pale, spindly creature. Its bare skin glowed through the fumes.

Samira didn't hesitate. A cold scowl on her face, she thrust her left hand up toward the monstrosity on top of the structure. Blue light blinded James as tendrils of lightning rocketed toward the creature from her fingertips. It leapt out of the way before the lightning speared the roof shattering the stone with a thunderous blast that shook the ground. Chunks of rock rained from the sky, and Roy barely had time to move before a hunk of stone landed where he had been standing. James rubbed his eyes and stared as Samira drew her hand back, her hand crackling with electricity. She held her sword at her side in her right hand, still surveying the rooftops for the three-eyed creature.

"Did you get it?" Roy whispered.

Samira shook her head slowly. "Astus strike me, lightning is always difficult to aim." She sighed and glanced toward the east. The flames drew nearer. "I was always shit with a bow too. We have to move. If they're here, things are about to get much worse."

"What in all the *scorching* world was that?" James squeaked. The only response was Roy's hand tugging him firmly across the bridge.

They crossed the bridge quickly, kicking up ash with their feet as they ran. James could just make out the path leading over the next few buildings to the

Sandstone Watchtower, a place where Temple clerics and some lamplighters lived. The clerics had said that there were four other watchtowers spread across the world, the birthplaces of each of the gods. None could say which gods were born where.

Samira held up the rear, scouting for the thing that had followed them. The inferno was almost to the edge of the city now, the smoke at its thickest. James could barely see more than a few feet in front of him. He, Samira, and Roy shuffled down the path, groping for direction in the smog. Samira listened intently to their surroundings on silent feet. Her eyes darted around with practiced caution for any movement in the smoke.

Frantic voices of over a dozen people started to come into focus. They were urgently talking over each other, attempting to maintain some coordination. Their shapes began to solidify as James, Samira, and Roy approached. Frightened townsfolk were passing pails, cookware, and bowls back and forth. They had torn the covering off a boarded-up well and were filling anything they could with the contaminated water. Even through the smoke, James recognized the long, forked beard of one of the people.

"Igard!" James called.

His pace quickened as Igard looked up, surprise and relief on his ash-streaked face. Samira and Roy jogged to keep up with him. The old lamplighter looked awful. His soot-covered clothes were badly torn, and there was a nasty cut on his cheek. A rare relieved smile touched his face as James and his companions approached. It was the happiest Igard had ever been to see him.

"I'm glad you're safe, boy. We need all the help we can get here." Igard panted. He pointed westward toward the Watchtower. "The flames are spreading to the tower. We need to put them out. As long as the tower still stands, the gods are with us."

Maybe no action is needed from me to burn it down then. James glared. "You need to leave. Everyone needs to leave right now."

His frown deepened when Igard shook his head and heaved a pail of water from the ground. The elder lamplighter strained as he hauled it into the smoke, and the gray water sloshed back and forth against its dented sides. Igard waddled a few feet before setting the cauldron down and wincing, clutching his back.

Samira marched through the ash and sand over to Igard. She gingerly laid a hand on his shoulder. "There's a devil out there, and it's likely the cause of this blaze," she called over the roaring fire. "The gods would want you to live so you can continue serving them. The city is lost, but come with us. We can help you find a new tower."

Igard looked at her stubbornly. "You have faith, girl, but I can't do what you ask. This tower is my connection to the gods and to my home. If I lose this, my purpose in life is gone. Iarus has set this challenge before me, and I won't fail him."

Roy shouted over the commotion, "It's just a place. Your connection is to the gods, not to a pile of stones." His face took on a brief desperation. "Dathos drown me, I need your help! Where are the clerics?"

The elder turned his gaze to Roy and squinted through the blowing ash. "Where do you think, boy? They're with the people trying to put out the Watchtower!" Igard pointed an exasperated finger into the swirling ash. Roy immediately strode into the churning blackness.

Samira turned back to Igard. "I know what this tower means to you, but we must go."

The old lamplighter motioned toward James. "Is that what *he* told you? He left the Temple years ago. He has rejected the gods as a heretic. How could he know their will?"

"They murdered my brother, old man," James spat, "at the behest of those gods you love so much. As far as I'm concerned, this whole scorching tower can burn to the ground and it still wouldn't be enough."

Samira's eyes widened with shock for the shortest of moments. James had nothing else to say. The Temple was responsible for his misery. He could have had a life; Gemmi could still be alive.

The lamplighter's forked beard swayed as shook his head and heaved the pail up to his hip. Roy's voice echoed through the smog, calling for the clerics. "May Iarus guide you." He nodded toward Samira and shambled off into the smoke. The smog enveloped him, and he disappeared from sight, joining the rest of the group. James could hear the splashing of water and the sizzle of extinguished fires.

Samira looked at him with a hurt expression. "You left?"

James fixed his eyes on the ground. "What would you have done?" he said bitterly.

She said nothing. Samira was obviously troubled by this, but there were more important problems. She took a rushed swig of her water skin and readied to throw it to James but stopped when the townspeople started screaming.

The screams lanced through the smog and pierced James's eardrums. Screams morphed into sobs and cries as they heard the survivors scramble through the sand, trying desperately to get away from the tower. James and Samira drew their swords. Swirling black smoke made it impossible to see what was happening.

"Roy?" Samira called.

The screams became fewer, silenced one by one. He shuddered as the last one was brutally and suddenly cut off. The smoky city was now doused in relative silence. Flames crackled and roared around them, but an eerie quiet now smothered the air.

"Sam!" Roy answered.

Samira took a step forward into the black air before her. Smoke swirled around her head, making her braid blur in and out of focus. James followed, sword drawn. James's hand shook. He had never had any formal training, but judging by what he had just heard it may not make any difference. They moved silently, carefully stepping through the ashy street.

They had gone about twelve feet before they saw the first body. The dead woman's head and arms were twisted to impossible angles. Ragged claw marks ran where she had been grabbed by something while trying to run away, as if from a predator.

The second body was a male cleric. The arms were missing, and a silent scream was plastered to his face.

Each grisly scene they passed became more disturbing, and James found that he had to clamp his mouth tight to avoid gagging. Samira got farther away from him with each wave of nausea.

James saw someone crouched over another body. It appeared to be a woman leaning over someone she had known, her back to him and seemingly in prayer. He wondered why she had been spared.

"Are you all right?" he called, stumbling over to her.

The figure's head whipped around, and James saw three gleaming eyes gazing back at him.

He stumbled away in the sand and tripped over a loose stone in the street. Wind rushed by his ears as his balance left him, and he fell. As James hit the ground, sending a plume of ash into the air, the three-eyed devil's silhouette drew upward to its full height, and the eyes peered through the smoke at him.

He couldn't see it clearly through the thick smoke, but the eyes gleamed brightly, as if they were flames of their own. His voice refused to work. A dry gurgle was all he could muster. The devil took a step toward him, its head cocked to the side in curiosity. Sand and ash covered his hands as he fell backward, scrambling away from the nightmare that stalked toward him. Heat from the burning tower behind him singed his cloak.

The devil's pale shape came into focus while it approached him. Sickly white, papery skin was tautly stretched over its gaunt female frame, slightly blackened by the falling ash. Curled horns sprouted from its angular head. Spidery fingers, dripping with blood, reached toward him.

James thrust his right hand out at the creature, a wordless scream flying from his mouth. His entire body shivered, and his muscles strained. Terrified energy cycled through him as he held his hand out in front of him, trying to keep the devil back.

His screams were replaced by the surprised shrieks of the pale horror when fire from the building leapt from the structure and engulfed it. James's stomach pulled inward, and the flames brightened. Intensifying wails from the devil rolled across the sand.

Realizing that he had a chance to escape, James bolted to his feet and tore through the ash toward Roy and Samira's voices. They were calling out for him. Smoke stung his eyes. He could hear their voices getting closer. He worked up enough saliva in his mouth to call out their names.

"Sam! Roy!" He could just barely see them through the fumes.

Samira's braid whipped around as she turned in the direction of his voice. A relieved breath escaped her, and Roy gave a slight nod when James finally reached them.

He panted, palms on his knees. "We need to leave. Now." He sucked in another breath. "The thing is here, but it's distracted."

A shape on the ground caught his eye. Squinting through the smoke, he saw a body. Its head had been twisted completely around. He breathed hard at the sight of the few remaining tufts of a forked beard sprouting from the dead man's jaw. His eyes closed for a moment. *Scorch you, Igard, why couldn't you have just left?* He steeled himself. The man was a foot soldier of oppression, a peddler of the Temple's terrible values, but lying there in the dirt Igard was a victim. Just like Gemmi.

"James, come on," Roy said firmly.

"The clerics?" Samira asked.

"Dead," Roy croaked.

Roy's hand closed around James's wrist and led him out of the burning remains of the city. James didn't look back at Boane. If he had, he might have noticed three glowing eyes atop the burning tower, blinking in the night.

⸺◆⸺

What Do You Want?

Sand covered everything. The two days' worth of desert between Boane and Epot Detharn crawled into every empty space, smothering all. James had given up trying to shake the sand out of his boots. He had already come to terms with the sand getting into his clothes. He had even accepted the sand that had somehow infiltrated the inside of Roy's water skin. Grit and ash caked into his hair and weighed his eyelids down.

He glanced at Samira and Roy. Both of them looked nightmarish, as if they had both bathed in coal. They scared him. Even though they had saved him, he could all too easily imagine their well-trained fury being turned on him. Perhaps leaving with them had been a mistake, but it didn't seem that he had much choice until they got to Epot Detharn. He would reassess then.

They had been walking for a little over a day. Though he couldn't see it, he could just barely hear the sound of the coast above the hot wind that whipped across the dunes. Squinting, he looked toward the south and into the desert. The Dunes of Knost rose and fell endlessly. Their yellow peaks rippled for as far as he could see. He had asked the clerics when he was young what lay beyond them. After scolding him for asking questions, they simply had said there had once been a great battle in the dunes. A war between the gods and a deadly cult of...something. He had been too young to remember. As far as he was concerned, anything could be across them, but it wasn't worth the journey to get there.

He tried to shake off thoughts of Igard. The fool had made his choice, and it wasn't James's fault that he went and got himself killed. He spat more sand out of his mouth and grimaced. Igard more than most had been keen on following the Temple to the letter, for all the good that came of it.

"What you said last night, about leaving the Temple..." Samira appeared beside him.

James looked up, startled. She had approached him silently. He had seen how well she could move, but it was still discomforting. A lot about her and Roy were discomforting, really. He nodded slightly. "A few years ago."

She grunted in acknowledgement, her brown eyes staring straight ahead. "What happened?"

"They said that it was justice, what they did to him," he said. "I grew up thinking that the gods were supposed to be perfect. The greatest beings to ever exist and that their punishments were always just, that people are never whole without their love." He ruffled his hair and wiped the ash on his pant leg while he walked. "But I guess you can't believe everything you hear."

Samira was silent for a moment as they trudged through the sand. She turned around and waved to Roy behind them, signaling that they would rest for a moment. Sunlight blasted everything around them. Pushing through the heat wouldn't do them much good. Samira turned to James.

"The clerics like to think of the gods as perfect. That's been a constant doctrine. Even though the Temple shattered into a hundred different sects long ago, it's been constant. But nobody is perfect, not even the gods," she said. "They do the best they can, and so do we. They're all that we have in the world besides each other. But we can't find the right path unless we have the faith to follow it. I have my faith, and it led us to you."

Roy caught up with them, and he knelt in the desert, untying the water skin from his belt. Sweat carved small streaks through the ash on his face. His scar shone through the soot.

James gave in to curiosity. "How did you get that?" He gestured to his face.

Samira stiffened next to him, uneasiness painting her sweating brow.

Roy tossed him the water skin without looking at him. "What does it matter? I have it. How I got it isn't relevant anymore."

His voice had a hard edge that made James regret his question immediately while still increasing his curiosity. Perhaps it was the tint of the sand around them, but James thought he saw a fleck of orange appear in Roy's eyes before returning to their cool turquoise.

Samira sat and leaned back against the diagonal slope of a sand dune, not seeming to mind the sand spilling down the back of her shirt. Her sword rested at her side. A sliver of the blade slid from the sheath, reflecting sunlight back toward the heavens. Samira's clothing couldn't have been doing her any favors in the heat. Appearing Kostran by design, the thick leather jerkin looked like its purpose was to protect the wearer from storms, not from the sun. A pendant made of shale hung from around her neck, a symbol of Kostra's watchtower.

"Why would he choose me?" James asked suddenly. He looked skeptically at Samira. He had been wondering about this for the last day since she had told him. "Why would a god choose someone like me as a champion?"

She squinted through the sunlight and shrugged. "Maybe he wants you to keep your faith. Maybe he thinks you're worthy of something." She examined her hands, ground with sand. "I can't really say what his reasoning would be. That's something you have to figure out."

James rolled his eyes. "You're starting to sound like the Temple. Vague promises and no answers."

"Could the Temple make flames grow or hurl fire?" Roy asked. He was still kneeling, cleaning the blade of his saber. "They may never have given you anything but false promises, but what Iarus gave you is real. I've seen it."

Samira chimed in, "What does Iarus do? What's his purpose?"

Silence reigned for the next minute as James thought about the question. His mind strained to remember the scrolls he had been forced to read. He frowned. "He's the Pathlighter."

She nodded. "It may take a while, but you'll find out why you were chosen. You just have to start down the path. I didn't know my path immediately, but I followed the signs and guidance from those I trusted, my father. Now my way is clear." She sat up, sand spilling off her.

"Fine. Whatever," James grumbled.

Samira and Roy both exchanged a glance. She motioned to Roy to let it go, but he walked to James and crouched in front of him, narrowing his eyes.

Scorch him, the man made James nervous. It was that ever-present tension in his otherwise tranquil face, hostile eyes looking from underneath a calm mask.

"What do you want?" Roy asked. His eye contact was suddenly painful.

"Excuse me?" James said.

"With your life, James, what do you want?" Roy tilted his head ever so slightly to the side. "Why did you leave Boane with us? You could have stayed and died there like the rest of them. Why go on?"

James hesitated. Roy had been keen to seek help from the clerics the night before. *Detailing my plans for revenge would not be the right move.* "I don't know." James shrugged.

"Don't give me that." Roy shook his head. "Dathos drown me, if you didn't have a reason to go on, why in the name of the gods did we drag you out of that sandpile?" His suspicious eyes pierced right through James.

His mouth dry, James looked down into the sand below him. Every day had just been a fight to wake up and continue his meager existence. Getting back at the people who killed his brother had seemed to be the only thing that cleared his head. Boane had been a terrible place. The consul, Temple, and the Garrison took from everyone, and the people had resigned themselves to it. Clerics preached of the goodness of the gods while cursing and stealing from their worshippers. Backstabbing and treachery were the real religion in Boane. It had made him sick, and losing Gemmi had confirmed his suspicions that good people were too rare to care about.

He sighed. "I want the Temple to pay for what they've done. They were the real disease long before the plague came."

Off to the side, Samira flinched at his words.

Roy nodded slowly, his eyes never leaving James's face. "I know that feeling, that hopelessness of knowing the ones who wronged you are still out there, unpunished. I won't stop you from confronting them, but then what comes after?" He shot a look at Samira when she started to protest.

James didn't answer.

Standing up quickly, Roy rolled his eyes and scoffed. "Figure it out then."

They waited until the sun had descended farther, casting its familiar blue haze over the dunes. Only when the azure had turned into a deep violet did they resume their trek through the desert. Overhead, the smoke from the still-burning city-state of Boane swirled higher and higher into the sky.

Paths Converge

They hiked through the night before they finally began to see the lights of Epot Detharn. The port city glimmered in the waning hours of darkness. James's stomach turned at the sight of the yellowed stone and chipped brick buildings. Only once had he been there, and his experience had been enough to make him never want to go back. Ships listed at the docks, barely larger than thimbles from a distance. One of these ships could take them across the sea. His throat clenched at the thought. He had once been thrilled with the idea of leaving this barren place, of getting away from the fanatics of the Temple and forgetting about them for good. A fantasy.

If Samira and Roy were telling the truth, the Temple was just as prevalent everywhere, and now he had this whole *Chosen* business to deal with. It was beyond his capacity to even fathom why Iarus would choose him as a champion. The gods were selfish. They were destructive and careless. Despite everything the Temple had tried to force upon him, he could see that much, but a man who conspired to enact retribution against the Temple? Hardly a fitting candidate.

Sunlight crept over the horizon and painted the dunes with lighter tints of purple before moving on to indigo and dark blue. Slowly, the lights in the city blinked out as daylight entered the area. As they set foot inside the port city, the sun had finally cleared the dunes and hovered in the sky.

It was exactly as it had been five years ago. But this time, the feeling of wonder while entering the city with Gemmi's hand on his shoulder faded in favor of revulsion. Every piece of this city was a blaring reminder of his brother, and not in the way that made him happy. The sounds of gulls warbled above. James, Samira, and Roy slinked into the city with their hoods up, avoiding anyone they got too close to. Epot Detharn was technically its own city-state, but it still often submitted to the will of Boane. Many of the problems Boane had faced would be present here.

The people here were sick too. It was a familiar sight as they passed streets packed with the ill. Their gray skin bled nonstop at a slow, viscous pace from a disease that dried the skin and organs of people who already thirsted too much. He pulled up his face cloth absentmindedly and coughed as he wound up with a mouth full of sand. Sweat and ash ran into his eyes.

Maroon and gray banners flew high overhead at the entrance of the city. Slightly below them on the flagpoles hung banners of a dark, mustard yellow, indicating low tide. Orange banners would replace them come high tide, and black would replace those in the event of a storm. James remembered seeing these tideflags and asking Gemmi about them when they had first traveled here years ago. Clerics stood at the street corners, shouting at passersby.

"Come, all travelers! Come and give thanks to mighty Wanderer Dathos so that he may bless your return journeys with swift seas! The gods provide for us! And we must provide in turn," bellowed a female cleric. Her ceremonial robes included less fabric than most clerics James had seen. After leaving the Temple, the actions of its members were extremely transparent.

Roy whispered to him and Samira, keeping his head down, "We should find a place to rest for now. Lay low. We can find a ship tonight."

Samira nodded and kept a hand on her sword as they waded through a crowd of traders, waiting to catch travelers at the entrance to the city like a fishing net. They sold everything. Expensive yet common trinkets lined their vision to the right. The left of the street smelled of fresh fruit, bread, and fish. Bards, performers, and dancers bumbled through the crowd, begging for coin or scraps. A sea of voices washed over the street. Everyone was keeping close watch of their wares and coins. The plague spreading to Epot Detharn likely caused an increase in thievery and crime. It was exactly what had happened to Boane.

James kept his eyes straight ahead and felt his stomach rumble. There was little to eat here that was in their price range and would still leave money left over for a charter. His hand jumped to his hip as he remembered the small pouch of coin strapped to his waist.

He nudged Samira as they trudged past a merchant frying strange fish over a fire. "Want something to eat?"

She accepted vigorously, eyes shining. He guessed that just as much time or more had gone by since she and Roy had eaten as well. Roy was at the other side of the crowded street, deep in conversation with a few sailors. There was precious little coin in his pouch, but Roy had been willing to help him. That meant enough to spend for a little extra food.

James peered around the street before stepping carefully to the fish merchant. Making sure to keep his eyes low, he studied the meat crackling in the pan suspended above the embers. The merchant smiled, revealing her few remaining teeth. Her tired, baggy frame gestured to the slow-cooking food.

"The finest spiced Scythefish in the world, sir," she croaked.

This was hardly likely to be accurate, but James had to clamp his mouth shut to avoid drooling all the same. The meat in the pan sizzled and snapped as she turned it over. Its blackened surface had a slightly orange hue, and the fibers were tender enough to melt. James untied the pouch Igard had given him from his belt and undid the leather cinch. Pouring a few bronze pieces into his palm, he held it out to the merchant. The crone shook her head slightly.

Grimacing, James shook the remaining few bits out of the pouch and clapped them into the woman's hand. Her toothless expression lit up her face warmly, as if she had not just cheated him out of his remaining coin. Wrapping three pieces of meat in a cloth, she handed it to him smugly.

He swiped the fish from her hand and walked back over to Roy and Samira, weaving through the growing crowd. Scanning the masses for any trouble, his eye landed on three men. Scavengers. The rabble stared at him, scarred faces trained on his position. Upon seeing him looking back, the men scattered. He shook his head quickly and hurried back to Samira and Roy. Epot Detharn had always been a thief's paradise. His companions were in the midst of a tired conversation as he approached.

"I'm just saying that I have no more options here," Roy said in a low voice. "Time isn't on my side."

Samira rubbed her temple with her thumb, obviously troubled. "We'll figure something out, Roy, but we have to get to safety first and regroup. That means taking the first ship off this continent. I can't abandon my purpose, but I won't abandon you either."

They both fell silent as James approached, obviously not keen on including him. Pretending not to have heard, he held up the food. "I got us some food. What now?" He tried to keep the irritation out of his voice.

Roy motioned toward the sailors he had been talking to. "I got us a ship. It will cost us most of what we have left, but the captain didn't have too many questions." He looked around, his turquoise eyes surveying the bustling market. "Let's find a place to settle in for now. The ship leaves tomorrow before dawn, plenty of time for you to visit the Temple, if you're still looking for passage afterward." His eyes settled on the food James was holding.

James gestured down the street, and the three of them began walking. They unwrapped the fish as they moved along and slipped into an alleyway.

"There should be an inn someplace." Samira nibbled at the fish, the grease soaking her fingers. "James, I don't think you should do this," she blurted out.

James wolfed down his food. The spices danced on his tongue and made his cheeks burn, but the taste was better than what he'd eaten for months. He scowled at her. "It's none of your business."

"This isn't what you were chosen for," she argued.

"And do you think my brother was 'chosen' for death? I'm doing this, Samira," James snapped.

"Sam, he's made his decision," Roy said. "It's not our biggest concern." Roy bit into his fish, and his eyes widened.

"What is it? What's wrong?" James looked into Roy's pained face.

Roy's cheeks had turned pale blue, and coarse hacking came from his trembling mouth.

"Hey!" James rushed to Roy, trying to get around him, get his arms around his navel.

Roy reached out and grabbed hold of James's throat, constricting his windpipe. They slammed against the nearby wall. Gulping at nothing, James's eyes rested on Roy. The Champion of Dathos glared at him with eyes that were no longer their calm turquoise. They gleamed a sinister orange in the shadow of the alley.

In an instant, Roy's hand released him, and he fell forward into the arms of Samira. Sand and dust spilled off his hair as she caught him. James wheezed, his neck still throbbing. James glanced upward to see Roy huddled against the opposite side of the alley, his hands on his soot-covered head and his again-turquoise eyes were darting in random directions with panic. Roy breathed shakily, terrified, as if his body had moved without his permission to nearly strangle James.

Hacking and spitting into the dirt, James finally breathed in a suitable quantity of oxygen. Kneeling by his side, Samira glanced cautiously at Roy. Her amber eyes betrayed nothing, but her voice wavered as she spoke. "Go."

Shivering and trying to stand, Roy backed away quickly. His hands trembled, and he glanced down at James. "I'm sorry." His voice was quiet and raspy. "I'm sorry." The black cloak he wore rippled, and he dashed away, leaving James and Samira alone in the alley.

Samira slumped to the ground, massaging her temple with her thumb. A sharp sigh escaped her, blowing away a stray hair that had escaped her braid.

"Wh—" His throat would not allow him to speak. He could only make a faint whistling as he tried to sound out his words.

Samira grimaced. "*That* is why Roy and I came to Boane. We're trying to find a way to help him, and the clerics at Boane were our last hope."

He tried speaking again but failed. He reached for the water skin, still on the ground from where Roy had dropped it, his vision swimming. The empty leather container crinkled in his grip.

"It's been getting worse, and we don't know how to stop it," she continued. "He's been a good friend to me ever since we were children, but he's turning into someone I don't know." Her voice started to crack. "It's a good thing he got a lid on it before he lost control completely. He could have killed us both."

"Where is he going?" James finally managed to say. His esophagus felt like sandpaper.

Working up her mouth, she heaved herself to her feet. "I don't know, but he can handle himself. When he calms down, hopefully we can still all get out of here."

She tried helping him to his feet but stopped after two attempts.

James's vision was still shifting in and out of focus, leading him to opt to stay put for a minute. After his revenge on the Temple, James would be finding his way off the continent on his own. He had no idea what was wrong with Roy, but he knew for a fact that getting on a ship with him would be a terrible way to die, and he would avoid this at all costs.

***

Merchants peddled their overpriced trinkets to pedestrians, and sailors drank their fill as Ariel watched from above. Several groups of thieves weaved through the rabble. Her keen blue eyes scanned the people below, looking for anyone who might be the Chosen of Iarus. Not that she knew what she was looking for, but she kept at it.

It was well into the afternoon, and the sun pummeled the hood of her dark-blue, sleeveless cloak. Her head was being cooked, but she didn't dare take off the hood. Her pale gold hair would reflect the sun's rays, making her too easy to spot. While normally she didn't do missions that required this level of secrecy, the emperor had been very clear that they didn't know who else was looking for the last of the Chosen. Why did she keep letting Leonard talk her into imperial assignments? All she wanted was to go home.

A warm breeze blew softly across the rooftops as Ariel exhaled slowly. This could take a while. Slung across her back was a quiver of arrows and a sturdy longbow. The bow was made of the Oreleaf tree native to Spiath. Hard as iron but still incredibly flexible. There was no need to use it yet, but it never hurt to be careful.

She remained crouched, pacing along the roof. Her boots barely made a noise against the clay, a welcome break from trudging through sand. There was too much of it here for her liking. A wave of smells traveled on the wind as she inhaled. Spiced fish, fresh imported fruit, and rum from Scourge Atoll graced her nostrils. She was tempted to jump down and see what this strange new city had to offer, bring something back for her family, but the potential for unfriendly run-ins kept the temptation at bay.

A flicker of movement caught her eye, and she whipped her gaze to the south. Something dark had just dashed across the corner of her vision. Maintaining her balance, she leapt to the next roof and prowled in the direction of the movement. Gliding over the clay rooftops, her eyes darted from sailors to merchants to city folk as she searched for that dark shape. A quick mental note of the increasing number of sick people was stored away before resuming the search. The dark shape had been vaguely familiar, but she knew that it was impossible. Heat swelled around her as she bounded to the next rooftop. The sunlight, absorbed by the bricks, made her feel like she was frying.

"Where are you?" she whispered. Her brow furrowed, wrinkling her lightly tan skin.

Her stare passed over an alleyway and froze. Something had been there. Her stare swung back to the alley, and she gasped. Samira stood in the shadowed alleyway, talking with someone a bit younger than her. A relieved grin struck her face. Samira was a welcome sight after expecting any number of dangers on this journey. Ariel didn't know the boy, but that fact that Samira was with him made him significant. His dark hair and brown skin were slathered with soot and perspiration. Samira didn't look much better. Even through the sand and grime, she could still tell that it was the Daughter of Astus. She thanked the gods and stood, ready to vault from the roof and join her. Before she could, a nagging guilt stopped her.

She won't want to see you, you know. The words rang in her subconscious and echoed painfully. Even after two years, the wound would still be fresh. A person couldn't just forget that the last time Ariel had seen Samira she'd gotten Roy killed, and nothing could change that. She sighed and backed away from the edge of the roof. After watching Samira and the boy wander off through the streets, she hiked across the harbor city by the rooftops. The trip back to the rendezvous point was a long one.

Under different circumstances, she would have loved to visit Epot Detharn. Come to think of it, she had never been to this continent before. But she had a job to do, and Leonard would not approve of any distractions. He was already waiting for her when she finally arrived, and the sun had dipped a bit lower in the sky. Early evening had begun.

"Well, you still have all your arrows, so I guess you didn't run into any trouble," Leonard said playfully, either that or his bright voice was injecting even more unintended mirth into his observation. He leaned against the absurdly tall spire of an ornately carved cathedral. Stone flames curled around the pointed tower. It seemed a place of worship for Iarus.

"No trouble, but I think I found who we're looking for," she said seriously.

His energetic hazel eyes widened beneath his bushy eyebrows. "You found them?" he asked, incredulous.

Ariel shrugged her tattooed shoulders. "Possibly. A boy no more than a couple years younger than me. But it's because of someone else that I saw with him." She swept the hood from her head, letting her hair spill over her shoulders. "Sam is here."

Leonard's eyes narrowed. "Why would she be here?"

"I don't know. But she's here, and she may not be happy to see us."

He sighed and stroked his stubbly chin. "We'll have to talk to her eventually if she's traveling with the last Chosen. Let's hope it goes smoothly. She was always the reasonable one, unlike..." He flinched, realizing that he may have struck a nerve. Ariel's hair danced in the breeze as she looked at him with narrowed eyes.

"Well, it's not *her* fault that Roy's dead," she said coldly.

Leonard ruffled his spiky brown hair. "I'm sorry, Ariel. I shouldn't have said that." He squinted back in the direction that Ariel had come from. "We'll go see her and this boy when the sun has gone down. Let's hope that she's happy to see us."

***

Roy stumbled through the packed plaza, his hands still shaking. Fury mixed with a horrified guilt saturated his consciousness. It had been weeks since the last time this had happened. In a moment of surprise, he had been tricked into attacking James. If he hadn't gotten a lid on it, he may have killed Samira too. He shuddered and drew his cloak around him. Even in the heat of the day, he felt chills rippling through him. This feeling, this anger, was all too familiar. *Charodon* was trying to wrestle control away from him. With Boane coming up another dead end, he was out of options to get rid of it, a terrifying notion.

"You're a drowning pain, you know that?" he said quietly. He knew that he must sound insane to anyone listening. Fortunately, everyone in this city was uninterested in one unstable stranger with a devil in his head. People coughed, and quietly wept, on the corners of packed streets. The plague from Boane had spread uncannily fast.

His pulse was still throbbing in his head. He needed to calm down. Walking quickly, he threaded through patrons and merchants toward the docks. It was nearly evening. The hoarse wail of an ailing man echoed in the vicinity. The thieves who prowled the port must have found something to take. Hopefully, James and Samira had found some place to hide out.

Roy's feet clomped across the cobbled street, and he quickened his pace as the sounds of the tide grew. Smells of salt, oil, and sulfur greeted his senses, becoming stronger, clearing his mind. The docks came into view as he rounded a corner. People became sparser the farther he strode past the docks and down to the craggy shoreline. Jagged rocks jutted from the surf, and the water swirled around it calmly. The tides were low for now, calmly trickling in and out of the rock formations that created a natural border to the docks. Ships waited patiently for the tide to come back during the night.

Several wooden poles with chains wrapped around them sat farther off in the surf. The water lapped around the posts, and barnacles clung to the deeply soaked wood. The tide only came halfway up the poles now, but when high tide was in full effect they would be completely submerged. Roy had heard of these types of sacrificial posts before, but he didn't think that they would still be in a major city such as this. He shuddered, thinking of all the people that the fanatics from the southern sect of the Temple had drowned to appease Dathos. The ocean could be unforgiving, but it was supposed to be a life-giving entity first. How could they not see this?

Roy trudged onto the rocks. Finding a place to sit, he removed his boots and reclined with his feet dangling in the water. The surf around his feet turned a slightly darker shade as the grime was washed away. The water was cool against his feet, and he could acutely sense miniature fish darting around in the water beneath them. Actually, he could sense fish much farther out, drifting by the pier more than seventy feet away. Allowing his thoughts to be consumed by the swelling of the tides, his breathing slowed, and the throbbing in the back of his skull began to fade away. A stiff, salty breeze ruffled his hair, and a brief daydream of silky, pale-gold hair swam through his mind. He shook his head slightly to dispel the image. It was best to leave thoughts like that alone.

He let out a slow sigh, exhaling to expel his tension. The tide swelled upward with his breathing, responding to his rhythm. Water crept up his legs and over his waist as he slid from the rock and waded into the surf. Leaning into the oncoming waves, his mind went blank, and the cool, foamy water covered his face. His remaining anger eroded away, broken piece by piece. From now on, he needed to be more careful. Charodon was getting more and more aggressive, and he couldn't afford to let it get in the way of him and Samira, especially since Charodon's old devilish friends were showing themselves again.

Now James was here, and there was a responsibility to make sure they got him to safety. It would be hard to regain his trust after what happened. They had just met, and Roy was sure that James would have a hard time accepting that it could be safe around him. Dathos drown him, *he* wasn't even sure if it was safe around him.

"No place is safe." Charodon's voice shot through his head.

He jerked his face from the water and gasped. The taste of salt trickled into his mouth. Shaking his soaked hair out of his eyes, he focused again on the flow of the waves. It didn't help much.

Senses

"I'm sorry, but I'm going off on my own. Whatever's wrong with Roy will backfire, and I'm not looking to get my neck wrung again," James said, exhausted as they trudged up the short wooden staircase. His voice was a hoarse whisper, and marks were beginning to appear on his throat where Roy had throttled him.

Samira shook her head. "We need you, James. I know we haven't explained much, but just give me a chance to do so." She tucked a now thinner coin pouch into the pocket of her brown cloak. "Roy has never once let me down, and I don't believe that he will anytime soon."

The air became decidedly damper and more humid at the top of the short staircase. A heavy wooden door awaited them at the landing. Small amounts of steam puffed through the cracks under the doorway.

Samira pushed the door open forcefully and steam billowed out of the inn's connected bath house to greet them.

It was all but impossible to see. James reached into the empty space in front of him and lost his hand up to the wrist in the fog. He could hear the sounds of padding feet, and low voices and splashing water reverberated through the mist from the silhouettes of people lounging in the bath. The condensation immediately settled on his face, carving paths through the ash and dirt that had been baked on by the sun. They stepped into the steam and closed the door behind them.

"What exactly is it that you want from me?" he asked quietly. He had no solid grip on his surroundings save for a few hazy lanterns hung in the corners of the chamber, but they made the mist even more difficult to see through.

"I think you've seen the reason we need you," she replied, sounding a bit annoyed. He could just see Samira kneeling to unlace her boots. "In case you forgot, there was a devil prowling the rooftops of Boane. These kinds of things aren't normally within the capacity for regular people to handle." A faint splash echoed against the walls as she sat and eased her feet into the water before them. James watched the shadow of Samira's shoulders slacken. She sighed, raised a dripping foot from the water, and pointed at her toes. "Feet. In."

Deciding to keep focused on the conversation rather than the stares of the shadowy people in the room, he removed his sandy boots and inched further into the space, searching for the edge of the bath with his feet. "I didn't forget. There are just a lot of things happening at once." His foot found the precipice of the water, and he carefully rolled up his pant legs and stepped into the scalding bath. He winced at the temperature as he submerged up to his knees and sat down on the wall of the bath. The mist coming off the water thickened and curled around him. "The Temple lied to me for my whole childhood. I can usually tell when someone isn't telling me something. And nobody tells the full truth, ever. It's why I'm better off on my own." He started swirling his feet. The water around him morphed into a deep black.

"I'm sorry. We'll try to be more honest with you." She sighed and leaned back. "Chosen have to look out for each other, and Roy and I will try better to do this for you. These Alderaye coming back mean a lot of trouble, and not just here. I wouldn't be surprised if they had a hand in Boane's downfall."

"What?"

"Alderaye. A cult of devils that date back before most of known history. Nasty ones too." Her voice held a great level of concern. "The legend is that the gods fought these Alderaye and banished them to the Dunes of Knost hundreds of years ago. My father called it the War of Lost Faith. And it's my oath, our task as Chosen, to keep them from starting another one. I'll be the one who ends this conflict, but I need your help to do that."

As far as James was concerned, his mind was made up, devils or no. Cupping water with his hands, he splashed water over his shins and viciously scoured the ashes from his knees. "What about the others?" he asked amid the mist, changing the subject. "You said I was the last one. Did you know the other two? Etah and Raslena's Chosen, I mean."

She spoke over the swishing of the water, "We knew them." Her voice had an edge of something he couldn't quite place. He couldn't see it, but he guessed that her thumb was kneading her temple. "But we haven't seen them for years. There was an incident."

James had no trouble guessing what happened in his mind. His hands were raw from scalding water and pawing through sand. "How did you find out? About being a Chosen?"

Samira chuckled. "My favorite thing to do as a child was guess where lightning would strike during a tempest. I got pretty good at it too, almost as if I had a premonition of where it would strike." Her voice brimmed with nostalgia. "There eventually came a day when I guessed wrong, and instead of landing a few miles away the bolt struck my arm." Footsteps smacked past them, and a hazy shadow passed in front of one of the lanterns. She whispered, "But then I threw it back. It was Astus choosing me, charging me to bring the other Chosen together."

Rubbing his eyes in disbelief, he stared into the fog. "How did you know?"

She shrugged. "I didn't. I don't even think I know now. It's like you feel this pull in your center. I feel the energy in everything. Everything around us has it, but lightning has more. It's just like how Roy can sense movement or energy within water. We have a connection to it."

Closing his eyes, James reached outward with his senses, feeling the temperature of the room. Heat blazed in the water below him. Within the water, several blots of intense heat radiated back to him. Listening, he heard muffled voices coming from the positions of the blots. "I can sense the heat from the people in here," he said, concentrating. "Seven, no, eight."

"Good. What else?"

He squeezed his eyes tighter, extending his consciousness beyond the bath. The air outside the water overwhelmed his senses with cooler circulation, creating a clear divide between the bath and the rest of the chamber. The colder flow of the air spread to all corners of the room except for a few blazing pinpricks of heat. "The lanterns. I can feel them."

James heard the slosh of water as Samira absentmindedly swished her feet in the pool. "Very good. You can use this along with what you've already done, controlling fire. Eventually, you'll be able to create fire from your own heat and energy. It will take practice, but I can help you if you stick with us."

The heat from the lantern's candle scorched his consciousness. He could feel it glowing in the base of his skull. A feeling of peace followed as if it were a flame spreading across parchment. James opened his eyes and exhaled slowly.

The flickering light in the corner of the room behind him went out. The water and fog around him plunged into darkness. He felt it. The burning at the nape of his neck slowly traveled through his body and into his center. It stayed there, soothing him for a moment before dissipating. Invigorated, he glanced in Samira's direction. Her silhouette nodded at him through the mist.

"You're learning fast," she said with approval. Then her voice became more serious. "I still don't approve of your plans with the Temple, but I also want you to know that I think what happened to your brother was wrong. We can find a way to make this right." She withdrew her feet from the water and reached for a rough cloth at the edge of the bath before tossing it to him. "Wash up, then we need something to eat," she said. James heard the patter of her feet as she left the room.

After James had bathed and dressed, he slipped through the door to the bathhouse. Taking advantage of the steam that billowed from the open door, James slinked from the bath down the hall to the cramped alehouse attached to the inn. The shoddy walls were a mixture of wood and stone. A pale barkeep stood at the southernmost corner, taking orders from patrons in various states of inebriation. Everything here looked cheap enough to warrant a meal.

He surveyed the dimly lit room for a moment before moving to an empty seat in a shadowed area near the entrance. Finally, a bit of quiet, a bit of time to himself. A little ironic, he guessed, that he had been afforded nothing but time to himself for the last seven straight years, but with the recent day and a half it was incredibly welcome.

"Storm's pushed our schedule forward," a gruff voice mumbled in the seat directly behind him. "We'll have to shove off before morning."

"Ain't wise, that. Gynn isn't even in town yet, and we were already a spot short to start with. Can't well push off without enough crew," a second voice said.

James's ears twitched as he picked up the conversation. It couldn't be this easy. A ticket out of the city just *happened* to be in the next chair over? He could just leave after justice was rendered, not even a second look at Boane or Epot Detharn. Samira and Roy had gotten him this far, and he was grateful, but he still didn't feel entirely safe around them. Samira was nice enough. The moment of pure calm and control in the bath and the comprehension of his power had been thanks to her, but what would she do if she wanted him to be something he couldn't? And Roy, how long before he snapped again and actually succeeded in murdering him?

Slumping over his chair, James contemplated his options. He could leave tonight with these strangers, barter for a spot on their boat, and start anew on another continent. But that glimpse of calm muddled with empowering heat had been enough to make him wonder just what the life of a Chosen could be.

Samira found him and sat across from him not two seconds after he had made up his mind. The two sailors sitting behind James cleared their platters and sauntered off toward the door, while James sat and waved the barkeep over.

"What's good here?" Samira asked.

They ate and left quickly. Night had fully arrived, and Roy had still not come back. Granted, he didn't know where they were. The inn was a good half-mile away from where he had run off. Soothed by the hot water of the bath, James's neck felt a bit better, but his voice was still a hoarse murmur.

Pale red moonlight stretched across the rooftops of Epot Detharn. The port city was still alive with activity. Merchants had packed their wares and left, but the bawdier sellers had emerged. Spiathi gin, Scourge Atoll rum, and a strange wine soaked the streets and produced a rotten, fermented odor. Brothel workers and street performers alike sidled the streets for coin. Some seemed to be in between professions.

James and Samira ducked under the arm of a woman stacking knives point-downward on her outstretched appendages. Looking around, he could see a few people hiding amongst the crowd, watching for an opportunity to swipe a trinket or coin purse.

Mustard-yellow flags flapped overhead in the breeze. Soon they would be changed to orange, and their ship would finally leave.

James wove through the various folk lining the street and went back toward the alley where they had last seen Roy. Heat was everywhere. He could feel it in every person, in every torch. He could even feel it in the brick rooftops, cooling from their long day in the sun. Since the bath house, he had been focusing nonstop on the energy around him.

It wasn't like he could see everything clearly in his head. The feeling was like being in murky water. He could sense that there were things out beyond his consciousness, but they wouldn't become clearer unless he reached for them. Glancing at Samira, a thought came to his mind.

"Where did you meet Roy?" he whispered coarsely.

She smiled briefly, carefully stepping around a man sitting against a stack of grog barrels. "About six years ago. The incident with the lightning had already happened. My father sent me to Cei to study with the priests."

His eyes widened. "You've seen the Frostspring Refuge?" The clerics had only mentioned it in passing, the most ancient and beautiful work of architecture in the known world.

Samira nodded, her hood flapping. "Oh yes! It's a sight I'll never forget. Striking near killed me to get there though."

"Why did you go?"

"Because I was getting hurt." Her voice took an unexpectedly serious tone as they neared the alley. "I couldn't control my gift, and my father was worried I never would. I left so that the clerics could teach me to wield it. We're given incredible gifts by the gods, but we can't use them to help the faithful if we can't control them."

Tilting his head in confusion, James pondered this. The memory of Samira hurling lightning at the devil in Boane flashed through his memory. "You seem to have a handle on it now."

Chuckling, Samira nodded again. "I do now, but there was a cost to it." Rolling up the sleeve of her cloak, she held out her right arm. Ugly, furious scars stretched up and down the skin of her forearm up to her bicep. "Our gifts make us strong, but all that power still is funneled through a human form. This is what happens to most people when they are struck by lightning." She rolled the sleeve back down and shrugged.

He peered warily at his hands. That scarring had looked incredibly painful. "Can that happen to me?"

"I would imagine it would be different for you," she said as they rounded the corner. The sounds of their footsteps echoed down the empty alleyway. "It affects us all differently. If Roy uses his power too much, his lungs will fill with water. He could drown even if he is miles from the ocean." She scratched her head and then clapped him on the shoulder before continuing down the side street. "Perhaps you would just burn up from the inside."

James stood for a moment, frozen in indignant horror before he followed. Samira looked like she was thinking of something. Stopping, she turned to James and said, "I noticed you don't have a very common name for a native of Boane. Come to think of it, your name sounds almost Spiathi or Collisun."

Nodding, James scratched his head. "It's not. When the Temple took me and my brother in as children, the clerics gave us the names of famous prophets from long ago. They named me after James the Tempest. They named my brother after Gemmi the Chasmwalker."

She cocked her head to the side. "Tell me about him."

"He was a couple years older than me," he said quietly and smiled. "Ruffled my hair a lot. Always let me win, no matter what we were playing. He was a good big brother." James got the sense that she wanted to ask more questions, but he shot her a look that he wanted the topic to be dropped. Blinking to show she understood, Samira continued onward into the side street.

Filth and garbage covered the inside of the alley, subtle signs of previous debauchery. Broken bottles and numerous smells littered the stone and sand. Rags and even an abandoned knife were strewn about, as if thrown by someone who had been keen to dispose of incriminating evidence. Samira kicked through the waste as they entered the pathway. The moonlight overhead couldn't reach into this crevasse between buildings.

James leaned against the wall. "Do you suppose he got lost?"

She leaned against the opposite wall and pointed toward the shadowed back of the side street. "He's here."

Roy stepped into James's dim field of vision, causing James to blink. Roy had cleaned up. He was no longer smeared with ash and sand. Smelling of salt, he stayed a few feet away from James. Turquoise eyes leveled and met James's gaze. "I'm so sorry, James. Are you hurt?"

James shook his head. He tried to sound more gracious but failed miserably. "We'll talk about this later, Roy. The Temple first."

The Champion of Dathos sighed, casting his eyes down. The expression on his face indicated that he had participated in a conversation of this sort before. Both of them looked to Samira, who reclined against the side of the alley with her arms crossed. Her amber eyes glinted beneath her hood, glancing between the two of them. Without a word, she pushed off the wall and turned in the direction of the street. Sounds of people milling about still persisted. This would be the best time for them to leave, and the best time for James to conduct his business at the Cathedral.

Staying in close proximity, they entered the street and began the journey across town to the north. The squares in the city were permeated with a tension that had not been there before. People were huddled together, traveling as a mass to avoid any confrontation. Most merchants had closed up their wares, retreating to hiding places within the city. Small groups around gave them wide berth as they continued north. The sick, having nowhere to go, clustered against the sides of the lane, wheezing and hacking into their sleeves.

Through parts in the crowd, James could see a man lying in the street. Blood pooled around the victim from a gash in his stomach, soaking the textiles he had been selling. He didn't bother telling Samira or Roy about it. He knew they had seen it too. The rest of the people ignored the bleeding man, as if acknowledging him would cause them to be targeted next. A cool breeze whipped through the square, causing the faint metallic smell of blood to reach James's nostrils. He pulled up his facecloth.

They heard scared murmurs and shuffling feet around them. Fear stretched through the square, taut as a bowstring. The three of them stood silently for a moment, cautiously waiting for trouble. People moved gingerly, heads down. The eerie echoes of footsteps and whispers swarmed like a tempest. James instinctively reached toward Samira to make sure he wasn't separated from them.

A hand slammed down on James's shoulder and forcibly spun him around. His eyes landed on a bald man with piercings covering his face. The horrible stench of grog wafted from his mouth. The rings on the man's chapped lips flexed as he sneered, putting a hand on the short sword at his belt. "Coin. Now," he hissed.

Before James could respond, Roy's fist crashed into the man's nose. Rings that had been improperly attached to the nostrils came loose and fell to the ground, tinkling lightly on the stones beneath them. The man's broken nose gushed as he involuntarily pulled a short sword from his belt. The scraping of the blade being drawn echoed through the square before Samira swept the man's legs from under him, causing him to topple to the ground with a loud thwack. The would-be thief was dazed and incapacitated before he even landed, but it was too late.

The sound of the sword being drawn was enough to panic nearby people. Screams erupted from those closest to James, and some sprinted wildly away. James felt panicked as a merchant in hysterics plowed into him. He reached for Samira and Roy, straining. From the corner of his eye, a squad of Garrison soldiers clambered into the street, wading into the crowded street and shouting, knocking people away. Already, fights were breaking out amongst Garrison and indignant, surprised townsfolk.

Scorch me, the soldiers are going to make things worse. Already, those toward the outside of the square were scrambling away from the skirmish. Caught between two shoving huddles of frightened onlookers, Samira attempted and failed to climb above the snare of arms and legs. Roy, bowled aside by the force of a fleeing man and his son, began forcing his way through the crowd with limited success. Both Samira and Roy had proved that they were stronger than most, but they couldn't compete with the writhing force of a hundred terrified and angry people fleeing the Garrison.

James was carried away from the docks by the momentum of the pulsing mob, back westward toward the inn where he and Samira had eaten. Gasping for breath, he tried to break through the bodies shoving him further away from his traveling companions. Flames began to lick at a wagon full of hay. Someone had knocked over a glowing torch that was perched on the street corner. The fire would spread quickly, as the buildings here were bleached by the sun and built with more combustible material than in Boane.

Trying to focus while being lifted off his feet, he reached with his consciousness toward the growing flame. He was forty feet away now. The torch was almost beyond the range of his senses. Straining, he tried to tap into the energy of the heat, tried to feel the power that it granted.

The fire slipped out of his reach. *This city is going to burn down too if we don't do something.* Rather than strain against the crowd, James decided to run with them. If he could get ahead of them, he could make a move back toward Samira and Roy. Sprinting in front of the mob, he looked back to see panicked faces and wide eyes. Several bandits had taken the opportunity of the chaos to make a move. The thieves weaved through the crowd with clubs, knives, and the odd short sword. Panic had invigorated the thugs, and now bold blood was pumping through them. He could see it in their eyes. Some of the crowd were going to be hurt by the hands of these bandits.

Without thinking, James bounded toward a dimly lit tavern. The outside of the building looked barely held together with sloppy extra mortar. A painted sign of a frowning sun hung just above the knotted wooden door. Throwing all his weight against the door, he burst into the tavern. The sound of cracking wood accompanied him as the door came off its hinges and fell onto the dirt floor with him. The cramped room erupted with startled cries as the roughly half-dozen patrons jumped from their chairs.

The thugs chasing the crowd had seen James's stunt, and they had turned their attention to him. Good. He had wanted them to chase him. By making such a drastic move, James had drawn attention to himself as someone who might possess a considerable amount of coin.

James quickly rolled to his feet and dashed behind one of the large circular tables. The surface of the table was an ancient shield, possibly the shield of a warrior from long ago. He turned the table on its side, spilling goblets and horns full of ale and rum. A few coins scattered on the floor as well. Some of the tavern patrons dove to scoop up the meager change. A single lantern shimmered at the corner of the bar, casting thick shadows on the walls.

"What do you think you're doing, boy?" the barkeep cried.

James was given no time to answer, as three of the bandits rushed through the door. More startled cries from drinkers reverberated through the tight space. The lead thug pushed to the front of the group, blood still trickling from his nose. It was the one who Roy and Samira had struck. The few remaining rings on his face reflected the dim torchlight of the room. Smiling as his eyes rested on James, he leveled his short sword at him.

"What happened to your friends, lad?" he mocked.

James shrugged and drew his own battered short sword, deciding to call this man Rings.

The thug shook his head and smirked as if it had all been a fun game. "Let's do this again. Coin. Now."

Rolling his eyes, James shrugged again. "I don't know what made you think I had any, but you won't find any with me."

Rings scowled, grimacing further as the glare caused the gash in his nose to open again. He glanced at his two partners, and the three of them rushed after James. Their eyes were aflame with fury and no small amount of humiliation.

Just as the first man was upon him, James kicked the overturned table the rest of the way over. The heavy wooden tabletop flipped and crashed downward on the knee of the first man. A sharp crack sounded as the man's knee was broken, and he collapsed, howling, to the floor. Rings and the other thief bounded over the table and struck downward at him. James rolled out of the way while the club and short sword clanged against the bar behind where he had been.

Glancing toward the lantern on the bar, James reached out with his consciousness. The lantern was a tiny prick of heat within his mind. He swung his sword and blocked a blow from Rings before ducking under a blow from the other man's club. Dancing around the overturned table so that he was close to the door of the tavern, James reached out again to the lantern and strengthened his concentration. The pulling in his stomach extended through his whole body this time.

Out.

The lantern went dark, plunging the room into blackness. This time he could see the action clearly. It wasn't blown out, yet the flame simply stopped existing, absorbed by his conscious command. This time he felt no fatigue, only a short burst of energy as the flame's heat transferred to him. Patrons, the barkeep, and the thugs alike all yelped in surprise as James rushed to the door.

Swearing as he bashed his hip on a table, he stumbled through the now doorless entryway and staggered out into the night. Compared to the darkness of the tavern, the moonlight outside was slightly blinding. Blinking, he glanced around the street. People were still running up and down the pathways, screaming. Fires took hold of buildings. He had been unable to stop the flames, and now they were going to spread to the rest of the town like it did to Boane.

A burning tideflag caught his eye as he looked above the tavern directly across the street from him. Smoke was already beginning to flow through the air in an ever-thickening cloud, warping the world before his eyes, turning into Boane all over again. Could the same thing really be happening?

A small reflection of light drew his gaze downward into the street. James's blood froze in his veins when he saw that it was from an arrowhead pointed directly at him. The arrow—nocked in the bow of a woman in a royal-blue cloak—was serrated on one edge. The other edge was filed to a razor's sharpness.

Sleeveless cloak flapping in the stronger breeze, the stranger's watchful blue eyes narrowed above a dark-green facecloth. Even at a glance, he knew that the archer would not miss. A strand of golden hair floated in front of her face. James held up his hands, extending them into the air. The stranger didn't lower the bow.

Roy and Samira were nowhere in sight. There was no way for him to dart out of the way of this shot. He was in close enough range, and the look in the stranger's eye conveyed the intent to hit him. In a last effort to spare himself, he decided to talk his way out of it.

"Don't—" he said.

The arrow flew, creating a ripping noise as it sliced through the air. James squeezed his eyes, expecting pain, but the arrow zipped past his ear, actually nicking the lobe. A thud sounded behind him, and he whirled around to see the shaft of the missile sprouting from the shoulder of Rings. The thug had followed him outside of the tavern and had been moments away from running him through. A clattering of metal on stone rang out as Rings's blade fell from his hand and clanged to the street.

Rings screamed in surprise, his face contorting in pain and shaking the last few piercings loose. A second arrow bloomed from the thug's leg. Momentum from the arrow swept the leg from under him, and Rings collapsed to the street face first. Wailing in humiliation and agony, Rings was unable to move, taken down by the stranger. He would live, but he wasn't going anywhere for a while.

James turned back to the woman clad in blue, bow lowered and already surveying the street for more threats. Having heard the importance of Chosen in the north, he knew that there may have been others looking for him. The question remained, what did she want? Why would she save him? He didn't get any time to ask the questions he wanted before the stranger spoke to him.

"Where is Sam? We need to find her." Her voice was smooth yet energetic. She could have been urgent or calm, and James couldn't decide which. "I saw her with you earlier. Where is she?"

"I...I don't know," he finally stammered. He realized that his hands were still in the air. Sheepishly lowering them, he tried to think of where Samira and Roy would have gone after they had been separated. "They may have gone to the docks."

The woman swept her hood back, revealing pale, shining hair. She hooked a finger around her face cloth and lowered it to expose a thin mouth that looked happy, even though her eyes were harder than steel, "What do you mean, 'they?'"

she asked. She couldn't have been more than a year or two older than him. Maybe Roy's age. Her lightly tan skin reflected the light of the fires burning at the end of the street.

He tilted his head, not understanding. His confusion deepened as her narrow lips turned upward and her teeth flashed white in an ecstatic smile. The wind blew at her cloak. Her attire was the strangest he had ever seen. She wore a rough wool shirt of the darkest green under the cloak, sleeves cut off at the shoulders. Her arms were covered with tattoos of unfamiliar glyphs. Her baggy pants were made of a thick material and extended to worn climbing boots. The attire was definitely foreign, possibly Spiathi or maybe even Cei.

"Roy was with you, wasn't he? Roy is alive." A relieved laugh escaped her as she stepped forward. Her demeanor was the exact opposite of what he would expect an acquaintance of Roy's to be.

James nodded, confused and impressed. "He was with me not five minutes ago. Before all of this happened." He gestured to the east. The left side of the street was completely in flames now. It was only a matter of time before it spread to the next block. Looking back at the stranger, her steely eyes now held a glimmer that hadn't been there a second ago. "We need to stop this fire or it will destroy the city like it did to Boane."

The woman slung her bow over her shoulder, and they dashed to the nearest structure, a stable. James's ear throbbed as they ran, and a light, stinging pain shot through his earlobe when he reached up to touch it. What else did he think would happen? Blood lazily dripped onto his shoulder.

The air around the stables was boiling as they approached. Terrified people still swarmed in the street, but no one was trying to put the blaze out. James was going to have to do this himself. Steeling his consciousness, he reached out with his mind to the stable in front of him. A white-hot wall of energy crackled before him. He could try to put it out like the lantern in the tavern, but would he be able to do it? The lanterns took a considerable amount of concentration. A flicker he could handle, but a blazing building was something else entirely.

Reaching his hand outward, he concentrated on the rumbling flames. The stranger's clear eyes widened as she watched him attempt to absorb the fire. Heat rolled through his body, blasting his nerves and rapidly crawling through his veins. This must have been what Samira was talking about, heat beginning to peak inside him. Trying to contain the intense energy, he shouted a command in his head at the flames.

Out!

The blaze did nothing. A deafening crack sounded as a support beam from the stable finally gave out and fell to the ground in three pieces. The building was falling apart. Scorch him, nothing he was doing worked. Closing his eyes, he tensed his muscles again and screamed soundlessly at the inferno.

Out, scorch you!

Another crack sounded, and a second beam fell from the stable ceiling. James reluctantly forced his eyes open to see that the flames had died down but barely by a third. If he waited a moment, maybe he could try three or four more times. That may be enough to put the flames out and keep the fire from spreading to the next block. The rest of the street was still aflame, though. He couldn't do the whole street.

Shadows danced across his face as he panted deeply, hands on his knees. His arm stung toward the back of his wrist. He looked down at his forearm and winced. Pink burns covered a small spot on his wrist. It was barely the size of a thimble, but Samira's words shot through his mind. *"Perhaps you'll just burn up from the inside."*

A stiffening breeze rolled through the street as the golden-haired stranger inhaled deeply. Bits of sand and trash fluttered through the walkway, and she gazed intently at the remaining flames on the stable. James watched, awestruck. What was she doing? Her cloak floated around her, and her hands, rough with callouses, pointed palms-first at the blaze. He could tell she was holding her breath, her gaze concentrated on the base of the flames.

Slowly pushing her hands outward, she released a sharp breath, expelling all of the air from her lungs. A short, hurricane-force blast of wind rolled through the square—killing the fire and sending a plume of ash leaping into the air above them. James grumbled as he realized he was now covered in soot all over again, but the feeling passed when he peered through the smoke to see the strange woman pulling up her cowl. Risking the chance of catching ashes in his mouth, he gaped at her.

Unshouldering her bow, she gave a thin smile. "That's one down. Name's Ariel. Who might you be?"

A Lost Friend

Limbs flew in their faces as they fought to get back to James. Roy and Samira were rocked and shoved eastward, back toward the city's entrance. Buildings passed by, and the mob eventually began to break apart. Roy hurled a larger man with a freckled nose and uncommonly light hair to the side and called out.

"Sam!" he shouted over the screams and groans of the terrified, fleeing residents. Smoke began to float above the rooftops of the port city, distorting the view of the closest tideflag. It was the same thing. Boane was happening all over again. *Tonight.* Dawn was too long of a wait. They would have to get to the ship and leave immediately.

A slight ache in his right hand persisted from striking that ringed bastard back in the square. Searching for Samira, he shoved through the chaotic crowd aggressively. There was no time for this. The cold anger he felt in the alley that morning started to ooze through the back of his skull. Like prickling ice, it poked at him, trying to set loose what had attempted to take over earlier that day. Fleeing townsfolk scattered like marbles dumped from a pouch, colliding with each other as they ran in nonsensical directions. Roy strained his ears for any sound that could be associated with his friend.

"Roy!" Her voice floated over the din of the street. Searching frantically for her, Roy's anger swelled again as frightened merchants staggered into his path, dragging a cart of wooden trinkets. The carving of the items was crude, and the men dragging the cart strained, sweat drenching their skin. A wheel had broken off the cart, causing the heavy body to scrape across the cobblestone, producing a piercing screech. It stabbed his ears. He could feel it behind his eyes.

Before he could stop himself, his leg shot forward and his boot collided with the side of the vessel. Wood clattered with the heavy kick. He threw the wagon over, toppling the trinkets and scattering them across the street. The merchants, dressed in faded blue robes with attached tassels, cried out in surprise, scrambling away. Cold fury swept through Roy as he brought his boot down on the cart again and again. The wood began to buckle, and he could see individual fibers on each board break. Snapping wood and Roy's incoherent roars joined the chaotic ensemble of panic. From the corner of his eyeline, he saw his hand as he brought his heel down upon the cart again.

The hand was covered in scales. Skin split as if molting to reveal dark green and gray, slimy and shifting as the shredding skin began to come free of his body. The frigid rage that had been sitting at the base of his skull suddenly became a buzzing terror. He was losing control. It was breaking out, and if he didn't calm down right away all of the people streaming around him would die. He clamped his eyelids together, trying to force down the ice in his blood.

"It's too late for that," Charodon laughed in his mind. *"Just enjoy the ride, boy."* Roy's body felt frozen. Droplets of water from his breath froze as he tried to slow his rapid breathing. The noise around him was deafening, drowning out his thoughts, giving way to the cold. Orange eyes darting around in terror, his vision began to blur.

Samira's hand clapped down onto his shoulder, grabbing his cloak and dragging him from the street. She strained and grunted as he struggled involuntarily against her pull. His boots scraped across the stones and sand.

The world came back into focus for Roy briefly, a room breaching through his swimming vision. It seemed that she had carried him into an old, crumbling storehouse. It was empty, half-eaten jars of expired goods only occupying a single shelf. Dust and sand gave the interior of the structure an ancient aesthetic. A dead family of scuttlers rotted near a wobbly table. Their arrow-like, hairy snouts and glassy eyes pointed upward toward the cracked ceiling. Each scuttler's six knobby legs were stiff, clearly having been dead for a while.

Lugging Roy inside the door, she gently placed him against the wall. Scales rippled across his neck. Ragged breaths escaped his mouth as his eyes, bright orange, began to wash back to their normal blue-green. Crashes, screams, muffled chaos echoed outside the walls of the storehouse. None of the mob attempted to break in, however. She knelt in front of him.

"You're okay," she said desperately. Her voice shook, praying for her friend to fight back against his tormentor. "Dathos, Wanderer of the Sea, please watch over your son. The Chosen of your gift lives to carry your will. Wash this intruder from him. Please," she pleaded rapidly, her hand still firmly holding Roy's shoulder.

It took almost five more minutes of Samira begging, but his eyes returned to their icy turquoise. As his splitting skin began to knit itself together over the slimy scales underneath, Roy's breathing began to slow. The dust particles in the air swirled around them in the pockets of crimson moonlight that spilled through the crumbling wall. To Roy, they looked like stars.

Leaning his head back against the wall, he sighed shakily. "Go find James and get to the ship." His eyes followed the swirling dust in the air. "It's going to try and take over again. You need to be gone when that happens."

She slapped him.

Roy's head flopped to the side, and his vision went out of focus for a moment from the force. Drown him, she was strong. He looked back up at Samira, surprise and annoyance painted on his face.

Samira's amber eyes glared at him. "Are you ready to talk sense now?"

He nodded slowly. A purple mark was already starting to balloon on his cheek.

"We're going to go find James, and then we're getting on the ship. *Together*," she said sharply. "No one is leaving anyone behind. Get your temper in check, get up, and let's get going." She shivered. "It's too dark in here."

His bones ached as he stood, but he got up quickly nonetheless. Dust particles sprung up around him. "Thanks," he said, a bit sheepishly.

She grumbled, rubbing her temple, "Astus strike me, I will slap you again if you say something foolish like that. Ariel would have knocked you senseless and dragged you along."

"And Ariel is normally the diplomatic one," said a light, jovial voice.

Roy and Samira whirled around, swords scraping as they drew them rapidly. Their eyes fixed on the entryway to the building. Leonard leaned against the brick doorway of the storehouse, his tall, muscled frame silhouetted by the moon. The large mace he held in his left hand rested on his shoulder. Roy and Samira both knew that the mace wasn't the weapon to watch out for. Leonard always kept a long hunting knife in his boot. Behind him, the mob still frothed outside. Shouts rang through the square, and the walls of the storehouse quaked as Garrison soldiers slammed bystanders against the building.

Like Samira, Leonard wore a leather jerkin, but his was dark blue, embroidered with a tree inside a sphere, the symbol of Raslena. He wore no shirt underneath, exposing his bulging arms to the night air. He had prepared for the heat better than Samira, however, his pants a light, breathable material. His square face was framed by his dark-brown stubble, and his thick eyebrows climbed his face as he leered at them.

"*You.*" Roy snarled, pointing his saber at Leonard's chest. The blade of the sword was unadorned, no markings of any kind. His hand gripped the leather hilt, one finger on the plain cross guard. He strode over to the man. His face burned in fury, flecks of orange beginning to reappear in his vision.

Leonard's smile flattened immediately. He had very clearly hoped to run into Samira by herself. It would have been much safer for him. Perhaps he had made the mistake of assuming that Roy was dead. Plenty had made that mistake, but only once. Bandits, hitmen, and even most soldiers had lost their lives after presumably killing the Scaleslayer.

"Roy, I just want to talk." Leonard carefully lowered the mace and held up his hands, fingers spread apart. Moonlight trickled through the gaps in his fingers, occasionally broken up by a fleeing townsperson.

"I don't care." The point of Roy's saber rested against Leonard's chest, poking into the leather of his jerkin. Once small specs of orange in his sights were growing larger. "You don't deserve to speak to us." Roy had sworn that if he ever saw the Chosen of Raslena again he would kill him. Those smug hazel eyes looked at him apprehensively. Roy's dreams had been haunted by those eyes, taunting him. He had dreamt of killing this man. Years were not enough to erase the scar that had destroyed his face, nor the devil that threatened to use him. Frigid rage began to build up in him again.

Samira carefully inched toward Roy and Leonard, her hand held up in front of her. The sound of her footsteps across the rotting floorboards felt as if they drowned out the chaos outside. Each creak and groan caused the three of them to stiffen, as if any sound may set off a bloody dance that would end with all three of them dead. Gingerly, she placed her fingers on the flat edge of Roy's sword and lowered the point to the floor. He let her but kept his eyes on Leonard. Glancing back and forth between them until she was modestly sure they would stay where they were, she peered at Leonard. "What do you want?"

Roy glared at him, unmoving.

Leonard sighed. "I know you found the last one. I want to help you get him across the sea. To safety." His eyes darted back and forth. Scoffing and rubbing his eyes with a thumb and forefinger, he clenched his teeth. "I would ask if you don't believe me, but you both are terrible at hiding your thoughts. Why would I want to harm him?"

"You couldn't have known that we found him until recently. We only found him last night, and that was an accident," Samira said. Her hand rested on the hilt of her sword, a purposeful move that Leonard had seen her use time and time again.

Roy's eyes narrowed even further. "You're here for the empire, aren't you?" A second, smaller crest was stitched into Leonard's collar. Dark-blue flames surrounding a gold sword. The Collisun Empire had made an errand boy out of Leonard. Collisun worshipped with similar fervor that they did in Boane, though not as extreme. *Dathos drown me, they're annoying*, he thought to himself. They'd tried to make a mercenary of him years ago, but he was no lapdog.

Leonard nodded again, flipping his spiky hair. "The new emperor is struggling after succeeding to the throne," he said. "He's not respected. The Chosen of Iarus blessing him would throw the support of the people behind him." He paused. "And he was willing to give me command if I brought the Chosen of Iarus back."

There's the motive. Self-centered as always. Roy bit the inside of his cheek.

The screams of the crowd outside had gradually morphed into the barking of soldiers. The Garrison had finally, amazingly, taken action in controlling the riot they caused.

Samira kneaded her temple with her thumb. "So they sent you here to find James and bring him back to stop an uprising?"

Roy could tell that she was thinking quickly, trying to decipher what was really at play here.

"No. Spiath and Kostra are both standing with him firmly. But Alaric is not his father. He needs the people's faith, and he hasn't won a war to earn it like his father did. People need strength right now."

Sneering, Roy stepped back. "And he sent you? I seem to recall that you have a knack for running away at the first sign of trouble."

Leonard's cheeks flushed, and he glowered at Roy, clearly annoyed. He began to reach for his mace.

Stepping between them, Samira searched every corner of Leonard's hazel eyes for deception.

Leonard stared back, unblinking. Even though moonlight shadowed their faces, she could see his eyes, what was behind them. He may be telling the truth, but it still might not be the best move to go with him. Roy knew that nothing was more important to Samira than her mission of bringing the Chosen together, of fulfilling the prophecy read to her by her father, and she needed James and Roy for it.

The only problem was that she needed Leonard too.

Her hand came off the hilt of her sword. She waited for something to happen, for one of them to attack the other, but Roy and Leonard stayed where they were. "James must know that our destination is the docks. If he got away from those bandits, that's where he'll be going."

Groaning as he bent down to pick up his mace, Leonard turned his head to the side, cracking his neck. Roy remembered all too well how much he liked to lord his age over them, always complaining about some ache or strain. Both of them had always ignored it as ridiculous. At only twenty-eight, he was just four years older than Samira and only seven years older than Roy. In Boane, it was considered much older, but across the sea, it was barely any difference.

The mace scraped off the stone doorway as Leonard heaved it up onto his shoulder. It was about three feet of steel, beautifully forged. A handgrip that he had wrapped himself clung to the narrow end of the weapon. The other end of the mace bloomed into what looked like a metal fountain, with ornate, steel pieces that fanned from the center. Standing back up to his full height, he was nearly a head taller than them. Leonard scratched his head absentmindedly against one of the prongs on the blunt weapon. "Ariel took off after him when you got separated. She should be able to look after him just fine until we can meet at the docks."

A tingle of electricity ran through Roy's body at the mention of her name. She was here? A vision of bright, gold hair swam through his vision as he sheathed his sword. His nerves buzzed with animation. It had been two years since he had last seen her, but it had felt much longer than that. He immediately squelched the exhilaration that had taken root in his stomach. There was a reason he hadn't seen her in two years, and he was sure that she hadn't forgotten it. They weren't the kids that played in the refuge anymore. She was a grown woman, one who he had grievously wronged.

"She's here," Leonard said, noticing Roy's expression. "Just try not to fall over yourself."

Roy scowled. Leonard's jests had not been missed.

Crimson moonlight spread over their faces as the three of them exited the building, Roy bringing up the rear. He had no intention of letting Leonard out of his sight. The bastard had his back turned. Now would be the best time to kill him. Roy's hand rested on the hilt of his saber for a moment before he let it slip to his side. There were more pressing matters, and he couldn't afford to waste time with a fight.

The fire to the west had stopped, and white smoke billowed from the still cooling buildings. The pale light of the moon illuminated thin wisps of smoke. Garrison soldiers, their rusted armor creaking, patrolled the disheveled street. Roy saw Leonard, the high and mighty bastard, shake his head at the way they marched. No self-respecting soldier would be caught with those gaps in their patrol. Well, military discipline wasn't everything. Even with the riot, someone had done their duty and changed the tideflags. The tide was high, and it wouldn't stay that way forever. The sailors he had bargained with to give them passage would not wait. Even though he would not pay them until they were on the boat, they were very clear that they were leaving at sunrise.

Incoming mariners had whispered of a massive storm brewing in the north toward the Kostran shores and moving south, not something that any smart sailor would risk passing through. If it went any further west, ships docked at Epot

Detharn could be stranded for another week. They couldn't wait that long. The thing that had attacked them in Boane was sure to follow them here. Putting as much distance between them and the devil that had killed countless people was paramount. Roy was fairly sure which Alderaye the thing had been, and the presence inside him all but confirmed it.

Shivering at the thought of the creature, he swept his vision over the considerably deserted street. Several people sprawled dead of either disease, thugs looking for anything valuable, or the soldiers. Putting down riots was something that bullies with too much power took to with glee. Epot Detharn was its own city by law, but it still relied on Boane to a degree that it used the Garrison force as city guard. Few of them could be spotted corralling people away, their rusty armor standing out among the huddled batches of bystanders. Roy nodded in the direction of the soldiers as they hid beneath a secluded awning.

Samira had already spotted them. "Best to steer clear," she agreed. A few strands of her hair had freed themselves from her tight braid and hung loosely in front of her face. Her keen eyes darted from corners, to rooftops, to alleyways, looking for the best possible route toward the docks. Her gaze finally landed on a relatively secluded side street lined by a few torches. Roy and Leonard followed her gaze and began to sneak out from under the ledge. Holding out her arm, Samira motioned for them to get back.

They shuffled backward, eyeing her quizzically. She gestured with her chin toward an open doorway within the alley. In the light of the sparse torches, a small shimmer poked through the darkened entrance. Even from this distance, Roy could tell it was the reflection off a dull blade. Someone inside that door was waiting for passersby with a knife, ready to pounce on the next oblivious soul to stroll by. The presence of the Garrison was not enough to deter the thieves of the city. It was only enough to make them hunt smarter.

Leonard looked ready to risk it. Roy rolled his eyes and scoffed, a sliver of cold anger manifesting itself within him. Two years had passed, and he was still as impulsive as ever. As if walking into an ambush was going to help them. Impulses like that were responsible for what had happened three years ago, when Roy and Leonard's friendship had died.

Feeling a light tap on his shoulder, Roy looked over as Samira pointed with two fingers toward a cart on the other side of the street. Packed with wooden crates of dropped supplies and tied to two Garrison horses, the wagon rested next to a mill. Bricks poked out from the mill wall haphazardly, creating an uneven surface up the outer walls. Nodding to show they understood, Leonard and Roy followed Samira silently across the street toward the cart. The street was too busy, crawling with people, friendly or otherwise, that could jeopardize their passage. Up high, none of the Garrison would be thinking to look for them.

Drawing his hood up, Roy strained to keep a low profile. The eyes of Garrison soldiers passed by without a second thought. The fire was out, and the soldiers assumed that their job was done. That was the difference between scouts and soldiers, Samira had told him once. Scouts never stopped paying attention. He assumed she had picked that up from her father.

Boots making the slightest scrapes against the cobbled street, they crept their way to the soldiers' cart. Blocks were placed behind the wheels in an attempt to keep the carriage in place. The horses whinnied softly as they approached, spooked slightly by their silent approach. Not good. Roy went to calm the horses while Leonard carefully hinged a foot on the wagon, hoisting himself up easily and clambering onto the payload of wooden crates. Roy stroked the first horse's muzzle, gently running his hand through its forelock. A sand-like hue.

"It's okay," he said, shushing the animal. Its baleful brown eye glanced at him. The horse snorted at him, and he cocked his head to the side. "I saw some apples back the other way." He shrugged and gave the beast a kindly pat. "They might still be there."

"Quit messing around," Leonard hissed. His arms bulged as he reached up for the next handhold, already halfway up the wall. Samira said nothing, placing her foot on a jutting brick, deciding not to get involved.

Roy felt the cold hatred seep into him again. Who was Leonard, the one who had always constantly been distracted by the nearest pub, blacksmith, or pair of breasts, to tell *him* to stay focused? Orange flecks sprung into his pupils once again. The numbness slowly climbed downward from the back of his skull. Suddenly, the horse's eye widened in terror, the orange in his eyes reflecting in its pupil. It began to shake in fear, squealing in a terrified neigh that echoed across the street. The other horse began to whinny fearfully, its eyes rolling backward in its head. They could sense it. They were afraid of him, afraid of *it*.

Roy quickly left the horses and mounted the wagon. Trying to make as little noise as possible, he climbed the stack of crates toward the wall. The horses were screaming now as he tried to push the cold back, tried to keep control. Sounds of clattering wood rang in his ears while the horses tried to pull away from the carriage, making the wheels clack against the wooden stops. Faint voices of alerted soldiers began to sound. Clacking, screaming, the cold, they all formed a vortex that swirled around him, within him.

The bricks of the wall were worn with pockets of air carved into them by the elements. It was a miracle that the wall was still holding together. He ignored this and tried to find a stable hold for his feet. Off to his left and below him, the horses shuffled restlessly. Samira was almost at the top. Leonard crouched on the roof, holding out a hand for her to grab so he could hoist her up the rest of the way.

It felt like his veins were freezing one by one. The screaming of the horses buffeted his eardrums, setting him on edge. He was barely holding Charodon back, trying to focus on staying calm while climbing. Skin was already starting to split on his left hand. Green-gray scales began to molt their way out of the tearing flesh.

A shout of alarm wafted from the street behind him. Roy didn't have to turn around to know that they had been spotted. He tried to ignore it and keep climbing. He looked up to see Samira and Leonard reaching down from the roof, their eyes both reflecting urgency and possibly panic. They suddenly both recoiled as something whipped past their heads. He glanced behind him and saw Garrison soldiers loading bolts into a crossbow.

Trying to climb faster, he positioned his foot to the right to get better footing. Suddenly, his right calf erupted in pain from a crossbow bolt tearing through his boot and driving into his leg. The brick that he had reached for came free of the wall and tumbled out of his grip. As Roy lost his hold on the wall, the cold spread throughout his body, numbing his every nerve as he lost control. The horses shrieked in terror, their dark eyes rolling white and pulling desperately against their rigging.

"*Roy!*" Samira yelled.

Roy didn't feel himself hit the ground. The cold had taken over, submerging him just below the frozen surface of a lake he couldn't break through. His nerves, limbs, and body were no longer his own. He could still see and hear as he crashed into the stack of crates and tumbled out of the wagon to the uneven stone street. Garrison approached him, spears and crossbows leveled at his torso.

Samira fought to descend the wall as Leonard held her back, shouting to him. Her words were indecipherable to him, but he could see her eyes. They were alight with abject terror. The horses, no less than seven feet from him, kicked and tossed danced in a panic. In the light of the torches, he could do nothing except watch as his skin unstitched itself from his body. Jagged scales pushed through the flesh as he grew in size. His bones broke and reset themselves, tearing sinew and muscle.

The soldiers scrambled backward, their faces contorted in horror. One of the men vomited at the sight.

Roy's gleaming orange eyes looked to Sam and Leonard in desperation before his vision went dark. Samira's mouth screamed silently at him. Her eyes glistened with tears. Leonard's mouth was pursed in grim dread. The voice, that terrible voice, boomed through the blackness in his head.

"*Food.*"

He screamed, but his mouth was no longer his.

"*Death.*"

The cold was all he felt. Memories of other sensations were lost. They no longer existed.

"Freedom."

Charodon

Samira gaped at the spot where Roy had been, but he was no longer there.

In his place now stood an abomination. Drawing itself up to its full height of twelve feet, it blinked its orange, reptilian eyes, eyelids sliding sideways across the membranes. Its crocodilian head bristled with broken, ragged teeth. Salt water pulsed through gill slits on the side of its neck, mixing with the slime and brine that covered its bulky frame. The scum-colored scales reflected torchlight with a grimy sheen.

It stepped on two legs toward the terrified soldiers, a deep-throated hiss emanating from its maw. A stench of death and decay floated on its breath. Mist began to draw around the monster, forming clouds that thundered with each movement it made. The soulless, reptilian grin froze the Garrison in place.

Still hitched to the wagon, the horses panicked, thrashing wildly in an attempt to get away from the monstrosity. Sentries for the Garrison tried to back away from the creature slowly. Rusted armor creaked, the only sound in an otherwise eerie silence.

On the roof, Samira and Leonard were sprawled backward, frozen in fear and hopelessness. It had plagued both of their nightmares for the better part of three years. Leonard's hand covered her mouth, but she could no longer make any noise. They had come to Boane looking for a cure but had found James amid a burning city instead. Gaining James had given her a lot of hope, her path was made clear, but it had inadvertently taken hope away from Roy. Now, seeing his body consumed by this demon, she knew that even if he was able to regain control he was running out of time.

The monster's massive hands unclenched, and knifelike claws extended from its webbed fingers. The clouds of mist swirled around it, as if it were the epicenter of its own personal typhoon. One of the soldiers' resolve broke upon seeing the claws of the beast. The man turned and attempted to sprint away, his armor clanking. Samira knew that he was a dead man. They were all dead men, just waiting.

In barely enough time for a person to blink, the devil lurched forward and snatched up the fleeing Garrison sentry, holding him in the air, squeezing him. The man's armor crumpled with a sickening crunch. He shrieked as the metal—rusted and old— bent into him, puncturing his skin and crushing his bones. He beat at the scaled hand that held him aloft, legs kicking in the air. The beast hissed and dashed him against the ground. Another crunch and a nauseating thud sounded as the soldier's bones snapped and his head smacked the stone. Blood and sea water trickled between the spaces in the cobbled bricks of the street.

Roaring in sadistic glee, the monster attacked the other stunned Garrison soldiers. Some tried to fight against the creature, throwing their spears into the armored scales of its body, but they bounced off or splintered. The thick, interlocking scales weren't even dented. It swiped at a spearless fighter with its claws, sending him sailing into a wall while also deeply cleaving him. Other Garrison men tried to flee, screaming for someone, anyone to help them. One of them climbed onto the wagon, desperately trying to keep his balance. The horses were straining against their traces, trying as hard as they could to get away from this terrifying predator. The man's rusted armor creaked as he balanced on the wobbling crates, calling up to Samira and Leonard.

"Help us! Help us! Please!" he screamed. His eyes were wider than thought humanly possible. Samira fearfully looked around for something that could give them an advantage.

Screams again reverberated through the square as the creature snatched another soldier. The man's head and shoulders disappeared into the mouth of the monster. Bones and sinew split as it wriggled its head, twisting the man apart. It was starting to pursue the Garrison further to the north. Soon it would run after them and be impossible to catch.

Samira gasped sharply as the solution came to her. "You need to trap it." She gestured to the stones and sand in the street. "If you can trap it, I can hit it hard enough for Roy to maybe regain control." This would be risky. Leonard's power took a tremendous amount of energy.

Leonard glanced at the uneven, cobbled street and nodded shakily. He was clearly terrified. Eyes darting from the ground to the rooftops across from them, he pointed along the clay roofs.

"I...I'll try to keep it close to these buildings. You can have a cleaner shot if you have height on your side." Every second they wasted would result in another casualty. Samira grunted in agreement before leaping onto the roof opposite them. Her braid whipped behind her. Up ahead, she watched as the monster attacked a cart with a man hiding underneath it. Its claws shredded the wood in front of it, whipping straw around the street. The bystander underneath the cart wailed, petrified. The cart all but disintegrated under the talons of the creature, leaving the poor man defenseless.

Samira grunted and swung her left arm downward, hurling lightning at the creature. The bolt arced from her fingertips and illuminated the street with a blinding flash. Even though she knew the monster could take a beating, Roy was still in there. She had to be careful not to cause too much damage. The bolt shot past the beast and blasted the building behind it on the other side of the street. Sparks rained from the point of impact, and a small flame sputtered to life in the doorway of the closed tavern.

Strike me! Even at relatively close range, it was hard to aim. The lightning was always powerful, and that made it hard to manipulate. On the street, Leonard dashed to the blackened doorway of the tavern and swept his foot through the sand on the cobblestones. The sand from the gutter kicked up into the air and landed on the fire, smothering it with a sharp hiss. He looked up in her direction and nodded curtly. Suddenly, Leonard's eyes widened.

She looked back to see the creature's orange eyes glaring up at her. The man under the cart was forgotten for now. Taking his chance to escape, the man darted away from the cart and into a narrow alley. One man saved. Samira's relief was short-lived. Snarling, the monster sprung toward the building and dug its claws into the bricks below her. It would be on the roof in a moment, and she would be at a disadvantage. Samira stumbled, the roof trembling beneath her. It was too heavy. The building was going to collapse. Perhaps they could use this to their advantage. Mist from the creature's storm swirled around her, making it difficult to see, but she could see its eyes glowing with animalistic rage through the clouds. She called to Leonard.

"Bring it down!" she yelled over the scrabbling of loose bricks below her. Nodding, Leonard rushed across the street, hurdling over the bodies of slain Garrison soldiers.

The orange eyes came closer to her. Determined not to be intimidated, she stood her ground as it grappled onto the roof, claws shearing the clay shingling. Sea water and foam dribbled from its cracked, yellowed teeth. The roof underneath it groaned, straining under its weight as it crouched no less than an arm's length from Samira.

Clasping her sword and ripping it from the sheath, she held it aloft in her right hand, electricity crackling in her left. The beast hissed a challenge. The stench of death wafted toward her, blowing her loose strands of hair off her face. She did not flinch, instead hissing a threat back to the abomination before her, the friend she had failed, "Give him back, Charodon. *Now.*"

Charodon opened its reptilian jaws uncannily wide and roared, its bloody maw revealing pink flesh leading to its gullet. At that moment, Leonard leapt over the splintered wagon and slammed his heavy mace into the bricks below the creature. Alone, the blow would not have been enough to bring the wall down, but Leonard channeled his power through the weapon, manipulating the clay particles within the bricks.

The bricks shattered under the impact, pulling the bricks above them inward. Charodon buckled under the avalanche of clay, unable to find purchase in the crumbling structure of the roof in front of it. The demon swiped its claw as it fell, missing Samira by inches. Leonard pounded the ground with his mace again just as the creature hit the street with a deafening crash. The bricks covering the monster melded together, pinning it in place. Charodon strained to get back up. Its mouth opened and a deep roar rumbled out of its throat in protest.

"Hit him! Now!" Leonard shouted. Samira leapt from the collapsing building and swung her left hand downward, aiming for the creature's monstrous face. Blue electricity arced from her fingers and shot straight into the side of Charodon's snout, stunning it and slightly darkening the scales. This wouldn't kill it, she was counting on that. All she needed was to hit it hard enough for Roy to retake his own body.

The lightning brightened as she hit it again and landed on the brick pile pinning its chest to the street. The stunned monster's mouth slacked open, unable to move. Flecks of turquoise began to show in its glassy, orange eyes. Samira hit it again, this time with a stronger blast, blinding white. The body started to shrink, the scales crumpling in on themselves like paper and becoming soft, fleshlike. The teeth straightened and fell out. New, more human teeth pushed through the gums.

Samira stared into the wilting face of the devil as it slowly transformed into the face of her friend. Skin finally knit itself together out of the remains of the crumpled scales, becoming Roy's pale face. His scar gleamed through his left eye, usually the last thing to return to normal after a transformation. It had been months since the last one. Roy's clothes were in tatters, and his boots had burst when Charodon's claws had sprouted from his toes. Samira glanced back to the horse cart and noted that his black cloak was the only bit of his clothing that stayed whole. She shook her head. Of all things, that awful rag had survived. He had been wearing it when she first met him, back when it was way too big for him. As far as she knew, he had always worn it, like a good luck charm. It was made of a common fabric found in Cei.

Hopping down from the brick pile, she strode quickly to the cloak and snatched it up. Astus strike it, it always had that damn salt smell. Leonard, exhausted and wobbly, strained to pull Roy from the rubble. He was alive, but it would be a while before he woke up.

Samira knelt and wrapped Roy in the cloak. She was going to have to carry him now. They couldn't wait for him to wake up. Anyone in the city who wasn't deaf would have heard the destruction, and they wouldn't wait long before investigating. She tried to haul Roy over her shoulder, straining with the dead weight.

Leonard leaned on his mace, wobbling to his feet. It had taken a lot of power to hold Charodon down, and the more power Leonard used the heavier and denser he became. Just the price of Raslena's gift, she supposed. It was a heavy burden, their power, but it was their calling to use it. Samira's eyes, with no small amount of gratitude, caught Leonard's. Charodon was Leonard's most persistent fear. Even fighting it indirectly was an act that restored her trust, mostly. There was still much for him to answer to, but it would have to be when Roy woke up.

"Let's go," she panted. "Ariel and James should be at the docks by now." Leonard limped after her, using his mace as a cane. With Roy slung over her shoulder, she shuffled north toward the docks. She wasn't sure how she would react to seeing Ariel again. Samira knew that Roy cared immensely for Ariel, but it had been a long time since she and Leonard had left. They had all been like family, but that was all gone now. Because of Charodon, it was all gone, and her mission was that much harder without them. *And because of me.*

They had almost made it to a secluded alley when a child squeaked behind them.

"I have to say, the Chosen are definitely the same as I remember," the young voice said, sounding bored. Samira attempted to turn around, straining with Roy over her shoulder. Before she could get a glimpse of the boy, a bright flash of pain crashed through her mind. Immediately, another presence invaded her thoughts.

It was one of *them*. A devil, another Alderaye.

She collapsed with Roy, banging her shoulder on the ground. Images cascaded into her vision: images of her worst fears, of her father, of her childhood. They overwhelmed her as she convulsed in the rubble. Leonard crumpled beside her and Roy, plagued by images as well. Samira saw the concerned face of her father after her arm had been mangled. She saw the body of Talia, buried after the explosion at the Shale Watchtower. She saw Roy and Ariel singing by the fire as Leonard piped at his flute. The memories and fears paralyzed her and washed through her consciousness over and over until she was no longer able to think. Her mind simply froze and went blank.

A Cleansing

Quiet had settled over the port city, blanketing the streets in a strange, unplaceable tension. The freak storm that had sprung up near the gates of the city had scared everyone into their homes. Nobody walked the streets. Vayne's blind eyes would not have seen them anyway, but he could tell that he and Rhaiga were alone. Her bare feet smacked lightly across the cobblestones. He could hear them just to his right. Quite loudly, now that they were one of the only sounds. His host body had become quite cumbersome, having to be led around like an ox.

Around them, tideflags whipped, impossibly still flying after the skirmish that had taken place. Rhaiga had told him what was happening as they approached the port city. It was apparent that there were more than just Chosen at play. The roars that had rolled across the sand toward them were unmistakable. Wispy hair floated around his soot-covered face as he shuffled down the empty street. The fires that had destroyed Boane were breathtaking to feel. He could still remember their heat even now. It was magnificent how quickly the arrogance of men and women could bring destruction, and Boane was just the beginning. After being banished to the dunes for centuries, it was time to restore the rugged world they had built, that *he* had helped build.

He heard Rhaiga's veil blow around her face as she walked. "This could only have been his work," she remarked at the dismembered soldiers scattered around them. Although Vayne despised Charodon, he knew that the soldiers had strayed into his path. Death was the only conclusion.

"It was. If Dhorh's intelligence is correct, it seems that the brute has taken a host in one of the Chosen," the old man said. Skin flapped around his mouth as he spoke. He rubbed his smooth, folding jowls in contemplation. "This seems ambitious for him." From what Vayne could remember, Charodon loved to overpower his hosts. The stronger they were, the more satisfaction Charodon got from it. Vayne didn't have that luxury. Tricking hosts into giving up their bodies made the husks last longer. Over twelve hundred years in, his current body was still upright, but barely.

"Why does he seek the Chosen?" she said curiously.

He shrugged, his shoulders shaking as he did so. "He does what he does because he wants to. What matters is that Dhorh found him and the Chosen. I doubt Charodon can be persuaded to reunite with our cause." The boy had reached them at the perfect time and was now holding them until the old man and Rhaiga reached the cathedral. He had long since stopped caring about calling Dhorh "boy." Even though he was ancient, Dhorh had always acted in a juvenile manner. It was up to him and Rhaiga to keep him in line.

Still walking beside him, Rhaiga grunted in acknowledgement. He faintly heard a grim chuckle pulling at her taut lips when she described the sick lined up against the wall of an alley. "You've outdone yourself," she said.

Vayne stood a bit taller despite his host body's hunched back. Mangler victims bled through bandages and coughed up blood. The air around them was saturated with disease, and it was beautiful. This sickness would be the stepping stone to a cleansing of this wretched place. After just a thousand years, the world had changed too much. He and the others had been all but forgotten. It was one of the few things that could still make the old man angry—or scared—after all these millennia.

They passed the sick as they continued toward the Cathedral of Iarus, ignoring the coughs and whimpers. Some prayed to the gods.

He sensed Rhaiga tense next to him, resisting the urge to lash at them. He stayed her hand. They were already on the path. It was not for her to interfere. Sometimes, Vayne wondered about the stability of Rhaiga's mind. She seemed committed as ever to their mission but had been prone to violent ebullitions of late.

A woman's stout voice mingled among the sick, ladling dripping water out to them. Vayne came up on the ladler, his brittle knees popping as he made a slight bow.

The ladler shuffled to move out of his way, her voice dour. "Best to keep a distance," she muttered. "This lot is getting worse, and it's spreading to everyone who isn't keeping covered. Not much time left, gods watch over them."

Smiling, the old man gently touched the ladler's forehead with a withered finger. "Nor much time for anyone, my dear." The ladler's dry skin went taut as a thin cut appeared on her forehead where the finger had touched her, the skin turning brittle. She scratched the spot. By the next day, her face would be split by dozens of tiny lacerations.

Rhaiga and the old man continued forward as the ladler went back to serving water to the sick. The port city would fall soon; Boane had done most of the hard work. As long as Dhorh did his job, the Chosen would be in their grasp. They'd kill the last obstacle that mankind could place in their way.

And then the old world, a world where they—the Elders—ruled, would no longer be a distant dream. Only then could Vayne live without fear of death.

A Smile in the Shadows

The cathedral loomed over the northeastern-most area of Epot Detharn. Not a half day earlier, Ariel had been here with Leonard, she had said. James stared at the flames carved into the south wall, a tribute to Iarus. High above the tallest roofs in the rest of the city, the two hundred-and six-foot spire of the cathedral glowed with a golden brazier. It was said that the flame atop this brazier was always lit, providing a path to Epot Detharn even in the darkest of nights. The last time he had been in the port city, James and Gemmi had stared at this light in awe, marveling at the mighty structure built in honor to the Pathlighter.

Following the fading trail of chaos and fires in Epot Detharn, James and Ariel had come across a score of wounded and nearly as many dead, seemingly all by Roy's hand. Ariel had insisted on lending aid to those unfortunate enough to have found themselves in Roy's path. In talking to some that were out of their shock, James and Ariel discovered that Roy was once again himself, but another more troubling development emerged—someone had taken them. Here, to the dim cathedral that stood before them.

The rest of the building was massive. Seven hundred feet across and a hundred feet tall, it dwarfed the rest of the structures around it. The glory of Iarus expressed through stone and sheer size. The outer walls of the cathedral created a crescent shape, and the ornately carved sandstone bore glyphs above the entrances, reciting prayers to the Pathlighter.

He could barely see inside the open entryway and into the cavernous hall, buffed to a shine. Torchlight reflected against the stone floor of the cathedral and danced before James's eyes. It had not changed in five years, and the sight of this ageless yet ancient building filled him with dread. He and his brother had visited this place in desperation years ago. It was in this building that he had walked in with a family and walked out all alone.

He realized that Ariel had said his name three times. "Sorry, what?"

She pursed her lips. "Whatever is holding them in there, it'll put up a fight. Are you sure you're up for this?"

James shook his head slightly. He hardly knew these people, but he was about to jump into what may be a fight with something he had no understanding of for them. It was madness, but Samira and Roy had saved his life. No one had cared for or even noticed him much since Gemmi had died. He at least owed them this, but he just wished that he wasn't *here*. His head perked up, remembering something from that day.

"I know a way we can go in," he said, motioning to the west point of the crescent. Straining his eyes, he peered toward the bricks near the ground where the two walls met. When they had snuck in years ago, he and Gemmi had found a door expertly carved into the stone at this corner. The intricate carving had been impossible to see, but Gemmi had been the one to find it, and on accident no less. He remembered how hard it was for the two of them to push this hidden door inward. They had both been starving and looking for any place for something to eat. Bread, scythefish, even the disgusting mushrooms that grew on the underside of the docks would have been devoured greedily. The cathedral had been their last hope for sustenance.

Ariel followed his gesture and frowned. "What is it?"

"Let me show you," he said, pulling his maroon facecloth over his nose. He wasn't defenseless anymore, but it would still be a bad idea to be seen. They had no way of knowing what was down there, only that it would be extremely foolish to just walk in the front door.

Their boots thudded against the sandy cobblestone as they lightly jumped from the roof. Ariel gripped her bow, her tattooed arms taut and alert. Her head swiveled from side to side, monitoring their surroundings. Drawing his gray hood up over his face, he quickly stalked to the right crescent point. The moon was well into its descent, and the first glimpses of purple were starting to grow to the east. They would have to move quickly, and even then it would take a miracle to make it to their charter in time. Finally making it to the wall of the cathedral, James pored over the stone.

The delicately carved slabs depicted triumphs of Iarus. He ran his fingers over the carving of his favorite childhood tale, admiring the craftsmanship in spite of himself. Iarus leading the other gods into battle and the monstrous girth of the insect-like beast sprawled across a stone twice his height. Other deeds of the Pathlighter were depicted to his right. Even his best attempts to purge the stories from his head with drink were not enough to forget them.

Directly to his right was the legend of Iarus's victory over the cannibalistic Altujan, violet-haired cannibals who worshipped devils. To the right of that, Iarus saving Raslena from the clutches of a demon. The carving of the demon had been scratched away by clerics, never to be gazed upon by a curious onlooker. James could only see horns curling from the top of the demon's shape. He tore his eyes away from the carvings and began to search for the entryway hidden in the stone. Ariel stood beside him, scouring the wall.

His fingers caught a camouflaged fissure in the carving, splitting Astus's face in two. He ran his hand along the fissure and realized that it went up and down along the slab, stopping at the ground. He waved Ariel over to him, fixing his gaze on the gap in the stone. This was definitely not any kind of stonework error. It had to be the door that Gemmi had found all that time ago. He gave it a halfhearted shove, not expecting it to budge. The wall shifted and slid an inch inward, startling him. It was indeed heavy, but he and Ariel would definitely be able to manage it. She placed her hands on the stone beside him and braced against it.

"All right." James crossed his arms. He had seen the destruction and heard from the wounded what the thing inside Roy was capable of. "This is as far as I go until I get the truth about what's wrong with Roy. I've seen his eyes, Ariel. Sam was *terrified* of it."

Ariel grimaced at this. but nodded grudgingly. "It's some kind of demon, using his body, his soul, like a parasite. The thing took him three years ago, and there's been no luck in finding a way to be rid of it. If it tricks him into losing his temper, it consumes him, and it will kill everything in sight." She shuddered. "It's like a living embodiment of savagery. Roy calls it Charodon."

Eyes widening, James leaned against the wall, massaging the fading bruise on this throat. So Roy and Samira had been in Boane to find a cure for this possession, and Samira had on no uncertain terms stated that it was getting worse. "Why is everyone acting like saving him or bringing him with us is the responsible thing then?"

Actual anger darkened Ariel's cheerful eye. "Because getting rid of Charodon will save countless lives, and because Roy never deserved *any* of this. It's not his fault. We are *not* leaving him."

James blinked, a bit ashamed. "Fine. But this can't be the end of it. Answers are owed."

"You'll get all the answers you want on the boat, *after* we've collected them. All of them," she said. "Getting away from large populations increases all our chances of survival right now."

It would have to be enough. Nodding, they both strained against the hidden door and thrust their entire weight against the carved surface. Low scraping sounds emanated from the entryway as the door slid across the surface. Beads of sweat began to form in James's hairline. Beside him, Ariel breathed deeply, filling her lungs and refreshing her limbs.

The door finally gave inward and lurched, causing Ariel and James to stumble forward. Stepping through the thick doorway, they found themselves in a dimly lit corridor. Triangular in shape, the walls of the pathway slanted upward and connected overhead in a point. Slivers of light flickered weakly toward the opposite end of the passage near the ground. Insects scrambled across the cracked floor, barely visible. Drawing his short sword slowly, James shuffled forward. In front of him, Ariel shouldered her bow and drew a hatchet from her belt. She led the way, carefully stepping over the cracks in the floor and toward the corridor's end. There were no forks in the passage.

Trying to shake off the memories, James followed the dim glow of Ariel's gold hair. He had followed Gemmi down this same pathway years ago.

The corridor led fifty feet to a sturdy wooden door. Its worn, splintering surface made James shiver, remembering the wood shavings that had bit into his hand when he and his brother had pushed against it. The door swung open to reveal a packed wooden chamber that simultaneously looked like it had been forgotten by time and had also been constructed that same day. Boxes and crates full of food, textiles, and trinkets were haphazardly stacked up to the low ceiling. Offerings to the gods from those who came to worship ended up here and were then left. Rather than being offered up to Iarus, the clerics kept the donations stored away. The trove packed the chamber, crowding James and Ariel. The room smelled of greed, and it made James's blood roil through him.

Two clerics were slumped against the wall on the east side of the room, apparently out cold. He had understood the corruption of the Temple for years, but seeing it first-hand always infuriated him. Zealots were all that they turned out to be. After the facade of taking in unclaimed children, building places of worship, and caring for the sick was cracked, the Temple could be seen for what it was, a lie. They were never in communication with the gods. They had no idea what the gods wanted, and the clerics treated the world as beneath them while using this lie as a shield.

"Are you okay?" Ariel had noticed him glaring around the room. She still held the hatchet aloft.

"Bad memories," James shook his head. He gestured through the towers of stashed offerings. "There should be a door this way." Weaving through the piles of trinkets, James remembered that night years ago. Gemmi had stood on the ground while he was climbing through the precarious stacks of donations, searching for food they could take. There had been only so much there that would keep for more than a few days. The clerics had always taken more than what was needed. Trying to stay as quiet as possible, his small feet had carefully stretched from one crate to the next, wobbling with the strain. It had been his feet that eventually gave out, sending him crashing through the stacks below in a rumbling of falling debris. He had been buried underneath a pile of wooden carvings and moldy bread.

Through the scattered mounds of treasures, a solid, decorated wooden door hung open. The light from the great hall of the cathedral shimmered against the flowing artwork on the door's surface. Another cleric slouched unconscious beside the empty doorway. It beckoned to them, daring them to move through it. This wasn't just a door to the next room. It was a door to the memory of Gemmi. The memory of what those bastard clerics had done to him.

Putting a hand on his shoulder, Ariel spoke softly, "We need to find the others. Then you never have to look at this place again." Her voice reassured him with the pleasantness of a cool breeze. There was undoubtedly a knowing tone in her voice. He guessed that she may have felt the same way about that village in the marshes. Pain had followed both of them, and it appeared as though the gods weren't too motivated to alleviate it, even for their Chosen.

Bracing himself, he followed her through the doorway and into the cavernous great hall. The ceiling stretched high overhead, glittering and shimmering as if it contained the stars themselves. Jewels lined the ceiling, placed in a manner that would reflect the torchlight to those on the ground, no matter how dim the light. Moonlight flowed through the only glass windows on the continent, streaming different colors due to the pigment in the glass. The five windows, each of them more than thirty feet tall, reflected a depiction of one of the gods. Etah simpered furtively from the far left, followed by the stern Dathos. Iarus stared regally from the center window, an orb of fire clutched in his hand that the moonlight illuminated fantastically. Raslena and Astus followed respectively, each looking toward Iarus.

Tapestries and other works of craftsmanship hung from the bow-shaped walls around them, each one most likely having taken years to complete. Gold embroidered the columns, and maroon-painted benches lined the east side of the crescent.

Everything in here was completely different from the rest of Epot Detharn, as if it had been brought from another country or from another world entirely. The marbled pattern of the floor swirled across the length of the cathedral, leading to lavish marble steps and an altar trimmed with gold and silver. Little more than a dozen torches lined the far walls. They cast enough light to see while still leaving heavily shadowed pockets of the intimidating space. Their feet clacked against the marble flooring, sending echoes reverberating down the curve and back to them, as if footsteps were following them when they came back.

He shivered and continued looking around. Carved statues of heroes and prophets lined the curved wall near the sealed entryway. Shivering as a sharp cold fear gripped him, James crept over to the gargantuan doors. The massive wooden planks that made the doors had to be as thick as a ship's mast and about as tall. How could they have been shut without them noticing? He was sure that the doors were open when they had been scouting from the outside. Memories of the clerics closing in on him and his brother began to encroach from his subconscious, trying to overwhelm his senses. Across the crescent, he heard Ariel groan.

His gaze flicked in the direction of the sound as it hit his ears. It hadn't been Ariel who made that sound. James looked in her direction to see that she had heard it too and was already hurdling benches and empty braziers in the direction of the noise. Echoes of their boots on the marble floors bounced off of every surface and created an eerie applause from an invisible crowd. Another groan floated from a pillar near the Astus window, and James saw a shape silhouetted in the red-orange light from the glass. Even in the darkness, he could make out the long braid stemming from the back of the shape's head.

"Sam!" he hissed, trying not to make any more noise. Sliding across the polished floor on his worn boots, he came to a hasty stop before her and knelt. His sword produced a faint clink as he gingerly set it down. Samira's head was bowed as if asleep. James leaned lower and peered upward into her face. His eyes widened. She stared directly back at him with unblinking amber eyes, yet she saw nothing. Her mouth moved soundlessly, as if at prayer. This was not a prayer. She had annoyingly done it enough for James to recognize when she was praying. She had not been bound.

There wasn't anything holding her to the pillar, but she sat loosely against the column in a haze, knowing nothing around her. James glanced over and saw Ariel shaking Roy on the floor near the column, an array of expressions fighting for control of her features, concern and happiness chief among them. Another man, a couple of years older than Samira, sat slumped against the other side of the pillar.

Assuming that this was Leonard, James knelt by his side and shook him. Leonard's spiky brown hair bounced. His eyes showed no hint of movement but instead gaped blankly in front of him. He rounded the pillar again and approached Ariel, still kneeling over Roy. He whispered frantically, "What do we do? Samira and Leonard aren't responding."

She didn't look up at him. "I don't know, but we have to get them out of here. We'll have to carry them."

"How are we going to carry all three of them?"

"I don't know, James! We don't have a lot of choices."

"We have to cut our losses, Ariel," James said.

"I'm not leaving him to die again!" she hissed.

He cursed, looking down at Roy. His face was as peaceful as he had ever seen it, scar and all. The Champion of Dathos's eyes were closed, as if he were sleeping. An angry bruise swelled on his face. James's eyes narrowed. "Why are his eyes closed? Samira and Leonard are both awake."

Shaking her head, Ariel unshouldered her bow, still kneeling, "Charodon may take a long time to force into dormancy. He could be like this for a while."

"And why would I waste the effort to trance him when Charodon is doing all the work?" a voice leered from the windows. Crisp footsteps echoed toward them, disquietingly loud. James scrambled for his sword near where Samira still slouched. Ariel fluidly raised her bow and nocked an arrow in the direction of the voice. The footsteps echoed more forcefully, sounding as if they were coming from every corner of the cathedral at once. The voice had sounded playful, mocking. Feeling outward with his consciousness, James searched for anyone who could have hidden in the great hall with them.

Massive cold areas dominated the space, only broken by tiny sparks of heat that must have been the torches. He couldn't feel any living presence. The torches seemed miles away. There would be no way for him to reach them from here. Pointing his sword at the base of Raslena's window, he peered into the shadows as they shifted.

A bright white smile materialized in the darkness. Each tooth fit into the next perfectly as if carved by a well-paid mason. It was a smile crafted for charming and deceit. The lips that framed it resembled a pile of shattered glass. Cracked and split, the pale red mouth widened, and the face around it slowly seeped into focus. It may be trying theatrics now, but it could attack immediately.

The face of the thing was a pale crimson, the same as its lips. Its pockmarked skin stretched thinly over bony features. The devil was bald with ram horns protruding from the back of its head, much like the scratched-out carving on the outside walls. But the most disturbing thing about the monstrosity was the hollow sockets where eyes should have been. Shadow passed in and out of the empty craters above its thin, pointy nose. Shivering, James realized that the devil appeared to be smirking directly at him. This thing was nothing like what he had seen in Boane.

It stepped forward into the moonlight cast from Raslena's window. Like the creature from Boane, this devil was tall. Its lanky form reached six feet in height. The rest of its mottled skin was the same washed crimson, and a great serrated claw protruded from the inner forearm of each limb. The darkness made it difficult to gauge the actual size of the thing.

"What did you do to them?" Ariel growled, drawing her bowstring back, ready to loose death in its direction.

Cocking its head to the side, it spoke with the voice of a young man, "It's nothing, really. I just plucked some threads of memory. However, I think they had some troubles when I returned them. I never put much work into sewing memories back together." He snickered, juvenile glee stretching his face grotesquely. "I think I may leave them like that for a while. Chosen are quite a nuisance when they're properly threaded, and we can't have them causing trouble for our guests." He took another step toward James and Ariel. Each foot held seven toes, the gnarled nails of each toe ingrown and swollen.

Ariel stood and drew her arrow farther back to her cheek, "Let them go, now." Her metallic eyes had a coldness that James had not seen yet. "Your guests will have to be disappointed."

The devil clicked his tongue and stepped backward into the shadow. The blackness enveloped him like a pool of ink.

James blinked. It was as if the scorching thing had never been there. He turned to Ariel, her arrow still nocked, "Where did he go?"

Ariel faced him and shook her head, leaving her back exposed to the dark behind her.

The devil's hands shot from the inky aether and grappled Etah's Chosen by the hair. Ariel was reeled backward like a fish. Her arrow flew high, zipping into the cavernous ceiling. Gnarled red fingers finally flicked her forehead, and Ariel slumped, wide-eyed, muttering. The devil dumped Ariel to the polished floor and sauntered back into the shadows, cackling.

James started toward her before catching something in the edge of his vision. The moonlight through the stained windows revealed the vague shape of the devil, standing smugly under the glares of the gods. James looked back toward Ariel. She writhed and gawked at nothing as the devil toyed with her mind.

"Twelve hundred years and everyone seems to have forgotten us except your friends," the devil said irritably. He pointed in exasperation to the windows behind him. The gods all seemed to be watching him. "At least *they* knew the way the world was supposed to be, who the *real* gods were. Vayne would be quite annoyed if he could see this." His mouth twisted as a crazed smile split his face again. "But that's okay. I can make them remember. And you get to be along for the ride."

James looked up from the other Chosen, furious. "Give them back!" Blood boiling, he charged the devil, his sword held high. The empty craters in its eyes widened as he sprinted up the stairs. Whipping his scratched sword around in an arc, he slashed at the seamless smirk. The devil's teeth flashed as it batted his sword away with its hand. It savagely swiped him aside, throwing him against a pillar several feet away.

James's arm stung where the claw dug into his skin. He could feel a thin dribble of blood, spreading, soaking into the sleeve of his shirt. His short sword didn't give him much of an advantage, and even if it connected the blade was chipped enough to possibly break after one blow. He had to get in close to hit it. The devil lurched toward him, crossing the distance in mere seconds. White teeth loomed over him in the semi-darkness.

"I must say, I never much cared for fighting. Would you mind sitting down and chatting for a moment?" It caught James's sword hand as he tried to swing again. The devil viciously struck him with the back of its hand. James's head reeled. "You must try to be more accommodating. We *are* in a holy place, after all." It sneered. Clicking its tongue, it reached a ragged hand toward his brow.

⟢⟡⟣

The Eye of Memory

As the rough, splintering fingertip touched his forehead, James felt a paralyzing, molten presence seep into his mind. The devil's invasion of James's thoughts slowly immobilized him, and he could feel the delight of his attacker slowly unthreading his memories. They blazed past him at frightening speed. He saw Gemmi pointing a twig at him while playing, challenging him to a mock duel. He saw poor Lenia just as she left to light the posts. He saw the terrifying three-eyed demon from Boane reaching toward him in the flames.

"So you're the one who burned Rhaiga." the devil said in his mind. *"Luckily for you, she isn't one to hold a grudge."*

James could say nothing back to the statement. He could only squirm there as it picked apart his memories.

"Dear me, you have a great many fond memories of this Gemmi. What happened to him, I wonder?" The voice came from every direction, and the memories spun faster. They blurred until he could no longer see anything. Blackness swam in front of his eyes.

"Stay here, James. They won't find you. Just stay put."

He opened his eyes. Gemmi knelt before him, beaming. His brother's long black hair was tied behind his face, and his green eyes shone. They were in the trove room. The hoarded offerings piled to the heavens. The room looked much bigger than he had remembered. He was back at that night, the night that Gemmi had been murdered by the Clerics. Approaching torchlight reflected off of Gemmi's brown skin. His brother firmly placed him behind a row of clay trinkets. Shouts of cathedral zealots began to grow louder. Unable to say anything, James could only watch in horror as his brother said the same thing as that night seven years ago.

"I'll come back." Gemmi ruffled his hair. "Promise." The torches grew brighter as the Clerics approached.

"I can make an assumption about where this is going," the devil said dryly.

James tried to scream at his tormentor to get out of his head, but he could do nothing. He watched hopelessly as Gemmi sprinted away, pursued by a group of Clerics. The sound of falling piles of offerings crashed after them. Metal clanged and clay shattered as young James cowered behind his debris pile. Shouts bounced off the walls and maneuvered through the offering piles like snakes in a field. He could hear the struggling of his brother as they finally caught him, the frantic kicking and pained grunting. His brother had never failed to come out of a chase unscathed until that night.

Young James peeked out from behind his hiding place to see the zealots dragging Gemmi out of the room and toward the secret entrance. When the Clerics had left with Gemmi and the room was finally silent, young James still cowered behind the clay pots and sculptures. For hours, he waited, not knowing what to do.

The devil spoke again, *"When you found out they had killed him, didn't you want revenge? They sacrificed your brother just for trying to help you eat, it's been years, and your little plan for vengeance was too pitiful to really be that serious."*

Its malice grew with every word, and the images of the day started to melt. Even through the liquefying memories, he could still remember sitting on the docks of Epot Detharn, staring at the drowning poles. Tideflags flew orange above as he watched the water lap at the submerged wooden posts. All the way to the left, long black hair swirled at the surface, the only image that came up anymore when he thought of his brother. *"I can give you courage,"* the devil said. *"Just wait until the old man and Rhaiga get here. You won't be a coward anymore."*

Head swimming, James tried to remain focused. Cruel satisfaction from the devil's consciousness still coursed through him, immobilizing him.

Roy's voice called from beyond his mind, clearing the noise, "Don't lecture about cowardice, Dhorh."

James's mind was suddenly filled with blinding pain. The molten presence of the demon flashed brightly, and the liquefied memories froze. Then they shattered. His vision swam back into focus as Dhorh's presence left him. The cathedral ceiling was high above him, still blurry, but he could at least see it was there. Dhorh's howls of indignant anger exploded through the cavernous hall, and James glanced over to see Roy standing beside him, saber drawn. His turquoise eyes were narrowed at the devil. He snarled at the pale red figure.

"I've heard about you, deceiver. Clever tricks and manipulation will only work for so long." He tapped his temple with a knowing finger. "I already have a voice in my head, and he's much worse than you. You're an insect, a weakling."

Dhorh's sculpted smile disappeared. White smoke poured from the wound where Roy had stabbed him through the bicep. His eye sockets betrayed nothing, and he stood up to his full height, towering over James and Roy. "This insect can still sting, boy. I may not be the Eye of Death, but I will paint this cathedral with your blood. You won't take my threads from me."

Gripping his sword, James slowly climbed to his feet. His face still throbbed from where Dhorh had struck him. He understood now, the devil was an ambush predator. Dhorh had probably been able to capture the others when they were distracted or at their weakest, but in a straight fight he may be outmatched. "I'm not letting anyone else die in this building." Leveling his sword at Dhorh, he nodded toward Roy. The Chosen of Dathos blinked and charged at the devil. James followed, their boots pounding the marble steps of the cathedral.

Scowling, Dhorh leapt back from their swords and attempted to disappear into the shadows. At that moment, the first rays of the sun streamed over the top of the building. The sunlight poured through the colored glass of the windows. Every corner of the great sanctuary was alight. James felt the familiar warmth of the sun on his face and sighed. He saw Dhorh's nervous face clearly for the first time. His bony, pale red frame looked sickly in the light, smaller than James had realized, the white smoke still curling out of his arm. The devil backed away slowly, getting too close to a torch bolted to the wall.

Roy glanced at James. "After you."

Feeling out with his consciousness, James probed the small flame at the end of the torch. The spark of warmth grew slightly as he merged with it and yanked his hand backward.

The torch exploded, cracking the wall and shattering Etah's window with a thunderous blast. Dhorh stumbled, flailing from the force of the eruption. His pale red skin blackened and singed.

Stepping forward, Roy whipped his sword around his body in a wide slash at the air. Water miraculously arced from the blade as if an extension, a whip of some kind, glittering in the sunlight. The heavy lash of water slapped against Dhorh's knees, and he lost his footing, tumbling to the marble floor. His horns clacked loudly as they hit the ground next to a stone pillar. James and Roy could hear the sounds of Ariel, Leonard, and Samira stirring, finally broken out of Dhorh's trance. The explosion must have broken his concentration.

While Dhorh struggled to get up, James rushed him, dragging his sword along the marble. The torch he had used to set off the detonation was gone, but maybe he didn't need a torch. Raising his sword as he approached the demon, he saw its eye sockets narrow as he drew closer. Heat built up inside him with every step.

The devil braced himself, ready to swipe the sword away when James attacked. Instead of slicing at Dhorh, James brought his sword down hard against the side of the pillar. Sparks shot from where the edge of the blade ran along the stone, showering both James and the devil. Its eye sockets grew wider as it realized what James was doing. Dhorh tried to scramble away, but it was too late. With the sparks hitting his cheek and singeing his clothing, James reached out to the tiny glowing dots of heat and bellowed, throwing his arms out in front of him at the devil.

The sparks grew in an instant, causing a massive fireball that sent shards of the Astus window pinwheeling throughout the space. James only saw a flash of red; a glowering Dhorh mostly dodged the explosion, but was still blown backward through the hole in the cathedral that James had created. The devil did not reemerge. It seemed he was conceding, for now. Metal around the explosion melted into steaming mush, and the tapestries and maroon carpets were engulfed in flame.

Roy was tossed backward down the stairs by the force of the repulse, landing at the foot of a bench. The others, just coming to their senses, were blinded as the bright orange and yellow flames expanded outward. The flash of light reverberated through the great hall as the fire dissipated.

Watching the Astus window, James finally lowered his sword. It didn't look as if Dhorh would be attacking again anytime soon. The area around James was blackened, and his charred clothing hung off him in tatters. Looking down at himself, he could see no burns. Instead, heat and warmth swirled throughout his body. A typhoon of intense energy within him. Breathing deeply, he calmed the rippling flames in his bloodstream and rushed over to Roy, who was sitting up slowly.

"Warn me next time you're going to blow up a holy place," he groaned. Roy shook his head in near disbelief at the power that had left James's body. His black cloak was singed, but he otherwise looked alright. Maybe a little annoyed.

"How hard did Dhorh hit you?" James asked, pointing to the bruise on Roy's face.

"That was Sam."

"Ah."

Out of the corner of his eye, Ariel approached the unconscious clerics, making sure they were not gravely injured.

Leonard stepped over to James eagerly and shook his hand with enough force to take his arm off. "Damn well met, James. Raslena crush me, couldn't have gotten a better introduction." The Chosen of Raslena grinned, still blinking his brown eyes from the explosion. His demeanor indicated no urgency or concern, as though this had always been the plan. James heartily shook Leonard's hand.

"Well met, Leonard," he said. He already liked this one. Roy looked less than pleased to see Leonard awake.

Glancing back further into the cathedral, his gaze landed on a pair of clerics glaring at him. They marched purposefully in his direction, righteous rage plastered on their brows. The damage he had done was certainly going to take much of their donations to repair. Destroying Temple buildings and property was a punishable offense. Gemmi had known that when he lured the clerics away from James all those years ago. He lunged at the murderers.

Samira rushed to James and snatched his arm in a crushingly serious grip. "James, *James!* Leave them. It's not worth it."

He raged against her grasp, her condescending tone. She hadn't seen what Dhorh had extracted from him, his hatred for this place and his disdain toward the ugliness it protected. "I don't care. They don't deserve this!" He gestured to the massive hall around them. "My brother's life was worth more than this whole *scorching* place. He was good! He gave up everything for me, and they butchered him! A holy place that kills young men for feeding their family can't claim to be holy." Tears welled in his eyes. "They can't get away with it. They can't, they can't, they..."

"Quell this dog's barking!" snapped the older cleric, a middle-aged man with patchy hair. He crossed his arms beneath his singed robe. "You've destroyed this place of worship, a place where the people come to offer prayer and hope for salvation. What will the people do now? You've doomed them! Who will the gods hear now?" He and the other cleric stumbled back as James lunged again, now being held by Samira and Leonard.

Ariel cleared her throat, calmly waiting for everyone's attention. "I think salvation is close for the people of Epot Detharn, very close. In fact, it may be as close as the next room." She nodded behind her. "Leonard, come with me for a moment."

No more than a few minutes later, James gaped at a yawning cavity in the side wall of the cathedral's hidden chamber. Sapphire sunlight streamed into the room, shedding light on the treasures, the food, the provisions. Onlookers attracted by the commotion shuffled cautiously into the street and up to the building.

Leonard stepped back and leaned his mace against a standing section of wall, admiring the crater that had melted into existence with a mere tap of his weapon. "Guess that nap Dhorh set me on gave me a little energy back." He chuckled. Waving to the onlookers, he beckoned them forward. "Come, friends! Experience the generosity of the gods. Take what you need, and persevere through this difficult time. Take what you need, and then take to the seas, away from these troubles."

Within seconds, townsfolk streamed into the building, dividing and scooping up the food and trinkets. James had difficulty believing that the room would ever empty. With the continually growing sunlight came a surge of life within the people. Smiles, voices, laughter, all but forgotten until now. James watched as Roy scooped up two loaves of bread and stalked to the two clerics, who stood by frozen in terrified fury.

"The generosity of the gods. Take it and go," Roy growled.

The clerics, not wanting to see what else Leonard's mace could do, promptly scrambled from the cathedral. It was a welcome sight for James, clerics leaving a crumbling cathedral while the people were finally freed from their dogma. The burning need for revenge still flickered, but this would do for now. Samira had said the Temple's influence reached all over the world. He took the tattered remains of his Lamplighter cloak and threw it down. It seemed, now, that James had a reason to go overseas after all.

He would bring the Temple tumbling down. Everywhere. For Gemmi.

The new day had begun, and they had already missed their ship. He glanced warily at Roy, who stood off to the side and away from the growing throng of people. "How do we get out of here now? Our ship probably went off without us."

Roy shook his head. "We will have to search for any ship left in the harbor. If no one is willing to take us, we'll steal one. There's no other way around it."

"We have a ship," Leonard said confidently. "Some of the best hired sailors that the empire could buy." Ariel joined them.

Narrowing his eyes, Roy regarded Leonard coldly. "They hired sailors? Why not just use some of the Imperial Armada?"

"Alaric has many enemies. Or at least, he *perceives* that he does," Ariel spoke up. Roy seemed to be working hard to avoid her gaze. "The ship and crew were hired from Scourge Atoll."

Samira rubbed her temple. "Astus strike me. The emperor hired a ship full of pirates to bring you across the sea and back with James? Was he mad?" She sighed and looked down, realizing there was no other reasonable option. "And you signed off on this?" she asked Leonard.

He shrugged. "I don't like it any more than you do, but these pirates are being paid a fortune. That's kept them in line so far."

James had heard of Scourge Atoll from several old mariners back in Boane. The large island was a criminal paradise. A deserter of the Collisun Empire conquered the islet and had established a colony of piracy and murder centuries ago. People who resided there seldom lived without enemies for more than a few years if they were lucky. Of all the places they could find a crew, why in the world would they hire brutes from a slimy death nest like Scourge Atoll?

Right now, though, it looked like his only way offshore.

"We don't have a choice," he said. The rest of the group looked at him. Ariel and Leonard both nodded, striding toward the entrance of the cathedral without another word. Roy, James, and Samira followed.

The fires set by James's blast had gone out. Gemmi's beaming face swam through his mind as he strode across the marble and out into the sunlight. Leaving this place didn't feel like it had before. The last time he had left the cathedral, he had been alone, his faith in the world and the Temple gone, his soul without a path. His eyes set in the direction of the sea as he stepped into the light. The sun hit his skin with an invigorating heat. There was a lot more skin exposed to the sun now that much of his shirt had burned away. The ashy rags hung off his scrawny frame. He silently hoped that this wouldn't be a regular occurrence.

Catching up to the rest of the group, he took up the back of the train with Roy. Ariel and Samira strode ahead of them. Samira stiffened as Ariel walked alongside her but didn't object. Adrenaline from imminent danger had given way to memories of a sore past, perhaps.

"I haven't seen your family in years, Ariel," Samira said, a bit forced. "How are they faring?"

Ariel chuckled artificially. "I saw them shortly before I left the continent. Mother and Father haven't changed at all since you last saw them. The two old Faders still help the young ones' home after all these years." She shook her head in amusement. "You should visit, Sam. They'd be overjoyed to see you."

Samira shrugged. "As long as I can bring them something that isn't a pallet fruit." The other woman chuckled as Leonard forged ahead, weaving through the now brightly lit alleys.

James turned to Roy, who had gained a sudden interest in the ground directly in front of his feet. "Where's home for you?"

"Up north." Roy was adverse to any kind of small talk. The man was tough to read. Then again, he may have still been exhausted from fighting Charodon into dormancy. Judging by how much the beast had scared Ariel and Samira, James was certain he didn't want to see it wake up. He brought his hand up in front of his eyes as the sunlight streamed through a gap in the squat stone houses.

As his eyes adjusted, he could see the sunlight reflecting off the shimmering waves. The Escrai Sea swelled before them, infinite in every direction. Most ships at the docks had cast off, leaving a fairly large row of empty wooden platforms jutting out over the receding waves. High tide was waning, and soon the waving tideflags overhead would be changed to their unpleasant yellow. A few vessels of differing size still floated at various points along the stretch of empty jettys.

James watched as Leonard stepped confidently down the sloping hill toward a modest ship. Its sails were in the process of being unfurled, the sun highlighting the holes that pockmarked the canvas. The mainmast of the ship leaned impotently at a slight angle. Sailors scurried across the deck to the tune of a bellowing, harsh voice.

The group trotted down the dock toward the gangway, five pairs of feet plunking against the wood. A salty gust of wind blew past James's ears, muffling the sound of Leonard's voice as he called up to the deck of the ship. Among the sailors rushing over the ship, several of them stopped and stared at the five young people standing at the gangplank. All of them looked like they had been in a fight, or several. Each one had a bruise or scrape of some kind. The shredded remains of James and Roy's clothing flapped in the breeze, barely clinging onto them.

As Leonard called upward, the booming voice abruptly ceased, and angry stomps pounded their way across the deck. A stocky man who looked to be in his forties appeared at the over-crossing. His rude black eyes darted to each of their faces.

"You said there'd be three coming back." His straight black hair was tightly wound into a bun, but the sea breeze had pulled a few strands loose. He rolled up the sleeves of his rough brown shirt and stepped down the footbridge, not even trying to hide his irritation. "Now I may not be a learned man, young master, but I can drowning sure count. And it looks to me like there are five pups. That wasn't our agreement." His narrow eyes landed on James, Roy, and Samira. Leonard and Ariel must not have updated him that there would be more passengers.

"Everyone, this dashing man is Mollis Vilch, captain of the *Greed Sun,*" Leonard said cheerfully. His confident smile infected some passing crew members. No one could say that the man wasn't charming when he wanted to be. "Captain Vilch, in our search, we not only found the last Chosen but also came across two dear friends." He gestured at Roy and Samira.

Roy grumbled, "Drown me, you worm."

Leonard shot him a glance and continued, "They can be of much use to the emperor. May I remind you that he is paying your wages for this voyage?"

"We didn't say anything about going with you to the empire," Samira hissed. "There are bigger problems."

Ariel whispered cautiously, "The biggest issue is getting away from this city. The rest can be haggled about later."

Samira growled and crossed her arms but stayed silent, unable to find an argument.

Vilch rolled his eyes. "The whelp on the throne didn't say anything about any others. I can't have them hanging about and getting in the way. Now we can sail from this sorry heap of rock with three of you or with none of you."

Sighing, Leonard pulled a pouch from his pant leg. It tinkled heavily with the sound of coins sliding against each other, a small plunder from the cathedral. Winding up his muscled arm, he tossed the weighty bag toward Vilch. The captain grunted at the weight as the shaking drawstring pouch hit his outstretched hands. His thin black eyebrows shot to the top of his brow when he opened the bag and viewed the contents. Leonard blinked knowingly. "If you take all of us, you get that much now, and double that when we get back to the empire."

Vilch crossed his arms. "Triple."

Leonard's eyes hardened as he shook his head. "Double. And these three will assist your crew." He pointed to Samira, Ariel, and Roy, who all regarded him with annoyance but said nothing. Even with the smile still on his face, Leonard's eyes projected a harsh warning to the ship captain. His mace rested on his shoulder.

Everyone waited as the sound of the tide became deafening in the silence. Vilch scratched his chin with consideration. It was apparent that he was used to haggling. James noticed the rest of his companions had slowly reached for their weapons as well.

Vilch noticed, a sly leer crossing his face. As someone who had been traveling with Leonard and Ariel for the past month, he likely knew how dangerous they could be. The crew of the ship had stopped their chores, gathering around the deck behind their captain. Skin peeling from salt and sun, the sailors waited for the standoff to break. Tideflags whipped and flapped overhead, chopping up the silence with sharp cracks.

"Fine," Vilch agreed through tightly clenched teeth. He waved his hand to the rest of the crew. The men and women behind him immediately rushed to finish preparations to cast off. Boots cascaded across the deck, and Vilch motioned with his head for Leonard to come aboard.

James watched Leonard and the others climb the gangplank and onto the deck. Without giving himself time to question, he moved his legs to follow. Everything he'd ever known was behind him. Better for it to remain there. It couldn't do anything more for him.

Ahead, Samira turned and wrinkled her brow, "You alright?"

The sea lay open in front of him, and with it a promise he could finally have a life after Gemmi. He would seek justice in his brother's memory, and keep others from the same fate. Traveling with the Chosen certainly had risks, but taking them was necessary. James nodded and followed Samira up to the *Greed Sun's* deck. He was finally being given a chance.

And he was going to take it.

Part II

Burdens, Lies, and Reckoning

The War of Lost Faith

Vayne hobbled up to the cathedral. Coughing and voices echoed around him. At the rate the sickness was spreading, it would overtake the city within a fortnight. Their work here was started. Even if Dhorh had failed miserably, it was no matter. Rhaiga described to him that the Chosen must have torn a hole open in the cathedral and fled, but they did not need the Chosen to finish this sacred task of tearing down the city. Though it would have been much easier without the Chosen getting in the way in the future. Vayne and Rhaiga had needed to stop halfway to the cathedral, for Vayne's decrepit body had been worn down.

The sunlight was directly overhead, frying his exposed scalp through the sparse hair atop his head. It wasn't like he could feel it. In fact, he hadn't felt little sensations in over two hundred years. Maintaining a host for too long had its disadvantages, but picking a suitable candidate for a replacement was something he took great care in.

Townspeople gathered around the shattered window of the cathedral, murmuring to themselves and stifling coughs. Glass peppered the sandy street, and some upstanding citizens were picking through the drudge to clean it up. The clinking tickled his ears. Foolish, perhaps, but the old man could understand preserving something one thought was important. He passed the crowd, running his hand along the building to keep his sense of direction. Rhaiga quietly stepped a few paces behind him.

They banked around the corner of the crescent and stopped. The old man's hand rested on a carving etched into the wall. He had felt this carving before on a palace far away from here. Iarus locked in battle with a demon. Smiling, the old man traced his fingers over the masonry. His fingers came to a stop and his sightless eyes blinked.

Half of the carving was scratched away, unreadable to anyone who came by. The monster that Iarus had been fighting had been scored off of the carving. Wrinkled skin folded on itself as he scowled. These animals were trying their best to forget him, a theoretical assassination. And what little carving that remained didn't even *look* like him. Multiple emotions stirred within the husk he inhabited. The Eye of Disease convinced himself that rage, not fear, was chief among them.

The woman exhaled through her nose. "They don't seem to remember the order of things, do they?"

Not turning around, the old man took his hand off of the carving. "They will soon, Rhaiga. They have chosen these new, inferior gods. They have already begun to walk the path."

Rhaiga bowed her head, her veil flapping quietly.

They continued toward the entrance of the cathedral. It had only been a couple of hours since the Chosen had left. Rhaiga had seen them sail off from the rooftops, though she had been much more discreet this time.

"If the Chosen's path is destined to intersect with ours, would it not have been better for me to pursue them? I wanted the one who burned me," she growled.

"They have their path, and we have ours. We can't give in to our base desires and pursue enemies when there is work to do eroding the structures of power these humans have built. Killing a Chosen helps our cause, yes, but killing one human makes much less of an impact than bringing down a system that thousands of humans depend on," Vayne cautioned.

Cold air emanated from the open cathedral doors as they stepped across the threshold. The hall was empty, cleared out and smelling of smoke. He sensed the familiar presence of the Eye of Memory.

Breathing sharply, the old man approached Dhorh, who was in the form of his host. Dhorh made no attempt to get up, waiting for the old man to lecture him. The Eye of Memory sat warily as Vayne settled into the bench next to him, uncannily silent.

They stared toward the windows on the far wall. The old man couldn't see them, but he knew they were there. If anything, it should be him up there. A twinge of rage pulled at him for just a moment before he sighed.

"What do you imagine they're thinking?" the old man asked.

"I'm sorry, Vayne," Dhorh stammered.

"I know you're sorry, but that isn't what I want to hear coming out of your mouth right now. What do you imagine they're thinking?"

Dhorh's frustrated squirming shook the rickety bench. "That the Chosen defeated me. That I'm not a threat, a weakling."

Shaking his head, Vayne spoke softly, "No, that's what *I'm* thinking, Dhorh. *They* don't think anything." He pointed in the direction of the windows. "They were fools that made people think that they had a greater purpose, that the world could bow to the whim of men and women rather than us. We were here before them, and they cast us aside." His blind eyes turned to the boyish face that Dhorh wore. "They will not replace us. We limit the chaos of life. Clean up after it. And what do they do? They burn and strike and flood. They crumble and blow everything we work for away. That is why we must throw what they have built into chaos and then birth order from it. *Our* order."

Vayne knew that Dhorh had heard this speech before, but the boy seemed too defeated to talk back this time. The old man was not someone to push when he was this angry. Rhaiga stood behind them.

The old man continued calmly, "The Chosen are not essential to our calling, but after letting them go they will be actively standing in our way. For thousands of years, you have killed Chosen in battle. And you let little more than children escape your grasp?"

Shivering, Dhorh spoke with a whimper, "I had them, but one of them I didn't unthread. He caught me off guard. Then I escaped through the broken window before I could be badly burned."

Rhaiga leaned from behind them. "Don't tell me that you've finally met someone you can't break." Vayne could hear her thin smirk plainly.

Dhorh turned and barked at the Eye of Death, "I was right. Charodon has taken one of the Chosen as a host. He was already unconscious. I didn't think I needed to unthread him."

"That savage brute," Rhaiga said nonchalantly. She gripped the back of his wooden bench. Elongated fingernails from her spindly hands bit deep into the wood. "Which one was it?"

Dhorh coughed slightly. "The scarred one. When I tried looking into his memories, there was no mistaking the other presence there."

Stroking his chin, Vayne turned his head back toward the windows. "So Charodon has not yet consumed his host? My, I haven't heard of a host giving him trouble before." This certainly complicated things. Everything became more complicated once Charodon got involved. The Eye of Nature didn't listen to anyone. Not Chosen and *certainly* not Vayne. That was problem enough as far as Vayne was concerned. Charodon yearned for carnage and nothing more.

The air around them became still. Rhaiga's nails still ground against the wooden bench, biting in deeply. Sighing, the old man clapped his hands to his knees and stood shakily. "We cannot change the course of our journey, and we cannot rely on Charodon. He has never been an ally to our cause, despite being the Eye of Nature. The chaos he creates would aid us, but he does not desire to rebuild order as we do. We finish our work here and leave for Collis."

Rhaiga nodded, unclenching her hands.

Dhorh stood with a cautious air. "We won't fail you, Vayne."

Vayne blinked his sightless eyes and exhaled deeply. The stench of rot and sickness hung on his breath. "No, I don't expect you will."

***

The Greed Sun was a modest ship. Two masts towered over James as he crossed the deck, the sails stretching tautly over the wooden structures. His feet wobbled beneath him. Roy had told him it would subside, but when? Two days wasn't long enough? It felt as if the whole world was tilting and lurching. He locked his legs and spread out his arms to keep balance, but the contents of his stomach were decidedly less sturdy at the moment.

Samira put a hand on his shoulder. "It takes longer for some to get over it than others." She nodded at the rising and falling deck. "Want my advice? Keep walking around the deck. It helps."

James wanted to nod, but even that small motion was too big a risk.

She gestured to his hands. "That blast you conjured at the cathedral was a lot of power at once. I can teach you to control it before we get to Collis. You came out of this fight without serious injury this time, but that devil won't be the last thing that you fight in your lifetime."

James watched Leonard walk across the freshly scrubbed deck with Vilch, deep in discussion. Something that Dhorh had said earlier was still firmly etched into his thoughts. "That Alderaye had said that nobody remembers them. That they were the true gods."

Samira rubbed her temple with her thumb before jerking the thumb toward the bow. "Walk with me." She stepped leisurely in the direction of the foremast.

Lurching a bit with the tides, the ship caught a brisk wind and continued on its way. James followed Samira to the bow and stared out in front of the ship to the north. The fresh air thankfully took the edge from his seasickness.

Samira leaned against the rail and squinted out at the horizon. Her braid whipped behind her in the wind. He had heard it could take near a month to sail all the way to the northern continent.

"Thousands of years ago, the Alderaye were the only beings on the earth," she said. "They predate everything we know, and it's said that as the world began to change, they sought to keep it the way it had been, their way. When the gods first came along, the Alderaye retreated into the shadows."

"I've never heard of anything like this," he said suspiciously. "The clerics never said a scorching thing about these creatures."

She shook her head. "Most of the other Temple sects around the world don't mention them either, except for the Shale Watchtower where I grew up, and even then it's kept pretty brief. My family has a long line of Watchers, so I was raised hearing bits here and there about Alderaye. Roy and I only found what little else is known of them while studying at the Frostspring Refuge. From what we could find, the Alderaye have been banished for centuries. The War of Lost Faith spanned much of the world as we know it now."

"What caused it?" James asked.

"Even Watchers aren't sure. Frostspring scholars say that these Alderaye started laying claim to the realms of men, with their disciples, the Altujan, killing everything in sight. A lot of people were killed, including Chosen of the time. It was only after the gods themselves joined the fray that the war ended and the Alderaye were banished. Much of the world has forgotten them over the years after the fracturing of the Temple, and that was a few hundred years ago. Now, different sects of the Temple could believe any number of different things and all claim they preach the truth. Chosen will only be born every four hundred years or so, but the Alderaye have been around since well before the first Chosen were documented.

These things are ancient. Best we can figure, there are still some 'Eyes' remaining after the war. Death, Disease, Nature, and Memory, to name a few."

It sounded that the Temple was also to blame for the lack of documentation on these devils. James wasn't surprised. "So if Dhorh wasn't the Eye of Death, he was probably the Eye of Memory. He was in my head..." James shivered.

"My guess is that he is the Eye of Memory as well," she said. "I also assume that the three-eyed devil we saw in Boane was one of them too, but I don't know which of them it was." She bit her lip. "We have to assume that at least two of them were at Boane."

James ran his fingers through his hair. "Dhorh said something about someone named Vayne. There may even be three or more of them." He looked over at Samira.

Nodding, Samira frowned toward the mainmast. "We'll have to be ready the next time we come across them. I doubt that we can catch them off guard like that again." Something in her voice hinted at knowledge she didn't feel like sharing.

"What about the fourth?" James asked. "That's possibly three accounted for."

Samira shook her head quickly. "I'm not sure."

"If it's your sacred task as a Chosen to destroy these devils, why leave the city?"

She grimaced. "The truth of the matter is that we're unprepared to deal with this. Look at how closely we came to all being slaughtered by the weakest one of them. We need all of us at full strength. The text that the Shale Watchtower passed to me are very clear about this. Can't very well charge into battle with Roy still harboring this demon of his and you only able to control sparks."

"I doubt anyone has ever described you as an optimist, Sam." James rolled his eyes. He bit the inside of his lip before the question spilled from him. "What happened? How did Roy end up like this?"

"It was a cruel chance. Charodon caught us unaware while we were working for a village's alderman. Roy tried to fight back, he got bit, and it's leeched off his body ever since." She looked down. "It's not his fault, but we'll find a way to help him. I swear we will."

The two of them watched as the crew members swarmed over the deck. Open sea expanded before the *Greed Sun* in every direction. Greens and blues swirled beneath them, flashing the occasional bright sunlight that was steadily growing. James watched Ariel climb the mainmast, her tattooed arms rippling as she expertly ascended. Roy stood below, holding a rope taut and glancing up in her direction frequently.

"What's going on with those two?" James asked, gesturing in their direction.

Samira snorted. "I'm honestly unsure if we have the time to unpack that."

Uncertain Waters

R oy tugged at the rigging, his palms ground to mash by the ropes. He had been at it for hours, and the sun was either on its way up or about to set. He had forgotten which one it was. It had been an odd day or two to say the least, and his mind was everywhere at once. Roy had lost control to Charodon for the first time in months, just after coming face to face with the man he hated more than anyone.

He and James had fought what was unmistakably another Alderaye, and Ariel had returned, making it very hard to exist normally. It was drowning near impossible to go about his life when she wasn't around. But now that she was back, her presence was intoxicating. It didn't make any difference though. He still carried the shame of his actions from two years ago, and he couldn't let himself off the hook.

Sea spray jumped from the swell outside the boat and spattered his face. The Escrai Sea was always choppy but now churned even more aggressively than usual. It was a welcome shock to clear his mind, and he hauled another foot of rope toward him, sweat and salt glistening on his face. The sleeves of his new white shirt had been rolled up, and he could feel the wind on his skin. It was picking up. His muscles and senses still felt heightened since his fight with Dhorh. Somehow, Charodon could sense the proximity to the other Alderaye, and Roy could still feel the residual contempt and adrenaline of his malevolent passenger. This could become useful later. If he could sense when the Alderaye were around, perhaps they could more easily be avoided.

He looked up at Vilch. The captain glowered down at him from the upper deck, clearly keeping an eye on him. Come to think of it, most of the crew had been watching him much more than the rest of his companions. Could it be that they had figured out what he was? Charodon had become something of a foul legend in the empire and across the sea. Some even thought that the devil was some kind of dragon, even though the ancient beasts mostly inhabited the tropics or the far north. He could always feel the nervous and suspicious eyes upon him wherever he went, and the whispering voices that called him that foul name. *The Scaleslayer.* A bit contrived perhaps, but the name did its job in making it difficult to exist around people.

"I don't think the rigging is going to come undone," Ariel said behind him. She had come up to him silently.

Electric terror ran through his body, but he maintained his composure and tied off the rope. How had she managed to sneak up on him? Perhaps she had caught on to the fact that he had been avoiding her. Turning to face her, Roy blinked as the last rays of the sun reflected into his eyes.

She leaned against the mast and gave a friendly smile. "You look different." The air around Roy felt thicker, more difficult to bring into his lungs.

He shrugged, knowing she didn't mean his scar. Desperately, Roy tried to think of something to say. "You have new glyphs." A tattoo on her left shoulder sported a swirling glyph in ink that was slightly darker than the rest of the tattoos that went up and down her arms. Her sleeveless wool shirt looked black in the waning sunlight. "Anyone I know?"

People native to Ariel's homeland of Spiath were incredibly interconnected, holding a philosophy of community and tradition. A village was not just a place that someone lived, but a sacred place. And the people who lived in one's village were considered extended family. To honor their township, Spiathi tattooed a glyph on their body for each person who lived there. New glyphs were added when new children were born.

She shook her head, still smiling slightly. "I expect I'll be getting more the next time I visit home. Were you planning on fixing nonexistent rigging problems all night?"

A grin tugged at the corner of Roy's mouth. "I suppose I was," he said with a hint of amusement. "Who knows when a problem might suddenly exist?" He tried not to make eye contact, but he could feel her metallic blue eyes trained on him. He continued hastily, "I mean, it's not impossible to think that something could happen."

"You're still a worrier." She chuckled.

"You're still an optimist," he countered. Three years ago, he would have done anything just to be around her. The corners of his mouth twitched again as he remembered a time when she had sat with him atop the Basalt Watchtower. He forgot who had challenged who, but they had engaged in a race to the top before Samira and Leonard could stop them. Perhaps knowing more than he had at the time, Leonard and Samira had stayed at the base, leaving him and Ariel to sit atop the tower through the night. Roy could still remember the keenness in her voice as she pointed out the Eleven Glyphs, sacred Spiathi constellations.

What was he doing? He was sure she was only trying to make polite conversation. No one could have forgiven him for what he had done to her. Charodon's consciousness chipped against the base of his skull, just as it had two years ago, one of the last times the Eye of Nature had ever pushed him into losing control. That loss of control almost killed Ariel. Any sense of happiness he felt from this fleeting conversation was immediately squelched.

"I should get some rest." He turned toward the staircase that led to the belly of the ship. "It's good to see you, Ariel." The wood of the ship creaked while he hurried down the stairs and disappeared into the berth.

***

Ariel sighed in disappointment as Roy went below. She knew it wasn't easy to get Roy to speak nowadays, but she had hoped for things to be different. How could they be though? There was little chance that he had forgotten that she'd left him to die that night, much less forgiven. She'd been scared, of course, but she regretted her actions.

Moving from the mast to port, she leaned against the rail, watching the black crests of the waves beyond them. She had seen a school of scythefish earlier, their sharp, thin fins cutting through the water as if they were slicing air. Just a few years ago, there had been such life behind Roy's turquoise eyes. His desire to help others had been a challenge for all of them, including her, to be better. Charodon had taken all of that away. To see a spirit like that so viciously killed, it was one of the biggest regrets that she had left.

Leonard leaned on the rail next to her. "What are you doing?"

She rolled her eyes. "What does it look like I'm doing?"

He smirked. "You know that isn't what I mean. Are you going to let him run away every time you get close?" Shooting her a knowing glance, he gestured to the stairs leading below deck. "Come on, it's getting painful to watch you two skirt around each other."

Ariel gripped the rail tight enough to hear the wood groan under her fingers. What did he know about it? Another new tattoo on her shoulder itched. She resisted the urge to scratch it. The one on her knee had finally subsided, but this one refused to go away. It had been a weight off of her to see Roy alive after two years, but their pesky history insisted on getting in the way. Mistakes had been made, and the consequences of those mistakes weren't ones that could just be shrugged off. She snapped at Leonard, "It's different. Things have changed too much. And if I recall, a lot of it is no thanks to you."

"Lots of things change, but this is one thing that's never going to," Leonard said. His spiky hair bristled in the wind. Her words had stung him, but she did have a point. "I know both of you pretty well. Roy may want to kill me, and the look you're giving me says you may want to as well, but I know that nothing's changed with you two." He grinned, trying to pass his optimism onto her. Ariel scoffed briefly, taking her weight off the rail.

"I'll admit throwing you overboard would be amusing." She punched him lightly on the shoulder. "And I don't think taking advice from *you* on this subject is going to be very beneficial."

Leonard feigned offense. "Me? What are you trying to say?"

"Are you forgetting about Lilia?"

"That was *not* my fault."

"Edmund?"

"That was an amicable ending to a relationship."

"Lady Clane?"

"I forgot about that one."

"August?"

"Okay, that one was on me," he admitted. Leonard chuckled sheepishly. His courting in the empire was legendary. Trying to be named head of an Aroch without a family name was a difficult task even as a Chosen, so it only made sense to try a different route. In the old days, a Chosen could have just taken the title, but Leonard stood firmly in support of the changes that Alaric was making. They just didn't know where being a Chosen would fit into those changes yet.

Trying to shift the subject, she pointed toward Samira, who was still talking to Vilch. "Are you going to help her with James's lessons?" She watched as Samira continued to speak at Vilch, who was rather disinterested in the conversation.

Shrugging, Leonard yawned. "I will if she asks me to. Not much point in it, if I were to state my opinion. Even with the use of only one arm, she has enough power to strike down a stronghold. I can't move much earth without becoming heavier than stone. What a stupid price to pay for the power to move the ground that you stand on." He started toward the stairs. "You going to get some sleep at all, or are you just going to wander around the deck all night?"

It was Ariel's turn to shrug. "Someone should take the first watch. Vilch accepted the extra coin we gave him, but that doesn't make him trustworthy." There was nothing about him that she trusted. Unlike the rest of the Chosen, Ariel had been to Scourge Atoll and had seen firsthand the grubby savagery that passed as a way of life there. Though the land was beautiful, the soil was permanently soaked with blood.

"Will you go back to Greade Harbor when we return?" she asked. "To see your mother?"

Leonard shook his head stiffly.

A shout from the bow yanked her out of the conversation. Ariel and Leonard approached Samira and Vilch, toward the sounds of bickering. The winds of the open sea were starting to chill her, despite the rising moisture and warmth in the air. That was what she could have expected from not wearing sleeves.

Samira's arms were crossed as she huffed at Vilch. "You need us, Vilch. Don't act like you and your crew could just throw us overboard if you wanted." She glowered.

"I won't tolerate speech like that on my ship," Vilch snapped back. "The only reason we took the lot of you was because Leonard paid extra. You and the Scaleslayer are lucky we even let you aboard."

Leonard sighed. "Why do you have to pick a fight with everyone, Sam?"

Samira whirled on him. "This dolt here could use a good smack across the face. He's sailing us right into a Dreadfront."

Ariel jolted at the mention of these legendary tempests. It was the season for them, but she hadn't thought about it when they had left the empire. Dreadfronts were especially fearsome due to their supercharged ferocity. Some even claimed that magic was involved. Few mariners had ever claimed to be survivors of a front, and even fewer could back up their claims.

She turned to Vilch. "Would you care to explain?"

The captain crossed his lean arms. "It may miss us yet, but it will be close." His black eyes darted back and forth between them like a dragonfly.

Samira's eyes widened at the captain's words. "You're insane! Why don't we just carve a hole into the ship now then? There are faster ways to drown, not to mention what surfaces during these storms."

Vilch didn't deny the stories that Samira was talking about. Because of the near supernatural strength of the storms, sailors had told tall tales of deep-dwelling beasts that came to the surface. Everything from giant amphibious creatures to incomprehensible horrors to merpeople supposedly arose during these storms, according to the stunned survivors.

"Aye, it's a risk, and I'm doing my best to skirt the worst of it and only clip the very edge of the front, but that's as far as my crew will go," Vilch insisted. "There's nowhere to port but the islands, and the crew won't sail there willingly. You know what folk have said about the Tarsals. We'd be getting too close to them on our current adjustments."

The Tarsal Isles were one of the few remaining places in the known world that remained wild. Out in the middle of the ocean, the mismatched cluster of landmasses looked vaguely like the scattered bones of a foot. It was anyone's guess what they could run into there, and somewhere between the documented accounts and the tall tales, it was likely that a trip there would bring catastrophe. Sailors in particular avoided the islands to an irrational degree.

Well, this was news that Ariel could have done without. "The Tarsal Isles may be home to a lot of strange things, Vilch. But we don't run the risk of drowning on top of everything else while we're there," she said. "You should have at least discussed this with us. How far away is the storm?"

Vilch shrugged and pulled a logbook from his shirt, flipping it open. His eyes became imperceptible as he squinted to read the parchment in the dim light. Ariel had seen storm logs like this before from other captains, made up of notes regarding strict observations. Cloud density, moisture in the air, swell patterns of the waves, behavior of the sea life.

The captain scoured the weather log for a few moments before looking up at her. "Maybe a few days." He pointed ahead of them to the northeast. "It's coming straight from this way toward the south, so our best chance is to sail sheer northwest and hope it barely misses us. It'll be close, but we might make it. This would add time to the overall journey, but it's better than the seabed."

"How close are we to the islands if we had to make an emergency landing?" Samira asked.

Vilch rolled his eyes. "Less than a week? I already told you that we can't go there. The crew won't stand for it."

Samira lurched forward and clamped down on Vilch's shoulder with her right hand. The scarred tissue of her arm tightened as she squeezed, making the captain wince. "Your crew can get over their superstitions and sail us there if needed, captain. The storms are real, and Astus strike me, we will not survive the storm." Eyes impossibly wide, the captain nodded, shaking from Samira's grip.

Releasing Vilch, Samira glanced curtly at Ariel and Leonard and strode off toward the lower deck. She still didn't trust them. Unsurprising as that was, Ariel still felt a little hurt.

Massaging his shoulder, Vilch looked incredulously at Leonard. "I thought you said you could handle them."

Leonard shrugged. "I know when to pick my battles, Vilch. And a battle with Sam is one that I would never pick." He turned toward the lower decks. "We'd better prepare for land if the storm pushes us too close to the Tarsals then."

Vilch shook violently and strolled across the deck. Several strands of hair came loose from his tight bun, much like the control he had over his own ship. He had been paid well, but even a hefty fee had its limit. Ariel knew that people ventured to the islands for discovery, knowledge, treasure, or other desires. Many never left the islands, and she had a good enough sense to figure that they didn't just settle down there. But at least on land they would have more of a fighting chance. She had enough understanding of Roy's power to know that he could only do so much against a churning sea. And Leonard's power was useless out here.

Ariel bade Leonard good night and made her way to the mainmast, eager for the ascent. It felt good to climb. It took her mind off things. Her hands expertly grasped every handhold as she hoisted herself up to the crow's nest, hands trained by years of climbing the trees of her homeland. Runes, carved to request the protection of Dathos, sprawled up the mast.

On their journey to Epot Detharn, the crew had learned that Ariel preferred an empty crow's nest as the sun went down. They grumbled about it, but they didn't protest. As expected, there was no one at the top when she got there. The structure was little more than an oversized barrel that had been tightly strapped to the mast, but it did the job.

Settling into the relatively cramped space, she brushed a strand of hair away from her face and looked out at the dark waters before her. They reminded her of the night she and Roy had spent atop the Basalt Watchtower. All Eleven Glyphs had glinted clearly in the sky, a constellation event that rarely happened. Overlooking the coast, the waves below the tower reflected the light of the Glyphs back up to the sky. Roy had excitedly claimed that the light was not a reflection but a refrain. Gentle beasts from the depths had risen to the surface to reflect the stars with a light of their own. He had been so happy. It was a good memory to hold onto.

The waves before the ship stretched on forever, but in a few weeks they would reach the empire. Then her job would be done. Leonard took pride in his service to the empire and the sense of purpose he got from it, but she was sick of it. It was a noble purpose, she supposed. But the emperor had Arochs to take care of problems within the land. Fighting wasn't supposed to be all that the Chosen did, but it felt like it was all she and Leonard were asked to do anymore.

Once she was done and back in the empire, she could return home and start a life that was peaceful. Just her and those she cherished. They wouldn't be around forever.

This dream was becoming less and less possible in her eyes, though. She had people she cared about on this ship too, and their fight seemed unlikely to ever end. And if that fight was unlikely to end, she would keep getting pulled into it.

"Just get everyone back safely, and then you can leave for good," she mumbled to herself. The words were lost to the wind.

The Simplest Form

James met Samira on the main deck the next morning before the sun rose. He dressed in a dark wool coat and roughly stitched pants to protect himself from the wind. Yawning as he approached her, James noticed that she was holding a single oil lantern. The heat from the captured flame registered at the edge of his drowsy consciousness and grew closer as he approached.

His awareness of heat around him had become sharper in the last few days. Before they had set sail, he could only notice it if he were in a room with fire or heat of any kind. Now he could faintly pick up on heat sources farther out, even if there was a wall in between. There were still things that he needed to improve, for his control over any manipulation was severely limited. Those blasts he had managed against Dhorh in the cathedral had been powerful, but it had been a life or death situation.

Samira was dressed in the same jerkin and brown cloak. Her braid was tucked into the hood of her cloak, and her eyes eerily reflected in the light of the lamp. Eager to begin, she smiled widely as he stumbled over. She had worked him to exhaustion the day before without much progress. He hadn't even gotten to interact with a flame yet. He'd climbed up and down the mainmast, lifted crates, and run the length of the deck for hours. What did that have to do with this power?

"Are you awake?" she teased.

James nodded halfheartedly as she chuckled. Putting the lantern down, Samira pointed to her chest.

"Breathe."

Doing as he was bid, James inhaled deeply, taking in the briny oxygen around him. It rushed into his chest, shooting brief energy through his body. His eyes looked at her quizzically. "What's this feeling?"

Tilting her head, Samira breathed in deeply herself. "Fire thrives when given oxygen. The more of it you have, the more fire you can produce or control. You are the physical manifestation of Iarus's power. So long as you can breathe, you have the energy and the means to control fire, whether it be one you manipulate or one of your own." She bent down and scooped up the lantern again, pulling the cover off of the flame. The tiny orange light sputtered a bit, but stayed alight as she cupped her hand around it, shielding it from the wind. "Breathe in."

James closed his eyes and took another deep breath, trying to hold in the air that cascaded through his system. The presence of the lamp's flame grew in his field of sense, as if the extra oxygen had heightened his awareness of it. Sensing it growing closer, he opened his eyes. Samira had taken a step closer and was holding the uncovered lamp out to him. An orange glow seeped into the corners of his vision as he trained his eyes on the pinprick of fire. The cold of the maritime wind had all but been washed away. His body was engulfed by the pleasant heat, and his continued breathing sped the convection through his mind. Feeling the familiar internal tug, he reached toward the open flame and caressed it with his palm.

Leaping from the uncovered lantern, the flame gently settled into his hand. It splashed against his skin like water. Holding his cupped hand in front of him, he watched, dumbfounded while the flame continued to burn. It sat on the heel of his hand, feeding warmth into his arm. Feeling strangely giddy, he laughed and looked up at Samira. Her eyes shone even brighter.

"Good, you can hold and maintain a standing flame. That's the simplest form. As long as you can do this without having to concentrate too hard, you can move on."

"Simplest form?" James asked, still staring at the small fire in his hand.

She nodded. "There are three forms using the gods' gifts. The first and simplest form is to hold and maintain the power within you." She again set the now-unlit lantern back to the deck with a metallic clink. "The second form is tricky. It's all about commanding or shaping the power to your instruction." She noticed his confused look. "Think of it as an extremity. You command your body to move a certain way or behave a certain way, and it's the same thing with your gift."

James stooped and picked up the lantern with his free hand, still holding the fire in his right. The metal of the lamp was incredibly cold, as was the wick protruding from the oil basin. It appeared that he had stolen all the heat from the lamp. Still holding the basin, he looked back up at Samira. "What's the third form?"

She jerked her head in the direction of the starboard rail. "Throw it."

Still holding the little flame in his other hand, James turned and hurled the lantern overboard. It spun upward into the sky in an arc. As it moved outward and over the waves, Samira grimaced and made a throwing motion with her left hand. Tendrils of lightning launched from her hand, rushing outward and smashing the lamp. The nearby horizon flashed blue. With an echoing bang, the oil inside the lamp ignited and expanded into a bright sphere of flames.

James watched the fireball disappear along with the blinding reflection of the explosion. He blinked, still seeing the flash burned into his vision. For a split second, it had been like the sun had come up early. Swearing and shouting followed from the crewmen and women. They had obviously been taken by surprise by Samira's display as well.

Rolling her left sleeve back down, Samira yawned. James glanced around to see the other crew members hurrying back to their stations, their heads down. Their captain had maybe not been very forthright with them about who she was. She shrugged and pointed to where the fireball had been. "That was the third form, inward creation. When experienced enough, a Chosen can use their own energy and power to create. This takes a lot of practice, and it takes the biggest physical toll out of all three forms."

"Is that why your right arm was hurt?" James asked.

Nodding, she tugged at her right sleeve, exposing the webbed pattern of scars that ran up her arm. The scars looked much like veins or cracks, as if severe dehydration and not electricity were to blame for her condition. "I tried too early to master the second form, and it was a horrible mistake." It looked as though she was remembering something painful. "I nearly lost the arm, and I can no longer use this gift with it. A lot of people were hurt that day." She sighed heavily. "Including someone I loved. Lightning is the most unpredictable of the gifts, and Astus sought to punish me for not being deliberate with each use of it."

"But why would he do that?" James asked skeptically. "Why would he punish you for trying to use the gift he gave you?" It didn't make sense to him. The Temple despised these questions.

"It's what he dictates, James. Astus is the most powerful of all the gods, a great equalizer. He can destroy an ancient tree with a single strike. Everything he does has a purpose, and power this great cannot be wielded with abandon."

He held his tongue, having heard similar answers in the past. The gods seemed to have too much restraint when it came to anything good but were just fine with unlimited punishment and destruction. Arguing with Samira was not going to help him. "Can the others use the third form?"

"Roy can in some capacity. Ariel and Leonard haven't mastered it yet. In some ways, Ariel may never need to. She is constantly surrounded by air. As long as she can breathe, wind can be shaped with her gift, much like you with fire." She gestured to his hand. "You seem to have a pretty good handle on the simple stage. The flame may have gone down a bit, but it's still there."

James looked down at his hand. The fire that had been in his grasp throughout their conversation had slowly diminished. All that remained were small embers that glowed against his skin, making the veins in his hand appear dark red. It was frail, akin to a bird on the verge of death. Heat throbbed at the very edge of his senses. Inhaling deeply, he extended his thoughts toward the dying flame in his hand, commanding it to grow. Light danced across Samira's face, and the fire in his hand expanded and fluttered outward exponentially before going out completely.

James gasped and closed his hand. The sense of warmth and energy he had felt mere seconds before had been drained from him as if by the fangs of a venomous spider. Holding and keeping the shape of the fire for that long was something that required more endurance. He now understood why Samira had ordered him to train his body so ferociously the day before.

Grinning, she pointed upward to the crow's nest. "Climb. You need to get stronger. You may have a handle on the first form, but the Alderaye have had thousands of years to hone and perfect their gifts." They had not been ready last time, and Dhorh had used that to his advantage.

The next three days went along smoothly. Ariel kept a soft wind blowing into the sails to keep the vessel going at a faster pace while Samira watched the sea for any threats. It didn't seem like anyone had been following them. Thoughts of vengeance and the Temple receded slightly in the back of James's mind. Out here on the waves, the rest of the world felt far away.

He could sense that the crew were curious about him, Roy, and Samira. They had grown used to Leonard and Ariel, but the new passengers on the ship were a very frequent topic of hushed conversation. A wide range of men and women, the sailors had avoided direct conversation with him. Not that they had a lot of time for conversation anyway.

The sky ahead of them to the north had grown increasingly dark over the last few days. James didn't know much about Dreadfronts other than what the clerics had said growing up, but from the way that Vilch and the rest rushed about, he could tell that there would be a struggle ahead. Of course, there was always the chance that it would miss them, but the chance of something good happening yielded slim odds given their record for avoiding danger.

On top of that, the crew had become more irritable since Vilch's announcement that they would sail toward the Tarsals to avoid the front. It had sounded reasonable to him when he heard it, but the crew had erupted in protest. Curses had flown for ten minutes before Vilch could get them in line again. Now the crew were openly hostile to James and his companions, not hiding the fact that they despised them.

James had also started to practice swordplay. Roy had him sparring twice a day. He supposed that calling it "sparring" was being generous. The reality was that Roy thrashed him each time he picked up his scorching sword. Even though James felt himself getting better, each session always concluded with a fresh bruise. His knee still throbbed where Roy had cracked it the morning before. Roy was patient but not sympathetic with James. That somehow made it worse. At least when he had play-fenced with Gemmi, his brother had been more gentle.

The fourth day, everything was going well, the wind blowing so strongly Ariel didn't need to tend to the sails. Samira stayed at the bow of the ship, scanning ahead for any trouble. James had noticed Vilch and the rest of the crew scuttling about nervously. Even in the mid-morning, the sky to the northeast swirled and churned with clouds the color of coal.

While the crew worked to prepare for the storm, Roy had insisted on trouncing him again.

"You have to move your feet, James. Otherwise you're just a dead man just waiting to get that way," Roy said, his sword pointed at James's chest for the hundredth time. Roy's face betrayed no emotion, but his voice had an exasperated edge. The sparring blade he had given James clattered on the deck, having been swatted out of his grip yet again.

James's shoulder stung as he reached down to grasp the hilt of his sparring sword. *I'm a dead man in proximity to you, more than anything*, he thought. The rough leather grip ground at the skin of his palm. "I think you enjoy kicking me around."

He could clearly see some of the crew members watching from a safe distance. The sea had grown fiercer in the last few days, causing the ship to rock more violently. The tolerance that he had built to the rocking of the ship suddenly had become no longer adequate, and he had spent the better part of the night before leaning over a pail below deck.

Roy rolled his eyes. "I'm not doing this to be mean to you, James. The world is one big nest of swords all trying to find their way into your heart. You can't survive by just putting on a light every time you're in trouble."

"I defeated Dhorh by doing that," James argued.

Roy nodded. "You did, but Dhorh wasn't using a sword. Most people who try to kill you will be." He motioned for James to attack with a wave of his sword.

"Is that a common problem for Chosen? People trying to kill you?"

"Not always."

"Altujan?" James asked.

"Nobody's seen one in centuries. But they said the same about Alderaye."

James took a deep breath and charged Roy with a slice to the shoulder. Roy fluidly dodged to the side and batted the blow away. James's sparring blade clattered to the deck yet again. James swore and bent to pick up the steel again. His fighting was child's play compared to Roy's technique.

Shaking his head, Roy held his sword in front of him, pointing his line of vision. "You have to dominate the area in front of you, James. Keep your sword in the space between you and your opponent." His dull sparring brand flashed even though there was very little sunlight penetrating the cloud cover. The storm could be seen off to the north, no more than a day away. It was almost impossible now that it would miss them. A slight green hue glowed from the darkness of the distant clouds, blinking with every flash of lightning.

Steeling himself to attack again, James held his sword aloft, maintaining his distance from Roy and keeping the weapon between him and his opponent. His swordplay experience had come entirely from watching Gemmi, and James was pretty sure that Gemmi had been making it up as he went along.

This time, Roy didn't wait for James to attack. His sword flashing, Roy slashed at James's flank. With barely enough time to counter, James sidestepped and knocked the blow out of the way. He didn't have time to be impressed with himself. Roy came at him again, the sword a fluid blur. The attacks flowed like water, and James felt as if he were drowning under each one. It was relentless, and all he could do was hold the sparring blade in front of himself helplessly. This time he managed to keep his grip on the sword, but he was trapped. Roy had expertly maneuvered him into a corner up against the mizzenmast and a stack of supply crates. Thoroughly annoyed with himself, James lowered his sparring weapon.

Roy lowered his steel. "You retreated."

"I get it, alright? I'm terrible. Point taken," James snapped.

Roy set his blade against the supply crates near him and sat against them. He motioned for James to sit. Shaking his head and ignoring his nausea, James sulked and slid to the deck. Roy looked at the horizon and the storm clouds to the north.

"You're a talented swordsman, James." Roy looked at him and rasied an eyebrow. "Untrained but talented. I mean that, truly. You have potential, just as you have potential in your lessons with Sam." His voice was its usual thoughtful, soft tone, but it had a hint of understanding.

Dumbfounded, James tried to find words to speak. The last thing he ever expected from Roy was to be nice to him, "I—"

"But I need you to be better, because of what happened with Dhorh," Roy continued. He squinted up toward the bow of the ship where Samira and Vilch directed crewmen. "There's more at play here than we thought. Dhorh appearing won't be the end. And I can't guarantee that everything will go the way it did last time. You know enough about what happened to me to know that things can get much worse for all of us. And they probably will." He looked back at James, somehow keeping his eyes open despite the growing wind. "This may come as a shock, but I would like for you to stay alive."

James smirked. He had no idea that Roy was capable of anything but backhanded, sullen remarks. Roy stood slowly, extending a hand. The wind swept across the deck of the ship. James took the hand, and Roy hauled him up. He scooped up the sparring blade from the deck, steel scraping off the wooden planks as he picked it up and handed it to James.

"Let's go again," Roy said. James nodded, ready to attack, but his concentration was broken by shouts of alarm toward the rear starboard of the ship. Immediately forgetting their sparring, James and Roy sprinted across the deck to the growing huddle of crew along the rail. Ariel stood on the edge, holding the rigging for balance. They all gaped breathlessly at the water below. Even the experienced sailors had shocked looks on their faces. James and Roy weaved through the steadily growing group of astonished mariners, trying to get a look at the waves below. James's eyes grew wide with awe and horror.

Circling less than twelve yards from the ship was a massive gray fin. It glided through the water, creating no ripple as the waves were sliced in half by the front of its triangular structure. The fin itself was attached to a terrifyingly large shape, lethargically coasting underneath the surface.

Moving slowly, the shape paid the ship no mind. Some of the crewmen weren't taking any chances and had gathered harpoons. The rusted weapons were in a pile near the rail, shifting with the rocking of the vessel. James had never seen such a large creature before. Even on land, the scuttlers that infested Boane had been little more than the size of a person's arm. The shape drifted lazily past the stern of the ship, taking an eternity to fully pass them. As if in a trance, everyone followed the creature, hurrying across the deck to port side.

"What is that? It's huge." James gaped. Several crewmen grunted in agreement of the creature's size.

"It's an imperator," Ariel said, ecstatic. Her eyes were fixed on the great fish. It circled back and investigated the large wooden structure that they all stood on. Barely obscured by the waves, its pointed nose pushed through the water effortlessly. Its tail propelled it through the swell with incredible power and yet with such little effort. Twin sets of pectoral fins protruded from its sides. Ariel stood on the port-side rail and beamed at the monstrous shadow below them. "It's a king among the deep, the bishops of Dathos."

"Dathos drown me, lass. A big shark is all," one of the crewmen, with a red beard, guffawed. The man's beard stood out in a crescent shape due to an unfortunately located bald patch on his jaw. His tone was light, but he glared up at her with a good deal of contempt.

Ariel shook her head vigorously. Golden hair floated around her head for a moment before settling again on her shoulder. "They only surface near dread-fronts, clearing the death that the storm wrought at the command of Dathos. Everything that surfaces in the storm returns to the depths because the imperator hunts them down." The sailor with the crescent-beard looked like he was about to say something else, but the fish drew closer, causing a hush to fall over the meager crowd. Even Roy was silent in reverence to the gigantic being that curiously swam alongside the ship.

Unbelievable. James's heart was pounding even though the animal had no idea he was even there. *It must be about thirty feet long!* The monstrous shark turned sharply and set its attention to something in the distance. Its forked tail pumped back and forth twice, silently and slowly propelling it forward. The blur of the waves above it caused the great fish to shift in and out of sight until it disappeared entirely. As quickly as it had shown itself, it vanished.

The crew around them dispersed and returned to their posts. Several of them began taking crates and supplies below deck. When the front came through, it would be important to make sure that anything not tied down was secure. The crescent-bearded sailor glared at them for a moment before disappearing down the stairway.

The water around them was already starting to grow to a boil, like a pot slowly gaining heat. James could feel the swell crash against the bow of the ship as it lurched forward through the water. Seeing the shark had almost made him forget how sick he had been feeling, but the nausea still lingered in the back of his throat. With the sky growing darker the farther north they went, he began to feel sick for another reason entirely.

Fury and Sadness

The bow of the ship plunged downward again, stabbing into the turbulent waters below it and ripping from the frothy wound. Samira stood at the bow with Vilch, blinking through the spray toward the north. She had heard the crew saw an imperator shark earlier. It made her a bit jealous. It wasn't often that one got to see a subject of tall tales. The storm was nearly upon them, and the islands weren't even in sight yet. At least, if they were there, they were obscured by rain. Her left arm tensed in anticipation of being around natural lightning. She would have to be very careful how to go about this. No one could get hurt. Astus had charged her with the safety of her friends. To complete their purpose, to defeat the Alderaye for good, all of the Chosen were needed.

"I've got the crew taking supplies below deck and readying the boats just in case," Vilch shouted next to her. The man's normally overpowering voice came out a bit smaller and more hoarse than usual. He had been yelling orders nonstop since the storm first appeared on the horizon. Like Samira, he was soaked head to toe in salt water and rain, and the tight bun of hair had unraveled to show long, graying strands that hung limp from his scalp. The captain looked exhausted, and the storm hadn't even hit them yet.

Samira waited for the next crash of the bow before shouting back, "Have you ever been in a Dreadfront before, Captain?"

Vilch looked straight ahead. "Once, but it was a mercifully short one. So short that it broke a minute after hitting us." Samira had to strain to hear the sailor's voice.

Vilch looked back at Samira. "The islands are another day ahead. Would have gotten there sooner, but this headwind had us near standing still for a while. Might actually be a good thing to avoid a lee shore and end with a shipwreck."

The strong headwinds had indeed been a problem. Ariel had tried her best to negate them, but even a Chosen would have a hard time stopping headwinds preceding a Dreadfront. Etah's Champion was sound asleep in the ship's hold, having basically collapsed after battling the headwind and then sprinting to the stern just to get a glimpse of that oversized fish. That had been just shy of a full day ago. Ariel overextended herself too often. It was one of the few annoying qualities that she had picked up from Leonard over the years.

Sea spray once again leapt from the surface of the waves and straight into Samira's eyes. Cursing and rubbing her face, she turned her back to the bow. She was going to have to get used to this happening for the time being. A familiar hand rested on her shoulder, causing her to smirk. "Guess I should have been more prepared for the striking ocean," she said loudly.

"I was going to say that avoiding the bow during a storm would be a start," Roy half-shouted.

"Then what are you doing here?" Finally blinking the last of the salt water from her eyes, she glanced at Roy's glistening face. He was also drenched from the ocean spray. His clothing given to him by the crew and his striking black cloak clung to him heavily.

Roy nodded toward the waves battering against the hull, brandishing a rope. "I'll be the failsafe, keep the deck as dry as I can. But if the waves get too big,

I won't be able to hold them for long." He set to securing the rope to the rail, presumably to tether himself.

"We need to get into a secure place."

He shook his head. "It's going to take three of us to get through this. I keep the waves at bay, Ariel redirects the wind, you watch for the lightning strikes. James should find a secure place or stay with the boats. Leonard can pitch himself over the rail for all I care."

"We're going to need Leonard if we have to land on the islands," she said.

"Why? The second we get in trouble, he's just going to run away again," he said a bit louder.

Leonard cautiously ascended the stairs to the main deck, "Where would I run, Roy? We're a bit stranded right now." He was irritated, the usual amused grin long gone.

Astus strike her friend's temper. Samira had forgotten how good Leonard's hearing was. The man had once claimed that was why he had such a keen ear for music.

Roy turned to Leonard. "You found a way to run off last time. And the time after that. You would think the emperor's errand boy would have a bit more courage."

The Chosen of Raslena reached for his boot. "I may be a coward, but at least I'm not a threat. Eh, Scaleslayer?"

Roy lunged at Leonard, fist aloft and fury scorching his face. Flecks of orange materialized in his eyes as Samira jumped between them and braced against Roy, holding him away.

"Both of you, stop it!" she shouted. "Your problems can wait, or did you not notice a striking *Dreadfront* only hours away?" It took a lot of strength to hold Roy back when he was angry, scaled or otherwise.

Sneering at Leonard, Roy shoved Samira away from him. "How about you fend off the waves, Leonard? For the empire, yeah?" He put a hand on the hilt of his saber and stormed toward the stairs to the lower deck. Leonard huffed and crossed his bulky arms.

Glaring at Leonard, she rubbed her temple with her thumb. "You couldn't have just let it go this once?"

He turned away from her and walked toward the rail.

Groaning with frustration, Samira rushed after Roy. Astus had granted her the power to destroy the whole ship if she wanted to, but she couldn't get the two of them to get along. It was like negotiating with the children she grew up with at the Shale Watchtower. The precipitation combined with the spray of the continually agitated sea had made the deck a precarious surface to walk across, and it took a moment for her to cross the deck and chase him down the stairs.

She called after him toward the stern, "You couldn't just play nice for the next few hours, could you? You had to start a fight with one of the people we need the most right now. I hope you're happy!"

"Couldn't be happier. Something to wipe that smile off his face," Roy snapped.

She finally caught him toward the port-side stern. Her amber eyes fixed on him, but he refused to return her gaze. "You can't let your anger control you," she said loudly. The wind was getting louder.

"I know." Roy grimaced.

"Leonard isn't our enemy, Roy. We can't afford to be fighting each other. We have to be united, or we'll fall," Samira said gently.

Roy stopped avoiding her gaze and looked at her. Fury and sadness fought for control over his face, and it looked like he was trying to find words cutting enough to get her to drop the subject. He sighed and looked down at the deck.

"It's all his fault, Sam," Roy shouted over the wind, "and I can't forgive him."

Samira didn't have to ask. Leonard and Roy had always looked out for each other. They never had to ask the other for help. Their group of four had been inseparable. And while life was never perfect, they had been happy. That happiness had been shattered on that day three years ago. They'd gone after a beast that was terrorizing a small town in the marshlands, hoping to slay it. Two days into the hunt, Samira had come down with a debilitating ailment. From then on, the whole operation had collapsed.

Samira remembered the day vividly, even through the green veil of sickness. She still felt ill remembering it, and not particularly due to the ailment. She remembered Charodon smashing through the trees and charging Roy. She remembered Roy swinging his sword, and the sword flying from his grip.

She remembered him screaming as the jagged teeth of the monster plunged into his shoulder. She remembered its snout being stained red with his blood. And as the beast consumed his energy and possessed his body, Leonard was nowhere to be found. He had run away.

"When I found him again, I was hoping we could make it right." Roy continued, "I wanted him to apologize for what happened. I thought we could be friends again." Roy traced his fingers over the scar on his eye and his face hardened. She couldn't be sure, but she thought that there were tears mixed with the sea spray. "But I was a fool, Sam. You can't count on anyone. Now, I'm a danger to other people. I needed his help, and he ran away."

"Leonard isn't as foolish as he used to be," Samira implored. "He's angry with you, but we all want to help you." Samira looked her friend in the eye for a moment, realizing that Roy's mind was made up. The shame and guilt bubbled into her throat, almost blurting out something to make Roy's hurt immeasurably worse. She had *known* that the creature they were after was Charodon, and she had *lied* to ensure her friends came with her.

She looked away. "We need to wake Ariel."

Roy walked out of the range of her voice, no longer interested in listening. Samira gazed into the swirling clouds ahead of them and tried desperately to think of something that could save her friend. The sickness of remembering that day swelled, and nothing she tried to distract her mind with could keep it down. Leonard wasn't at fault for what happened to Roy; she was.

A short time later, Samira stalked across the deck with Ariel wobbling after her.

Exhaling sharply in a stifled yawn, Ariel stretched her patterned arms outward. It was a miracle that Samira had been able to wake her at all. Ariel had always been the last of the group to get up when she could find sleep, even if she hadn't just pushed an entire ship along for four days.

Each raindrop across Samira's face stung like a tiny ice pick. Growing up in the presence of constant storms normally would have helped her ignore this persistent nuisance, but things that annoyed her were amplified in Ariel's presence. Samira had tried to shed grudges and be friends with Etah's Chosen again. Some grudges just ran too deep to let go, at least without time. There was still a part of Samira that cared for Ariel, but remembering that Ariel had left her and Roy when they needed her the most made the raindrops sting even more. Roy wouldn't have the scar, and they might have remained a family.

"I was having a good dream. Is there a chance I can still wake up?" Ariel yawned.

Crossing her arms, Samira looked up to the swaying mainmast. Sails, normally aflutter in the breeze, were tightly furled. Tying her waist tightly to the mast, Samira spoke loudly, not having Ariel's tiredness, "Can you break the front?" She left about five feet on the rope to ensure a range of motion. Anticipating lightning strikes would require it.

Ariel shook her head and grasped the mast to stay upright. She must have been exhausted after pushing the sails straight through the last four days and then sleeping for a fifth, but none of them were feeling extraordinary in the face of this storm.

By all accounts, it was mid-afternoon, but the clouds above blotted out most light. Clear blue water had been rendered black from the absence of illumination, and the darkness around them was occasionally interrupted by the bright-green lightning that rumbled through the sky. James, Leonard, and the crew had all been sent below deck, stuffed alongside everything else that could counterweight the ship against the feral winds.

Vilch stood at the upper deck, tied to the mast and appearing to mime orders to Roy. It might as well have been what he was actually doing, because his words were snatched by the storm and hurled into the sea.

She caught a glimpse of Roy at the bow, his back to everyone. His dripping cloak was cemented to him by the rain, and his arms flung water with every motion. He bent and swayed with the water as it charged the vessel, guiding it to the side with each wave. It wasn't going to relent soon. Roy would have to keep this up for a while.

"Go on, but be careful," Samira said. She turned, realizing she was talking to no one. Ariel was already half way up the mast. *Striking typical.*

This storm was like nothing she had ever experienced. Dreadfronts started in the Moth Mountains of Kostra as simple thunderstorms. Samira had seen them from the Shale Watchtower, nonplussed at their lack of severity. As they crept through the mountains, however, the tempests picked up something that corrupted and supercharged them into an unnatural and deadly entity. Samira could feel the raw power as the sky tingled with lightning, wind bombarding the ship and ripping the waves from the surface of the water.

Samira peered into the sky, her left hand extended out to her side, ready for the slightest hint of a charge that would bring a lightning strike upon their heads. She glanced at Ariel, now halfway up the mainmast. It was an incredibly stupid thing to do in normal situations, but there was no choice here. There was no possible way that Ariel would be able to control the skin-peeling wind from the deck. Bracing herself and getting a good grip, Ariel began to climb the mast, ascending toward the crow's nest. The only way to subvert this deadly wind was to get into the thick of it and steer it away from them. Even though the wind was stronger near the top of the mast, she just might be able to redirect it.

From below, it looked like Ariel was climbing without difficulty; Samira knew better. Rain pelted Ariel's sleeveless arms, needling her fingers, wind practically stripping the wood from the mast the higher it went. Samira could tell just by how much Ariel took her time that anyone else would have fallen immediately. Growing up in the forested land of Spiath gave Etah's Chosen a stark advantage.

Just as Ariel reached toward the cusp of the nest, a feral blast of wind knocked her back, nearly sweeping her off the mast entirely. Samira sucked in her teeth, hand on her knife, ready to cut her rope and dash to catch Ariel if she fell. Ariel's grip barely held before she regained her footing.

Trying again, Ariel finally hooked her fingers around the rim of the crow's nest and hauled herself into the platform. Samira let her breath go finally.

Great care would be needed. If Ariel used too much of her strength or was overwhelmed, she would asphyxiate, her breath taken from her. Breath regulation was how she used Etah's gift. Without controlling her breath in this storm, she would be dead in minutes.

Samira turned to her own duty. Instinctively, she calmed the pace of her heart, shutting out the roar of the storm around her. The steady building of energy coalesced above her. This storm would put up a fight, but it would get one in return.

The torrent of wind around her slid off of the deck and into the sea beside them. Ariel must have begun her work. It would be impossible to stop the gale from going downward, but if Ariel could divert it to the side and away from the ship she would only be fighting it slightly.

Samira closed her eyes. *We'll make it. We'll make it. We'll...*

Dreadfront

Drips of salty water plunked against James's head. The droplets seeped through the old rope and tar that filled the crevasses between the planks of the deck. Stowed with Leonard and the crew in the belly of the ship, he had stood maintaining a frail sputter of flame in his hand for no more than a minute. The look in Samira's eyes when she had ordered him to remain below had been more serious than he had ever seen her. To keep himself busy, he assisted Leonard and the crew by tying down everything that had not been already. With most hatches and openings to the outside firmly secured, James stifled gags and coughs due to the lack of clean, fresh air. This would have to do. At the very least, he was still breathing in air and not seawater. He held a crate in place while the crescent-bearded sailor fastened it in place.

"Keep her steady, lad. There we are. It won't be going anywhere now," the man grunted.

Leonard stumbled to James and braced himself against the hull with a thick arm. "That's the last of the water barrels lashed down, Joskine."

"Did you make sure we can still get to them easily?" Crescent-Beard asked.

Leonard nodded. "We can cut them loose in an instant if we need to. We have men manning the pumps and the rowboats prepared for the worst, just like you said."

"Good." Joskine clapped Leonard on the shoulder. The middle-aged sailor's disdain for them had been suspended in light of more pressing matters. He looked toward James. "Now help me gather the harpoons, lad."

James clambered after Joskine, confusion tossing him as much as the waves outside. "What do we need those for?"

"For whatever is out there." Joskine growled, not turning around. "With Dathos's blessing, we might make it through the storm alive."

"If he didn't send this storm to sink us." James rolled his eyes, trying to keep his heart from fluttering. Whispers of Dreadfronts and their mysterious, yet terrifying traits had made their rounds below-deck several times while preparing for the storm. Sandstorms had eaten away at Boane for centuries. His whole life, he had understood them to be an unavoidable part of his world, but this storm was not natural. It wasn't possible to run to a sturdier shelter when these kinds of storms hit. The flame in his hand shivered with every wave that the ship slammed into, its warmth slowly fading. Thunder boomed above their heads. But the thunder failed to completely drown out a sound much closer.

"What was—" James started.

"Shush," Joskine hissed.

Scratching, tapping, and gouging rippled its way along the hull's outside, mere feet from James and Joskine, akin to rapid skittering. The noises crawled over James's skin, bringing his hair to a pointed stand everywhere on his body. Nothing resembling a storm could produce such a phenomenon, which meant only one alternative...that something was crawling on the outside of the ship.

Joskine and Leonard shot him foreboding looks, shaking their heads. James thought of the remaining Chosen above deck, fighting the storm, oblivious to whatever was waiting just below the surface. He knew that the delicate operation they had implemented on deck couldn't afford any distractions. That very much included him getting in the way. Getting through this storm alive meant being as useful to the collective group as he could.

But whether or not he was of any use, he wasn't going to be the one to determine that usefulness by sitting in the dark while those things roamed the deck. Admittedly, the sentiment had lost some potency once he had thrown open the hatch and gotten a good look at the storm.

The sky frothed above him, mirroring the black water below him. Despite Roy's attempts to steer the waves away from the ship, they rammed the hull again and again, creating a shattering quake that ran through his bones. Every sensation of the wind or rain hitting his body had an aura of raving fury, and he had to lean into the wind to keep from blowing over. It was the most powerful thing he had ever felt in his life. The flame he had held in his palm had been instantly snuffed out when he had emerged from the ship's belly.

He quickly slammed the hatch closed behind him. Everything around him was cold. He pushed his senses outward, feeling for the slightest spark of warmth, but found nothing. His gift would be of no help here.

Looking wildly around him, James's eyes landed on Samira, tied to the main-mast and peering into the sky, and her left hand outstretched beside her. Her fierce eyes locked on his in shock and scolding for a moment before she turned her attention back to the churning clouds. Thunder fulminated from the heavens, and a flash of green rolled throughout the clouds for a brief moment. Samira was clearly not happy that he had come up, but there was nothing she could do about it without ignoring the skies.

Another deafening crack of thunder buzzed James's eardrums. He resisted the urge to slap his palms over them in reaction. That last thunderclap had sounded much louder, much closer.

Leonard's hand clamped down on his shoulder, frantically, painfully. "Get down!" Leonard screamed.

Whiteness enveloped James's vision. The beaming flash turned green as a bolt of lightning arced downward from the clouds. James and Leonard dropped flat to the deck. The tendrils of energy rolled straight toward them. Their light reflected in James's eyes, and he stared in incredulous shock at the lightning reaching for him. In that moment, he felt nothing but instant, unfathomable heat.

With impossible speed, Samira charged from the corner of his vision and stretched outward with her left hand. The strain on her face was highlighted by the bolt of light, and the heat of the shaft evaporated the rain and perspiration. Her fingers groped forward. Barely snagging the heavenly projectile with her fingertips, she snatched the lightning from the air and hurled the bolt out over the waves using its momentum.

Samira winced and spun from the force of her redirection, her heavy, soaked braid whipping upward in an arc. Glancing at her waist, James realized she had cut her tether and was now stumbling carefully along the planks. The only thing keeping them all from being blown overboard was likely Ariel's intervention.

Unable to move from shock, James knelt in the quarter-inch standing water on deck, blankly staring at Samira. Her power was far stronger than anyone had let on. Samira's eyes landed on him, looking worried. She wouldn't be able to do that more than a few more times. Powerful as she was, she would eventually tire. The storm would do no such thing.

Kneeling in front of him, she shook him by the shoulders, hard. "Get back below, *now*," she said loudly into his face.

James didn't move. His vision still blurred after the searing lightning blast that had narrowly missed him.

She shook him again, making his head flop forward. "James! *Go back below!*"

His name reached his ears and perforated the shock that had immobilized him. Standing shakily, James leaned on her as she helped him up. The cloud cover had become too murky, making it difficult to even see or remember where the hatch had been. Leonard half-crawled back in the direction from which they came, searching with his fingers.

Stumbling on shaky legs to Leonard's position, he caught the muddled, bewildered shouts of Raslena's Chosen. Glancing in his direction, James registered a faint glow coming from the water. The glow appeared to morph between two hues, creating a pale red and purple sludge from beneath the waves. He blinked and slogged on toward Leonard. Whatever this was, the noises they had heard below deck had to have some connection.

"What are they?" he shouted toward Leonard. The wind snatched his words away before Leonard could hear them. Both of their bodies tensed as the lights not only kept up with the ship but began to move and surround the entire port side of the ship. Toward Roy.

Leonard seized the front of James's shirt and hauled him within hearing distance, which was just shy of a foot at this point. "If they get to Roy, we can't stay afloat. You *have to protect him.*" He shoved James, skidding in the direction of the stairs to the forecastle, placing a rope in James's hand before doing so.

Gripping the railing with the tight grasp similar to that of a determined drunk, he took to the stairs. He glanced back to the quarterdeck and caught a glimpse of where Vilch stood, staring in horror at the waves before them. His bun had been deconstructed by the wind and now tossed wildly around his head. Vilch's face, tanned from months in direct sunlight, was now paler than bone. His eyes looked straight ahead, toward the black torrent of water that charged the ship. The captain's white hands gripped the helm stiffly, trying to keep it steady at a perpendicular angle to the waves.

James reached the forecastle and set eyes on Dathos's Chosen. Roy's breathing was ragged. Hunched over and gagging, he swept the growing swells to the side with increasing difficulty. The waves were now ten feet above the deck. The cryptic glow of the water was beginning to intensify, dimly illuminating Roy's face.

Shielding his eyes from the spray, James approached Roy, straining against the force of the wind. It buffeted him as if giant, unseen hands were thrusting him back, causing him to slide backward and kick up water. He assumed Ariel's control over the wind was weakest up here.

Roy glanced back at him for less than a second before turning back and hurling an incoming wave to the left. Exhausted and swaying back and forth, he focused with some difficulty on the next wave ahead of them. Even from behind, James could tell that Roy would not last through the coming minutes. Still, Roy blocked wave after wave, staying on his feet as if in defiance of the storm. As James looked back ahead, his blood felt as if it had stopped altogether in his veins.

A new massive swell rose above the ship, dwarfing the ones that had come before it. Nearly thirty feet above the deck, the black wall of frigid, indifferent aether charged to engulf the craft. Wobbling, Roy positioned his feet on the deck and threw his arms forward in a stabbing motion. The wave slowed slightly but continued its advance. Roy's whole body shook, writhing under the force of his adversary. Continuing to rush forward, the dark swell yawned open like the maw of an imperator.

A harsh, guttural scream forced its way from Roy's lips, and he ripped his arms outward, as if tearing the space before him in two. The wave before them shredded, parting and collapsing on itself before flowing past the ship on either side. Roy crumpled to his knees, choking and coughing up water and foam. Roy's tether tightened against his sagging posture. He was drowning. Using his gift this much was causing his lungs to fill with sea water. It sprayed from his mouth as if he had just surfaced from the bottom of the sea.

Hoisting Roy upward like a grain sack, James tried to shout encouragement into his ear. A crashing shudder rumbled through the ship as the waves, only loosely held at bay by Roy, pounded the bow. Water washed the deck and took James off his feet. He gripped Roy tightly, taking them both to the deck. The strange glowing around the ship had intensified, creating a false halo below. Boiling black water became ablaze with false light, and James's entire body trembled.

Still coughing, Roy rasped, "The lights. We're all going to die."

"I won't let that happen," James said quickly. If Leonard and everyone else had done their jobs, the ship only had the waves and these lights to worry about. There was still a chance. Roy and Samira had gotten him out of Boane. He would do whatever he could to get them out of this alive.

"They're following the ship," Roy insisted, still leaning on James as he knelt. His stern eyes darted from the deck to the water. James took a precious few seconds to lash himself to the rail. The rope dug around his waist.

Ariel was no longer visible above them in the crow's nest, and Samira and Leonard were only barely discernible. Samira impatiently trained her eyes on the sky in the middle of the main deck. Her braid had all but frayed apart like a knot that birds had relentlessly picked at. Leonard hurriedly ducked into the hatch he and James had come from, potentially calling for help from the crew, tying himself to the railing. Vilch still manned the helm, trying desperately to keep the ship on course through the growing swells.

Water continued to flow over the deck as the increasingly violent waves crashed onto the bow. The deck tilted combatively, and James struggled to stay on his feet. Thunder growled above them, and Sam tensed. Her instincts read plainly on her face, prey that had caught the scent of a predator nearby. Leonard also noticed her body language and motioned desperately for James to help him.

Lightning rocketed from the ashen clouds toward the mainmast. Leaping from the deck, Samira reached for the flashing projectile. James and Leonard covered their eyes as the world was washed out by green light. Reaching out with her left hand, Samira hooked her fingers into the bolt. She attempted to pull the lightning away from the mast, but her hand couldn't get a strong enough grasp to move it. The lightning bolt crashed into the base of the mainmast, just shy of taking Samira with it. The wood of the mast splintered in a monstrous explosion, sending her sailing backward. She rolled across the deck as the spar crackled, blackened and brittle.

James and the two other Chosen screamed for Ariel's attention. The mast was going to fall, and she would be dumped into the sea with whatever was creating those lights. James staggered and grasped the rail just as the ship crested a steep wave. Roy attempted to soften it but was too exhausted. The deck tilted upward, and several crew cried out while they slid toward the stern. Samira skimmed across the polished and wet wood of the deck, streaking downward as the bow of the ship continued to soar upward. It would be a miracle if they made it to the islands. As the ship crested a wave almost ninety feet up, a faint red glow seeped into the corner of James's vision. Turning his head to face the glow, he saw what only could have been described as a nightmare.

It crawled using hardened bristles that protruded from its body, about five feet long. The creature's translucent skin revealed the outline of its skull. Its slippery body, the size of a man, exuded a pale red bioluminescence, covering every surface near it in a shade of bloody crimson, mirroring what moonlight would look like.

Staring in horror at its cosmic, lidless eyes, James reached for his sword as it shambled toward him. Its slack lower jaw hung open, exposing needle-like teeth. Ripping the short sword out of the scabbard at his waist, James swung wildly, hacking at the long bristles that the creature used to crawl on land. Its tail fin flopped behind it uselessly as he swung desperately, slicing two of the appendages and causing it to stumble. The creature made no noise, simply staring at him with those black, bottomless eyes. A thin liquid pumped from the monster's sliced bristles, and it continued to charge him. Keeping his sword in the space between him and the deep dweller, James slashed again, this time at its face.

As he lurched forward in attack, the ship cleared the crest of the wave and plunged downward toward the trough of the next one. James and the monster fell forward and crashed into the rail right next to Roy. The rail cracked with his impact, and the creature landed on top of him. James pointed his sword upward, and the deep dweller was pinned onto his blade. A bristle or two found its way to flesh, sticking shallowly into his thigh. James bellowed and heaved over his head. The sound of the bristles clicking on the wood of the deck made James's skin shiver. It could make no sound, but he could hear its gills clapping against its neck. Using all of his strength, he hauled the monster over his head and into the waves, where it was promptly squashed against the hull.

Next to him, Roy held his hands out in front of him and braced for the upcoming trough of the next wave. The ship shuddered, but broke through to a considerably shorter swell. The wind tore at Roy's cloak noticeably less. The squall was gradually diminishing, but the creatures assailing the ship were not letting up.

Lightning cracked overhead again. The mainmast drooped to the starboard side. James looked up and saw Ariel dangling out of the crow's nest over the water.

Roy steadied himself, constantly looking up to her location, his scar highlighted every time the lightning struck. Samira, Leonard, and a few crew members fought through an onslaught of the glowing sea dwellers. Some of the crew must have been called up to assist with the defense. Leonard's mace crushed the fishlike bodies of the attackers, splattering their incandescent fluids across the deck and mixing it with the sloshing water. His jerkin was torn to ribbons, deep cuts in the leather sporting a small amount of blood.

Samira swung her longsword in quick maneuvers, efficiently incapacitating creature after creature. She used the flat of the blade and the hilt as blunt weapons to stun them before plunging the sword into their colorless skin. A sea dweller charged at Samira from the side, attempting to bite her left arm. Without hesitation, Samira raised her left hand and slammed it downward on the beast's head with a loud squelch. Electricity charged through her hand as she conducted lightning into its soulless eyes. The creature squirmed in terror and pain before its head blew apart with an audible pop. Purple glowing liquid spattered over her face and clothing. She whipped her head back and forth in disgust.

Samira noticed James running toward them. The relief in her amber eyes turned to fear as she shouted, hand outstretched. Her voice was stolen by the wind, but her mouth told him all he needed to know. *Get down!*

Lightning slammed down on the ship once more, the sheer weight of it cracking the wood and finally jarring the mainmast loose. It fell toward starboard quickly. Ariel toppled from the crow's nest, using what little breath she still retained to blow herself back over the deck. She hit the planks hard enough to chase the wind from her chest. Ariel rolled over the deck, finally coming to a stop as she collided with the starboard rail and grasped it to keep from rolling over it and into the waves.

Leonard, struggling to get up, slogged his way through the rapidly dwindling deck toward the fallen mast. If the mast continued to drag behind the ship by the rigging, it could turn them sidelong to the waves, and they would be rolled over. Even though the waves were waning, it would still be enough to sink them. His mace dragged against the wooden planks. Other crew members followed him with axes, desperately chopping at the downed and tangled ropes. The falling mainmast had squashed some of the creatures. Samira mopped up the rest with extreme ferocity.

The old rope and tar that plugged the planks of the deck together had been worked loose by the storm, and a growing amount of water filtered its way into the *Greed Sun's* hold. Faced with the fear of the attacking creatures, James had temporarily forgotten his inability to swim.

Roy gripped his arm. "Cut me loose! I can see if the water can be forced out." As Roy said this, the ship shuddered violently and slowed to a near halt in the waves.

James gulped as the waning waves around them seemed to be getting taller. It took only a moment to realize that the swell wasn't picking back up. In a few minutes, they were all going to have a lot more room to swim. "Are we…"

Taking his saber and cutting himself free, Roy gritted his teeth, "The mast wasn't cut loose in time. It was dragged around and cracked against the hull. That's too much damage for me to manage the water coming in. We need the rowboats, *now*."

"Do we have enough of them?" James squeaked. The rain still pelted from above.

Roy shook his head. "I saw only three. They aren't meant to evacuate everyone, just to carry goods to and from shore."

They rushed to the main deck and joined Leonard in wrestling the three boats from the rapidly filling hold. Crew members raced over the deck, trying to wrestle together provisions to take on the boats. Vilch, finally having cut himself free of the helm, sprinted to the first of the boats, scowling at James and Roy. Before James could shout after them, the rowboat, carrying Vilch and six crewmen, had hit the water to port side and was tossing through the rain and slowing waves. Tragically, the *Greed Sun* hadn't been able to stand even the very edge of the storm. While the worst of it had perhaps been a few hours, the Dreadfront had been determined not to let the ship escape.

Rain struck Samira's face, mixed with the glowing fluid from the creatures. Half of her face and hair resembled the glowing embers of a dying fire. The hardened bristle from a dead sea dweller protruded from her right shoulder. She said nothing.

The second rowboat hit the glowing water, carrying more crew of the *Greed Sun*. They cursed at the Chosen as they rowed through the lurching waves after Vilch's boat, off toward the last known direction the ship had been headed, toward the Tarsals.

Leonard and Samira wasted no time in hauling the last rowboat to the rail, readying it for launch while Roy swiped a fresh water barrel from the rapidly filling bilge of the *Greed Sun*. James could see Roy biting the inside of his cheek, no doubt steeling himself after seeing the bodies of several sailors that hadn't been able to fend off the creatures. The next moment, Ariel had flown across the deck to assist Samira and Leonard with the rowboat. It was a seven-person vessel, sturdy at a glance.

"We'll be taking that now, lad," a voice said.

James blinked in the waning flickers of lightning as Joskine stepped forward with around a dozen remaining crew members, all brandishing harpoons, all with somber grimaces.

"Joskine, hold on just a minute." Leonard held up a hand, desperately trying to prevent the inevitable.

"Nothing personal, lad." Joskine was lit from behind with purple light. He and the other sailors took a step forward. "But in a minute, all of us will be swimming, so we'll be taking the boat." The light shifted behind them, accompanied by coarse scraping.

"Behind you!" James shouted. He readied his chipped sword.

The sailors turned to witness a stampede of scrabbling deep dwellers, all exuding crimson and purple light, descending from the starboard side. Jaws hanging open in greedy, gaping hunger, they collided with the starboard-most sailors. Bristles crunched against flesh, the sound comingling with screams as the sailors swung their harpoons. Ariel reached into her quiver for an arrow but found it empty. The storm must have blown them all away.

As more creatures from the deep swarmed the deck, Samira and Leonard prepared to launch the rowboat. Roy coiled a tether rope around his shoulder, ready to hurdle the rail. The sea still churned below, but Roy could keep it steady enough for everyone to board. Essentially stagnant now, the ship was incredibly low in the water. It wouldn't stay up for more than a minute longer. Water poured through the hole in the hull and the cracks in the deck, and anyone working the bilge pumps were either dead, fighting, or had already shoved off.

"Come on!" Ariel bellowed toward the sailors as Roy hurdled the rail with the boat. She jumped the rail next with only a mere four-foot fall before landing in the vessel.

James leapt from the railing of the ship with Leonard close behind. They landed square on the center keel. The strong metal braced against their feet, and the boat jostled under their weight, but it held. Red and violet hues dominated the water now, as if sensing that this smaller mass would yield the easier feast. Ariel held out her arms, signaling for Samira to jump. Samira braced herself quickly before springing from the side of the ship. The *Greed Sun* groaned. Samira landed hard toward the stern of the rowboat. Ariel grabbed her by the shirt collar and pulled her in closer before she could lose her balance. James looked on at the

Greed Sun sinking with growing momentum. Its still-tethered mainmast floated alongside. He looked on numbly.

A thud jarred James out of his shock as Joskine, followed by another three remaining sailors, all but crashed into the keel of the rowboat. The vessel strained under the weight of now nine people, but it held under Roy's will, barely. Behind them, the *Greed Sun* had finally slipped beneath the waves, still swarming with the horrors of below. The mast would soon be pulled down with it.

Samira looked infuriated by the sailors' presence, but Roy interrupted before she could say anything.

Roy turned to the rest of the boat. "I'll do what I can to get us through the waves, but I need everyone to row!" he instructed, squinting through the rain. His clothes and hair were plastered to him. Pointing to a pile of oars lying in the center bow, Roy pushed past the other passengers and knelt at the front, readying himself for the next wave as it loomed ahead.

Samira immediately scooped up the oars and tossed them to everyone else. James settled toward the stern with Leonard and Joskine, brandishing his paddle. There was a chance they might make it out alive. Hopeful, he inhaled deeply, clearing his mind for the grueling journey ahead. He could clearly see the boundaries of Roy's influence around them, as the infuriated sea calmed to a heavy simmer within five feet of the boat.

As he breathed, his senses expanded outward, causing him to stop. Puzzled, he felt further, catching the tiniest hint of heat from deep below him. The heat grew, becoming much larger in the span of a few seconds. Looking ahead to the front of the boat, James could tell that Roy sensed it too. Suddenly, everyone noticed that the lights below them had begun to disperse. The bristled deformities that had plagued them since the storm hit were leaving, and quickly. Something had alerted them, and that something was causing them to flee. All passengers on the rowboat paddled ahead through the storm, making it a few feet before the water beside them thrashed.

A huge mass passed through the few remaining light-bearing creatures below, snuffing out the red glow as it went through. Shuddering, James realized it was an imperator. The great fish circled below them, its keen senses searching for further morsels. Focusing on the heat that its regulated body exuded, he joined the rest of the crew in rowing toward the west. The tarsals were close, he hoped.

The imperator fluidly angled itself toward the boat, alerted to the oars splashing in the water. Ahead, the next wave rose above them. Weaker than before, but still more than enough to capsize them if Roy wasn't able to stop it. It couldn't be said that the crew were cowards. As they rowed toward the wave, many of them looked straight ahead through the rain, unblinking and unbent. They had seen their path to survival, and it was one they would not stray from. Foam bubbled around them, the imperator shark still circling the boat. Its swordlike fins sliced through the churning waves. The behemoth was a creature of the waves, and its muscular tailfin propelled it between the boat and the detached mainmast.

By this time, the remaining rowers had become aware of the great predator. As thick as the mast it swam under, the thirty-foot fish effortlessly glided through the savage current. One bite was all it would take to snap up a single one of them. If any of them ended up in the water, it would be the end. The shark was ignoring them now, investigating the sinking mast and sail. Why couldn't it just have stayed away like it did earlier?

Heat flared in James's consciousness, and he felt the imperator shudder. Even from several yards away, the force of the creature's tail propelled the boat a few feet to the right. A moment passed as James struggled to determine what the increase in heat was. Pushed backward by the approaching wave, the raft started to drift closer to the wriggling shark.

It's stuck! he realized. It must have swam through the ropes underneath the mast and become tangled, dragged downward. As the next wave approached, James glanced backward to see the shark flailing. Fins slapped the water. The dagger-shaped body of the fish rolled, tangling itself further. Trapped in the mess of slack rigging, the imperator was panicking. Heat was rolling off the frightened body as the boat drew closer and closer.

Roy braced at the front of the boat, waiting for the wave to get closer. Holding his hands in front of him, he prepared to rip the wave just enough to let them pass through. The power that he held was staggering. Though he may not possess the raw strength that Samira used or Ariel's accuracy, his emotion and will granted him the ability to bend the elements to his command. It would just barely be enough in this circumstance, but his gift would lead the way out of this nightmare. The oncoming swell of the wave pushed the boat a few more feet back, right into the path of the imperator.

As the wave swelled, the shark had found its path to freedom, open sea ahead of it. Attempting to propel itself away with one mighty stroke, the imperator swung its tail in a wide arc. The fin, as tall as a man and sturdier than tempered steel, clapped into the side of the boat, wrenching it to the side and sending Joskine tumbling into the waves. Crescent-beard yelped and choked on the surf as he thrashed in an attempt to grasp the side of the boat. Roy only turned for a moment before focusing on the wave again.

"Ariel, don't!" Leonard cried. Before James had a chance to register what had happened, Ariel dove headfirst into the black water after the crewman. With a soundless splash, Ariel's feet disappeared under the waves. James had seen this before with the wounded that Charodon had left behind at Epot Detharn. The sailor wasn't dead yet, and Ariel was intent on making sure he stayed that way.

With a deafening crash, the wave rolled over the small vessel. James clenched his eyes and teeth together, waiting for the salty cold to infiltrate his bones.

Hands swinging over his head in an arc, Roy grunted. A vast hole punched through the center of the wave and cleared a path for the raft. A rampart of water hurtled by on either side of them. The rush of the wave blew past James's head, narrowly missing him. Roy sat back in the boat, gaining some brief respite between swells.

A shimmer moved across the waves as another crack of green lightning tore its way across the sky. It was farther away than the previous strikes. Seeming to confirm his assessment, Samira turned away from the lightning and leaned over the edge of the boat, staring downward into the violent water. Ariel and the unfortunate sailor were invisible beneath the surface. James's thoughts raced from one terrible thought to the next. Had they been pulled away by the current? Had the panicked crewman pulled Ariel down to her death with him? Had either of them been eaten by the imperator?

Another shimmer at the tumultuous surface caught his attention. A hand protruded above the pitch-black water not fifteen yards from the boat. Frantically pointing to their position, James called to Leonard to get something to throw.

Looking immediately to where James was pointing, Leonard snatched the length of tether rope from Roy's shoulder. He took a moment to wind up his arm and launched the knotted end of the rope toward the splashing hand. Ariel's tattooed arm flailed in the swell as the rope slapped downward into the water, kicking up more white spray.

Ariel's hand closed around the rope and pulled wildly. Viciously shoving the crewmen out of his way, Roy joined Leonard in reeling her in. Both grunted desperately while they strained against the line. Samira and James watched anxiously as the line drew closer and closer to the edge of the boat. Roy may have hated Leonard, but he worked alongside him to bring Ariel back. James struggled to keep his balance as Roy released his focus on the waves.

The line finally ended with Ariel's hand. Grasping her forearm, Roy hauled her into the boat, the rapid smack of water droplets hitting the floor. Ariel hacked up water and rested her forehead against Roy's shoulder. He kept an arm around her as she regained her breath. Leonard's muscles bulged, and he lifted Joskine onboard. The man was unconscious.

One of the few remaining crew members, a teenage boy, knelt over Joskine and immediately started pounding on the man's chest. Water trickled from the sailor's mouth and over his chin. The boy pressed downward on the Crescent-Beard's chest once more, forcing the water out of his lungs. Air rushed into the abdomen of the drowned man, his eyes grotesquely wide, soaking beard clinging to his neck. Shaking their heads in what was mostly relief, the remaining two mariners clapped the exhausted boy on the shoulder.

"What were you doing, strike you?" Samira roared at Ariel. The amber of her eyes crackled with electricity.

Ariel, still purging the water and foam from her body, said nothing.

Furious, Samira rounded on Ariel, maneuvering through the crew members straight toward the front of the boat. It rocked in the turbulent waters. "This is *not* the time for you to be a hero. Astus strike me, you never learned *anything* after two years, did you?"

"Leave her alone, Sam," Roy hissed, glaring at his best friend. A speck of orange even surfaced in his eye, a grim warning. Still clearly angry, Samira carefully stepped back to the center keelson and sat. Another wave approached from the front-left. Even so, Roy stared pointedly at Samira for another few seconds before gently sitting Ariel down in the flat bottom of the raft. He turned to deal with the oncoming swell as the crew took up their oars. James followed suit.

The storm had shown them the limits of what they could do in the face of death, and he had barely been able to do anything. At least Leonard had his strength and courage to row his fair share. They paddled through the waves for hours. Roy flattened each wave as they approached, water trickling from the corner of his mouth as they went. Even with his airway filling with water, he struck each wave down with narrowed eyes and a set jaw. Leonard shouted encouragement to the crew members, trying to keep their spirits up as the storm waned. He even had them singing halfheartedly after an hour or so. Samira said nothing, rowing with her back to Roy and Ariel, expressionless.

The hours blurred, and as the storm continued to thrash about them like a nest of frenzying snakes, James forgot about everything. He forgot about his friends. He forgot Gemmi and his vengeance. He forgot the Alderaye. All that he remembered was rowing, rowing, rowing.

Unrelenting Domains

The waves lapped at Vayne's bare feet, covering the blue wrinkles of his papery skin. He tried to remember what the touch of water had been like. Had it been smooth? Perhaps it had felt "refreshing" as he remembered humans describing it. Now he was trying to remember what being refreshed meant, what was so appealing about it. The surf rushing over his feet, the wind caressing his face, they all wafted through his mind like stories of an experience told to him by a stranger, like a secondhand fable that he questioned the validity of. Even now, with his wispy hair floating in the breeze, it felt like a lie. The old man he lived inside had felt, but his soul was gone. It was just Vayne in there now, and the husk was deteriorating too quickly to waste time on such things.

Rhaiga had been gone for some time now. She would be getting close to the islands, close to where their remaining loyalists were, maybe. It *had* been a few centuries since he had seen them. Twelve centuries in fact. He sat on the mostly destroyed dock, thinking to himself.

Dhorh could be heard behind him. He was hopping around the wreckage of Epot Detharn, taking memories from those who still clung to life, murmuring to himself. Those who had died no longer had memories to give, so Dhorh let them lie. Vayne knew that all Dhorh really cared about were the memories that he gathered from living things. As long as Vayne could convince him that the memories would be safe in the world Vayne envisioned, Dhorh would stay loyal.

It had taken longer than Vayne had wanted to cull the port city. Less than two weeks was still far too long for him, shameful. If Rhaiga were still with them, it would have been over much sooner. Her ability to kill was quite impressive. *As long as she remembers her path and contains herself. Unlike that Charodon.*

He shook his head. As much as he hated Charodon, his brother of sorts had such a hunger for violence, which could be useful on occasion. He needed no convincing. But he was too erratic and couldn't see the bigger vision, hence his title as the Eye of Nature.

Dhorh hadn't made up for his failing with the Fire Boy and the rest of the Chosen, but Vayne still needed him, so he had pretended to let it go. He turned back to where Dhorh loomed over a coughing lad. The lad's hacking indicated he was succumbing to Vayne's power. The Mangler, he had heard some call it. It wasn't often that he respected the silly names that humans assigned to his work. The fruit of his labor, nearly two hundred and fifty years in the making, was doing a fine job.

Vayne waited as Dhorh needled the lad's forehead with uneven fingernails. Vayne had heard it described to him by Dhorh in the past, like reliving a memory that was unraveled and spooled back up. Dhorh was able to give memories to other living creatures as well. As the Eye of Memory took his fingers off the lad's forehead, the shallow breathing ceased, life no longer inhabiting the human.

Something unnatural bubbled inside Vayne's lower chest. It startled him, placing a hand on the sagging abdomen his head and shoulders were attached to. What was this? It was…bad. It felt unpleasant. The displeasing sensation wormed inside his ribcage, making him turn away from the dead youth. Gnarled hands shaking, he maneuvered his withered body into a standing position, careful not to collapse the already unstable dock. Why had hearing the lad die given him this feeling? The teenager had meant nothing to him, still meant nothing, but Vayne's mind had reacted to something when the boy died. That something had been terrifying, and the source of the terror came to him like a candle exposing the shadows of a room.

An unpleasant sensation rose into his throat, but he stoppered it. Vayne was actually feeling sick! *Him*! He could not die. He was not like these humans. He *would* not die.

Not unless the Chosen found a way to kill him, like they had killed the others. It was a mystery that he could have sworn was solved ages ago, how the Chosen had done it, but the answer eluded him. The time spent banished in the Dunes had worn on his mind as well as his host body. Perhaps he should have asked Dhorh to unthread the memory and save it.

"Are you done not looking at the sea?" Dhorh complained. "The threads are all frayed here."

Vayne said nothing but shambled toward the sturdiness of land. His glazed, unseeing eyes were pointed straight ahead, straight toward the smoldering wreckage of the port city. A single blackened tideflag remained above them.

"I still don't understand why Rhaiga got to sail off before us," Dhorh pouted. He really did act like a child. Though Vayne supposed that telling someone to "act their age," as the humans said it, was difficult if the subject of your ridicule was many thousands of years old. Yazdra had been the only one that could silence Dhorh's incessant whining, but she hadn't survived the last war.

He finally sighed and spoke after a long internal debate on whether to ignore him, "Our domains move slowly. Disease, Death, and Memory are unrelenting, but there are times when swiftness will gain the advantage. Sending Rhaiga north is a means to utilize swiftness, to gain allies that move more quickly."

Dhorh shrugged. "Can't you just say what you mean?"

Another sensation gurgled in Vayne's chest, this one warm, hot even. He resisted the urge to snap at the boy. "What I *mean* is that human civilization is swift. Though it may take a lifetime for a human to build something, they are all rapid when compared to us. We must stay ahead of them. Look what they have done to our world, Dhorh." He gestured with a wobbly hand. "Stone monstrosities, metal trophies robbed from the ground. They are disobeying the precedents that *we* set. They must be set right, or the world that we built will no longer exist." He shuddered. *We will no longer exist.*

"Shouldn't we have gone with her then?" Dhorh loudly scratched his bald head. For some odd reason that Vayne couldn't explain, the hair had never grown back since the Eye of Memory had taken that particular host hundreds of years ago. When the eyes for Vayne's host had worked.

"Possibly." Vayne frowned. He didn't much care for these questions. Shuffling down the walkway toward the shipyard, he took a deep breath in, feeling nothing. A sudden noise caused his hair-filled ears to twitch, and he smiled. "But a healthy mix of patience and swiftness may prove to be the right path. My power moves slowly. Creating effective diseases takes centuries, but they work quickly when perfected. They create a baseline for destroying a city. With you unthreading and causing mania and Rhaiga providing a few well-timed deaths, we can effectively dismantle civilization one settlement at a time. Only then when they are scattered, without leaders, without structure, can we step through the ashes and impose our rule. Even though it was diverted, the path still stays firmly beneath our feet."

He began to shamble at a slightly elevated pace toward the shipyard, his bare feet pressing silently against the uneven stone paving, another thing he disliked.

Up ahead, a group of rasping survivors carried precious few supplies toward the last few boats. Only one looked fit to sail, by Dhorh's whispered description. It was a small, two-masted vessel shaped like a scythefish, as if it was designed to slice the water itself, making it a fast charter.

The six survivors tossed whatever they had over the rail and began to extend the rigging with urgent voices. What sounded like a man was busy uncoiling the rope from the standing end, getting ready for departure. Vayne and Dhorh approached, still in their host appearances.

The man with the rope gave a surprised grunt. "Thought everyone up and died during the night, Dathos drown me. Are you two all right?"

Vayne assumed the character of a kindly old man. "We've been hiding under a pitched wagon all night. My grandson and I were the only survivors." He gestured to Dhorh, who had better have been doing his best to look sad. "Those devils, those *things*, they left around dawn. This one's mother, my blood…" His voice wavered.

The man grunted in a show of sympathy. "Dathos sail her to the edge of the sea. She is at rest now." He patted the hull of the boat, "Come with us. The city's gone to the devils," he spat. "But we're still alive. We can look after you. What's your name, elder?"

Bowing to flatter the man further, Vayne searched the thousands of names he had heard over the years. "I am Yomon. This is my grandson, Konh."

Taking Vayne's brittle arm and leading him toward the ship, the man grunted again. "I'm Gronnik. Don't you worry. We're going to make it."

Tarsals

S amira didn't remember who first spotted the Tarsals on the horizon. The darkness of the storm had faded, allowing for a minuscule amount of sunlight to penetrate the black ceiling that hovered above. Changing slightly from black to a midnight blue, the water below their lifeboat had ceased its endless attempts to capsize them. Samira was not sure how long they had been rowing; the storm made any attempt to discern the time of day meaningless. Leonard and James had taken up the oars immediately, redoubling their efforts to leave the sea behind. This show of strength had roused the crew members to attack the water with renewed vigor.

They made landfall within the day, feeling the welcoming sturdiness of land against the bow of the rowboat. The Chosen and the sailors had leapt from the raft, limping through the surf onto the coarse sand of the short beach. One by one, they promptly collapsed after emerging fully from the tide.

Face-first in the sand, they still crawled forward, dragging themselves up the rocky beach and into a line of swaying trees. The bright green foliage blocked the setting sun, soothing them all with its shadows. Still, they crawled further into the tree line, covering themselves in mud and leaves. Samira clawed through the silt until she reached a nearby tree. The spiky bark dug into her back as she heaved herself into a sitting position.

Every muscle in her body tingled, and the fingers on her left hand were involuntarily pressed together, forming a tight beak that she was unable to open. Trying to catch several direct blasts of lightning had definitely taken their effect. Her adrenaline must have kept her body working all this time, but now it was shutting down. She glanced around at the rest of the party. James was already unconscious, his head inside a fern that fanned outward like the tail of a bird attempting to attract a mate.

The crew members were scattered around the cluster of trees, all of them asleep except the young boy. He tended to the wounds of the bald one, ripping leaves off a shrub to use as bandages. The boy would come in handy. Leonard and Ariel had some skill with medicine, but another healer was always welcome. Samira wasn't about to try and remove the shard of bristle in her shoulder by herself.

Deep-blue sunlight reflected off the water and filtered through the trees like radiant spear shafts. Roy slept on his side like he always did. Even in his state, his hand was at his boot, ready to draw his knife. Somehow, Leonard had managed to hold on to his mace. He slept against a tree toward the beach, the hefty weapon resting in his lap. She had no idea how, but his spiky hair still pointed straight up in the air. Even caked with mud and brittle from the sea spray, it poked outward in stray quills.

They were alive. That was the most important thing.

Samira leaned backward, ignoring the prickly bark of the tree. She allowed her eyelids to slip closed, gently embracing sleep.

A sharp snap of a branch caused her eyes to fling open. Her hazy vision cleared as she blinked the snares of sleep away.

Ariel sat near the edge of the tree line, stripping a fallen tree of its branches. She held the sharpened hatchet that she kept on her belt. Her light-gold hair had become a dingy copper from the muck they had crawled through. Even the tattoos on her arms had been caked over by silt and leaves. Ariel glanced up at Samira and continued stripping the bark from the wood.

"What are you doing?" Samira asked, trying to keep a civil tone. It was a hard thing to do when she was annoyed. She had seen a friend, a *Chosen*, so eager to throw her life away. They had a purpose as Chosen, and Ariel couldn't fulfill that purpose if she was dead.

"I lost most of my arrows in the storm," Ariel mumbled. Her metallic blue eyes drooped through the mud. She was clearly exhausted, but her hands expertly scraped the bark off the wood from memory.

Samira exhaled through her nose, massaging her temple with her thumb. "It can wait. You need to rest." Instead of leaving it there, she spoke without thinking, "I'm sure you'll find a way to get yourself killed in the morning."

The hatchet made a loud thunk in the fallen tree. Ariel's steely gaze glared at her, suddenly no longer dazed. It was amazing how stubborn she could be about these things. Ariel threw the half-finished arrow down and leaned forward, "Don't give me another one of your lectures, Sam," she hissed across the thicket. "We aren't children anymore."

"Jumping into a Dreadfront headlong *is* childish!" Samira said harshly. "We need you to get across this forsaken sea. The world needs the Chosen to bring peace and keep it out of the hands of the Alderaye! And you would throw it all away just to be a striking hero for a fleeting moment. You could change the course of the empire, become an ambassador for Spiath, or train a generation of warriors. You're wasting the gifts and responsibility that Etah gave you."

Ariel rolled her eyes. "He would have died if I hadn't!" she said indignantly.

"Does you even know his name?" Samira balked.

"Joskine." Ariel crossed her arms.

"You despise people from Scourge Atoll."

"Correct."

"Then why would you risk drowning or being eaten by a striking big fish for him? He's a brute that you hardly even know or like!" Samira raised her voice, causing a few of their companions to stir in their sleep.

"It doesn't matter!" Ariel snapped. She knew how seriously Samira took her faith and her task, but this was obviously—blasphemously—important to her, more important than being a Chosen. "It doesn't matter if he's a pirate, or a criminal, or a heretic. The man is someone's son. He's someone's friend. He's someone's neighbor, maybe someone's father. He is important to *someone*, and if I can keep him alive then I will. You know as well as anyone that I will fight to protect the ones I care about, but standing aside and letting someone die or killing someone is out of the question. No life is worth taking away."

Samira bit her lip. That striking Spiathi upbringing of hers made Ariel a pain to argue with. Why couldn't she realize that life as a Chosen couldn't be this way? Samira had learned as soon as she could walk that life had choices where you couldn't win. Working to control her power had forced her to leave her home and all she had known. It was a choice she had refused to make for years. And as a result of that choice, her inexperience had killed Talia and crippled her right arm. She was reminded every day of her mistake that had cost Roy his happiness. The lives of Chosen were supposed to be difficult. It made them worthy of their gifts. Lives would be lost, as they were all the time. What mattered was if the gods' will continued to be served.

None of this was going to change Ariel's mind. It looked as though Samira would lose this battle, again. *Strike me, I have stubborn friends.*

Samira sighed. "Fine." It was best if she made peace with it now and moved on. Eventually, they would see the way. "Just be careful. You're some of the only family I have. We care about you." She glanced at Roy sleeping fitfully. "Some of us very much so."

A reluctant smile pulled at the corner of Ariel's mouth. "I know, Sam. I promise to give you more warning before I do something stupid."

Samira rested her head against the prickly trunk of the tree. "Save the warning and just thank me for helping you out instead. It'll save you time."

They both reclined against their respective trees and listened to the waves, a sound that was now comforting from dry land. But the discomfort was still there.

"I know what you're going to say," Ariel spoke up. "Now is as good a time as any." The rest of the party was now out cold.

Tilting her head slightly, Samira narrowed her eyes at Ariel. She had played nice in front of Roy, but she had known the niceties couldn't go on forever. "You left us."

"I made a mistake."

"You watched Leonard nearly kill Roy, and then you left." Samira was starting to tremble. All of the repressed resentment she had pushed down for the sake of survival welled to the surface. "And you call it a striking mistake."

"I don't expect you to forgive me, Sam," Ariel said, head in her hands. "I wanted to come back the next day. I didn't have the courage to."

"Then what *do* you expect? You just pitch up and try to whisk James away to the empire and drag Roy and I into it too? You know that I love you like a sibling, Ariel, but you have no right to ask us this after what you did."

"That was Leonard's task. I came along because he asked me to," Ariel stressed. "After this, I'm done with missions. I'm done with all of it."

Samira sat straight up, perhaps a bit too fast. Her head spun, but she ignored it. "You're going to just give up on your responsibilities? Give up on being a Chosen?"

Ariel rolled her eyes. The whites of her eyes stood out prominently against the mud on her face. "Chosen aren't just supposed to be warriors, Sam. But you grew up listening to your father's ramblings and believed it was some kind of prophecy. Chosen are meant to shape the world through other means than just bloodshed. We've seen too much of it, and I don't want any more part—"

"The other Alderaye have come back, Ariel. What about that? A fight is coming whether you like it or not. Dhorh was just the start, and the last two will show their faces before long." Samira looked intently at the edge of the tree line. "We need all of us for this. We were unprepared to fight just one of them. When the rest come for us, when Charodon makes his move, we'll need you."

Swiping some of the caked mud from her arm, Ariel pondered this. "If that's true, then maybe the empire is the safest place for us to go right now. The new emperor has expanded the reach of his Arochs in his desire for change. And he's actually appointed generals with some sense. With Spiath and Kostra lending their forces, we would have all the strength we would need."

Indeed, the Collisun Empire had become more progressive in some places since the death of the old emperor and the appointment of his son. Samira had seen some of the early signs of this before leaving for Boane. The empire's Arochs, special companies of bannerets, had visited the Shale Watchtower to offer their respects. They had never traveled that far just for a pilgrimage before.

That being said, the young emperor hadn't experienced a crisis yet, and it would be anyone's guess how he would handle it once one came along. Politics and Chosen business did not blend well. Anyone with a record of history and basic common sense would be able to see as much. Many Chosen had sat on the throne of the empire before, but never for long and never without struggle.

"I wouldn't count on it," Samira said, picking a spec of mud from her eye. "We don't all have the patriotic sentiment that Leonard does. Politics will just get in the way." Samira leaned backward against the tree. She would have to keep a close eye on Ariel and Leonard still. Sorry or not, Ariel had still left them when they needed her.

Now with James in the mix, they couldn't afford to split up after finally becoming whole. The Watchtower's prediction must come true. Only when Astus's Chosen had the rest around them would they be able to kill the Alderaye. She *would* have them all together. There were just too many things in the way, some of them with the blame resting on her shoulders. Leonard's loyalty to the emperor, Ariel's desire to leave, James's heresy, and Roy's dwindling time in control of his body threatened to doom them all. It was her task to save the realm of humanity, and she couldn't fail.

Scarred

James dreamt that he was in a forest, a different one from the jungle he fell asleep in. The needled branches stretched far overhead, and dense snow graced the grassy floor of the woods. He suspiciously inched his way through the trees. Even in a dream, trees were a curious concept. The trees shimmered if he got too close to one. His feet made no noise in the freshly fallen snow. He couldn't feel the flakes that came to rest on his skin. The woods around him were surreal, as if they were warped ever so slightly.

"There's something you should see," said Dhorh.

James wheeled around to see the devil sitting against a tree. His ram horns were sprinkled with snow, and the empty, eyeless sockets bored into James. The cracked lips beneath them split into a psychopathic grin. Dhorh had James afraid and that was exactly what he wanted.

The Eye of Memory was clothed differently this time, wearing a rough-spun dark robe. What was he doing here in James's dream?

He tried to sound intimidating, "Did you want me to burn you again?"

Dhorh chuckled and rose from the base of the tree. "It was quite painful actually. I would rather not do that again." His robe billowed around him as he took a step past James and into the forest.

James scowled. "Get out of my head."

"I have half a mind to. It's rather bleak in here." Dhorh smirked. "When I unthread someone, it gives me certain...privileges. I can give them memories at the time of unthreading, and I can make infrequent visits afterward. But for now, why don't you shut up and move along? We have somewhere to be."

James reluctantly followed Dhorh into a clearing. The snow fell more freely here, and the moon occasionally found a window between the thick clouds overhead. He noticed Dhorh facing the trees and followed the devil's presumed line of sight, not expecting anything useful. There was a person stalking through the tree line. The person was clothed entirely in black, and James could only see their faint outline among the trees. There was something familiar about that person, but he didn't know what. He tried to call out to the figure, to ask for their name, but he suddenly couldn't speak. He glared at Dhorh. The Alderaye's lips split again as he grinned, pressing a finger to his mouth.

The figure finally emerged from the tree line and into the clearing. James suddenly realized that this mysterious person was not alone. At the end of the clearing, there was someone else. The two strangers kicked up the loose snow as they rushed to each other and embraced. The hood of one of the strangers fell to reveal a head of golden hair.

"I thought you wouldn't come," Ariel said with relief.

The other figure brushed the hood from their head. It was Roy. James looked on in shock. Roy had no scar. His face was completely healthy. He looked about twelve years younger without it.

"Did you find him? Is he coming?" Roy asked, clearly agitated. They finally separated. They both looked a bit younger, now that James looked closer. This must have been a memory Dhorh had stolen.

Ariel nodded. "Sam found him, and they're on the way now." She held his face. Her brow folded with concern. "What are you going to do?"

Roy sighed and looked at his feet. "I'm not going to do anything. He's going to apologize, and then I go on my way."

Her eyes widened. "You're leaving?"

He turned away, pacing around the clearing like a wounded animal. "What else can I do? I can't stay in the empire after that village..." He took a shaky breath.

Ariel followed him, their boots left shallow prints in the snow. "So you're just going to leave Sam, your best friend? You're just going to leave—"

"It's the best for all of us."

"You don't believe that."

Their argument abruptly ended at the sound of a snapping branch toward the other end of the clearing. Roy drew his sword. Ariel quickly nocked an arrow and aimed toward the direction of the noise. Their eyes both locked on the edge of the trees, and a few seconds passed. A few more passed before two others cautiously entered the glade.

Samira removed her hood. "Good, you're both here." Ariel gave a brief nervous smile. Roy didn't answer. His cold turquoise eyes followed the other traveler who came with Samira.

"How long has it been, Leonard?"

Leonard swallowed and said, "Nearly a year, I think, Roy. You look...different."

Roy stepped toward him. "I suppose I do," he said in an ice cold voice. "Where were you, Leonard?" He stepped forward again. James knew what would happen. He tried to yell at Roy to stop, but he couldn't speak, couldn't move. Dhorh snickered beside him. Samira tried to step forward and intervene, but Roy just marched right past her.

Leonard stepped back and raised his hand in denial. "It was your own fault that—"

Roy lurched forward and snatched Leonard's wrist in an animalistic motion. Leonard yelped, and James could see the muscles in Roy's hand tighten and squeeze Leonard's beefy wrist, crushing it with Charodon's strength. "Painful?" Roy asked Leonard with gritted teeth. "You don't know how much worse it can get." Despite his size, Leonard was doubled over from Roy's grip. His wrist was starting to break. James tried to scream at Roy to make him stop, but as before he couldn't speak. Dhorh stood next to him, unable to contain his contempt.

Ariel tried to stop Roy, stepping in between Roy and Leonard. She seized Roy's arm and tried to wrench it free. "Roy, stop!" she yelled at him. James saw that she was crying, the tears sliding down her cheeks and dropping to the ground. She put a hand on Roy's face. "We can help you! Please don't!"

Roy released Leonard's wrist and looked at her angrily. His eyes flashed orange, lighting the falling snow. "How? How can you *possibly* help me? You know what happened. I killed those villagers, and so many since then. Nothing you can do will change that!" He turned away and faced Leonard, who was clutching his wrist.

Leonard let go of his wrist and reached for his mace, plucking it from the frosty ground with some difficulty. His brow was furrowed in resentment. "Is that what you wanted? To lure me into the forest and threaten me into apologizing?"

Roy drew his saber out of his cloak. "I was trapped inside that *thing* for a year! And I'll have it inside me for the rest of my life! And what did you do? *Nothing*!"

James saw the look in Roy's spotted eyes and was about to yell at Roy to stop, but Ariel beat him to it.

"No!" she cried, but it was too late.

Roy charged at Leonard, intending to deal him a fatal blow, but Leonard whipped his mace up in defense. The weapons clashed together with a loud clang and a screech of metal on metal. Roy dealt another furious blow, which Leonard barely deflected. Roy pushed him all around the clearing, slashing and ducking. He attacked with a blind rage, his sword an icy blur.

Leonard used the shaft of his mace to block Roy's sweeping attacks. The blunt weapon was too heavy to match the fluidity of the sword, so he had to make short, quick movements. Roy's face never wavered from a cold snarl, and he put all his strength into his attacks. It was like watching an angry storm blowing over everything in its path.

Roy dragged his sword through the snow, using his power to fling the ice shards into Leonard's body. Leonard dropped his mace and clutched his face as the ice fragments tore into him. The ice caught him in the leg, the shoulder, and the bicep while leaving slivers all over his body. Leonard cried in pain and raised his leg in the air. Roy saw what he was going to do and rapidly tried to scramble away.

The foot of Raslena's Chosen came down and shattered the earth underneath it. Roy barely had time to leap over a crevasse before it swallowed him alive. He turned and glowered at Leonard, who was still clutching his wounds. James gaped at the quick burst of power that Leonard had wrought. He had never seen the man use his gift before. The Champion of the Earth growled at Roy and looked for his weapon. Roy wouldn't stay put for long.

Leonard suddenly lurched backward, a whip of seawater slapping him across the torso. Using his power had made him heavier, momentum threatening to take him down.

Roy stood across the crevasse with a fist pointed at his enemy. He had summoned the water himself. He leapt across the pit and charged Leonard, who had just put his hand on the knife in his boot before Roy was upon him. He'd barely brought up his hand to defend himself when Roy's fist slammed into his face.

James winced at the ferocity of the blow. Leonard fell to the ground with Roy on top of him, fighting to keep his consciousness. He tried to punch back but with little effect.

Roy continually drove his fists into Leonard's face, punching harder each time. If he kept up, he would kill him. Leonard tried one last move to gain an advantage. He took the knife from his boot and slashed upward in an arc. Roy cried out in pain and fell back holding his face, writhing. James knew what had happened. Leonard was the one who gave Roy the scar. Roy's hands were already slick with blood.

Dhorh snickered beside him. "This is the best part."

Leonard stood up, broken nose bleeding profusely, and leaned over Roy. "You gave me no choice, Roy," he cried. Rapidly swelling, his face shuddered.

Samira and Ariel ran over to Roy and knelt beside him.

"What have you done, Leonard?" Samira demanded. She saw the cut on Roy's eye. It was bleeding fiercely, and he was losing consciousness.

Leonard looked grim, his face bruising and changing color from the blows Roy had dealt him. "I didn't want to hurt him, but he was going to kill me." He sighed, and a tear went down his face. "I can't stay here. He won't forgive me, if he lives."

Ariel looked up, shocked. "What do you mean?"

Leonard held up his knife. The edge of the blade was a sickly green color. Poison. Ariel looked down at Roy and saw the flesh around the cut already starting to turn gangrenous. She put her hand over her mouth and exhaled so violently that it sounded like a sob. She gently placed her fingers on Roy's forehead.

Roy jerked awake, gaping around wildly through his one good eye. James jumped back as Roy's hand shot out and grabbed at Ariel's neck. Roy's good eye had a look of hatred, already bright orange, the eye of Charodon.

Ariel swatted his clawing hand away and slid backward, instinctively drawing her bow. Her arms drew the arrow all the way back, ready to loose directly into Roy's skull. Moonlight reflected in Ariel's watchful eyes, and her thin lips were drawn into a deadly grimace. A single drop of blood ran from the very thin scratch across her throat. Ariel didn't act this way. Fear and training had taken over.

The arrow began to slip from her fingers a split second before she regained her senses. She desperately swung the bow to the right into the woods, terrified of herself. Air tore apart as the arrow sped off into the darkness. Roy's body was crouched in front of her, ready to pounce.

James saw a look of shock cross Roy's face as he realized what he was about to do. Roy sprawled backward and moaned, disgusted with himself. Ariel tried to speak but was only able to stammer an apology.

"I'm sorry," she said desperately.

Roy howled with misery. He tried to sit up but fell back again, and the screams turned into sobs. He had come close to killing one of the only people who had ever cared about him. Ariel knelt in the snow and wept.

No one moved. Even though he was not really there, James felt bile rise into this throat. They had been hiding this from him the whole time. Every resentful pause, every hateful scowl, every shameful look his companions exchanged had been because of this night.

Leonard put a hand on Ariel's shoulder. "We need to go." He got up and started walking away. Ariel didn't move, still frozen with the shock at what had just happened. "Come on!" Leonard yelled. "I don't want him to hurt you!" Ariel got up, tears wetting her face, and followed. They soon disappeared into the gloom.

Samira knelt at Roy's side and frantically tore a strip from her coat. She wrapped it around Roy's eye, trying to stop the bleeding. Roy's consciousness was failing.

Dhorh clicked his tongue and knelt beside Samira as she bandaged Roy's head. "This is quite the mess." He smirked, "Are these really the people you want to die with? If you don't think you're headed that way, you're a fool."

Dhorh's withered hand shot forward unnaturally far and touched James's brow.

James thrashed awake and sat up, sweating, heart galloping. Now he knew why Roy hated Leonard so much, why there was a noticeable rift between them all. He knew why Samira defended Roy so much, and why Roy and Ariel—despite their obvious feelings—avoided each other. He needed to do something about it. But what? Roy clearly hated Leonard enough to want to kill him. This couldn't end well, and the state everyone was in could result in something like this happening again.

The Chosen were supposed to be emissaries of the gods, the mortal representatives that did the gods' will. It turned out that they were petty, backstabbing wrecks, barely able to function as people. Perhaps they fit the role a bit too well, and the gods didn't seem to be bothered enough to intervene, as usual. He looked around the dark, jungly space that passed for their camp. His new traveling companions slept at opposite corners of the area. Only the sailors trusted each other enough to be near one another.

He tried for hours to lean back and forget about what that worm Dhorh had shown him. But despite his best efforts, sleep refused to welcome him for the remainder of the night.

A Fresh Start

Awaking early the next morning, the Chosen sat by the sailors under the foreign, leafy trees and contemplated what they had been able to smuggle off the ship in the storm. Despite the mundane quality of the items, they still lent a fair range of adaptability to the new, tropical environment. The entirety of their survival tools included a length of rope, four water skins, a roll of gauze, fishing tackle, and a tinderbox. Roy immediately handed the tinderbox to James.

Embarrassed, James took it. He was barely even able to attempt the second form of his gift. He was the mortal embodiment of fire, and they had to rely on tools to provide one of the most crucial survival provisions instead of him. Leonard shrugged, as if trying to say it didn't matter. Heavy, dark circles weighed down James's eyes. The dream from last night had not allowed him a single moment of sleep.

The crew members acted much more comfortable around them after Ariel's rescue of one of their own. Joskine drew a number of oblong shapes in the mud between them.

"The Tarsals form a string of islands that stretch toward the north, no more than a day apart from each other at the most. The farthest one to the north is naught two weeks sail from Collis." Joskine carved a line above the circles to show the upper continent and the gulf that housed Greade Harbor.

Leonard stroked his lengthening chin stubble. "So you think we could jump from island to island until we get within pissing distance of our destination." He grinned. "Well done, Joskine."

Joskine shrugged. "Supply runs go from Collisun to Spiath by sea all the time. The best chance we have to be noticed is there."

The bald sailor, the man who had introduced himself as Kahb, shook his head. "I don't like this, you don't mind me sayin'. Nothin' good on these islands." The bandages around his chest needed to be changed.

Roy pointed at the solidifying map on the ground. "We can't just take a rowboat out to the open sea. At least with this route we can stop and plan as well as hunt for food."

Clicking his tongue in agreement, James looked inland. The ground sloped upward at an increasingly steep angle. Most of these islands had apparently formed as a result of volcanic activity. It was possible that the slope led to a large crater.

Distractingly green trees barred their eyesight from penetrating much more than two-hundred feet inward. They still registered as outlandish to James. Boane's only tall objects had been buildings, and sour nettles the only plants that grew. These plants towered above everything, imposing and *green*. The only variety of color he was used to seeing was the odd patchwork of clothing that a foreign traveler wore into Boane. And even then the traveler would be robbed of it immediately. Anything with color was considered in the same value range as gold. Feeling outward with his senses, he felt heat swell around them as far outward as he could reach. There was so much life and heat around them. A forest of torches.

Badlai, the lone female sailor approaching thirty years, fiddled with the end of her lengthy auburn ponytail. She didn't seem too keen to speak and instead nervously watched the tree line. Her gaze flitted from branch to branch, looking increasingly wary of the encompassing canopy. The bridge of her nose suggested that it had been broken multiple times. James recognized her as someone who frequently had watched training sessions between him and Samira.

Ariel stood up from her crouching position, rolling her shoulders. "Well, if it's going to end up at a vote, I say we go with Joskine's plan."

The sailor turned as red as his moon-shaped beard.

Nodding, Roy stood as well, dried mud cracking across his pant legs as he straightened his knees.

Kahb and Badlai were the only ones who seemed to object. The young boy with them shrugged in agreement to Joskine and the Chosen. James watched as Ariel trudged into the green haze of the jungle with Roy and the sailors in tow, all of them shuffling like animated mud creatures. Why couldn't they go more than a few days without being covered head to toe in something?

Samira and Leonard scrubbed the map from the mud and prepared to follow the group. Leonard coiled the rope and fishing tackle together before slinging them over his shoulder. Samira tied one of the water skins around her waist. Ready to march after the rest of the party, they took no more than one step into the foliage before James spoke.

"I know what happened to Roy's face," he said.

Leonard froze, panic lighting in his confident brown eyes. James waited for Leonard to ask what he meant, to refute the statement, or to say anything at all, but there was no response.

"I know why you've been acting so careful around each other, and it's threatening to rip this whole thing apart. You've asked me to *trust* you, to go along with you to the empire, and to fight against something I don't understand." James looked back and forth between them. "Scorch me, the *Temple* is more transparent than this."

Neither of them looked particularly happy to speak. Even Samira, one of the most direct people he had ever met, did not look at him. "We needed you to come with us. I was afraid that you wouldn't if you knew our whole past. We've made a lot of mistakes. Mistakes unbefitting of the gods," she said, shamefaced.

"We've done the best we can since then," Leonard added. Samira glared at him briefly. He scratched his mud-speckled neck. "There just hasn't been any time to address what's happened."

James shook his head, frustration burning through his eyes. "Well, then now's the time. We all have to trust each other if we're going to make it out of here alive. I don't care what you've done to each other, *fix it*. Because if you want me to come the rest of the way with you, I want to know I can trust you, and I have a right to know what's going on. The Temple lied to me my whole life. You aren't much better so far."

Seeming to come to some kind of nonverbal agreement, they motioned for James to help them with the rowboat they had dragged ashore. It was needed for Joskine's plan to hop from one island to the next. As much as James had gotten used to being on a boat the past week, he still didn't know how to swim. They towed the raft through the leafy floor of the jungle. Damp soil and mud squelched beneath their feet. Outlines of the rest of the group were still faintly visible through the shady canopy. Small pockets of sunlight needled their way through the thick leaves overhead.

The young boy from the crew, Amry, hacked through the vines ahead of them with a hunting knife, staying close enough to listen in on the conversation. His thin, rusted wire glasses hung off his nose. The green rag that was always wrapped around his head was starting to slip off, exposing unevenly cut hair, suggesting that the boy had done it himself.

Rays of sunlight crawled over them as the day wore on. James listened to Samira and Leonard without speaking until they had finished completely. The emperor's wishes, the story of Roy's possession, and the feud that led to the group's separation.

"So the emperor wants me to be a mascot for him," James said skeptically.

Leonard bit his lip, pondering this for a moment. "I was going to say 'not exactly,' but yes, now that you've put it that way."

Samira glared at him.

"But I've been serving the empire for years. I grew up there." He backpedaled. "They respect me, and you will have their respect as well. More importantly, the empire would be the safest place for us to be right now. The emperor is expanding recruitment for the infantry and Arochs twofold."

"Ariel made the same suggestion last night. I don't like the idea of throwing in with politicians," Samira mused, rubbing her bandaged shoulder. "But it isn't like Spiath or Kostra have a force centralized enough to repel a large attack. We also can guess the Alderaye won't stay in Epot Detharn for long, if they are still there. They spread like disease. All of us must fight together in order for what I read to be realized."

"And you read in this *Temple text* that with our help you can kill the Alderaye?" James frowned, anger stirring at the mention of religion.

Samira nodded, her braided hair swaying. "It was a text passed from generations of Shale Watchtower devotees. It was eventually passed down to my father, who is the current Watcher. It said that the Champion of the Astus must have the other Chosen at their side in order to finally destroy them."

Sighing, Leonard reset his grip on the wooden lip of the lifeboat. "You still believe that?"

She whipped her gaze over to him. "We found James, didn't we? When was the last time in recorded history that all the Chosen fought alongside one another?" Her eyes shone with prophecy.

"I don't know, Sam," Leonard said exasperatedly. "The ones before us died four hundred years ago. Before that, they were all too busy taking sides in wars and trying to outdo each other. It's probably why none of them lived very long. It's a mystery how we've even survived until now. If the rest of the history wasn't lost, we may know more, but the shattering of the Temple ended with a lot of the past being scrubbed."

James cocked his head to the side. He could tell that Amry up ahead of them was also listening intently. "I still don't understand what good it'll do to have me as the emperor's talisman," James said. "From what you've told me, Collisun rules over Kostra and Spiath, but they don't seem to be as fervent as Collisun does. What good does a mascot do to unite three whole kingdoms?"

Leonard pondered this, "Alaric's father made a lot of changes, changes that gave Kostra and Spiath more power and more say, and Alaric has expanded them even further. Even though Alaric is still emperor, it's gotten to be more of a Triumvirate of late. In the long run, I fully believe that it will make the empire stronger to give more people power, but there are many, mostly within Collisun and the Temple, who will take convincing. They're used to how things have run, namely the emperor dictating Spiath and Kostra's way of life. The one thing that can change that is if the Chosen of Iarus steadies their fears."

Samira strained with the weight of the raft. They had been dragging it for the better part of the day. "Do you remember what Roy and I first asked you when we found you?"

"You asked me what I want," he recalled. He swore that he could feel half a dozen splinters in each hand. "I still want what I've always wanted, to see the Temple become nothing more than an outdated ruin. They've ruined just as many lives as the Alderaye."

Setting down her side of the raft, Samira massaged her hands. "I know you're angry, James, but bringing the Temple down will not bring you peace. Destroying the institution will make you no better than the enemy. It's childish, not to mention that it would create chaos in Collisun."

"What would you know about it?" James spat. Samira's righteous spouting had been encroaching on his nerves. "The Temple is just as much a blight on the world as the Alderaye, the way I see it. You just heard Leonard say that they're hindering progress in the empire that would help people. With the Temple gone, the world would be a better place. They are also the enemy. You won't convince me of anything else, Sam." It was what needed to happen, to keep children like Gemmi from meeting the same fate. He fastened his grip on the rowboat, ignoring Samira's protests. She didn't understand, was too blind to understand.

But she would.

***

Roy clawed the dried mud from his hair and stood. Without a word, he scooped up the squat cooking pot and stepped carefully out of the camp toward the west. The voices of his companions faded into the deep hum of the jungle around him. Insects chirped as he walked by, alerting others to his presence.

The swampy ground underneath him was eerily similar to the Draypond Marshes. Three years had passed, but he still remembered every detail of that day before it all went wrong and Charodon appeared. Roy massaged the bite scars on his shoulder. They still pained him from time to time, never truly leaving. He rubbed his eyes, banishing the memory. It was no use to dwell on that day, not when their current situation was what needed his focus.

A mossy pond of modest size sat between a gauntlet of knotted trees. Its glossy surface was impossibly still. Stepping closer to the edge, Roy inhaled deeply through his nose. Immediately, he felt a rush of life and calm seep into him. The pool before him was alight with life. He could feel the movement of small fish, the flitting of bugs across the surface of the water, and a large, motionless mass at the center. It drifted closer to him, stealthily.

Roy looked directly at the beady eyes that watched him from the surface. The crocodile halted, sensing that it had been discovered.

"I see you," he said, raising his eyebrows knowingly at the creature. The eyes stared back at him, giving nothing else away. The face of the animal looked much like the face of the devil he had been taken by all those years ago. The difference was the eyes. Charodon's eyes carried the rage and callous side of the natural world. They saw the world indiscriminately as playthings for slaughter. Looking into the round, black eyes of the crocodile, he saw nothing but calm patience. The natural world at rest. It no longer drifted toward him, listing lethargically to the center of the pond.

Sighing, Roy held his hand over the surface, closing his fingers as if grasping a needle. Brown, silty water flowed upward and into the cooking tin. The muscles in his wrist tightened with every drop of water he lifted. It wouldn't be enough for everyone to drink much, but it was better than nothing.

He looked again at the water, the crocodile. How long before Charodon stopped being placid and began fighting in earnest? It was all he could do to keep the devil at bay now, while it was still dormant most of the time. Three years of constant battle had left him hollow, scratched raw inside. Would he make it to another three? And what about the empire? Suffice to say he was not well-liked there, which tended to happen when the Elder devil possessing him carved a bloody scar through the countryside. That *could not* happen again.

"It will. Despite your efforts, it will."

He often had to ponder at length if a voice in his head had been his or Charodon's. They were starting to meld at the edges, angry thoughts from him becoming insane actions from Charodon and the people around him paying the price. There had been times, not as long ago as they felt, when he couldn't sleep, all the promises of people he could help, protect, shearing through attempts at rest. These dreams had been replaced by a rasping dread. In his sleep, he could hear the hissing of the Eye of Nature, following him. Nights were spent crouching with a knife in his hand, ready to slit his own throat in fear of the monster suddenly making a move.

Two years, he and Samira had traveled to the corners of Collis, searched every athenaeum, sought out every religious leader in hopes of finding a way to purge Charodon from his being. Samira had her mission, and he had his. Clerics from the Sandstone Watchtower in Boane had been his last option, the only hope that was left. That, like everything else, had ended with death and disappointment. At what point does a mission become a fool's errand? Even at Frostspring, his childhood mentor had not been there to help him when he sought a way out.

A Chosen protects innocents. It's what he had learned as a boy growing up in Cei at the Refuge. Roy wanted desperately to be this, to make amends for the Eye of Nature's acts done through him.

Charodon couldn't escape the prison he had made for it, not ever. He would die before that happened, and increasingly he knew that the time may reach him soon. The sand in the hourglass would never run out; he would break it. Familiar, light, and rigid, his dagger pressed against his ankle within the sheath in his boot.

Trying to think of good things, happy things, he stood and trudged toward the camp with the water tin. His night with Ariel at the top of the watchtower or dinner with Samira's father were swallowed by the cavern. These days were gone, and so was he, nearly. One foot after the other. Each step, the dagger pressed against his skin.

Soon. Clarity came through. There were still some things to do. He would have to hold on, help Samira complete her mission as best he could. But then, it may be time.

***

It occurred to James this was the first meal he'd really shared with someone since Gemmi had died.

The sunlight no longer peeked through the canopy overhead by the time Roy had come back to the camp. Night had come all too quickly, and yet it was not a moment too soon. It had been a long day, and sleep had started to pick away at each of them. It was only when Ariel had calmly strolled into the wooden grove holding three furry carcasses, arrows all piercing directly through the eyes, that everyone briefly forgot about their exhaustion. Each of the creatures Ariel had shot were covered in matted gray fur. Strong back legs and a ridged spine suggested that they were gifted climbers. Ariel confirmed that she had shot them out of the trees. No one in the group knew what they were, but the species no longer mattered as they ate voraciously. The stale bread and spoiled fish on the *Greed Sun* were not missed.

James gulped down the greasy food. Not even the scraps thrown out of the Boane consul's court and into the street tasted as good.

Their journey across the islands had borne fruit in the form of long-discarded, sporadic supplies left behind by explorers or the marooned, including a jug of grog. Finally relenting to Kahb's pestering, Joskine fished a few flagons from a nearby crate and filled them with drink. The cups slowly drained as they were passed around the fire. Taking a whole cupful to himself, Kahb grew redder in the face with each passing minute. Joskine elaborated on voyages past. Leonard competed to spin a taller tale while enjoying the rum himself.

"It's true! I saw one, as sure as I'm sitting here!" Joskine blurted. His patchy beard cast misshapen shadows across his face. Grog sloshed from the mug, spilling too close James's pant leg.

"Are you absolutely sure that you are in fact sitting here?" Samira jabbed with a small smirk on her face.

Laughing a bit too enthusiastically, the sailor sloppily passed the cup to Leonard. "A good one! I may have drank my fair share, but I'll never forget a Khavanh whale. They're nightmares to behold. Bone white and like a skeleton, they are. But there was never a gennler...gen...*gentler* creature that graced the sea!" He stood abruptly and bent over his legs, reaching down to his boots. "I had it scribed on me so I'll never forget it!"

With a dramatic flourish only accomplished by a drunk, he yanked his pant leg up to his knee, exposing a bare calf. Swearing, Joskine rolled up the other pant leg, revealing a crudely drawn tattoo. The faded ink showed a skeletal marine figure. Haunting and yet strangely beautiful, the whale tattoo curved around his calf, stopping at his crooked kneecap. He sat and grinned in Ariel's direction. "I guess that makes us similar, eh lass?"

A wry smile touched Ariel's lips. "I suppose it does." She had scratched off the dried mud from her arms, and the dark ink of the tattooed glyphs absorbed the light of the fire. She sat beside Badlai and Roy, the latter of whom seemed keenly—and somewhat uncomfortably—aware of where she was sitting. She clasped her hands, noticeably devoid of any markings. Stories from James's homeland had claimed that some Spiathi die without an inch of bare skin left.

James turned to Badlai, who sat with her hand in her lap, eyeing the trees as always. "Where are you from, Badlai?"

She looked at him, startled. Wide green eyes regarded him. Looking like she wanted to speak, Badlai sheepishly averted her gaze. Everyone around the crackling fire sat in awkward silence. Confused, James felt a tap on his shoulder from Amry.

"She don't talk." The boy whispered. "Never told anyone why. Might have been born that way for all anyone knows." Badlai looked down, embarrassed. James passed the grog to her, guilt washing through him along with the warmth of the drink. She took it graciously, giving him a forgiving nod.

"I knew someone a lot like you, Badlai," Samira said gently. "Her name was Talia, and she was also quiet. Wonderful person, the pride of the gods." Samira's amber eyes crinkled. "She actually wanted to sail, to see the world like you do." Looking fondly into the fire, she sipped from a flagon.

Badlai grinned and tapped Samira's shoulder. Her lips mouthed the silent words, complementing the glimmer in her look, *thank you*. James discerned something in Badlai's eye that he'd seen in some of his lamplighter brethren, but he wouldn't be the one to bring it up. That was Badlai's business.

Sensing that the energy of the camp had come to a halt, Leonard stood and strolled to James, clapping a sturdy hand down on his shoulder. His grip was a hair too firm and as solid as stone. "James here defeated a devil with a single blow! Now who here can top that story?" The sailors around the fire gawked at him in awe. They reminded James of the children he grew up with at the Temple, amazed by stories they had heard a hundred times.

"It was nothing." James shrugged.

"It was amazing," Roy interjected for the first time that night. All heads swiveled to him. "He saved our lives. And he did it without thinking."

James straightened slightly as Roy nodded at him. Dathos's champion raised the cup that Ariel passed him. Her blue eyes were beaming. Roy acted different than before, like there was life in him. But it seemed forced, rehearsed.

"To you, James," Roy said. Everyone echoed the toast and drank deeply. James couldn't be sure, but through the shifting light there appeared to be a subtle smile on Roy's face.

They continued to sit for another hour, joking and passing the grog amongst themselves. Sifting through the remaining mossy crates with limited coordination, Leonard triumphantly held up a crude wooden flute, proclaiming he had used music to propose to many a paramour.

Chuckling at his childlike delight, Samira and Amry requested every song they could think of. Though the wood of the instrument had begun to rot, Leonard still produced a mellow, soothing tone. It sang through the trees, perfectly resonating with the ambient buzz of the jungle.

James felt his stress dissipate with every note. Joskine and Kahb droned along to each tune, whether they knew it or not. Ariel, Samira, and Roy talked quietly amongst themselves. Badlai sat with them, stealing glances toward the Chosen of Astus.

Feeling the effect of the grog, James set down his flagon and basked in the contentment of the night. Not since Gemmi's death had he ever forgotten himself in a moment. There had been no need, no point. His brother had taken the whole world with him when he died, as far as James had discerned. But watching his new companions—maybe even his friends—unconsciously laid a path in front of him that he could follow. The past was not fixed. It might never be fixed, but his future and theirs held something he couldn't quite elaborate on.

In watching Leonard and the sailors dance to the flute, in watching Ariel and Samira laugh at old memories, and in watching Roy serve Amry and Badlai more meat, James decided he could stay with them, maybe for a long time. His brother was gone, but he was no longer alone.

Brothers No More

Leonard waded silently through the sea of ferns and trees that surrounded him, tense and alert to his leafy surroundings. Looking back on the beginning of the night, he should have stoppered the grog barrel much earlier. It would take too much time to even think about getting the sailors up in a few hours. And Ariel may not wake at all. It was a foolish thing, to waste time and energy when their best was needed. But perhaps the meal around the fire was needed as well.

Despite his headache, his eyes didn't droop. It had been drilled into him long ago that waking up early was just part of life. His commanding officer had assigned latrine pit duty to anyone who was not awake at the proper time. The night had a habit of making the insects and creatures of the jungle bolder, and his ears bristled with each whine or crackle that sounded too close. Crush him, this was a time when he even missed home. The voice of his mother still reverberated through his head. *"Useless."*

Scowling despite himself, he combed his fingernails through his hair. The brown spikes shot back upward. As much as he feared Roy's unrelenting hatred, her frigid contempt was worse. With his father going off to war and getting killed before he was born, Leonard had been a constant reminder of her grief. The whole town told him every day how much he looked like his father. He grew to hate it. A great hero his father was, getting himself killed and leaving his wife to take her frustration and hopelessness out on her young son.

"You're going to get yourself killed, just like he did." Those had been her words when he left to join the infantry. Before he had met the others.

"I won't," he remembered saying.

Her glare had been enough to peel the bark from a tree. It had finally come to him after he had left their shack of a house that it hadn't been an assessment; it had been a request. He had visited again some years later, after the border skirmishes with Cei had subsided. The town had welcomed him back as a legend, a hero, but his mother's home was firmly locked. She hardly left the house when he lived there. Nothing had changed. Years had passed, and a few unanswered letters. At least he had Ariel and James, and even Samira was starting to trust him again.

He continued through the brush. In the darkness, the deep green was now washed-out black. The grog had worn off with sleep, and his nerves spiked through his throat. All he had to do was take over watch, but any interaction with Roy could become deadly without Samira or Ariel around to stop him. Leonard had seen some of the old Roy tonight, but it was no more than a ghost. The man he had once called his friend was dead.

It took him a moment to pick out Roy's dark outline in the foliage. That trademark cloak could be annoying at best. It often wasn't the best case, however.

Roy noticed Leonard looking at him and broke the silence. "Anything of note over here, Leonard? Please enlighten me," he said through clenched teeth. The tension wasn't from the sinister rainforest around them. Both of them knew it.

Leonard refocused on the blurry jungle in front of him. "My apologies," he said with equal irritation, "I thought that being civil was a possibility."

"I wouldn't expect it to be," Roy barked. He wasn't interested in mending whatever friendship he and Leonard had once had.

They continued in silence for another few minutes. The jungle around them sounded with a cacophony of noise, as if the whole place were a colosseum filled with insects, birds, and other wildlife waiting for the next pit match. Leonard spied Roy taking a piece of a dead branch, no bigger than his index finger, and tossing it into the air directly above him. The twig sailed into the air and drifted backward. The stick landed about eleven feet behind Roy. There was a subtle wind blowing through the trees. This meant there was a clearing somewhere close by. Leonard had seen Ariel do this trick many times before and guessed Roy had picked it up from her.

"She missed you," Leonard said. "She did a good job of hiding it, but I could always tell."

Roy looked at the ground and gave a slight nod, avoiding a verbal answer to Leonard's attempt at conversation. He stepped away from his post, pushing through a green, twisting cluster of vines.

Leonard stewed. A bitter taste developed in his mouth, drowning the already bitter taste from the grog. So it was finally going to come out. Fine, better to have it out now. "I know you don't particularly enjoy my company, but do you think you could stop being an ass for *one second*? It's not like it helps anything."

Roy stopped and looked Leonard in the eye. "And finally you speak up," he spat coldly. He had probably been waiting for when this would finally happen. His hands clenched at his sides, trembling ever so slightly. "I don't give a *damn* what you want. Everything is wrong because of you."

Leonard jabbed his index finger at Roy, no longer interested in keeping peace. "Don't put that on me, Roy. You charged the crushing thing and got bit. You think you're the victim in this, but everything that happened was your fault!"

Roy's eyes flared orange, contorting the scar that had destroyed his face. "That isn't the point! I needed you, and you let me down, Leonard. You were supposed to have my back, and you left me to die, possessed by that monster."

"I...I didn't know what to do."

"When I finally woke up, you were gone." Roy took a step toward Leonard. A wet tree branch cracked under his boot. His fists were clenched dangerously tight. "All I wanted was an apology. All I wanted was for you to *look* at me and say that you were *sorry*. And what did you do instead? You gave me this!" He pointed to his face, the long scar gleamed in the dim light of the jungle floor.

Leonard shook his head vigorously, his eyes blinking away tears. "You attacked me."

"I did. And don't think for a moment that I wouldn't again. You wouldn't dare try to make that excuse if you knew what it was like." Roy was furious now. Orange patches within his turquoise eyes began to solidify and grow. His voice sliced through the canopy. "I'm a monster." Then it wavered. "And it's because of you."

"*I'm sorry!*" Leonard wailed. "What else do you want from me? I'm sorry I left. I'm sorry I didn't take responsibility." His words shook with barely contained tears. "I'm sorry I cut you. I'm sorry I made Ariel leave with me. There's too much I'm ashamed of!"

Roy stood, wide eyes incredulous as Leonard regained his composure. The noises of the jungle slowly seeped back into the wilds around them. The echo of their outburst was smothered by the intense green of the forest. Leonard looked back at the man who used to be his friend, his brother. He wanted to want Roy to forgive him, but he knew that was an idiot's wish. The possibility of forgiveness had died years ago.

"Get out of my sight." Roy looked away with disgust. It didn't matter if Leonard was taking watch. Roy refused to move.

Leonard slowly turned and trudged ahead into the jungle, farther from the post. Roy stood frozen in place for a few moments. He then lashed out, punching the tree to his direct left. The trunk shook and a creature that had been sitting in it above him squawked with protest. He hit the tree again and again, crunching the bark. The tree groaned and Roy finally stopped, knuckles bleeding and breathing heavily.

From the shadow of the canopy, watching, Leonard sighed. Their first real conversation in years had gone about as well as he had expected. Better, actually. Thanking Raslena that he was not that tree, Leonard settled into the brush, ready for a long watch.

***

It had been a thousand years since the thoughts of Rhaiga's host had died out. Not that it was too terrible of a loss. The woman had been a nuisance, prattling on about the immorality of Rhaiga's charge. Granted, supervising death wasn't exciting. It was a chore.

As the schooner cut through the waves, taking her closer to the islands, she wondered if the followers she had been tasked to meet were still there. Vayne had been confident, but she wasn't as sure after having been gone so long.

Rhaiga tied off a line and banished the uncertainty. He was never wrong. There was no reason to doubt him about this.

The carnage of Epot Detharn had already been forgotten in her mind. It was just another point on their path, even though it had been slightly exciting. There had been a confusing yet exhilarating moment when she'd taken apart a group of soldiers. She didn't remember *enjoying* the dealing of death before. Ever since the dunes, her mind had felt...disjointed. As if a fog inconveniently covered something simple.

Her fingers worked expertly with the rigging of her stolen vessel. Dhorh had decided to prove useful, providing her with the memories of a sailor. Even though she had never sailed, she had the experiences of a lifelong mariner. It was ridiculous that she even had to learn. Before their banishment, there were those who would sail them to all corners of the map purely out of devotion. The devotion had given her the power to travel anywhere she desired. Now that they had returned, the stuck-up humans had forgotten all about them, a fact that had driven Vayne mad.

A large storm had lurked up ahead until a few days ago, vanishing quickly as she got to the edge of it. The natural entities of the world, while still brutal and powerful, were fading, much like Rhaiga and her bretheren. Storms such as these would be a hundred times worse ages ago. They would keep up well into landfall on occasion. Her thoughts again turned to her host. The woman had always gone on about how much she wanted to see the ocean. What had her name been? Stoya, perhaps?

Rhaiga wondered what had caused her to start thinking about the host again after all this time. Her mind always turned to odd things when she was alone to converse with it. Each host was the same, a sack of jelly and bone that she had tricked, pretending to be some benevolent goddess. No reasoning behind it other than the fact that they were normally easier to trick.

Once they let her in, she would take over, slowly eating their souls until nothing remained, just driving an empty husk. Some had protested. Some resigned themselves. It was all the same in the end. A great many of them had an aversion to death though. Perhaps that was why she didn't particularly enjoy handing it out most of the time, preferring instead to watch paths expire organically. If someone's path was at an end and they tried to extend or cheat it, well, she would put that down immediately.

The silk robes she had worn for the better part of a century had been replaced with a long wool coat that had three missing buttons toward the bottom and ragged trousers. The sailor's memories and clothing had been given to aid her in her journey before she had driven her hand through his chest. She had to pull the drawstrings of the trousers especially tight, as the man had been much bigger than her host body. The coat hung loosely over her shoulders, itching terribly, but it was much better suited to the sea wind than what she had before. Her black veil still flapped around her face, the only garment that she had kept. Thankfully, the sailor's blood had not gotten on it, only the coat. There had not truly been a reason to keep it, for she just liked it. It made people nervous around her, and she liked it when people were nervous.

This new clothing might also help her to be more inconspicuous around other humans in case she ran into any. Dhorh had shown her the few bits of memory he gleaned from the Chosen's heads before she left. His residual presence in the mind of someone he had once unthreaded was invaluable, almost worth ignoring his asinine behavior.

The Chosen had been headed north, Dhorh had said. Potentially toward her destination and the home of the last followers of the Elders, as she and Vayne called themselves. Perhaps the remnants of the other Eyes, the ones that had been killed, would be there, or even the last of the Altujan. The race of beings had been a wide-ranging force before she had been sent to the Dunes. Many had served, and now most were gone. For centuries, she and the others had slaughtered the Chosen with ease, but it was harder to do now. The very thought made an unusual feeling stir in her chest, like a pit being opened.

Those who opposed them had to die. It was her duty. They opposed the natural order of things. Death, disease, nature, memory. These were all constants that made the world what it was. The world bent to these things, or it must be made to bend. Men and women were standing in the way. Civilization, human order, it prolonged people's paths. Rhaiga saw this as an affront to her very existence, unacceptable. The path was not to be bargained with or subverted. The feeling of the pit deepened. For the briefest of moments, she felt a strong desire to lash out at something, end its path right there, but there was nothing around. The feeling passed.

Wind blew through her veil again as a gust swept across the surface of the waves. Rhaiga would do her duty, as Dhorh and Vayne would do theirs. The path to sow chaos was set. They just needed some assistance from old vassals.

Reunion

They had crossed three islands over the last day and a half. By now, it was ingrained into James's body how the procedure went. Carry, shove off, row, repeated for hours on end. In addition, they now had some of the supplies from the abandoned camp. Most of the islands they trekked across were small, allowing them to cut across with not much time. Their resemblance to the plentiful bones in the foot is what earned them the title of Tarsals. When asked how many more times this routine would have to be done, Joskine replied with a simple shrug. At some point, the islands would run out once they reached the northernmost point of the vast chain.

The mud that they had been slathered with on the first day was repeatedly washed off and reapplied every time they rowed to the next island. It was a grueling process, lugging the rowboat up the beach and into the dense, marshy jungle.

Traveling through such a compact and humid environment had also alerted James to the insects that provided no end to small bites. None of his friends could confirm his sighting, but he could have sworn he saw a massive bug at least five feet long with legs that stuck out like branches. The fact that something like that could be blending into the trees gave him real pause to even walk near one.

As they hauled the rowboat up another sludgy bank, Samira's eyebrows perked upward. A different sound penetrated through the dull hum of the jungle.

Foraging ahead into the trees, Samira and Ariel searched for the source of the sound. It reached James's ears, sounding promisingly like running water, although he couldn't be sure since the waves lapping against this island could still be heard behind him.

Shouts of excitement came from ahead, sounding like it was more than just Ariel and Samira in the thicket. Joskine ran ahead, recognizing some of the voices. Come to think of it, James was sure he recognized them too.

Dropping the boat, James hurried into the thick jungle with the rest of his friends. Leaves slapped at him, but he ignored their assaults as a clearing came into view up ahead. Coming from just past a string of fallen trees, the voices intensified. Leonard hurdled the trees and sprinted further. The blur of foliage finally gave way to a measly glade, an oblong reservoir glistening in the far northern corner. The ground throughout the clearing had been torn by just shy of twenty pairs of feet. Shouts of happiness had transformed into a tense argument. Samira and Ariel were surrounded by the remaining crew of the *Greed Sun*.

In the center of the group, Vilch stood inches from Samira, sword in hand. The captain's face was in a state of blind loathing. Samira stood callously, one hand resting on the hilt of her sword. Even with her swordplay training, it would take too long for her to draw. Vilch's sword was already out and was pointed directly at Samira's throat. The rest of the crew members surrounded them menacingly, all of them in various states of disorder. Several were missing shoes, and injuries were rampant within the group. Every face in the remaining crew seemed to agree with the captain. Some were even reaching toward their weapons.

Leonard and Roy attempted to break through the circle to stand with Ariel and Samira. Two crewmen turned and held them back. One of them, a man with a large scab on his cheek, placed a hand on Roy's shoulder.

"Not another step, slayer," he growled.

Leonard smirked. "You are seconds from death, sir. Not even the animals would find what's left of you if you stand in Roy's way."

"For once, listen to this man," Roy said, nodding toward Leonard.

Vilch leered at them from the corner of his eye. "We're in this mess because of you, Chosen. My ship is at the bottom of the sea with those drowning fish crawling all over it, and two thirds of my crew are dead!" His wiry black hair was strewn around his head in clumps, stuck together with mud. The sword hovered closer to Samira's neck. Her grip on her sword tightened.

James instinctively reached for his sword. Amry stood, shocked, gaping at the standoff.

Vilch wasn't thinking rationally at this point. It didn't matter if he had chosen the heading that led to getting caught in the Dreadfront; Vilch wanted a scapegoat for his anger. And one just happened to drop out of the jungle for him.

Joskine approached the crowd. Some of the mariners recognized him and nodded, still not taking their attention away from the captain and the Chosen. He held up his hands and shouted to Vilch, "Captain, Ariel saved my life. They aren't here to do us harm. They can help us!"

"They saved your life, but what about everyone else?" Vilch bellowed. "Should we wait for another storm to hit, for more bugs to descend from the trees, or perhaps for us to run into a dragon's nest? They are a plague, a curse! If we don't deal with them now, we will all die!"

"No, Vilch. Just you," Samira growled.

"Sam, don't!" Ariel cried.

Before Vilch could react to the threat, Samira swiped the sword from the captain's hand and shoved him backward. Vilch fell into his crew. The Chosen of Astus threw the short sword point-downward into the mud and drew her long steel. The blade glimmered as she pointed it toward the crewmen circling her and Ariel, who removed the hatchet from her belt, looking sick.

Vilch spat and pulled himself up using the shoulders of his crewmen. Every weapon was drawn. James glanced over to the sailors who had traveled with them the last few days. Amry looked desperately toward the captain. Kahb glanced around uncertainly, clearly wondering which side he should take. The sound of boots squelching in the mud came to a halt while everyone stood completely still. A desire to fight coursed through the people there, but none wanted to be the first to begin. Badlai gazed worriedly at Samira, a hand over her knife.

"Stop this! All of you!" Joskine shoved through his mates and stood between Samira and Vilch, boots planted firmly in the mud. The crew stiffened, looking more than a little betrayed. Some blinked, keen to listen to him. Joskine drew himself up to his full height and set his jaw, crescent-beard jutting from his chin at an angle. "Captain, this isn't right. We lost the ship, but we're still alive. We're alive because of them."

"That ship was my life," Vilch said, his voice hardening, "and they made me abandon it."

"No, Vilch. The storm did. You want to punish someone for your decisions, and it's making you not think straight. You're going to get us killed, not them," Joskine said firmly.

Amry's glasses were fogging up. "He's right, Vilch. You aren't fit to be captain. We need them."

Joskine shot a look of approval toward Amry. Badlai looked like her mind was made up too. The bearded sailor raised his chin, pointing his beard straight at Vilch. "Give up, Vilch."

Every pair of eyes watched the captain, some holding up their weapons expectantly. A majority of the crewmen and women expected him to give the order.

Spitting and swiping a knife from a nearby crewman, Vilch uttered a harsh, guttural yell. The captain charged Joskine and Samira, murder bubbling in his black eyes. His feet kicked up mud. James tightened his grip on his sword.

Vilch's scream was short lived, smothered by a blinding punch to the side of his head. Ariel had struck him, and the dazed captain stumbled backward. There was no pause between the first punch and the second. Another blow from Ariel caught Vilch in the stomach. The third hit was blocked by the shipmaster, catching the knee of Etah's Chosen before it could batter his ribs. Vilch shoved her backward with an angry grunt. Ariel's boots skidded backward through the mud.

As if activated by a spring, the crew devolved into violent chaos, the clash spreading throughout the glade. Some sided with the captain, charging James and the rest of the Chosen. Others, persuaded by Joskine, intercepted and fought back. It was as though the jungle had detonated around them. Bodies rushed and coursed in currents as strong as a runnel.

James blocked a sword that came his way and thrust back at the arm that held it, but the sword was already gone before he could follow it.

His vision, blurred by the constant motion around him, landed on his friends, twisting and shoving through the chaos. The mud around the ankles of several crew members began to slowly creep upward, like some tentacled leviathan reaching upward from the earth. The tentacles slapped onto the legs of the sailors and wrestled them downward. Leonard twisted the head of his mace in the mud to lock the earth in place. His victims were pinned.

Another assailant leapt toward him, a rusted hammer in his grasp. James ducked under the first swing and rolled through the mud. It glistened against his skin and shirt. When he looked up, the man with the hammer was gone, swallowed by the whirling skirmish around them.

Brief glimpses of his friends came into focus. Roy slashed toward a woman's boot, causing her to lose balance and sprawl into the mud. Samira charged her fist and struck an overweight sailor. The lightning charged in her hand ran through the man, stunning him for enough time to plunge her sword into his gut. He saw Ariel, covered in mud, on top of Vilch, bringing down one fist after another.

Mud squished in front of him as Kahb stepped to where he crouched. Breathing a sigh of relief, James reached toward the bald man's outstretched arm. There was a quick flash of steel before his wrist bloomed into a sharp pain. He had failed to notice the knife Kahb was holding. Looking into the man's eyes, James saw contempt and resentment roll over one another.

He dodged the next slice, turning his body sideways. Taking advantage of the sailor's exposed torso, James punched Kahb in the center of his chest. The worn bandages around Kahb's sternum peeled backward, and the wounds opened. Blood blossomed through his shirt.

"Drownin' wretch!" Kahb frothed, furiously swiping at him again. The knife nearly shaved a bald spot into James's head. He deflected the next stab with his sword but was too clumsy for how close they were. Kahb stabbed again toward James's throat. He caught the sailor's wrist before the knife could sever his neck.

They struggled for half a minute, neither one able to leverage the other. Squeezing Kahb's wrist, James felt his muscles contract. His stomach lurched with the familiar pull. A sizzle and the smell of burning flesh entered his senses, and the sound of the bald sailor screaming infiltrated his ears. Kahb fell backward, clutching the angry scarlet hand mark on his wrist.

Was that the third form? He hadn't even been thinking about it. Kahb snarled and picked the dagger back up gingerly. Roy's lessons took over as James established distance between him and Kahb. He used the sword to maintain space, pointing it directly at the curling bandages. As James readied himself for another attack, Amry leapt onto Kahb's back, aggressively pushing a knife through his torso. The already red bandages on Kahb's chest darkened as blood gurgled out his mouth. Shoving the traitor to the mud, Amry threw off his green cap and rushed to James. The boy hauled him aside.

"Thanks." James whispered. Clamping his grip even harder on the hilt of his sword to keep from shaking, he rushed forward to help his friends. His feet slid through the softening mud as he looked around wildly.

Ariel stood over Vilch, who was disoriented and breathing heavily. The captain's nose was squashed from where she had struck it, and Ariel didn't seem to pay much mind to the battle around her. Her wet, mud-caked hair smacked her shoulder, turning at the sound of Samira's voice.

"Ariel! You have to kill him," Samira shouted.

James saw Ariel's defiant stare, even through the winded haze. They all knew the type of person Vilch was. Leaving him alive now would mean a knife in the ribs later.

"When he wakes up, he'll just follow us."

Samira's amber eyes pleaded with Ariel, who still panted. The wind strengthened through the glade as Ariel's breaths became deeper. The water in the pond began to ripple.

Samira screamed at Ariel, "*Kill him!*"

Ariel shook her head slightly. Her eyes glanced toward Roy, who returned her stare from across the glade.

Exchanging a nod, the pair turned to the oncoming crew. Of the seventeen who had attacked them, ten still stood. Wind swirling around her, Ariel released a hurricane of air in a course howl. It rotated through the clearing with a force that rivaled the Dreadfront. Trees and vines whipped around as if they were mere blades of grass in a breeze. Cries of alarm escaping them, the attackers immediately covered their faces, still trying to creep forward. Weighed down by his previous power usage, Leonard twisted his mace in the mud again. The viscosity of the silt increased, and it caused the enemies to stick.

Holding an open hand above his head, Roy stood in front of the reservoir, his hair dancing. The water whisked behind him, growing white with froth. James's eyes widened as Roy's hand began to plunge downward.

James had no more than a moment to tackle Amry out of the way before Roy hurled the entire reservoir of water at the sailors. The water blasted the Scourge Atoll natives backward into the trees toward the south. Some were barely able to avoid the wave before it pummeled the clearing. Stirred by the wind, the shimmering green water assaulted the trees at the edge of the glade, all but splintering them. Bits of rock and mud from Leonard's attack were swept up as well, whooshing between gaps in the foliage.

Sensing that the improvised storm was beginning to wane, the remaining crew rose from the ground. Some even emerged from between the trees, reentering the glade after the Chosen's attack had banished them. Their fear had not quite overcome their hatred.

"We need to go!" James yelled. They all looked at him. Joskine, Amry, and Badlai all were shivering on the ground, terrified by the power that had been displayed. Hauling them upward, James and Samira dragged them along into the trees. Leonard, Roy, and Ariel followed. The jungle thundered with rushing water, swirling wind, and the raucous screeches of the wildlife up-rooted by the fight. James's labored breathing wheezed in tandem with those of his friends. More excruciating time passed before Samira finally stopped in a mossy grove toward what was assumed to be the center of the island.

Joskine and the other sailors dropped to the carpet of moss, still in shock from the display of power. The trees were more spread apart in this area. A rugged formation of stone sat in the west corner. Like everything else, the rocks were blanketed by moss and vegetation.

Letting out a roar of frustration, Samira drew back her left fist and slammed it into the trunk of a nearby tree. Lightning conducted through her hand, discharging into the wood and snapping the trunk cleanly. A silencing crack echoed through the jungle and briefly stifled the ambience of chirping wildlife. The thick trunk of the tree fell outward, rocking the floor of the grove.

James heard the popping electric charge under the skin of her hand. He slowly approached Samira. She panted angrily, and her shoulders were hunched in agitation. Glancing at Leonard, he received a warning stare. Leonard backed away from Samira slowly. His expression begged James not to say anything.

The group collectively held their breath as James approached. "Samira," he whispered, "it's all right."

She didn't look at him, instead rubbing her brow. "We are all going to die before we even reach Collis. I'm tasked by Astus with bringing all the Chosen together to confront the Alderaye, but we won't even make it out of here alive. Strike me, everything has been *wrong* from the start."

He glanced at the rest of the group. Ariel looked away. Roy and Leonard grimaced. "We won't let that happen." He tried to reassure. "We're all alive. Your mission still has purpose."

Samira's crackling hand came dangerously close to striking him as she spun around. "And what would *you* care? A heretic who left the teachings and abandoned the gods. You've been chosen for a gift beyond most people's comprehension, and still you despise the gods and all they stand for!" Only an inch or two taller than James, she still somehow towered over him. He stood frozen in the shadow of her anger. "You're faithless! You don't deserve the power you have."

No one dared speak. Glancing downward, James shuffled uncomfortably in the moss. "You're right, Samira. I'm a heretic. I don't have any love for Iarus. My observation is that the gods are cowards. They're asking us to die for a cause they don't have much interest in helping with." He tried to stand up straight, meeting Samira's eyes.

"I don't have faith in Iarus or Astus. I have faith in *you*, and in Roy. You both saved me from that Alderaye in Boane. You saved me from the Dreadfront. I have faith in Leonard and Ariel. I have faith in them." James gestured to the sailors, still coming out of their shock. "Amry just saved my life. The gods and the Temple have done nothing for me, but you have done everything. So you're not giving up. Astus and the Temple have nothing to do with it."

Samira's shoulders drooped, and she hung her head. "I told you to call me Sam." She trudged angrily into the woods, eyes still fixed on the ground. James started after her before he felt a hand grip his arm.

"Leave her. She needs to cool down," Ariel cautioned.

They watched the Daughter of Astus walk until the canopy covered her in shadow. Samira then leaned against a rotting tree and slid to the mossy ground.

Ariel gestured to the tree that Samira had splintered, the trunk sinking slightly into the moss. "Will this do for firewood?"

Smirking slightly, he nodded. "Barely, but I'll make do," he said.

***

Slumped against the tree, hiding in the shade, Samira forced angry tears from her eyes. One dripped down her face, then two, but no more would come after that.

This frustration, this utter feeling of failure permeated her every thought. From the start, this voyage home had gone wrong. She was supposed to end the suffering of thousands of people. Hundreds of thousands. *Millions.* It was destiny, prescribed to her by centuries of expectation. This future had been passed down through her ancestors until finally their prayers were answered and she became a Chosen. The day she had caught and thrown back a lightning strike in front of her bewildered father, he had gone mad with pride.

"The War of Lost Faith ends with you," Samira whispered the words of her father. "Find them and be a hero for the rest of time." The damp moss covering the tree trunk seeped through the back of her shirt. Slivers of azure sunlight needled through the dense canopy above her, creating a blazing kaleidoscope beneath her eyelids. Her father's pride in her was the greatest gift she had ever received other than Astus's gift itself.

But his pride was also a terrible curse.

Her childhood as she had known it was scrapped and rewritten. Hours of play and school lessons were replaced with full days atop the tower, waiting for the next storm so she could catch more lightning. It had taught her patience, tranquility, and the determination to see things through. Years passed. Friends she had known grew up and moved away, members of the town whispered behind her back about her power, making up far-fetched and sometimes hurtful speculations about her.

But it had mattered a mere pebble's worth compared to the praise she got from her father. It nourished her more than food ever could. And in the times when it was withheld, she wasted away.

"I thought I was raising a hero." His disappointed voice cut through her thoughts. She winced, knowing that Astus had given her this power for a singular

purpose, the same as every other Chosen of his. She would be the one to finally do it. If not, the failure of disappointing her father would be far more painful than any end that came at the hands of the Alderaye. She wouldn't be able to face him if they didn't return in one piece.

But her quest was balancing on a sword's edge. Ariel wanted to give up the fight, James despised the very religion that bore this prophecy, and Roy's remaining time—a result of her negligence—was dwindling. Any one of these things could ruin everything. She had tried to be firm but risked pushing them all away.

A slight disturbance in the moss beside her caused Samira's eyes to flutter open in annoyance. She wasn't interested in listening to anyone. Not Leonard's attempts at levity, not Ariel's words of encouragement, nor Roy's sullen silence. She didn't even want an apology from James, not that he could ever hide his contempt for her upbringing or faith.

The one she never expected to see was Badlai. Gently, the sailor knelt beside Samira. A look of understanding softened her face.

Samira shook her head and wiped the moisture—a salty union of sweat and tears—from her cheeks. "You don't need to worry, Badlai. I'm all right," she said.

Badlai's emerald eyes blinked. *No, you aren't*, they said.

Tears already cleared, she exhaled. "Really, I'm fine."

Badlai sat in the moss next to her. Then Samira's head was on her shoulder, no tears, no rage. Calm. It was the first real calm she had felt since the day she threw the lightning back. Badlai did not attempt to comfort her but was simply there. The things Samira's father had said were gone for now. She was not a hero, nor a god, nor an instrument in this moment. She was just Sam. Even through the constant noise of the jungle, Samira found a bit of repose. Silence was what she needed, not comfort or a rousing speech. In the shade, Badlai's kind green eyes glinted, a pretty, reassuring sight.

She didn't have the slightest idea if they would make it, but nestled quietly next to Badlai in the shade, it looked a bit more hopeful.

Finding Trouble

The camp had gone silent save for the gentle patter of rain. Ariel held out a hand into the soothing downpour. While still large in volume, this rain fell compassionately compared to the Dreadfront's torrents. Save for Joskine, Ariel, and Roy, their hasty camp had succumbed to sleep.

Crescent-Beard stood watch, perched on a large, mossy rock. None of the Chosen were keeping an eye on him. After the sailor had stood up for them, they fully trusted him. Even Samira, who would have slit Joskine's throat if Astus had told her to, slept with no reservation. Scourge Atoll may be an island run on blood, but Ariel silently rejoiced to see that it still was home to some honorable people. Joskine, Amry, and Badlai could just as easily have grown up in her village.

Letting the rain roll off her head, she leaned out from under the leafy shelter she had constructed. The others were completely asleep. Joskine still manned his post, though his eyes drooped. Ariel looked past all of them and spied the object of her search. That black cloak.

He sat under a tree, eyes closed and one knee drawn up to his chest. She knew better than to think that he was sleeping. And that knee at his chest wasn't something he did for comfort either. It just gave him easier access to the knife in his boot.

Smiling quietly to herself, she slung her bow over her shoulder and shuffled out from under her low-hanging fern roof and into the rain. Luckily, the canopy overhead had some hand in mitigating how much actually made it to the jungle floor. With the dim thrum of the rain, treading quietly was a simple task. Moss thicker than ornate rugs cushioned her feet, making it all the easier. She almost wished that she wasn't wearing shoes.

Still slinking on the balls of her feet, she crossed the camp and came to Roy's tree. He could tell she was there, and Ariel heard him speak before she could alert him to her presence.

"I'd forgotten how hard you could punch." He glanced at her. "I doubt Vilch will forget after today," he said.

Ariel smiled discreetly, crouching in front of him. "Oh? You forgot the night I beat your head in for cheating in Omens?"

"I did *not* cheat in that stupid card game," he insisted. "You were just angry because I won all of your gin money." There was a sliver of levity in his tone. "And if I recall, you tried to steal someone else's bottle and started a tavern brawl."

She scoffed in mock annoyance before snickering at the memory. It had been a blurry night. There were many gaps, but the constant was him being there. "You and I still cleared the place out."

He exhaled in a quiet chuckle. "They threw us into the chicken coop. We woke up covered in scratches."

"I remember it differently." Ariel looked down as mirth gave way to guilt. "Was Sam right? Should I have killed Vilch? I keep fearing that I've made the wrong choice. What if he and the rest come back? We can't afford to just fight them off every few days."

Roy was silent, which could have meant anything. Her instincts told her that he was thinking. Even under his drawn hood, she could visualize his creased brow.

"You would have done it," Ariel whispered.

It was an observation, but as it left her mouth it sounded like an accusation. She cursed herself. This was her chance to make things right, and all she had done was insult him.

"I would have," he muttered. "But that wouldn't have made it the right thing. You spared a life. It's not something someone like him deserves, but you did it. It doesn't mean you're wrong. It means you're merciful, and it's one of the things I've missed about you the most. You're honorable, and you're kind." His words mingled with the plodding of rain. "But your kindness is wasted on me, Ariel. I attacked you, and I've killed, and devoured, and I can't take any of it back. I'm sorry. For everything. Leonard may be to blame for this curse, but I'm too weak to resist it. And that weakness hurt you."

"You don't have to be sorry. I forgive you," she said gently. "We both made mistakes that night." The unbearable memory of her drawn arrow, pointed between his eyebrows, made her wince. It had been close, *too close*. "I'm sorry too."

"There's nothing to forgive," he reassured.

Neither had a response. The jungle and its symphony of wildlife had unexpectedly quieted. Ariel suddenly held out a hand. Joskine's head drooped further over to their right.

"Going off to find some trouble?" Roy said, glancing at her calloused fingers. Those words had greeted her every time he'd caught her trying to sneak into the Frostspring Refuge wine cellar as youths.

She replied with her favorite saying, "A chance encounter wouldn't hurt."

Firebreather

James woke to Samira's hand over his mouth. Her silhouette loomed over him, and all he could see was the faint glow of her eyes. She signaled for quiet. He nodded, reaching for his short sword at his side. The rain had stopped, and the quiet swishing of the leaves above them persisted in a quiet drone. Based on her movement, James could immediately tell that something was wrong. He furrowed his brow in inquiry.

"They're here," she whispered, "Vilch followed us, and I can't find Roy or Ariel." The grogginess immediately drained from James's body. He jolted upward into a sitting position, hand on his sword.

"What do we do?" he stammered.

Samira rubbed her head and put a hand on the hilt of her longsword, "We greet them. Our top priority is making sure that Roy and Ariel aren't hurt." She pointed to where the remnants of their campfire still smoldered. "Go now. Have something where you can make a fire. We may need it if a fight breaks out." James rose and rushed to the center of the camp. His boots slipped a little in the moss, bumping into Leonard.

Raslena's Champion stood with Joskine and Badlai, grimly looking out into the shadowy brush at the edge of the camp, leading to a steep incline back the way they came. James followed their vision. Around a dozen figures stood just outside the area. One in front had clearly distinguishable black wiry hair.

So it was true; Vilch had followed them. The beating Ariel had given him was not enough to deter a pursuit. And now Ariel and Roy had been captured. It was only speculation if Vilch would negotiate before killing them. Or possibly worse, perhaps Vilch would cause Roy to let the creature out. He didn't know if that was even possible, but the mere thought of it was enough to terrify him.

He fished a smoking branch from the fire pit that they had dug earlier. Using his senses, he was still able to determine that it was hot enough to reignite a flame. Closing his eyes, he reached into the heat with his mind and willed it to grow. James felt a flash of warmth across his face and opened his eyes. The branch was now alight with fire. Grim shadows crossed Leonard's face, nodding approval. Coming into view, Amry groggily looked at their stony faces and immediately reached for his knife.

James followed Leonard and Joskine to where Samira stood. Badlai and Amry tailed gingerly, a few paces behind. Samira's arms were crossed, her head lowered as she glowered at Vilch, who stood with a sword in hand. The captain of the *Greed Sun*'s face was disfigured and blackened by the blows Ariel had landed earlier that day, and the bruises showed no sign of shrinking. Standing in the flickering light of James's torch, the welts were even more pronounced. He and his crew stood with their backs to the slope, knowing they were trapped against it but not caring. This sent James's nerves into a frenzy.

"What a wonderful surprise, Vilch. You should have sent word ahead that you were coming," Leonard said, his swashbuckling tone having a harder edge. Vilch said nothing.

"What did you do with 'em?" Joskine demanded.

"Shut your mouth, drowning traitorous wretch," one of the enemy crewmen spat.

"I would very much like to know too, Vilch," Samira hissed. "Where are Ariel and Roy? Tell us now."

James noticed Vilch's eyes narrow slightly. The captain had clearly been hoping to catch them while they slept. Something about his reaction to Samira's question seemed odd, as if he were surprised to hear that Ariel and Roy were missing as well.

"It's too late for them," Vilch shrugged. Samira and Leonard stiffened. "Your blood will water the jungle too, and your traitor friends." He scowled at Joskine, Badlai, and Amry.

"He's lying," James said. "He has no idea where they are." The man reared his hateful stare at him for a moment before turning back to Samira and Leonard.

The metal of James's sword hissed quietly as he drew the weapon from his scabbard and pointed it at the enemy sailors. Leonard hefted his mace. Samira silently drew her sword. Her left hand began to sputter with electricity.

The sound of cracking wood rang through the camp. Samira's head turned, analyzing the noise. James could see her scout's mind working furiously to determine the source of the crash.

Leonard gasped, feeling the reverberations through the earth. He dropped to one knee and placed a cautious hand upon the moss. James struggled to remember how Leonard had put it when he had asked about his friend's gift. He was able to feel vibrations of anything moving on the ground in a close vicinity, but there was a limit. Pure earth was easier to hear through, and he could only register large disturbances if he was just using his feet. If he had felt the tremors before using his hand...

"Well, that is not ideal," Leonard muttered.

James's questions were ripped from him as the trees to his left were splintered by a gigantic pale green mass. Yellowed teeth clacked together with excited starvation, and an eye the color of soured milk blinked in the direction of its new prey. The thundering steps the creature took shook the leaves on the trees. It looked to be in the shape of a gigantic lizard with a large, jagged hump on its back. As it shrieked, James stared in horror into its black-gummed mouth.

"Striking dragons," Samira cursed.

The great beast's wail resembled two dissonant screams that pummeled the ears and froze the senses. It was nothing like the mighty roar of fables. Teachings of the Temple had always portrayed dragons as majestic yet powerful creatures, the pinnacle of the natural world. It was taught that even the gods respected the creatures enough to leave them alone. But the beast he saw before him shattered those fantasies. The off-green skin that covered the animal hung loosely and had a dull sheen. Its vaguely reptilian features were distorted by the sagging skin that covered it, seeming to dangle from the four prominent horns on its head.

It crashed through the grove on four legs toward the standoff of Chosen and mariners. The front legs were much bulkier and taller, giving it the appearance of having hunched shoulders. Its black gums pulled back from the yellow needle teeth, and a barbed tongue the color of dried blood slithered through the air. The putrid smell of the creature's gaseous breath reached James just as Leonard tackled him to the slimy ground.

A blast of bright blue flame erupted from the dragon's mouth and eviscerated the spot where he had been not a moment before. Samira, Joskine, and Badlai leapt behind the trees closest to them. Leonard hauled James behind the craggy rock formation. Amry was separated and fled behind the trees to the right of the dragon with Vilch and his crew. The mossy floor of the grove was aflame in an instant. Fresh green growth became ash, and smoke sprung into the air. Clothing singed by the fiery attack, James gawked in horror as the behemoth set its opaque eyes on the members of Vilch's crew that were unlucky enough to be caught in the open.

The next burst of blue fire enveloped the trapped sailors immediately. James guessed that this monster exhaled a colorless gas that it then ignited. Not even having an opportunity to scream, the crewmen were incinerated, eyes and teeth melting in an instant. They fell to the ground, blackened. James sensed bile rising in his throat. A deep snort left the dragon's mouth, and it craned its long neck forward, the folds of its wrinkled skin stretching outward. Using its needle-like fangs to skewer its prey, the beast swallowed the charred humans whole. A sickening, gelatinous slosh emanated from the its throat as it gulped its prey one by one like a pelican.

An arc of lightning rushed from behind a tree and bashed the dragon's shoulder. James looked closer to see Samira crouched behind the tree. Stumbling, the beast bellowed but did not fall. The pale green skin had torn where the lightning hit it, revealing a deep green gloss underneath.

"She hurt it!" James exclaimed over the screech of the dragon.

Leonard shook his head quickly and clutched his mace. "No, she just made it angrier. This thing must have just left its cocoon. It's supposed to shed the skin over time so the scales underneath can come in. That's why so many dragons don't make it to adulthood. Because the skin is so soft. But those scales are basically as hard as diamonds."

James looked and saw that Leonard was right. The scales underneath the skin gleamed in the firelight. Samira rolled from behind her tree to another as the creature ignited another blast, melting her previous position. Part of the blue flames licked the shedding skin of the beast, causing it to be set alight. How was anyone supposed to kill it? The dragon continued to pursue Samira as the flame spread across its body, shriveling and burning the dead skin as it went and exposing the unyielding scales beneath.

"What do we do?" James's mind raced. He had been so frightened that his torch had burned out.

"We don't get eaten, and we build from there," Leonard said, fumbling with the knife in his boot. "It's a bad idea to engage a dragon, even indirectly. We can maybe run away and lose it in the trees, but we'll be looking over our shoulders all night." He looked back to where Samira ducked away from the beast. "Sam will know which way we're going. She won't be far behind."

Surveying the raging glade, now aflame and building in smoke, James saw an opening. The dragon had given up pursuing Samira and was now seeking easier prey. Vilch's crew members scattered in terror up the slope behind them. Screams of the men and women wafted through the smoke. With the beast distracted, the north opened up behind it. He could already see Joskine and Badlai inching toward the opposite direction of the battle. Locking eyes with him, the man beckoned him to cross.

Azure and orange flames raced across the moss on the ground, scorching soil and cracking mud. Its skin was almost completely burned off now, showing sleek scales. The hump on the creature's back had not been a hump at all but wings trapped under the skin. They stretched as the skin burned free, the color of dark earth and shadowed emerald. Its wings expanded ever outward, bumping against the nearby trees that still stood.

He felt Leonard's solid hand grip his shoulder. "Run!" James was shoved forward into the fray. Catching his fall, his feet began to move of their own accord, sprinting toward the opposite edge of the grove. The dragon swung its massive tail to the side. It was still pursuing the sailors. James dropped to the dry ground, sliding underneath the tail. Thick as two tree trunks lashed together, it passed overhead by mere feet. Leonard rolled under the tail and immediately righted himself, still sprinting toward Joskine and Badlai.

James scrambled to his feet and followed. The sound of his own breathing was muffled and overpowered by the dragon's stomping, its deafening wail. Another blast of fire rocked the jungle. He could feel the heat rattle his senses. It disoriented him. He could see nothing when he felt outward.

A wall of flames taller than his waist loomed ahead of them. Focusing on the sight of the fire, he drew his arms outward quickly. Sputtering, the flames parted just fast enough for him and Leonard to dive through. They rolled through the scalding dirt and clambered toward the tree where Joskine and Badlai waited for them. Soot was smeared over their faces, but their eyes were white with horror.

James could see the reflection of the gruesome scene behind him in their wide eyes.

"Where are the others?" Joskine cried out. A few embers rested in his beard. Badlai's green eyes darted around the trees.

"We don't know!" Leonard shouted back over the blaze, coughing. "We could use Ariel and Roy to put this out. It doesn't matter. We need to reach Samira and get away from here."

Crescent-Beard looked around wildly, as if just realizing he lost something. "Where's the boy?"

A deep, cold fear stabbed through James's lower back. They had lost Amry. He had been separated from him and Leonard. He looked at Leonard, his face taking a hard expression. "We need to go back," James said.

Leonard's shout of protest was rendered silent by another explosion, lighting up his worried face. James turned to Joskine and Badlai. The pair nodded and rushed to follow him as he sprinted back into the burning glade. He could hear Leonard swearing loudly behind him and scrabbling to keep up.

The dragon was still visible, leaving a trail of flames and ash that carved an open wound into the jungle. Flashes of radiant light flickered near the beast's head. Samira was still fighting. The fight's path of destruction had transformed a once uneven and luscious terrain into a level wasteland in the middle of the jungle.

James's focus was on the dragon ahead to such an extent that he almost missed the silhouetted figure of a person jumping into their path. His boots skimmed across the cracked earth in protest as he halted.

Still holding his sword, Vilch stood in front of him, atrociously burned. His shirt melted into his skin. Patches of hair stood on end atop his head. Steam rose from burns on his welted face. James only recognized the black eyes glowering at him.

"You did this," Vilch rasped. "You brought a curse on us. But if I'm going, I will see you drowning come with me." He pointed his sword at James.

Drawing his short sword, James glanced to the side at his friends. "Go help Samira and the boy." Nodding, Leonard and the sailors ran after the battle raging to the west. Leonard looked back over his shoulder once and then charged off.

Flames still crackled around James as he assumed the stance Roy had taught him, pointing his sword into the space between him and the captain. The chipped blade still shimmered when he turned it over, catching the blue and orange flames that devoured the life around them. Now that the dragon had moved farther away, his senses began to pick up the heat sources around him. He could feel the fires, the scorched ground, Vilch.

Trusting his instincts and Roy's teachings, James leaned and parried a slash from Vilch. He responded with a jab of his own. The two circled each other. Vilch's breathing was labored, wheezing.

James attacked with a downward cut, trying to catch the captain off guard. Vilch blocked his attack and whirled with a vicious swipe toward his stomach. Even in incredible pain, Vilch fought with the intention of seeing him dead. Vilch attacked again and again, each time putting hatred into his swing. Watching his opponent, James readied himself.

Stepping forward into the captain's downward slice, James batted the sword arm away with his left hand. His right hand ran Vilch through with his sword. Vilch's dark eyes lit up in pain. James drew the sword back, causing those black eyes to flutter. The fight had been remarkably short. James knelt in the dry, dusty earth next to the captain. Vilch collapsed to the ground, gasping.

"I'm sorry," he said, looking sternly at Vilch's clouding eyes. "But you can't threaten them."

Vilch turned his head away from him, refusing to look at him before going limp. The ground around them steamed. James groaned as he got up. His joints cracked and popped along with the fires he stood amongst. Vilch had given him no choice. The flames produced a great whoosh, growing slightly. It didn't make sense. This wasn't his doing. His mind clicked to the answer just as the foul gas breath met his nostrils.

Diving to the ground, James slammed against the singed dirt, and the ignited gas bloomed into a blue fireball. Feeling the back of his shirt catch fire, he rolled over, smothering the flame and commanding it out with his mind at the same time. The adrenaline coursing through his stomach overwhelmed the pulling feeling in his gut as he used his gift. It hadn't felt scorching but still warm and growing hotter every second. He could tell that his gift wouldn't save him from whatever fire this was.

A second dragon, even larger and still covered in the hideous pale skin, pushed through the trees and shrieked at him. Not even Dhorh had sent such a sharp, paralyzing scythe through his nerves. Covering his ears, James looked frantically for anything he could hide behind. The burned jungle had been cleansed. Bare earth stretched too far for him to stumble to safety, as if he were lost at sea again. But no one else was here this time.

Like an idiot, he had shooed his friends away, and now the consequences of his decision would quite literally fry him. Smelling the gas again, James ducked and scrambled backward, missing the next blast by a mere handbreadth. His hair singed and produced the uncomfortable smell of himself being cooked.

The ground bent underneath the behemoth's heavy, six-clawed feet. Each of its claws was the size of his leg, pointed and gripping the newly molded earth beneath it. James's arms twitched helplessly, going limp as the beast inhaled, ready to smother him in its flammable breath. James couldn't move, couldn't scream, couldn't blink or close his eyes. All he could do was watch. A forceful gust of wind whirled its way through the dragon-made clearing. He tensed, waiting for the heat that would envelop him. The wind intensified.

As the dragon clicked its barbed tongue, igniting the gas, the flurry of wind spiraled, swirling the flame. It disrupted the path of the explosion, causing blue licks of fire to roar through the air in a spinning column that doused itself on the dragon's face and neck. Screaming in frustration rather than pain, the beast reared backward away from James. Fire spread rapidly over the green skin, exposing the shimmering scales beneath. A voice called to him.

"Why are you just standing there? The fire! *Use the fire!*"

The next instant, Roy and Ariel were beside him. Her gold hair blazed in the light of the fire, and her tattoos rippled as she drew an arrow back. Letting it loose, the shaft zinged toward the beast, hooking into its nostril. So there were parts of the dragon they could still hit. Startled, it thrashed its long neck in every direction.

Roy's hand seized James's shoulder, jerking him out of his daze. "We can't let you stumble your way through this one, do you hear me? We need what you did with Dhorh. Show me that it wasn't a fluke!" Roy barked. James couldn't tell if it was the different colors of firelight, but Roy's eyes were shifting between blue and orange. Roy's words from the desert punched through his head. *What did we save you for?*

Jostling his head quickly, he nodded at Roy's eyes. "Leave it to us," he said, nodding toward Ariel. A brief, approving smile appeared before Roy turned toward the other battle, still leading away. James saw Roy meet Ariel's eyes, then his fellow Chosen whirled and tore off to the west.

Coming out of its surprise, the dragon bellowed at James and Ariel, stretching its newly unrestrained wings and blotting out the smoke-filled sky. He slid his sword into its sheath as she nocked another arrow.

"I have an idea," he yelled over the creature's stomping. They both dove away from a blast of its breath. The fireball burned in his vision, turning everything blue. "Can you do what you did before, disrupting its breath?" He blinked, eyes tearing up from the brightness. "If you can keep it from roasting us, that leaves an opening for me."

"To do what?" She raised an eyebrow.

James reached out behind him with his hand, and at the same time he felt outward with his senses. Samira's lesson from before the storm spoke to him, and he grasped at the knowledge. *Like an extension of my body,* he thought. Closing his fist, he felt his soul grapple with the flame that popped behind him. The pull in his gut no longer felt like an exertion but a burst of adrenaline. He could feel the flame feeding him and feel his hold on it. It was warm and powerful.

Before them, the dragon exhaled, coating the air in its noxious wheeze.

"Go, *now!*" he yelled. Without hesitation, Ariel thrust her hands outward and whipped them to the right. Wind roared across the battlefield and scrambled the air. The gas swirled away from them again, causing the fireball to miss them entirely. Tightening his physical and spiritual grip on the fire, James hurled a blazing projectile of his own at the dragon's face. It caught the beast in the side of the neck with a thunderous shockwave. Stumbling, it turned its milky eyes toward him, glaring with animalistic hatred. Black gums parting to bare its teeth, it gave a screeching hiss. The earth rocked back and forth as it righted itself.

Just as he had figured, the fireball hadn't punctured the scales, but the force had been enough to push it back. It dug its back claws into the dirt, using one of its front paws to grip a nearby tree. The tree snapped off at the base and slapped the ground under the weight of its foot. Ariel glanced at him with approval. Heat, warm and calming, circulated through his veins, as if his blood was made of sunlight. The creature drew air into its lungs, intending to saturate the clearing in fuel.

This time, Ariel needed no prompt. Her tempest buffeted the dragon and dispelled the gas streaming from its mouth, disarming it once again. Another ball of flame, thrown by James, slammed into the beast's flank. The warmth within him was still growing, becoming hotter with each movement.

Blast after blast, Ariel and James countered the dragon's attacks, sending fire back at it in strikes that it had no experience in defending. Its shrieks drowned out the thunderous cracks of the explosions, and the force of them was keeping it from getting back up. *We can keep it from killing us, but it's all we can do,* he thought. It was one thing to keep the beast down, but they couldn't make it stay that way. There was no other choice. They had to kill it. It was too big to trap, making the fight extremely simple. The problem was that it was so scorching *big.* It looked up from the last attack James had thrown at it, bubbly, dark blood oozing from its black gums and mouth.

That was it, its *mouth*. Its scales were too hard to puncture, and it covered most of the creature's body, but the maw of the beast was soft and exploitable. Even so, James doubted any of Ariel's arrows could do enough damage on their own to gravely injure the dragon. Despite how effective they were at keeping it down, his technique of hurling fire at it didn't seem to have the results they needed either.

Ariel shouted at him, snapping him out of his thoughts just before the beast shook its massive wings, causing a blistering gust to roll over the dirt they stood on. James ducked as Ariel charged in front of him and ripped her arms downward, splitting the wall of air in two. Trees far behind them were blown over. They cracked with strain. The sudden scramble for defense had given the dragon all the time it needed to right itself, and it now lumbered toward them.

Ariel's buffeting winds had blown out all but a few of the fires that crackled around James. His ammunition was largely depleted. They didn't have enough power to kill it, but that meant one possibility.

Only the dragon had enough power.

Prickly teeth lunged at him hungrily as if they were needles intent on stealing his blood. James leapt to the side, skidding through the dirt on his shoulder and tearing off his sleeve. Hot soil and ash rubbed against his skin, sanding it down, making him grunt at the gritty sting. The dragon turned, shaking a carriage's worth of earth from its jaws. It was too close, *much* too close for his taste. The odor of gas hit his nostrils.

The blast exploded directly in front of his face. Scorching blue heat charged toward him as he instinctively held his hands out in defense. His stomach felt as if it were being inverted, and his nostril hairs singed. But as he held out his hands, his forearms and biceps strained, holding the flame back. James's senses took over, grasping the heat and holding it away from himself, between him and the behemoth. The hand of his soul gripped the licking flames.

Rearing back, the dragon's chest puffed as it inhaled deeply.

James screamed straight in the direction of the creature, not knowing where Ariel was, "Make him swallow it! Send it back!"

Ariel understood immediately. As the dragon wheezed a rush of gaseous breath straight at James, she thrust her hands together in a conical gesture. The gas retreated and funneled back into the creature's black jaws, causing a deep, metallic rasp to sound from within its throat. Its milky eyes bulged as it choked on its own vapor, darting around in panic.

Throwing his hands over his head, James loosed the flames back in the direction of the animal with a hoarse cry. The sky turned a bright shade of blue as the fireball arced toward its target. Ariel threw herself to the ground, hands over her head. James followed suit.

The fiery bolt flew straight into the mouth of the dragon, igniting the gas that Ariel had just choked it with. The resulting eruption vaporized the beast's head and neck, and the few standing trees in the area caught ablaze, blowing away to ash in an instant as if they were already made of dust. Soot and dirt plumed into the air, sent aloft by the crashing of the creature's body.

James squirmed in the ash, dumbstruck by what he and Ariel had done. It shouldn't have been possible. Just two and a half weeks ago, he had barely been able to keep a *candle* alight. Their continuous slog through the jungle had been more effective physical training than even Samira's sadistic regimen. Even through the adrenaline, he could feel the inner heat eating away at his muscles, his innards. He couldn't just let loose like that. Some burns, pink and angry, were showing on his now sleeveless arms, and they weren't from the dragon's fire. They would heal, but they served as a reminder of what could've happened had he gone too far.

Ariel staggered over, gagging on the smoke. The air had become noticeably thick. She held out a hand, straining as she hauled him upward. "Good thinking there. A little messy, however. I doubt we can pull that off a second time." New fires blazed around them.

He smirked. "Not with that attitude we can't."

She rolled her eyes but returned the smile. "Perhaps our luck will stretch a bit further."

***

His boots slid in this semi-molten soil too easily. Roy was struggling to keep his pace without falling over his own feet, slipping every few yards. He had heard explosions behind him but had forced himself not to look back. James and Ariel would handle it. James had seemed confident, and Roy's instincts had told him that the newcomer would handle himself. Plus, he had Ariel helping him.

Trees blurred past him and fires flashed, making his surroundings flicker. The dragon loomed ahead, still razing the jungle around it in an attempt to kill the remaining humans that evaded it. Brightness glared around the beast, and the earth rose and fell, trying to throw it off balance. Samira and Leonard were still alive then. However, it didn't look like they were making any progress. Neither of them had a power that could directly penetrate those scales. By all accounts, the fight that he was rushing into looked hopeless, and that hopelessness made him furious.

Every fight, every kill, every injury he had taken, they had all been in the hopes for a better life at the end. He had seen a glimpse of that future just tonight, and these great drowning dragons were dangerously close to taking it away. His thoughts struggled to keep up with his feet, and his adrenaline and emotion clouded his mind.

That split second, he made a choice. Perhaps rashly.

"Help me kill this dragon," he said, panting as he ran. He felt the icy presence stir within him. He threw off his cloak as he ran. It billowed behind him before coming to a rest in the heated soil.

"I want freedom."

"You won't get that," he rebuffed, "But you will get a fight. Just this once." The dragon wasn't going down. A beast that big could only be taken down by something closer to its size.

"And if I refuse?"

"Then we both die."

"I'm not easily killed, boy."

Roy glared at nothing, his turquoise eyes slowly melting into a bright, malevolent orange. "Are you willing to risk it? Because you know that I am." Charodon's silence was the only answer, but Roy could feel the frigidness steadily spreading throughout his veins. His senses were dulling, and his feet pounded harder into the earth. Dathos drown him, he was probably making a deadly mistake, but in the moment he could think of no other option. A miniature storm brewed around him, swirling and darkening his vision.

Monster Against Monster

His mace shattered the ground beneath it as Leonard brought it down again. Earth flowed, solidified, shifted, and changed at his whim, staggering the dragon. Its green scales were covered in dirt and soot, and smoke curled off its body where Samira had struck it. No matter what they threw at it, the scales had not cracked or even wavered. Meanwhile, the beast had been dismantling the jungle around them, making it nigh impossible to hide. A number of felled trees sat to his direct right. The branches had been seared off by the heat around them, but the trunks still remained intact. He and Samira fought the dragon at the bottom of a steep incline that extended to his right. Toppled trees and those that remained upright were still a bit further up.

Near those trees, the crew of the *Greed Sun* cowered. Joskine and Badlai, having found Amry with them, stood before them. Joskine screamed at the remaining sailors to get up. It looked as if they were standing on the edge of two different dimensions, one being lush, green utopia and the other a fiery desolation.

He willed the earth underneath him to liquefy, swallowing the dragon's back left foot before hardening it again.

Trapped, the creature pulled ferociously with its hind leg, cracking the ground. Its ironlike tail came sweeping around before catching him in the ribs and sending him soaring backward. Leonard landed on the balls of his feet, but the momentum still caused him to somersault backward, dragging his face and back through the dirt up the steep slope. He grunted as he slammed into the trunk of a thick, viny tree. The air rushed from his chest.

A grimace split his face, feeling a few of his ribs break with a sharp stab as he slid to the base of the trunk. Another crack of lightning sounded, and the rainforest around him lit up. Samira's lightning caught the dragon in the snout, making it reel backward but otherwise doing no damage. Its eerie eyes glowered in her direction, igniting another explosion of blue fire into the tree line.

This was just one creature, yet it caused apocalyptic destruction. Leonard peered into the trees further down the slope and caught a glimpse of Samira diving behind a massive tree's wide girth. Catching this movement, the beast lashed at the tree with its claws, slicing deep into the wood of the trunk. The tree moaned as it drooped, not yet falling. Fire devoured the once-green vicinity of the battle. Where was James? *Don't tell me that he can't beat Vilch with a sword*. Raslena crush him, he would never hear the end of it from Samira if he left James to die.

Frustration continued to well up inside his throat. This was getting them nowhere, *less* than nowhere actually. Samira was down there fighting a dragon all on her own, and he couldn't even take care of himself.

"*Useless,*" his mother's voice snarked, "*You're of no use to anyone. Thank the gods that your father couldn't see his useless excuse for a son. You disgrace his memory.*"

"Shut up." He knew that the voice was just a memory, but he said it aloud anyway. He'd joined the Imperial Infantry to prove he was worth something, but a not insignificant part of him had done it to prove her wrong. He had learned discipline, forced himself to shut the words of his mother out. It didn't matter if he was useless. He had only to be worthy of his squadmates' trust, and he would prove to someone that he was worth something.

The training, the battles, the realization that his power could be used to help his company, all of it had proven his mother wrong. One day, he would return home, the commander of his own Aroch, and show her. He had become strong, and she had taken no part in it.

"You abandoned them. You betrayed them. You're nothing more than the same coward that ran away from my home." Her voice insisted. *"You want to leave them, even now."*

He realized that he *did* want to run away. The dragon's snaggle-toothed maw turned upward toward the sky, unleashing an air-splitting howl. It made him remember the roar of Charodon three years ago and the unshakable terror that had consumed him. The terror had moved his feet before he could think, and before he could decipher what had happened he was sprinting in the opposite direction. It had cost him everything. His friendships with Samira and Roy, his standing in the empire, even Ariel was terse with him when Roy was mentioned. The same terror shook him now, but a greater terror held him in place. The terror of his friends dying and not being there to help them.

Standing quickly, he flinched again as his broken ribs prodded at his innards. He could see the crew still cowering behind fallen trees and sweating rocks. His spiky hair bobbed, his head turning in the direction of the beast. It was directly below him with about a dozen trees in the way.

Infantry training taking over, he strode to the sailors, back straight and resting his mace on his shoulder. "Form up! We're taking this dragon down, and I need all of you to follow my orders exactly!"

They gaped at him, still in shock, not able to say anything.

He brought his mace down against a boulder a quarter his size, turning it to dust with one swing. "I said *form up*! Otherwise you can hop down this slope and serve yourselves up to the beast. I don't crushing care either way, but choose quickly!"

Joskine and Badlai immediately stood straight and nodded at Leonard. Amry followed, then another four soldiers. Two women and two men. *Soldiers? Is that what they are now?* The remaining three stayed where they were.

He gave a cocky chortle, the same kind he'd gotten from his commanding officer his first day. "Very good. Now, we'll have one shot at this. If we take its mobility away, we can possibly make an opening for Sam to kill it. That's where you come in. We're going to make a rockslide." He squinted at their determined faces. "I need you to find all of the heavy rocks and fallen trees that you can roll to this exact spot. I'll trap the beast by holding its legs. Then, once it's trapped, you release the rocks up here. This should be enough force to break its legs. Look for my signal. Sam will light up the sky, and that's when you release. Any questions?"

Leonard was answered with determined stares, all of them looking toward the dragon around a hundred and fifty feet away.

"Good! Now get moving!"

As his new soldiers dashed off to take care of the debris, Leonard propelled himself down the slope toward the fight. Gritting his teeth, he hardened the ground underneath his feet, allowing him to push off harder, gaining speed with each step.

The dragon was too focused on Samira to see him coming. Trees flashed past him, sometimes a little too close. It was getting harder to control his direction at this speed, but he couldn't slow down. His limbs began to feel a bit heavier, slowly being weighed down by the toll of his power. That was why he relied on the soldiers to start the rockslide. He could do it himself, but it would take all of his concentration to keep the dragon pinned in place. The air was thunderous in his ears.

Another bright flash crackled through the trees. Samira hit the creature with another bolt of lightning, causing it to flinch in acknowledgement but not in pain. He could see other black spots in the ground around the monster where she had missed, still struggling with her aim.

Leonard neared the base of the slope, dragging his mace behind him with one hand. The metal head of the weapon bounced as it struck off rocks and earth, creating a narrow canyon in the ground. He was close, within twelve feet of the beast when he attacked its flank. Swinging his mace forward, Leonard willed the earth below him to attack. A gargantuan spike of rock grew rapidly from the earth, sharpening to a point and stabbing at the dragon's belly. The earthlance cracked and broke as it crashed against the deep green scales, but it pushed the monster back, off balance. Leonard brought the mace straight down, head first, commanding the earth below the dragon to liquefy.

Bellowing in confusion, the dragon thrashed as its clawed feet sank into the dirt like quicksand. Leonard pushed the head of his mace deeper into the ground in front of him, sweating. Seeing an opportunity, Samira dashed through the trees and ran to him. She was panting and had several burns on her clothing. Some of the fire looked like it had made it through her right sleeve, adding an angry-looking burn to the web of scars already there, like a coat of paint on split wood.

"What are you doing?" It was not an angry question.

"I'm trapping its legs. The soldiers up above are about to start a rockslide to break its legs and immobilize it." He grunted. "Then we can figure out how to kill it." The dragon released a blast of flame into the air above it in protest. Its legs were submerged in the soft ground up to the knees. "When I say, throw lightning in the air. That's the signal I told them to watch for."

Samira nodded before going silent, her eyes looking beyond the dragon, "No." She gasped. "No, no, no, no *no*."

Leonard could sense it before he saw it, a heavy pair of running footfalls on the earth, too heavy to be James's. He looked into the swirling smoke and dust behind the flailing dragon and saw two orange pinpricks of light, rapidly growing larger. A rage-filled, murderous roar assaulted his ears. The roar had persisted throughout his nightmares for years now, but this time was very much real.

"Signal now, *now!*" he shouted.

Samira flung lightning straight above her, illuminating everything within a mile. The radiance of the lightning reflected off Charodon's gray-green scales but failed to shine brighter than the bloodlust in its eyes.

Barely able to move, the dragon looked up just in time to see Charodon crash into it. Leonard hardened the earth around the winged creature's feet with a sharp twist of his mace. A jarring crack rang through the clearing as the dragon buckled under the force of Charodon's attack, its knees snapping out of place with startling force. Leonard could feel a shockwave rumble through the earth as Charodon, much smaller than the dragon, still clobbered it with terrifying savagery. The Eye of Nature cut off the beast's wail of pain with a viscous swipe to its jaw, swatting ten of its ragged teeth from its gums. A thick swirl of mist whipped around Charodon, furious and giddy. The teeth clattered to the ground some feet away like a bushel of reeds.

Charodon struck rapidly, strengthening with each blow, claws screeching off the crystalline scales of his opponent. Even he was proving incapable of getting through its tough exterior. Leonard watched, dumbfounded as Charodon continued to roar in malice at the dragon, spewing water from the gills on his neck, punching in vain at the dragon's scales, even trying to bite at its throat.

Grunting as Samira tackled him, Leonard felt rather than saw the rumble of rocks and debris cascade past him and collide with the dragon and Charodon in an ear-splitting crash. His vision rattled along with the ground beneath him. He lost his hold on the handle of his mace. Samira gripped his arm painfully. They shielded each other from the rockslide as it rolled past them, piling up against the dragon's ensnared body. Ash and soil were flung into the air by the momentum of the spinning boulders. As the last of the debris crashed to a halt. Leonard and Samira looked upward at the dragon. His eyes widened. *It's not possible.* he thought.

The behemoth still lived, staring directly at him with its milky eye. Even battered by the rocks and immobile, its wings stirred and tail whipped. Water from Charodon's gills dripped from its body, the coldness of it making the beast shiver. It wheezed, inhaling shakily, intending to breathe more death in their direction.

"Hit it now!" he screamed to Samira.

Samira hurled lightning overhand straight at the dragon. Even with the velocity of her attack, the bolt would not have made it through the scales, but Charodon had given her an opening. The salt water from his gills had seeped between the impenetrable scales, creating a pathway for the electricity to travel.

The lightning ran through the water and then through the dragon, scorching its insides. Its lengthy body shimmering and convulsing, the creature did not wail.

Samira hit it again and again rapidly. Involuntarily thrashing, it was already dead, steaming after just two bolts of lightning. Samira lowered her hand and bent at the knees, vomiting from the smell of the carcass, a smell that closely resembled rotten fish and burned skin.

Leonard's hair swayed on his head as he retched, reacting to Samira's sickness. Battlefield wounds didn't bother him in the slightest, but watching someone vomit was sure to make him do the same. He wiped his mouth with the back of his hand and spat. The taste of dirt lingered on his lips as he had just pulled that hand from the soil. Looking back up at the dragon, he saw the steam from the carcass begin to clear enough to focus on what stood behind it.

Charodon was still there.

The Eye of Nature stood on top of the rubble, malice painted clearly in his crouch. Water still pulsed through the gills on his neck. Dark orange eyes were fixed on him and Samira. They had stolen Charodon's kill, and now his bloodlust and fury would be directed at them. Mist curled around the devil, and was that more *lightning* flickering around it?

"Roy," he whispered, holding his hands up at shoulder level, "I know you're still in there. We need you back."

Charodon's reptilian sneer regarded him coldly. Had he killed Ariel? The thought turned Leonard's stomach, twisting it with a rage of his own. No, he could feel that hadn't happened. No matter how Charodon had wrestled control away from Roy, there was no way that Roy would let Ariel get hurt. Leonard's heart was galloping in his chest. A familiar, shameful fear clasped a hand on his throat.

Samira had stood up to her full height. She held her left hand behind her, ready to hurl lightning at the slightest movement. A slight smell of ozone crept into Leonard's nostrils. Her arm twitched and shook as she held it aloft. She was nearly at her limit. "Roy, please," she pleaded. Her voice cracked.

He took a deep breath, letting the urge to run leave him. The terror stayed, but today he would face it. Leonard's face stretched into a grim line, his stubble bristling, and he gripped his weapon tightly.

Scrabbling could be heard behind them. Leonard turned his head slowly to see the soldiers making their way down the slope, making an unbelievable racket. They kicked over stones and banged their weapons against trees in triumph. They had won. The dragon was dead. They had not seen the horror—in many ways a *worse* horror—that stood just beyond the dead reptilian. He held up a hand to signal for them to quiet themselves, but it was too late.

Like a string from a bow, Charodon charged in the direction of the soldiers. Samira and Leonard protectively stepped into his path, weapons aloft. Her shaking hand buzzed with electricity. Charodon's blazing orange eyes again settled on them.

Ready to swing with whatever strength he still carried, Leonard held his mace aloft. Something changed just then. A spec of blue appeared in Charodon's eye, slowly growing against the orange. Roy was fighting back!

As the Eye of Nature drew closer, Leonard charged forward, holding the mace in two hands at his side. The leather grip of the handle dug into his calloused palms. His heavy limbs threatened to drop altogether, but still he held them up.

Dense thuds from Charodon's feet jarred his heartbeat and shook his broken ribs. He ignored the pain and horror as best he could.

Using all of the energy left in his legs, Leonard sprung from the ground, extending the earth below him to propel him further upward, cracked ribs shrieking. He sailed upward, upward still, until he was level with the false crocodile's grin of the monster. He screamed a challenge at the terror he had run from. Swinging with every ounce of strength, he pounded the mace into the side of Charodon's head. At the impact, the monster's orange eyes reverted to Roy's calm turquoise, and it dropped to the ground, legs still pumping. The blow had been what Roy needed to take back the reins. Only when Charodon's body began to shrink and transform did Leonard realize that he was still in the air, his feet still hovering.

Wind swirled and pulsed around him in a frantic burst. Knowing this trick well, he looked toward the east and saw Ariel. She and James were trudging through the rock and sparse fires toward him. Releasing him to the ground, Ariel clambered through the debris toward Roy. Now completely transformed, he shivered unconsciously in shredded clothing. James followed her, rubbing what looked to be burn marks on his arms.

Leonard closed his eyes, inhaling deeply, and tilted his head upward into the sky. The soldiers cheered behind him. In his mind's eye, he was back in the infantry, their first battle won. Just like then, it was clear that while they had won the day, the victory would be short-lived. His senses reached downward into the earth, past the flame-heated rubble to the cool mud below. It soothed him for a quick moment.

Samira staggered to where Leonard stood, hands on her hips, as she looked at Ariel, who knelt in the dirt beside Roy. He looked like he would be fine, but Raslena crush him, it had been close. Ariel covered Roy in his black cloak. At this point, Leonard was convinced the garment was indestructible.

"It would have been striking nice to know that you hadn't been captured and killed by those Scourge Atoll rats," Samira said through clenched teeth. Her voice got louder as she went. "Astus strike me, *why* do you have to always run off? We can't afford to lose each other. This luck is going to run out, and if you aren't around someone will *die*! Where were you two?" she yelled.

Ariel blushed and looked away. Roy, still unconscious, had his head cradled in her lap. A knowing smirk appeared on Leonard's face as he assembled the pieces. He glanced at James, whose eyes suddenly widened with understanding. James shook his head and chortled briefly. Ariel finally looked up at them, setting her jaw upon seeing that Samira didn't look amused.

Samira kneaded her temple with her thumb vigorously, as if she were attempting to gouge her own skull. "I don't believe this. What is wrong with you both? You two have the *worst possible timing!*" She threw her hands upward in exasperation. "Find a way to get him up. We need to leave this jungle." Samira turned and stalked toward the north. "And if we see any more *striking* dragons, I'm feeding you to them. Ridiculous!"

Leonard grinned after Samira. She may have been angry, but he could clearly picture the relief on her face as she strode away. The soldiers curiously began to make their way over to them through the rubble. Leonard started toward them to head them off, having to slow down on account of the ribs, which were making him wince. Best to get everyone else moving. Roy was well attended to.

"James, help her get him up," he called. The lad nodded swiftly and crouched next to them, ready to hoist him upward. Ariel still sat with Roy's head in her lap, clasping one of his hands. She was no longer looking at Leonard or James but staring with dread at Roy's face.

Still unconscious, his eyes fluttered and opened just enough for Leonard to see the pupils. Calm turquoise blinked except for a tiny patch in his right eye. Even in the flickering light of the fires still burning around them, Leonard saw the glow of orange in the corner of Roy's eye. His latest lapse in control had just cost him dearly, giving the creature the foothold it had been looking for. This would make it easier for Charodon to break through Roy's defenses, shortening whatever time

Roy had left. Despite winning the day, everything had become a great deal more dire.

The orange corner of his eye was permanent.

247

The Beach

After several hours, the group came to the edge of the island. The blue sunrise, just barely climbing over the waves and other islands to the east, banished the remnants of the night's rain. Now consisting of the Chosen, Joskine, Badlai, Amry, and four others, the remaining survivors of the dragon attack waded into the surf at the edge of the powdery beach. This beach stretched for miles to the east and west, much larger than the ones James had been accustomed to on the islands so far. Cold had never been so appealing to him in his life.

As he stepped up to his waist in the swirling, salty water, he felt his senses and exhaustion slowly melt from him. The minuscule burns on his shoulders, persistently stinging, were soothed by the chill. His clothing clung to him gently, and his bare feet—he had taken off his boots and set them on shore—descended into the sand beneath them with each wave. He sighed at the pleasant feeling of sand grinding softly between his toes. To his left, Samira splashed water over hear face, washing away the ash and tension. Bright-blue sunlight reflected off her dark skin as she stared toward the next island with drooping, defeated eyes. Coming to the islands had been nothing but disaster. Getting on a ship had brought nothing but disaster. Samira noticed him standing near her and smiled tiredly, sloshing through the surf toward him.

"Ariel tells me you accomplished something today," she said, not hiding her satisfaction.

He shrugged. "It took me too long to figure out. I could have helped so many times before this." *I could have kept Gemmi alive too.*

She gave him a look of understanding. "But you helped now, and that is what we focus on. If you had not been capable of using Iarus's gift, that dragon may have killed us all. You've grown. And that growth saved us."

Uncomfortable, he nodded while staring into the foaming water beneath him. James didn't have the heart to tell her that he didn't think of Iarus once. It had been Roy and Ariel's faith in him that ultimately spurred him to action. Their trust had fueled a refusal for him to let them down because he could tell that their trust was real. His brother was dead, so he could make no more promises to him, but he could honor Gemmi by avenging him and looking out for those who trusted him now.

Seeing that he didn't want to answer, Samira continued, "What did you feel? When you used the second form, what did you feel?"

Struggling to remember the feeling of his soul grasping the fire, of his body and spirit hurling the flame, he pondered. "It felt as if I was holding the sun." He glanced at the horizon and the brilliant orb above it, spreading warmth across the surface of the world as it rose. "It felt warm, and I felt like I could attack the dragon bare-handed."

"And what does the sun do? What does the flame do? It illuminates what is before us, James. Iarus is showing you your path, little by little. You will find out who you want to be before the end."

His brow furrowed uncomfortably. "Before the end of what?"

She turned away and picked up her knees, trudging through the water back to the beach. "This great struggle, James. The Second War of Lost Faith. The enemy most certainly won't stop. Neither will we. Neither will the gods."

James shuddered, thinking of Dhorh and the three-eyed devil from Boane. Just the two of them were a force comparable to the dragons, and they hadn't even met the third and fourth Eyes yet. They had defeated Dhorh, yes, but the devil had underestimated them and was sure not to make that mistake again.

A chill moved through him, but not from fear. A large shadow had overtaken him, blocking the warm sunlight. Shirking his troubled thoughts for a moment, James turned to see Leonard's large, muscled form blocking the rising sun. The Champion of Raslena was grinning widely. He slapped his hands down on James's shoulders. James could have sworn that his feet were pushed a few inches further down into the sand beneath him, and he grimaced from the burns on his shoulders.

"Tell me how you did it! You're one of only five people alive I know of who can call themselves Dragoneaters now. You'll be famous in the mainland!" Leonard beamed.

Stunned, James stammered, "I lit the gas it breathed when it was still in its mouth." He gestured to where Ariel sat, having just climbed from the waves. "I couldn't have done it if Ariel hadn't helped." What Leonard said still sounded odd to him. *Famous?* It seemed like something that was reserved for great heroes of past ages, not an upstart from Boane. *Certainly not a heretic.*

"Roy and I helped Sam, but she finished it off." Leonard said sheepishly. "We have two Dragoneaters among us now. Almost half of the world's population!" he laughed. "It's a pretty elite demographic you're in. You'll meet the others when we get to the empire."

"And when we get there, what am I going to do? I don't think I can become something like what the emperor wants. I don't even know if I want to." James frowned.

Leonard's expression softened. "It won't just be you. We'll be with you every step, no matter your decision. Perhaps your mere presence will be the confidence boost the emperor needs to rule competently and push progress. The man has a good heart, but he sees the love his people had for his father before him. It would be difficult to have the trust of the whole empire after ascending to the throne that a great man once sat on. He's only a few years older than myself." He patted James on the shoulder gently, but even when being careful, the force of the gesture made James wince. "True character speaks in actions, James. And from what you did today I know that you won't let anyone down."

"And what of your actions, Leonard?" Roy said stiffly. James and Leonard both whirled around and saw Roy standing some few feet to their right, his hair and strange cloak suctioned to his skin from the water.

"Roy, please don't do this now," Leonard mumbled.

"Sam told me what you did tonight. What you did to help me." Roy rubbed his right cheek. "Thank you." It looked like it was painful for him to say.

James spied Ariel up the beach watching them, a satisfied smile on her lips.

Roy sighed and continued. "This doesn't make up for what you've done in the past, don't forget that. But I'm thankful for what you did back there."

An uncomfortable silence fell upon them. Waves slithering up and down the shore dominated the conversation. James shivered, his sunlight still being blocked by Leonard.

Hair swaying a bit, Leonard nodded toward Roy, knowing that this concession didn't come easily. The permanent orange blotch in the corner of Roy's right eye disrupted his already scarred face. Even so, Roy stood, fairly relaxed. James reckoned that he could infer why that was.

"So," James said, a smirk appearing despite himself, "You and Ariel were..."

Roy abruptly turned and sauntered toward the sand. "We're done here."

Leonard closed his eyes and shook his head, smiling. They followed Roy out of the water toward the spot where Samira sat, halfway between the waves and the tree line. It afforded them about ten body lengths in each direction.

Joskine and some of Leonard's new soldiers had gathered as much dry wood as they could carry from the edge of the rainforest. Dropping them with a clatter in the sand, they acknowledged at the Chosen before descending the beach. Leonard had gained their trust by counting on them to help him trap the dragon.

Despite their original hostility toward him, he had saved them, and they gave no indication of forgetting any time soon. The group stripped their clothing before inching into the surf. Some kept their trousers. Others did not. James turned away, embarrassed as the men and women bathed themselves in the salty water.

"That can't be cleaner than the muck we've been slogging through," Samira remarked. James pretended not to notice, working on assembling the pile of wood into something that would make a strong fire.

"They've spent their whole lives at sea." Leonard snorted. "This water might be some of the cleanest they've seen in years." Badlai and Amry sat up the beach toward the trees, resting in the shade of low-hanging foliage. They had no interest in the water. Badlai, however, seemed to exhibit much interest in Samira's activities.

James knelt and pulled the flint and steel from his belt. Holding out a hand to stop him, Samira moved to sit next to him, amber eyes fixed on the wood now expertly stacked in front of them. "Try starting it on your own."

He looked at her skeptically. She wanted him to use the final form after just barely figuring out the second?

"What you told me about using the second form a minute ago, you said it was like grasping the sun," she said, snapping her fingers. A compact pop of electricity flitted across her smooth left hand. "If I were to catch a lightning strike and throw it back, I would feel as if I were holding an entire storm in my hand. But now that I've mastered the final form of Astus's gift, it's like I have *become* a storm myself. I can sense the lightning every moment of every day. The charge is docile when I want it to be, but when I will it..." She flexed her left hand, causing small sparks to fly outward from it. "I change its course into something powerful, aggressive, or deliberate. I want you to think of that feeling. Use that deliberate emotion to create a sun of your own." She noted his unsure glances. "I know you don't think it possible, but you have this power."

James looked back at the pile of wood he had stacked, gently placing the flint and steel back in the pouch at his waist. Rays of aqua sunlight illuminated the crevasses of the stacked branches, slowly, deliberately. Imagining the sunlight circulating through him, James held his hands, palms outward, toward the kindling. He didn't feel much difference between his idle state. It wasn't the same exhilaration he had felt before when engaging the beast.

Thinking of the feeling from grasping the dragon's flames, he held onto the memory, allowing it and the sensation to fill his senses. The stinging in his shoulders began to grow, spreading down his arms at a leisurely pace. He opened his eyes after hearing Roy and Leonard gasp.

His hands were smoking. James blinked, astounded at the white vapor curling from his fingers. *He* had done that! His excitement was short lived, for the smoke dissipated, followed by a sharp sting in his forearm. Raising his hands to eye-level, angry pink burns were already beginning to appear on his skin. Even in this capacity, using his power in this way had taken a large toll. He would have to be careful.

Samira sat back, approving. "Good. Go cool yourself in the water. You'll find that using this form takes far more effort than the first and second forms. Your body must be prepared for it, otherwise you will be annihilated by your own power."

James hastily stood. The water sounded like an excellent idea to him, especially now that his old burns from hours previous had begun to flare up. "How long did it take you all? To master it, I mean?"

"It took me months of practice," Roy said, rolling a bead of water between his fingers. "Everyone is different. It took me the better part of a few years to master the second form. I originally had very little control. But the monks were persistent with me. They were able to help me realize that swordplay and my gift could go hand in hand. The flow of a sword is like that of water." He nodded to James. "Or of flames. Studying the sword helped me to gain more ground in my training."

"And it took me less than a year to master my gift up to the second form," Leonard added. "But I've found that it's stronger when I channel my intentions and senses through an instrument." He gestured toward his mace, shining in the sand a few body lengths away.

Nodding, Samira massaged her left hand. "It took me six years to master the third form, but my circumstances were much different. One can have fire, water, or earth readily available. Waiting for lightning to strike is tedious, and I made many mistakes while learning to control this gift." She gestured to her scarred right arm, but James thought he caught something different in her voice, as if her arm had been the least of her mistakes. It struck him that Samira was often the one fighting the hardest to keep them all alive, and she often did it at the expense of her own well-being.

He squinted against the sunlight. "I'll keep practicing. Roy, will you spar with me? Perhaps some swordplay will help me along as well, and it would do you good to rest, Sam. You've been pushing nonstop since we've left Boane."

Immediately, Samira shook her head, trying to stand. "Absolutely not. We've so much work to do. You *just* came to the cusp of attempting the third form. You'll need my help to master it."

"You're right, but I'm not good enough at the second yet. As someone who studied it for years to master it, Roy can take over for one day. Scorch me, Sam. You're going to run yourself aground. Rest. We can resume your sadistic methods later. You can have me climb a tree and then burn it down while I'm still in it if that makes you happy. But today, you rest. Maybe focus your attention on someone else, yeah?" He nodded in the direction of Amry and Badlai.

Samira glanced backward and caught a glimpse of Badlai looking away quickly. She spun around, her braid loudly slapping his knee.

Rolling her eyes, Samira finally admitted defeat. "Strike it, fine. I'll let you train with this pushover for the day." She jerked a thumb at Roy. "We'll camp here through the night too, get some much-needed rest."

"First, you should cool off, James," Roy insisted. He glanced at Leonard. "Go get control of your soldiers."

James waved his hand and treaded heavily toward the creeping waves. The tide grew lethargically. Roy followed him, holding a water skin and tapping his shoulder. Taking a swig of water as he waded back into the surf, James looked over his shoulder to where Samira sat, but she was no longer there. A trail of sandy footprints led up the soft slope toward the tree line. He smiled to himself and continued into the soothing water, shielding his eyes from the blue radiance of the shimmering waves.

***

Night had fallen quickly over the islands, Leonard remarked. The one day that they had any time to rest, and it had drained through the hourglass in what had felt like a few hours flat. Even Samira had grumbled about the shortness of the day. That was how they knew it was too little time to rest. Low-tide waves sloshed against the fine sand underneath his feet. He was grateful to have some time on land.

Leonard trudged along, following the steadily eroding footprints that Amry had left in the sand. The lad had been on watch the shift before him. Raslena crush the youth, he was supposed to patrol up and down the beach, not stay off to one side. A fair chance he was off relieving himself into a fern. It was the price he should pay for guzzling half of the water skins whenever they had just been filled. But Leonard supposed it was better than some of the people he had known, draining bottle after bottle of spiced beer. The stuff wasn't even that good.

The indentations were getting a bit deeper, heavier. Scratching his stubble, Leonard crunched through the sand, now a few dozen body lengths from the flickering fire that James had maintained all day. The boy had gotten exceptionally good at that. Soldiers and Chosen alike settled around the fire, drinking in its warmth. Ariel, opposite her lively personality, slept like a corpse. Leonard rubbed his eyes, shuffling farther. Maybe it was a good thing to take over watch now.

Samira's booming, thunderclap snores had become a bit too hard to ignore, although Badlai didn't seem to care. She slept near Samira without being *too* near.

Black water shimmered with a dark red glare from the moon above him, turning the ocean into one expansive pool of blood.

Amry, this had better just be a long piss, Leonard thought as he huffed further still down the beach. The camp was out of sight now, and the prints kept going. What did the young man think he was doing? The point of watching over everyone was to actually *be* where they were! Puffing despite his athletic physique, he glued his sight to the tracks, tuning out everything else.

The prints eventually curved away from the shoreline and went up to the trees at the edge of the beach. He felt the sand against his boot grow rougher as he ascended the shallow slope to the foliage. Green leaves looked black and brown by the light of the moon, and he squinted into the thicket no more than a few feet away. The shadow of the boy's head with accompanying cap stood among the darkness.

"And what in the Raslena's crushing quakes are you doing way out here, Amry?" Leonard demanded. "Nearly pulled something walking this far to find your secret piss spot."

Amry said nothing.

Leonard reached forward and grasped the lad's shoulder. "I'm only fooling, Am. Go back and get some sleep." Wobbling, as if shaking his head, Amry remained in place. He jostled the boy a bit harder, and an appalling crack sounded as the boy's head bent backward, too far backward. Amry's eyes stared straight into Leonard's with an abrupt surprise. Leonard looked down at his hand, feeling a thick, sticky substance. It looked black in his hand, but he already knew it was blood. Something had killed the boy. His glasses, still clinging to his face, were speckled black-red.

Leonard's legs refused to even tremble, locked with fear and grief. The boy hadn't deserved this.

The others are still in danger, his mind bellowed.

He lowered Amry to the ground gently but quickly. "I'm sorry," he whimpered, "I'm sorry, Amry." Hands still slick, he turned and scrambled down the beach. Something rustled behind him, but he did not chance meeting whatever waited in the bush. As he kicked up sand, orange firelight came into view, gently washing away the moon, the blood, from his vision. Leonard's mouth opened to scream, to warn them, to wake them, but no sound escaped his lips. A thin, stinging gash on his wrist dripped a skinny line of blood down onto his fingers. Had he been cut? He couldn't remember.

Blurring shapes straining his eyes, he peered ahead, dropping to his hands. Several figures, indistinguishable black wraiths in the night, gathered up the camp, carrying away the limp bodies of his companions. They had been ambushed.

"Ghh..." He gurgled. The veins on his head were throbbing enough to explode. Sweat and tears rolled as one down his face.

"I think this one's about to have a fit," a gruff voice behind him snickered.

Leonard's limbs failed him, sending him face first into the sand. Grains of sediment ground against his left eyeball. He couldn't close his eyes, couldn't move in the slightest. Calloused hands gripped his limbs and hauled him upward as if he were little more than a bag of the sand still in his eye. Grit filtered the light of the blood-red moon into his vision, showing him what surely awaited him: blood and blackness.

Gods and Men

There was a sprawling city touching the horizon from where James could see. The clouds around him churned and parted with the wind to show the magnificent stone structures and cathedrals taller than he could have ever imagined. He stood at the very apex of a mountain. Even from up here, he could see the vast population of the city below, more people than could possibly exist in the world, he thought. Colorful banners flew from the windows of every conical structure, looking like threads from the mountaintop.

James didn't remember entering this dream. He looked around for Dhorh, expecting the eyeless bastard to be behind this. The sheer rock beneath his feet felt jagged and unstable, and the wind whipped his clothing and hair ferociously. He squinted against the wind and saw two other mountains on either side of him. James could barely make out a figure standing at the peak of one of them. The wind assaulted his eyes, causing him to force them shut.

When the wind finally let up and he dared open his eyes, the figure was gone. He turned to the other summit to see two people standing on his mountainside just below him. James nearly lost his balance and fell. His heart felt as if it were dropping and leaping out of his throat at the same time. Whose memory was this? Neither of these people were Dhorh. They looked too normal—and hornless.

"I see the Son of the Pathlighter has joined us," one of the people said. He was an old man, hunched and wearing coarse rags. What little hair he had left blew in the wind as if they were part of the wisps of cirrus clouds in their midst. His kindly, milky eyes smiled even though they could see nothing.

James peered at the man's pleasantly wrinkled old face. "Who are you? What do you want?"

The old man shambled up the mountainside a bit further. He held no cane and didn't use the arm of his companion, an adolescent boy. His grandson? The bare feet of the elder prodded rocks and pebbles out of the way, causing quiet clacks to echo over the mountain peak. Stopping just before James, his already angled back bent just an inch more in a weak bow. "I am Vayne. It is a pleasure to meet you, my boy."

That couldn't be right. Vayne was an Alderaye, otherwise Dhorh wouldn't have mentioned him. Deciding already that he didn't like this liar, James held out his hand up to the man as he started to shuffle closer. "That's far enough," he shouted. The wind was starting to swell again. "You never answered my question. What do you want?"

The man nodded and stayed where he was. His sightless eyes still managed to shine as he looked in James's direction. "I wanted to meet you, child. I'm thankful to Dhorh for the opportunity." He motioned toward the child, who was no older than ten. The boy wore a faded gray tunic and was looking down at his feet, not making eye contact with James or the wrinkled man. Cloud vapor glistened on the boy's tan, bald head.

James wasn't impressed, rolling his eyes. "I've met Dhorh, and you can't fool me. I know what he looks like. Now, I'll ask you agai—"

His voice caught in the back of his throat when his eyes swept over to the young boy again. James's horrified eyes watched but barely comprehended as the boy's skin began to both bubble and split at the same time. The split skin knit itself together with a stomach-turning scraping and crawled over the skeleton and clothing of the boy until he no longer stood there. Dhorh perched where the child had been. No, where the child still was. Dhorh was using a trick of some kind. It looked exactly like what happened when Charodon took over Roy.

The devil turned his empty sockets to James and bared his teeth in an insane grin. "Still quite dreary in here, your head. You ought to think about freshening it up a bit," he said.

"You will not speak out of turn," Vayne said.

Dhorh's eerie cheer faded for a hair of a second before solidifying.

"The Elders know how to blend with the race of men, child," Vayne said. "As beastly as they are, they make wonderful hosts."

Repulsed, James's eyes widened. "You mean these forms are actual people?"

Vayne nodded, his kind face flapping a bit in the wind as he did. "Yes, child. Dhorh's host was a boy from Boane who was believed to have a certain clairvoyance. Poor boy only had nightmares, nothing more. Rhaiga's host was a priestess who lived hundreds of years ago. I do wish that you could have met her, but she is away on an important mission."

James continued to stare in horror at Dhorh.

"Our true forms can be a bit unsettling. Particularly true in his case," Vayne continued, smiling sympathetically.

"What about your host, who was he?" James demanded.

Vayne held his hands out at his sides as if in prayer. "He was a dying man. A sick, lonely man. He decided that rather than succumb to the disease, he would become the disease himself. He gave himself to me willingly." He shook his head as if fondly remembering the man. "I'm afraid only a dying man can see the race of men for what they truly are. Selfish, violent, crude beings. Animals that refuse to coexist with anything else. I would thank the man for his vision, if I could remember his name."

"The gods are said to have wanted humankind to live and thrive," James shot back quickly, disgusted by what he was hearing and slightly disgusted by what he was saying. Was he resorting to Temple preachings? "They sent you away all those years ago, and they'll do it again."

"My dear boy, you know the truth," Vayne said, shuffling up to where James stood. He stopped level with James, his wispy hair dancing in the breeze. His withered face was painted with a sad understanding. "You've always known the truth, haven't you? Always had it in the back of your mind. You know it but don't want to believe it." The sightless eyes peered into James's thoughts.

The nagging truth that James had carried his whole life came crashing to the front of his consciousness, and he said it before he could stop.

"There are no gods," James said blankly, throat dry.

Vayne sighed solemnly. "A fiction. A way to explain away the unexplainable. Iarus was a man, like you. He possessed a power that none could match or explain, like you, but he died just the same." The old man reached out with a spotted, shaky hand and touched James's face. "Just as you will."

James felt a draining sensation seep into him. His forehead burned and began to throb as if a smith were hammering it. "I don't understand. Why would you tell me this?"

Vayne turned his head away, as if looking downward toward the city below. The spots on the back of his head seemed to be shifting in James's pulsing vision. "You were an orphan, born into a brutal world. Those who sought to control you told you of indifferent, uncaring gods, as if to explain the reasoning for your suffering. They believed it themselves. They believed they were pleasing the gods when they beat you, when they told you that you were broken, and that all you needed was them to be whole again." Vayne directed his blind gaze back to James, who was swaying, lightheaded. "They believed it when they murdered your brother, just for trying to provide for you. You wanted to believe the lie too. You wanted to believe in it with all your heart, because if there were no cruel gods, if there were no such beings..."

James's heart plummeted from his chest, as if it were tumbling down the mountainside, yet still beating unnervingly fast. *All of the Temple was a lie. I knew it.*

Vayne sensed James's realization. "If there were no such gods, then humans slaughter each other, brutalize each other, and *lie* to each other for no reason. No reason, other than *wanting* to."

Behind him, Dhorh pressed a fist to his chin and turned his head, cracking his neck with a sharp pop.

"I'm telling you because you understand these things. Your friends, who can barely keep from murdering each other, have spent their entire lives believing in the lie. Living the lie themselves." Vayne shook his head.

"But we can't just have this power for no reason!" James argued. "Why can I grasp the flames or sense the heat of living things?"

Shrugging, Vayne rubbed his mostly hairless head. "Why can I create or cure disease? Why do I need to infect a host to survive? I have no answers to these either. I simply found my rightful place among the order of things. We are the real gods. We've controlled this world for thousands of years, bent humans and beasts to our natural order. But one day, humans gained the ability to harness power unlike anyone had seen. They were revered as gods, and for years we exterminated them like insects."

"Until they banished you," James said. That made Vayne's bravado twitch ever so slightly. Sensing that this was something the Elders—as they had called themselves—didn't like to think about, James smiled grimly. "Is that still a sore subject?"

Vayne drew in a shallow breath, still leering, "Indeed, they banished us to the dunes. They were strong ones, the Chosen who sent us away. Had my brother Charodon been there, we would have won."

James blinked as if he had been slapped. The others had never mentioned that Charodon was an Alderaye. *They lied to me again. They scorching lied to me, right to my face.*

Vayne continued, "We stumbled through those forsaken sands for over a thousand years, our bodies slowly decaying. My body most of all, since I had already not taken a new host for a few centuries. And when we returned, the race of humans had taken this beautiful world. Those who followed us had been wiped from existence. The cities of men and women had taken root, and they run deep, but even a sturdy tree can be uprooted. We will tend our garden accordingly to rid it of pests." Blinking his dead eyes, the old man's wrinkles formed a face of hopefulness. "I hope that you will see the nobility in our cause. You who have seen some of the worst of what men and women do. Pledge yourself to the Elders, become a host. I will give you the vengeance you crave, tenfold."

A moment passed and then several more. James stared blankly at Vayne, vision flitting to Dhorh, who—despite his hideous appearance—was trying to look earnest. The need for revenge still seethed inside him, but he wouldn't become the puppet of some ancient devil just to get what he wanted. "I don't think so," James said, putting a hand to his sword.

Sighing, Vayne gingerly stepped backward. "You believe they can change? Humans are animalistic, brutally unintelligent bacteria that disrupt the natural order."

"They may be, but your petty hatred for them isn't as noble as you think. And you don't sell your lies nearly as well as they do. I can tell that you believe them though. Well, scorch you. You're no better than the ones who murdered Gemmi."

"Very well." Vayne's white eyebrows were knit together in frustration. "In centuries past, I may have offered again, but the time for that is long dead. A great sickness is coming, and it will purge the greatest sickness of all, the race of men."

James started to sway more violently. Vayne's leering face became unfocused, and the mountaintop spun. His shoulder felt weak from where the old man had touched him. The Eye of Disease.

James looked down in horror at his arms, spouting pox and spores, the skin turning a sickly gray. He tried to speak, but his throat and mouth could no longer make noise. All that escaped was a dry gag as his vision blurred exponentially.

Vayne's kindly features faded in front of him as James vomited over and over. The bile began to change color from a dry yellow to a dark red, chunky and bubbly, splashing against the rocks below him.

"I cannot promise a painless end for you, child," Vayne said, his voice muffled. "All I can promise is that it is coming."

Black Smiles

The last thing James saw was Dhorh's fissured face peering at him from the rocks below when he suddenly woke up, jerking to a seated position. The world swam into focus around him. James squinted, noticing the ground did not look like the sand he had fallen asleep on. More like stone, on which he promptly vomited.

His feet brushed against metal bars, producing a slight ding. The craftsmanship on the bars was detailed, made with interlocking shards that produced a sturdy barrier. A diamond-shaped lock of silvery metal was attached to the door of some kind of cell, keeping him locked inside. Smooth stones in the shape of a valley locked together to construct the wall behind him and to his right, making him guess that he was near the end of some hall. But a hall in where? There hadn't been any sign of civilization anywhere on the islands. He touched the wall, running his fingers across the peculiarly-shaped bricks.

They were expertly crafted, smooth to the touch and symmetrical. Nothing in Boane had ever looked like this. Shoddy craftsmanship had been the norm where he had grown up. The same smooth gray stones covered the floor of his cell, now sprinkled with sand from his relocation off the beach. Other cells populated the hall to his left, containing the other Chosen. The sailors were missing.

Ariel was awake in her cell, two over from him. The two cages between them were empty, as if their currently absent captors didn't trust putting any of them close to each other. He looked at her expectantly, seeking answers, but only received a shrug as a reply. Ariel looked as if she had just been roused as well, her gold hair disheveled, inspecting something on her glyphed wrist.

A slight throbbing in his own wrist drew his gaze downward, landing on a scratch just above his hand on the outside of his forearm. Something must have snipped at his skin, or someone. Could this have poisoned him and the rest of the group? Farther down the row of cells, two cells in between each, he could catch glimpses of Samira, Leonard, and Roy. Still no sign of Joskine, Badlai, or Amry. Leonard's soldiers were nowhere to be found, either. They were captives of an adversarial stranger, and half of their friends were missing.

He stretched his senses outward, searching for heat anywhere that could give him better bearings. The dull hum of sunlight beaming against the other side of the wall at his back came to him first. Turning his attention to the hallway on the other side of the bars, James's senses stumbled across a ring of red torches glowing toward the end of the corridor near Roy. The air directly to the right of the ring contained less heat than the surrounding area. That most likely indicated a door at the end of the path. James realized that his sword had been taken from him, as well as his flint and steel. They did not seem to be in the corridor. If he had his flint, he could make the sparks hot enough to melt the lock on his cage

Shuffling and groaning echoed, indicating someone else had just come to. Leonard rubbed his neck and leaned against the V-shaped bricks behind him.

"Waking up behind bars gets old after the first few times," Leonard moaned.

"Few times?" James asked, his voice reverberating back to him.

"Got in quite a few fistfights when I first joined the infantry. I didn't always lose, but I was always unlucky enough to get caught brawling."

"It didn't stop after you left either," Ariel added.

"I wasn't the one who started those fights," Leonard shot back. "And I would say getting ambushed in our sleep is a bit different."

James let his attention drift from the conversation to his ethereal meeting with Vayne. What the old man said still prickled through his ears. *There are no gods.* He had suspected this multiple times in his life. After Gemmi had died, his doubts had become real, a dark stain on his worldview that had grown from the inkblots of questions past. In his grief, he had decided that the gods had demanded his brother's life out of spite, or perhaps out of cruelty. His desire to know why had finally been met with an answer, and the answer made him feel even worse. Gemmi's murder, Samira's prophecy, even his supposed importance to the empire were based on a lie.

From the corner of his vision, he noticed Samira wrestle herself awake. Her hands were covered by heavy stone shackles, perhaps meant to negate any attempt at shocking herself free. James's revelations about her beliefs made his mind race. She believed with her whole being that she had a sacred task to end the Alderaye—or the Elders—for the gods. And her misguided belief would possibly get them all killed. She was just like the Temple, maybe worse.

Samira saw him looking in her direction and raised her eyebrow, as if asking what was going on.

He scowled and said nothing.

James knew himself well enough to determine that he wouldn't be able to stray away from his realization about the gods, and he knew Samira well enough by now to figure that she wouldn't believe him anyway. James glanced at Roy, a not insignificant amount of anger flaring within him. Even after they had promised not to lie to him anymore, they had never mentioned that Roy was the host for an Elder or how the Elders could hide among humankind. *Where was the honesty they promised?* Disgusted, he leaned his head against the smooth bricks behind him. They weren't his friends and never had been. He was just their stooge, strung along from the beginning.

Hours passed. Roy finally blinked awake, surveying the room with a calm disposition. He leaned forward and felt the bars in front of him. Whoever their captors were, they had taken his cloak and weapons. Taking his hand off the bars, he listened to the slight ring of the metal and placed a hand on his boot. "I don't like this."

"You don't say?" Leonard sighed, exasperated.

Roy shot him a look. Even from the opposite end of the corridor, James could see the glowing corner of his eye. "I remember something about this kind of craftsmanship from my time at the Refuge. Whoever built these cages is not good news."

"Of course they aren't," Samira said. Her shackled arms kept her from kneading her temple.

"I remember seeing that book too," Ariel mused. "But the ones who used this kind of architecture and metalworking have been extinct for years, centuries." Before James had the chance to follow up, the door near Roy's end of the corridor squealed open. No dust billowed from the doorway. Whoever had captured them seemed to value a clean dungeon.

Two figures strutted in, tall and imposing, yet there was also something strangely wrong about them. Appearing to be one man and one woman, they inspected each of the prisoners. They both wore long coats, open at the front with a reddish-brown and black checkered pattern. Samira glared at them as they passed. Leonard shrank back in his cell, horrified by their captors.

Silk shirts with a gray slash down the front billowed underneath the coats, even though they were tucked into the trousers. With each step, James noticed their appearances became even stranger. Their skin was sickly in color, sallow and gray in some places. Dark-red hair the color of thick blood was swept toward one side and fell over their left shoulders, and their necks bore an odd pigmentation, seeming to sport what looked like a black V across their throats.

The female looked toward him and leered. James shuddered as her violet eyes flitted over him as if sizing up an animal for slaughter. Her teeth were pitch black, still somehow glinting in the dim torchlight. Even though they vaguely resembled humans, they were so profoundly alien in their appearance.

"You're Altujan," he whispered, aghast. He had heard the dark tales at the Temple, cannibalistic ghouls who marauded the upper continent, and—at one time—the whole world. *The one time the Temple was correct about something.*

The male turned and bared his black teeth in satisfaction, as if reveling in the recognition. "Indeed," he said in a shaking deep voice. The corners of his extremely wide mouth curled downward as he spoke, giving him the most peculiar accent. It was difficult to decipher. His vowels stretched and rattled James's eardrums. "So odd that you would gape at us like we we're beasts in a cage while you're the one behind bars."

James fumed.

The male Altujan's eyes narrowed. He ignored the snickering of the female. "Bah! It's what I get for trying to communicate with the likes of humans. The others you were with were even less capable of conversation."

Ariel jumped upward, gripping the pristine bars. "You killed them!" Her eyes were alight with horror. The bars creaked slightly, but didn't move.

The female smirked in her direction. "One or two. Examples have to be made. We can't allow such a resource to revolt before our people have had a chance to put them to use." Her voice flowed like a velvet scarf in the wind, but there was a threatening edge to it, as if the scarf could just as easily tighten around his neck.

"You put on quite a show for our scouts the other night," the male continued. "To think that all five of the Chosen were just an island away from our colony. Luckily the dragons forced you to show yourselves before you could infiltrate us. The Elders were banished more than a millennium ago, but you can't leave our people to live on their own, even without masters to follow. You have the audacity to call *us* bloodthirsty." His anger grew with each syllable.

"An ignorant world raised them, Zatran. A world that is oblivious to the *real* gods," the female mused. Her eyes had something in them that terrified James. There was a glee for violence not quite hidden behind them, a violet hunger.

"We were shipwrecked trying to sail north," Samira insisted. "We had no knowledge that you were here."

Leonard spoke up, "If you release us, the empire will remain ignorant of your location. I swear it." Samira looked at him angrily. There was no way that a devoted Chosen like her would actively help the followers of their enemy.

The female shook her head vigorously, her hair like a spray of blood, "You must think us fools or savages. You won't leave this island. You are ours now, better start acting like it."

"I am the host body for Charodon, the Eye of Nature," Roy called from the end of the corridor, face pressed against the bars of his cell. "You will release us by command of the Alderaye."

Zatran and the female approached Roy rapidly, inspecting his face through the bars. Zatran's wide eyes grew wider upon seeing the orange sliver of Roy's otherwise turquoise eyes. He turned to the female in excitement. "He's telling the truth, Mastreh. Look at him!"

Mastreh crossed her arms in dissent, her white lips frowning, "He speaks of his own will. Charodon may be in there, but this one is still in control. The Eye of Nature is dormant."

Glaring back and forth between them, Zatran shoved Roy away from the bars, backward into the cage. "The Eyes damn you! How *dare* you deny Charodon what any of us would gladly give him!"

Roy stepped back up to the bars fluidly and thrust out his fist. A concentrated jet of sea water exploded from his hand, throwing Zatran backward and into the wall a few feet behind him. Mastreh dodged the blow and lithely rushed the cage. Her veiny, gray hand grasped Roy by the throat, squeezing. Roy immediately released his water attack, letting the droplets fall to the polished floor. Roy gasped for air and held up his hands in surrender.

"Stop it!" Samira shouted.

"Leave him alone!" Ariel called.

Leonard tried to bend the bars of his cage, tried to escape to help Roy, but the metal was expertly crafted. Mastreh looked at him, a skeptical expression painting her face. Leonard dropped his hands. Finally, she let go of Roy's neck, dumping him on the floor of the cell, hacking.

"I think we'll take this one with us," Zatran said, dripping water, eyes narrowing vengefully at Roy, "and see if we can't assist the Eye of Nature ourselves." He turned to his fellow Altujan. "Mastreh, will you be so kind as to subdue him so we can take him to more... *suitable* quarters?"

Mastreh's wide mouth grinned her white and black smirk. Fear streamed through James, and Ariel pressed against the bars of her cell. They meant to torture him to lure Charodon out. Roy scrambled backward in his cage, squeezing his eyes shut, trying to block out the devil as Mastreh undid the cage's bolt. The rest of the Chosen screamed in protest, pleading with the Altujan to stop. She wasn't listening. Mastreh lunged forward, her foot connecting against Roy's stomach with a heavy thud. Roy flopped backward with a desperate wheeze. Holding out his hands, Roy caught her next kick, only to receive a savage swipe to the face from her clenched hand.

Leonard grasped the bars of his cell and started to pull again. "Don't touch him!" His normally calm brown eyes shook with rage, as if caused by an earthquake. He strained again against the cage, actually budging the metal an inch. Zatran turned and hurled something in Leonard's direction. A clang and a swear rang throughout the dungeon. Leonard stumbled back, clutching his left hand, looking at the ground.

A throwing knife clattered to the stone floor, its edges smeared with a blue, inky substance. James looked on in fear as Leonard slid to the floor against the V-stone wall, a dizzy swirl in his eyes.

Zatran stooped in front of Leonard's cage and plucked the knife from the ground, waving it tauntingly before he dazed Chosen. "You may be distracted by Mastreh's methods, but I became Blood Herald of this colony by the strength of my mind. There is a tree native to these islands that produces a certain paralytic sap. It has no effect on us Altujan, but it is quite potent to other living creatures." He chuckled and slid the knife into a sheath at his belt. "We actually use the sap to make a very formidable drink. Consider this a warning, Chosen." He gestured to Roy's unconscious body, "This one is of use to us. You are simply meat in a cage. You will *behave* as such, and we will make your end quick. It's as good a deal as we will give you, and no more than what you deserve for what your kind did to ours."

Leonard slumped, eyes going blank.

James felt his head whirling, overwhelmed. Leonard's mace was gone, so his manipulation of the earth, the stones, the metal, was limited. Samira was incapacitated by the stone gauntlets, and Ariel could do little more than circulate the air in this space. The memory of Kahb, stepping backward after James had grabbed him, a red hand mark burned into his skin, flashed through his mind's eye. He had to do that again, melt the bars and escape to help Roy.

He gripped the metal latch to his cage and strained, but his thoughts were too scattered. The coldness of the bars spread along the skin of his fingers, immobile. He snapped his head up to the sound of Ariel and Samira's screams. Zatran and Mastreh hoisted Roy's listless body upward, blood trickling from his lip, and dragged him from the room. The water from Roy's attack had extinguished the torches near his cell. When the Altujan closed the door behind them, the room became black, swallowing everything but the sound of their cries. James hurled insults after their captives, cursing them, spittle flying from his teeth. This would end in the razing of everything that lived on this island.

"No, no!" Ariel screamed, anguish tearing at her voice.

James heard stone and metal scraping from Samira's cage. She was trying to rip her restraints away.

"Wait!" he screamed after their captors. "I carry Vayne! The Eye of Disease is dormant in my head! Take me instead!" He repeated the lie again and again, hoping his words could reach Zatran and Mastreh.

"James, what are you doing?" Samira shrieked

He ignored her, shouting enough to unnerve a madman. He shook the bars to his cell, kicked them, howling after the Altujan. "I carry the Eye of Disease! I carry Vayne!"

The door crashed open, flooding the corridor with dim blue light. Zatran burst in, hair flipping wildly as he scanned the room for who had spoken. His violet eyes landed on James, and a black smile spread his mouth apart. Zatran marched directly toward him, knife out. Horrified shouts came from Samira and Ariel's cells. James held his hand outside the bars of the cage, offering his flesh to be cut. He realized as Zatran approached that he didn't care if Roy lived. If Charodon lived, they all died. They had lied to him again, but he still needed them to escape, and it was much easier to do that if they weren't in Charodon's belly. Tuning out Ariel and Samira's protests, he waited for the *snick* of the knife. They would find a way to get out of this once he woke up, and he would do anything he could to kccp Charodon from turning loose.

Zatran held the knife outward, squinting into James's eyes, perhaps looking for a trace of something telling of a host. "How do I know you're telling the truth? How do I know you carry him?"

James's mind raced. The bastard had probably been learning about Vayne since he was born. What had Vayne said to him?

"I was sick, dying," he said quickly, trying to sound sincere. "He came to me, and I chose to become the disease instead of succumbing to it." James held his breath, still holding out his hand. Samira and Ariel were too stunned to speak. If he could save Roy from being overridden, they may all have a chance to make it out alive. *And then I'm done. They can find someone else to be their emperor's puppet, to fight the Elders. Lies killed my brother. I'm not going to let them kill me too.*

"Why are you fighting him now?" the Altujan inquired, still not convinced.

"Because of my guilt. I didn't know he planned to raze the world of humans. I just don't want to die." He tried to sound convincing, even adding a break to his voice. The eyes of his captor considered him for a moment.

The knife flashed and Zatran slit James's palm painlessly. Immediately, the wall began to blur in front of him. Sitting down hard, he heard the cell door swing open, Ariel and Samira's muffled shouting, and the clack of Zatran's boots on stone. Muddled thoughts of how he would get out of this raced through his mind, getting slower by the moment. At no point did he consider what would happen to him, but it would occur to him later that he definitely, absolutely, most certainly should have.

***

Vayne opened his eyes and saw the world. Slanting downward to his right, the ragged, crystalline slopes of the Bo'Shk mountain glistened with blue sunlight. And blood. He looked out across the ocean, feeling the warmth of another sunset, drinking in the sight as the white sun morphed to a deep cobalt, one of the things he missed the most. It was not real, just a memory. He knew this, but he dispelled the thought for now. Best to wait until Rhaiga arrived. Until then, he would bask in the fondness of the recollection he had requested Dhorh to unthread.

Feeling something soft against his foot, he kicked outward absentmindedly. The corpse of a Chosen, he had forgotten which one, tumbled a bit farther down. The mountain covered the entire miniature continent, so everything looked entirely too small. Some of the islands that surrounded the great mountain were likely greater now, having formed for thousands of years after this memory.

Things had been simpler then. If he squinted his functional, perfect eyes hard enough, he could make out the burning villages of the humans who lived here far below. Animals, frightened by a storm. Frightened by true gods. Vayne could see the others, the ones no longer alive, as ghostly mirages among the flames. He sighed. *If I could only find out how they killed you, I could prevent it from ever happening again.* Often, he tried to fill in the gaps of the days leading up to his banishment, but so much time in the Dunes and his deteriorating husk had rotted the echoes of that time. This memory remained clear, however. It was the happiest one he had.

Light rippled and bent as Dhorh and Rhaiga emerged into the memory, both of them in their true forms, as they had been that day. Those days, they hadn't needed hosts to live. They were free to roam the earth as they had come into being. Over time, the natural balance of power had shifted. Other entities had grown stronger, while the power of the Elders had faded. Vayne glanced downward and saw that he was now in his own true skin, dried, cracked, blackened. There were several toes missing from his left foot, but he paid that no mind. He rolled his neck to the side, chin brushing his shoulders. Even back then, he hunched.

"Here again?" Rhaiga mused, crouching near a woman's body, covered in pox, another Chosen. She played disinterestedly with its coarse black hair. "Nostalgia seems to be more and more your defining trait, Vayne. I'm starting to think you're taking too much after those old men who host you."

"I could say the same for you," he said. He could feel his slack, dead jaw droop even more. "For a being of death, you seem to have an aversion to it."

"A lack of interest, more like," she corrected. "Death happens. Paths end. Watching things come to that end, however. That is a worthy pastime."

"Unless that path intersects with ours."

She snapped, "Yes, I've made that clear. If something's path opposes ours, or is prolonged unnaturally, it is an automatic end. These humans have been doing a lot of that lately with their...I believe they call it *sciences*."

Vayne wasn't going to hear her grievances today, but these outbursts were getting worrisome. He turned to Dhorh. "Thank you for bringing her. You've proven yourself useful these last few weeks. And your memories are that much safer as a result."

The Eye of Memory bowed his head, ram's horns curling upward. He had been crucial in getting Vayne an audience with the FireChosen. The youth had been at odds with the humans' false religion. Shattering this by giving him the truth would pit him against the religious one and fracture their merry band. Dhorh's frequent visits to the FireChosen's mind had solidified the steps toward disunion.

To add to that, Charodon would break the control of his host soon. While he had never been interested in their cause for Elder rule, the brute would work to their advantage this time, for once.

Vayne gestured to the bloody battlefield on the mountainside around them, "I like to revisit this day from time to time, the glory of it. The Chosen could not match us then. We outnumbered them two to one, and we succeeded in preserving the world as it was." Peering up toward the apex of the mountain, he spied the silhouettes of jagged figures, made of angles. The crystal-clear memory couldn't even bring the other Elders back. It was as if they had been wiped from existence, past and present. *Why can't I remember them?*

"What does that have to do with what we're doing now?" Dhorh gave the impression of rolling his empty sockets. "Things have changed. The Chosen have power now."

A slight chill slithered between Vayne's shoulder blades. Fear? No.

Well, perhaps. He couldn't argue, as Dhorh was correct. But this fear enraged him. The world had been simpler, but the humans and their Chosen had made it complicated.

"They have power, yes. So do we. Less so than in days past, but still enough to kill any one of them, every one of them. We must be smarter. Ripping down humankind from the top is no longer feasible, but our method of making it crumble on top of itself has proven effective. But Boane and Epot Detharn were disconnected, outliers. It will take much more effort to bring down the empire."

A surprisingly chilled gust of wind threatened to scrape them from the crystal surface of the mountain. The three gods did not flinch, as they had refused to flinch that day. Vayne's rotted maw pulled itself into a smile as it looked downward at the corpse he had kicked. Astus. That had been the man's name. Mouth gaping as wide as the hole in his chest, the carcass stared blankly at the sky, his clouded eyes drinking in the sun, beard filled with dirt. They had met the first

Chosen here, millennia ago, killed them like rats. He wished humans could all see this day and witness what their gods had been. In a word, frail, exactly how he felt now. It would break the fabric of their society.

Rhaiga stopped twirling the hair of the slain woman—Raslena, the Builder—her bone-white skin reflecting the last rays of sunlight. "The islands are even better than what you predicted. Altujan colonies have held onto their foundations, dozens of them. And they have captured the Chosen."

Vayne smiled. The Chosen wouldn't be getting in their way, after all. "So the old world clings to life. This is good. No, it's fantastic. Make contact with them. Give the orders that I have relayed to you. They can catapult this great task of ours into motion at a pace we could have only hoped for."

"And then?"

"Lead them to the mainland. They can give us the means to hobble the empire."

She nodded and stretched her skeletal arms, flexing the skin enough to make it look like it might rip. Dhorh stood a bit taller, sensing that the conversation was ending.

"You may take us back now, Dhorh. Do not fail us, Rhaiga."

The royal-blue sun disappeared as if it were a lamp, snuffed. Blackness overtook Vayne's vision, and the warmth left him. As he felt himself drift from the vision Dhorh had brought him into, he sighed. Would that he could stay in that blissful memory forever. Alas, a god's work could not wait.

Darkness now ruled his eyes as Dhorh helped him up among the swaying floor. The belly of the ship had served as a place they could communicate with Rhaiga undisturbed. Coughs and whimpers could be heard above them, lifting Vayne's spirits. The Mangler was spreading among their traveling companions as intended. It was mild for now, slight pain. He just hoped that some would survive to their destination. What a terrible thing that would be, to arrive in a strange land all alone, having to start over with new victims.

Bloodbreathing

What was that light? Piercing blue stabbed Roy's eyes, bringing him from the ledge of unconsciousness. It did nothing to help his headache. Dathos drown him, the Altujan woman hit harder than anything in recent memory, assuming she hadn't just beaten his memory out of him too. Pointed directly at his face, the light obscured his surroundings, eliminating any chance of discerning where he was. He could hear the crackling and feel the warmth of torches around him. Scuffling echoed through the space to his left, sounding as if a few pairs of feet were shuffling across the stones. Held behind him in the air, his arms and shoulders burned intensely. He must have been here for a few hours now. Trying to move his arm, he felt only thick leather strapped around his wrist. A slight metallic smell persisted throughout the chamber.

His legs were strapped down as well. Panic engulfed him for a moment as he remembered the knife near his ankle, his safety net, was gone. It became clear he was sitting on a stool, arms suspended behind him—Dathos drown him, that made his shoulders sore—and his legs securely fastened to wooden posts in the dirt floor. Could that be sunlight hitting his face? No, he was looking down. So what was it?

"You don't have to concern yourself with this prison if you let me out," Charodon mocked. He had become more and more talkative since Roy had given him ground. Idiot. He could have used his own power to cover the dragon in water. Why didn't he think clearly in that situation? No, trickery from Charodon. The reality was that his own lack of judgment had led him here, like a fool.

"If I let you out, I'd be in a different prison," he said in a raspy whisper.

"What will they do first? A beating? A lashing? You know I could kill them easily."

"Don't take me for a fool. They worship you too."

Charodon's hiss shot a sharp spike of pain through his brain. *"They follow Vayne and his lapdogs. They're prey. All prey is the same."*

"I won't let you out either way, so get used to the boredom of torture." Roy sighed.

"Well, yeah, that's why I'm here with you," James croaked.

Roy turned his head to the left with some difficulty, blowing his increasingly long hair out of his eyes. James was strung up in the same way on another stool next to him, looking disoriented but relatively unhurt. More than Roy could say for himself.

They had replaced James's clothing with a shirt and ragged, short trousers that had been made out of cloth sacks. In fact, the shirt was just a sack with extra holes cut in it. He squinted down at himself and realized they had placed him in the same sackwear as well. Roy might have noticed had his head not still been throbbing.

His friend looked as if he were trying to concentrate on the torches, their heat, but whatever the Altujan had extracted from that sap was strong. It made his thoughts a haze. Roy found that he couldn't sense much moisture or water at all.

"Dathos drown me, James. What are you doing here?" he hissed.

"To make sure you don't scorch up and let the beast loose."

Roy felt a stirring of ice in his belly, anger shooting through the fogginess of the sap. James was enduring torture or worse just to babysit him? He couldn't be harboring another Elder, otherwise Charodon would never have shut up about it. "Your faith in me is so encouraging, James."

"You lied to me. You never told me the truth."

"What difference would it have made?"

"The difference is that I would trust you, but it turns out you can't trust anyone, can you?" James spat.

Roy didn't get the chance to respond. Zatran crouched in front of him, eerie, violet eyes peering into his, somehow managing to twinkle while torturing someone. The Altujan cocked his head, assessing Roy's bruising face and bleeding lip. "Eye of Nature, if you can hear me, come forth from this body."

"*He's direct,*" Charodon mused. "*I'll eat him first.*"

Roy shook his head slightly, wincing. "Not happening." He gritted his teeth at Zatran.

Zatran exhaled sharply through his nose, flexing his nostrils. "You can't dictate the will of a god, boy."

"He's no god. He's an animal."

"Yes." Zatran shrugged. He stood and stretched, yawning. "The Eye of Nature is a force that none can control. He is the living embodiment of the natural world and its mercilessness. He's the Dreadfronts that ravage the seas to the west, the dragons that prowl these islands. Even the winters in that frostbitten gash you call home—your cloak was a dead giveaway. Nature is not meant to be contained. It must ravage as it pleases, and you, in your lack of vision, seek to rob nature of the freedom it is entitled to."

"Is this the torture?" Roy muttered.

Zatran crouched again and slapped him, hard. Roy's head lolled to the side, bright flashes appearing before his eyes. Vision spinning, he looked downward. Fresh blood trickled from his mouth.

"You're a strong one. That much is clear, human. I can see why he chose you, of all people," Zatran growled. "But we *will* unleash him, and Charodon will exact his fury on the race of humans as punishment."

"And when he's killed his fill of us, where do you think he'll turn? He's a monster, one that views the whole world as prey. If he's released, then all of us are dead, starting with you and me," Roy wheezed.

The light in Roy's eyes suddenly went dim as Zatran turned and kicked at the mirror behind him. It had been reflecting the light of the sun from a hole in the ceiling, disorienting him. It spun away and cracked against the floor with the sound of tinkling glass. Roy's eyes flicked around the room, taking in the clear chamber. Circular walls surrounded them, made of those trademark V-shaped bricks, cleaned and spotless. Torches lit troughs of filmy, glistening, blue liquid lining the walls. He and James were trussed up in the center, a bit more than four feet from each other. Mastreh was busy tightening the restraints on James's arms. James winced at the strain. His blazing green eyes didn't leave Roy's, and there was a noticeable anger there that he had not seen before.

Stomping back up to Roy and gripping his face, Zatran hissed through his black teeth, a sickly sweet stench wafting from his mouth. His other hand cut Roy's wrists loose. Mastreh lurched over to assist her Blood Herald, leaving James to watch, helpless.

"Don't give in, Roy," James said. His voice was furious, accusatory.

I shouldn't have kept this from him.

They hauled him to the edge of one of the troughs, his feet dragging across the V-stones. The inky liquid glistened in front of him.

"*Here is your chance. Let me kill them,*" Charodon growled. "*You can spare yourself this pain if you give me what I want.*"

Roy's face hovered over the trough of blue sap. "I don't want to be spared," he said through tears. It was what he deserved for hosting this foul creature. It was Leonard's fault that Charodon lived in him, but the deaths were his.

An explosive punch to the stomach from Mastreh chased the air from him. It was as he gasped for breath that they shoved his head and shoulders into the trough, submerging him. As his lungs heaved, crying for air, the bitter, cold liquid rushed down his throat.

The sap tasted like blood, thick and filmy. It coated the inside of his throat, his eyes, his teeth. Blue became all he could see. At that exact moment, Charodon roared in his mind, attacking his consciousness as if it had been lying in wait in the trough itself. He felt his mind, his veins, his limbs, turn to ice. Roy could barely think. Pushing back blindly against the cold, he screamed into the trough of sap, bubbles rushing past his ears.

Sweetness overtook the rusty, briny taste of the ichor. His tastes became feral, relishing it. No sound reached his clogged ears as the Altujan pulled his head from the trough. Gurgling liquid gave way for oxygen. A precious few seconds of air rasped into his lungs before Mastreh and Zatran plunged him deep into the basin again.

"Let me out! You're mine! The world is mine!"

Thrusting his fist out blindly, he attacked with a jet of water, but he couldn't know if it connected or not. Roy choked on ichor. He could fight Charodon or the Altujan, but he couldn't do both. It was the moment he had been dreading since the beast had taken residence.

He stopped struggling, focusing all his energy and willpower on keeping Charodon back, thrusting the frost from his system. Letting the sap into his lungs, purging the monster from his senses, his vision began to darken. Feeling began to fade from his limbs. Zatran's hand still held firmly to the back of his head.

Charodon surged again into his thoughts, bellowing threats, thrashing. Roy screamed as the Altujan hauled him from the trough once more. Even through the blood—sap, whatever it was—he could feel James's horrified eyes on him as the scream morphed, becoming deafening and savage. His own voice tore apart and reknit itself as Charodon's, echoing off the stone. An icy hand gripped Roy's throat, and the screech intensified even as they threw his face into the basin again and again. Raw throat slicked by the vat, Roy screamed in Charodon's voice at the hands of the Altujan, pushing the devil back and swallowing more. How much time had passed? His feet scrabbled on the slick floor beneath him. He no longer remembered smells, his nose plugged by ichor.

Realizing what he was doing, Charodon strayed to the corner of his consciousness, staying back. If Roy died before Charodon had the chance to take over completely, then the essence of the monster would die too. Roy knew this much. Through the blue, he saw faces, hundreds of them, maybe even thousands. They stared at him as if waiting. A young boy with a bald head, a woman in a black veil, a blind old man with wispy white hair, a girl with a sharp chin and nose...

Roy didn't feel himself hit the sap-spattered floor, nor did he feel the raw grinding of bile against his throat as he purged the contents of his stomach. Numbness consumed his body, refusing to give sensation back for the moment. The only thing he felt was the quiet rage of his passenger, sitting defeated in the corner of his consciousness. In showing his willingness to die, he now had power over the Elder. It was a victory, a hollow one. A brief one.

"Roy?" he heard James's muffled, shaken voice call to him gently. He didn't answer, trembling on the stones, sackwear caked in bloodsap, hair plastered to his head. A shadow leaned over him, grasping his arms and dragging him toward his stool, trailing ichor.

"I respect your strength, godspawn," Mastreh said, her voice more clear. "But we are a patient people. You think you can die to defeat the Elders? Fine. We will keep you alive."

Clinking sounded to the right of him. Zatran was undoing the straps on James's restraints. A second trough glistened in anticipation next to the first.

Wrong

Samira tugged at her chains once again, more out of habit now. The expertly crafted metal was spotless, no rust and no weak points to exploit. Stone was not something that would just crumble with lightning either, and shocking her way free would risk serious damage to her left hand. She would need it to get out of here alive.

She tried to keep her mind off her restraints, but she kept coming to a more disturbing problem as she did so. Why had James claimed to host Vayne? Was he attempting to fool their captors into letting him go? No, they had taken him using the poison sap. They would not do that to their god if they thought the Eye of Disease was in control. He was being tortured, certainly, along with Roy. A day ago, Samira had heard the shrieks of Charodon attempting to break free. They had no way of knowing if Roy was holding together, nor did they know how James was faring. No rational thought would bring someone to *voluntarily* be dealt such suffering. Methods of the Altujan were mostly unknown, but judging by the way Ariel had panicked at the thought of Roy and James going through it, she had found some things in that book that were horrid.

Ariel herself sat in the back of her cage, head bowed as if in prayer, her legs drawn up to her chest. In the dark of the hall, the prisoner sackwear that they had been forced to don made her look like one of those pallet fruits she went on about. A pale gray shape with a tuft of gold silk at the top, and tattooed limbs looking like roots. It had been maybe two days since the Chosen had woken up and the Altujan had taken two of them, still no sign of the other crew members.

Another pang of fear struck Samira when she thought of that. Mastreh had said one or two of the sailors had been killed, maybe eaten. Was one of them Badlai? Just another person that she had likely gotten killed. A person she liked, maybe a bit more than she let on to herself. After Talia had died because of her mistakes, Samira had tried to ignore that kind of thing, focusing on training. Once she had read the prophecy passage at Frostspring, it had been all she had let herself focus on. That afternoon spent with Badlai on the beach had given a brief respite, a glimmer of something simple, happy, but now it seemed that she had destroyed that too. The thought deepened the sorrow she already felt.

Leonard had regained relative function of his limbs the day before. He paced restlessly in his cage, pulling at the cloth of his sackwear, shivering, as the arm holes were cut too large. After trying to tear the bars of his cell apart had proven fruitless a second time, he had attempted to manipulate the bricks beneath him. Without the use of his mace, he was not able to do much more than push a few stones downward. It would take a while before he could do anything meaningful.

"What are we going to do?" he said, repeating himself yet again.

"I don't know, Leonard," Samira replied, the same response she had given each time he had asked the question before.

"That can't be it. There has to be something better than me moving a few bricks around."

"If there is, I can't think of it," she snapped.

Samira glanced at where Ariel sat. The pattern of her glyphed arms and legs were barely discernible in the dim light. Normally the optimistic one, Ariel was incredibly quiet, and that worried her.

Leonard scratched his head, fingers combing through his spiky hair. "What if you try to shock the gauntlets off you?"

"I've already told you this. I could risk blowing my hand off, and then I'd be of no use to anyone." She sighed. This wasn't getting anyone anywhere, and Leonard was starting to get on her nerves. Helplessness was not something she could claim much experience with until now. Most times, there were at least *some* options.

Astus strike her, despite her experiences, the last time she had felt this way was when Talia died. It had been her own fault, showing off for the girl she had grown up with, trying to be a great hero of the histories after barely learning about her power. Talia had gone with her to their favorite outcropping, as she normally did during a storm. They watched the rain roll over the hills, the boiling clouds. They had made a game of Samira predicting when and where lightning would strike, as Samira had told Talia everything.

In an ignorant disregard of her father's advice, she had held out her right hand, intending to catch lightning for Talia. And she'd caught it, but was unable to handle it.

Now the reminder of that day greeted her every time she raised her right hand to eat, drink, greet someone, or draw her sword. The path of scars moved up and down her arm in the exact way she remembered, before it had leapt from her arm to the next conductor, Talia. It had killed her instantly, burning her eyes and lighting up her teeth. She had left the Watchtower Villa the next day, the day after she trudged back into town, one arm hanging uselessly, the other carrying the dead girl she had loved.

A jarring roar pierced through the air, slightly muffled by the stone walls around them. Samira retreated from her memories and attempted to bolt to her feet, forgetting momentarily about the chains around her wrists. The restraints yanked downward, and she sat down hard, cracking the back of her head on the bricks behind her. Charodon's roar was unmistakable. It carried deep, unrelenting hatred and insanity like nothing she had ever heard. The torture had either begun for the day or had started producing results.

"No!" Ariel sprang upward and attacked the bars of her cage, pulling on them with all her strength, failing to budge them. Desperation gleamed in her normally cautious and watchful eyes. Leonard strained against his own bars, attempting to force them apart and shouting.

The door to the chamber flew open, making way for shy of a dozen Altujan guards posted outside. Brandishing short swords and glaives in a flow of rust and black, the sentries halted at their cages, sap-coated weapons at the ready. Leonard backed away from the bars, palms facing outward. He scowled at the Altujan. Their violet eyes viewed them all with contempt, blood red hair immaculately, eerily so, combed over one shoulder.

Ariel ignored them, still struggling against her cell. As two of the guards approached her, she thrust her hand outward, exhaling in a hoarse yell. A sudden gust of hurricane-force winds slammed into the Altujan, crunching them against the wall a few feet away. The two sentries slumped to the spotless floor, gasping for the air that was banished from their chests. One of the captors brought the pole of a glaive down against Ariel's shoulder with a swift crack.

Ariel grunted sharply before grasping the handle, yanking the guard into the bars of her cage. The guard's sallow face dinged against the metal loudly. He stumbled back, clutching his forehead. Brandishing the glaive with un-characteristic menace, Ariel chopped, hacked, and pummeled the bars of her cage. Steel screeched in a twisted harmony with Charodon's roar, still sounding through their ears.

"Roy!" Ariel bellowed. "Stop it! Please, stop it!" she shouted at the captors. An unfortunate Altujan guard attempted to wrestle the polearm out of her hands through the bars and received a deep slash through the back of his hand. The appendage dripped dark violet blood that smelled of sulfur. Samira watched Ariel beat at her cell again and again, puffing with exertion, all while calling Roy's name. Guards gathered around her cage nervously. The rods of metal held firm against the curved blade of the glaive, and cracks began to etch into the weapon's edge.

A sharp crack and tinkling of metal was produced from the shattering polearm, blade fissuring into a dozen pieces, shaft splitting down the center. From the other side of the bars came a jabbing butt of a guard's spear. Driving squarely into Ariel's forehead, it sent her stumbling, dazed to the floor. Blood trickled along the stones as her hands were scored by the shards of metal. It mingled with the thick dark blood of the guard with the sliced hand but did not mix, like water and oil. Roy's screams—and the screams of Charodon—had stopped.

"Stop! She's done. Leave her alone!" Samira pleaded. Gathering up the pieces of the broken weapon, the sentries filed from the chamber, slamming the ornately lacquered door behind them. Samira trembled. Everyone she cared about got hurt because of her, her ambition, her striking hubris. Believing her father's fervor about some cryptic prophecy had set everything wrong. Her pride and arrogance had caused Talia to lose her life. From then, it had been one stupid decision after another. It had been at her suggestion that she and Roy travel to Boane to find secrets about the Alderaye, trying to find secrets that could prove her prophecy right, while also trying to correct her mistake of Roy's unwanted passenger. All of that had been disregarded the minute they had accidentally happened upon James.

Now she had pulled James into her fool's prophecy, risking his life for a cause he had no faith in. Her goading mixed with selective truth-telling had caused James to distrust her and *voluntarily* be tortured by these monsters. She pushed her friends against their will or ability in her selfish desire to accomplish her mission.

Wrong. All of it, wrong. She was a woman who had wanted to save the world, make her devoted father proud, and prove that her mistakes didn't matter. But they had mattered, more than anything she had done right. And now her mistakes would get everyone she cared about killed. Roy, James, Ariel, Leonard, Joskine, Badlai, poor Badlai.

She wasn't worthy to be a Chosen. The gods had given her a gift, and she had squandered it on a vague promise and her father's expectations, maybe on a lie. Why did the gods give this power to humans? She cursed them, cursed them vigorously. Astus, Iarus, Etah, the whole lot of them were cowards. She had said the words, followed the scripture given to her by her father, and she still ruined everything.

Samira bowed her head, shame spreading to every corner of her body. It made her stomach crawl. "This is my fault. All of it." Tears flowed steadily down her dark cheeks. "I'm so sorry. I've failed you, all of you." She turned to Leonard. "I do nothing but put you all in danger."

Shocked at this sudden apology, Leonard shuffled on his knees to the edge of his cage. His sackwear rustled as he adjusted his bag-shirt. They were used to strong emotions from Samira, but never outward despair. "We're Chosen, Sam. Danger just sort of finds us. It's not your fault."

Samira shook her head vigorously, blustering. She couldn't keep it down anymore. "I knew we were chasing Charodon."

Ariel, still dazed, lifted her head. "*What?*"

"When we went to the Marshes, I knew that it was Charodon. I wanted to be the one to kill it, to prove that the prophecy my father believed was true. I was afraid that you wouldn't come, so I lied. A believable lie, a Saltboar, a group of marauders, something manageable. It was supposed to be a turning point, my time to leap into a destiny I wanted." There was no stopping the tears now. She wept openly. "Instead, I fell ill, and I soldiered on like a fool. We got lost, and it attacked Roy. Strike me, it's my fault. My fault. All my...fault." Great, heaving sobs filled her throat, choking her. "And then I let my pride and guilt hide this shame. I let Roy blame you, Leonard. Every *striking* thing that's happened since that day is because of me."

Stiffening in quiet rage, Leonard turned from Samira as the information sank in, exhaling forcefully. "I mutilated him, left him to die. He almost killed me, and you're telling me that you could have prevented this?"

"Roy and James are being tortured to death as we speak." Ariel clenched her teeth. "The sailors are being killed one by one, and you think an *apology* will fix anything? All you ever did was spout about the virtue of Astus and the rest of the gods, and you didn't even have the spine to follow it yourself. James has heard nothing in his life but lies, and now he can't trust us because you've been lying to him, and we've stupidly followed your lead." Her voice broke, "And Roy's whole future was stolen. He probably won't last another year even if he survives."

Samira closed her eyes, clamping down on the flow of tears. "You love him."

"From the day I met him."

The tears didn't stop. She could feel them surging through her eyelids and down her face, unable to even use her sackwear to dry them, hands restrained. This pride, this shameful craving for a true prophecy had caused Roy's possession and the eventual fracturing of the Chosen. Everything she had ever done was wrong.

Samira had thought she could kill the Eye of Nature herself. *Wrong.*

She had let Roy blame Leonard to escape both his rage and her own guilt. *Wrong.*

Then she held the truth from James, perhaps killing his faith in everything. *Striking wrong.*

"I've damned us all."

Heaving herself into a sitting position, Ariel refused to look at her. Instead, she fiddled with something in her bleeding hands. Samira blinked through her tears. What was that? Blood dripped from Ariel's fingers as she held up a thin gleaming object. It was a shard of steel from the broken glaive, about two inches in length. She had hidden it from the guards in her hand when she fell. Shakily stepping toward the lock on her door, pinching the shard between her fingers, Ariel spoke firmly.

"I will *not* let them die. We need you to escape this place alive, but then I never want to see you again, do you hear me? No one else will die today, and after today you're on your own. Sort out your prophecy if you want, but our lives won't be disposable so you can fulfill your destiny," Ariel snapped. She unlocked Leonard's cell first. The two of them glowered into Samira's cage, waiting for her response.

No words could come out. She could only nod. Nod and weep.

An Empty Cage

James sat, arms bound with heavy chains before a massive steel cage. Roy slumped beside him, breathing heavily. Why they had been brought here was beyond him. After blistering torture, the bloodbreathing had broken him. Shivers continually ran down his body, as if in rhythm. Gone were any memories of what food or wine tasted like. Even water, if there was such a thing, no longer held any place in his memory. His smells were of sap, his tastes of blood. Everything was tinted dark blue. The sensation of blood rushing down his throat sickened him; he gagged on his own thoughts. It had been enough to send his mind spiraling for the better part of the following day, only to be further broken down by the subsequent horrors that Zatran had to offer.

Still, James had to be faring better than Roy, as his fellow captive hadn't spoken once since the first bloodbreathing. James regretted volunteering to support this liar. He could take a beating, but this was maddening. He had tried relentlessly throughout the torture to tell them he had lied, but the ichor choking him had made it impossible to speak.

The room extended far beyond the faint ring of light provided by the crack of a closed door behind them. An Altujan—Zatran or Mastreh, James had forgotten which—stood near it in silence. Blood sap still sluggishly circulated under his skin from the scratchy lacerations Zatran had made to his arm, rendering him too drowsy to move quickly. It seemed to only affect those who had the sap in their bloodstream. As he glanced around sleepily, wincing, the dried sap on his head and shoulders cracked and flaked off.

The spotless stone floors did little to reflect any light further into the chamber. Extremely tight, the space on the floor they occupied was mere feet from the cage, its bars like metal fangs.

Something sinister struck him about this place, gaping, endless, seeming eager to swallow him and Roy whole. In truth, James had no idea how large this chamber was, for the cage stretched onward forever. Maybe it was just his depth perception askew, as he was only able to see out of one eye for now, the other one swollen shut. Hard to think of a part of his body that wasn't bruised though. The chains ground against the skin of his wrists, and his one-eyed vision still blurred slightly, throwing off his senses. Whatever tree that sap had come from, the Altujan kept it in very ready supply. He tried reaching outward with his senses but only managed to make it a few feet.

He glanced at Roy, still caked with dried resin. Indeed, the trauma and shaking were not enough to bank the anger that he felt. Cursing himself for ever thinking that standing up for Roy was a good idea, he boiled. What kind of scorching nonsense that had been, to endure the agony and morally support a liar, a *traitor*? Even Vayne, the enemy, had been more honest than his supposed friends, and Roy was one of the more honest ones! Roy's increasing silence was making him nervous, and it was making their captors, Mastreh in particular, more frustrated.

Rather than fighting back and becoming enraged, Roy had just taken the torment, silent for more of it every hour. They weren't able to move much in their restraints, but James still shifted enough to look behind him. Mastreh eyed him with an expression that definitely *looked* like hunger.

"Is there a point to this? If you're offering a bigger cage, I'll take it," he snarked, trying to act unfazed despite his quite obvious trembling.

Mastreh stepped forward and shoved him back in the direction of the yawning cage, deciding not to speak. She had folded the checked coat and now stood in trousers and one of those odd silk shirts with a gray slash mark down the middle. It billowed around her, making James wonder if there was some kind of air circulation in this chamber. If there was, he couldn't tell. Even though she had lost her infantry jacket, she didn't look any less warlike. He glanced back at Roy, hoping to see a change in his mood, and was unsurprised when there was none.

"That cage is already occupied, Eye of Disease," she said, annoyed. They had started calling him and Roy by their "true names" instead of their host names. So far they had not noticed that James was not, in fact, a host for Vayne.

Mastreh walked casually to the door of the cage and traced a finger along the bar with a reverent, nostalgic air. "We have a great gift for the Elders: the very last of your pets. We bred them for centuries, trained them as attack dogs for you, sometimes fed our own people to them to keep them alive."

James squinted into the cage with his good—well, *semi*-good—eye. Fuzzy darkness was all that greeted his sight. Beyond the reinforced, fanged bars of the pen was only blackness. Shadow. Roy was not paying attention, looking down, or at least had his head bowed. Bastard.

"With the absence of you and the rest of our gods, the beasts grew more and more feral, and we couldn't keep them in captivity any longer. Unfortunately, many had to be killed because of the danger they posed. But this one, this *one*, is the last one we ever were able to breed. It waits for orders. It waits for you." Her light-violet eyes reflected some light that wasn't there, flashing briefly in the darkness. "And I have a sense that you've been waiting for *it*."

James felt outward, weakly, with his senses. They wobbled, held at bay by the toxic sap, reaching no more than five feet inside the cage. Nothing. No heat. No life. There was nothing in there. He feigned a smirk, letting it evolve into a forced chuckle from his salty, blue-stained lips. It bounced off the polished walls of the chamber, distorting and coming back to him before finally dying out.

"You think we're scared of an empty cage?" he jeered, spitting the taste of blood out of his mouth. "Two of us are Dragoneaters. A friend of mine tells me that's pretty significant. I don't like history lessons either, so you can scorch your story about the Elders." His eyes darted quickly about, praying that Mastreh didn't sense his posturing.

Roy suddenly looked up, the orange corner of his eye shining through the inky void. His pupils widened, and low growl vibrated at the base of his throat. The sliver of orange clawed its way across the turquoise, enveloped it. From the depths of the blackness behind the bars rang a short, guttural cackle. The laugh crawled across the stone walls. James's skin felt as if it were crawling itself from the trembling, askew sound. Just human enough to pass, but with an edge of something unspeakable. With no thought to stop himself, James moved to cover his ears, only to be stopped by the chains slathering his wrists. Roy's breathing became ragged, hostile. *Whatever is in here, it's having some kind of effect on Charodon*, he realized. The cackling faded, stretching thin and seeming to shred in his ears. It made his skin prickle.

"You're welcome to spend the night in this 'empty' cage if you feel so strongly." Mastreh leered. "It won't protect you from the attack dog in there or from your friend out here." She laid a hand on Roy's right shoulder, fingernails digging into his skin. Another bellowing cry launched from Roy's mouth, overlaid with the sharp hiss of Charodon.

Still spreading across Roy's right eye, the orange gleamed dangerously. It didn't seem like the devil was responding neutrally to whatever presence was here. The Eye of Nature was posturing, overriding Roy's control to do so. The thing in the room with them was no friend. It wasn't a pet, more like a threat. Mastreh bared her teeth. In the dim lighting of the chamber, her mouth resembled a void, ready to swallow him and everything he knew.

James shuffled to Roy, trying, failing to ignore Mastreh's psychotic grin. He spoke slowly. Deliberately. Desperately. "You can't do this, Roy. You can't let him win."

"And what do you care?" Roy rasped. The voice that left him deepened, sounding as though gravel were being poured into a barrel. "I've seen your face, James. I know that face. You've given up. We mean nothing to you."

"I..." James fumbled. Lying wasn't going to help. They had lied to him, misled him, and would probably get him killed. The only thing he could count on was that if Charodon never broke out, he would live that much longer. He thought Roy had been one of the honest ones, but it turned out that he had been keeping secrets too. James was trying to save his own skin. *That* was why he cared.

A pang of guilt was quickly smothered by the indignant anger he had felt for nearly a week. None of this was his fault. He wasn't the one who whisked himself away into peril after peril, almost dying and getting covered in every scorching substance conceivable. Roy may be one of the better ones, but even he wasn't worth it. Doing the noble thing had been a foolish, naive, idiotic choice.

"I'm sorry this happened to you, Roy. You didn't deserve this. But you lied to me. You didn't tell me that what you hosted was an Elder." Mastreh's eyes narrowed as James continued. "I can't trust any of you. People have lied to me all my life, and what did putting faith in anything get me? They murdered my brother, claiming the gods willed it. There are no gods, Roy. It's just us. Samira is going to get us all killed, and I don't intend to follow her prophecy to the grave. Scorch me, I've almost died just sticking up for you. So go ahead, give in or don't. Just do it far away from me."

Roy shook, sweat trickling down his forehead. "I won't lose, not without taking him with me. If he and I both lose, then in a way I win." More cackling reverberated against the walls. Roy struggled to face him. That single orange eye burned an afterimage into James's sight. "I've been ready for this for a long time, and that is no lie. But I can sniff out lies too, and your mouth is betraying you. It doesn't matter if Dathos or Iarus don't exist. You've always been faithless, pathless, wanting nothing but revenge, and I feel sorry for you."

James sneered indignantly. "You're sorry for *me*? I've only survived this long because I know what trusting someone, anyone, will get me. You trusted Leonard, and I don't see you reaping much benefit. Go ahead and let yourself die if that's what you think is best. Leave me out of it. You all think you have this noble purpose, don't you? But it's just what you think is best for *yourself*."

His shoulder flared as Mastreh's hand clamped down, squeezing painfully. The pressure against his collarbone was immense. He whimpered in pain and squeezed his eyes shut. From the back of his mind flooded the sensation of breathing in ichor. *Don't. Please don't send me back. I'll do anything.*

"You lied, didn't you?" Mastreh snarled. "You don't host Vayne. You're just some upstart godspawn." She growled in disgust and hurled him to the floor, chains clanking, leaving specs of rust on the spotless bricks. Mastreh snagged James's chains with her fingers and hauled him to her side, dragging him. "Why don't we go back and give your friend some time alone? You boys don't seem to be getting along anyway."

She cast the heavy door open, making way for dim blue sunlight. She grumbled while pulling him along, "Zatran's going to bitch about this for days, only having Charodon and being tricked into thinking Vayne had returned. With any luck, he'll at least let me peel the eyelids off you. Blink now so you remember what it was like."

James looked backward toward the structure they had just left and watched the door slip shut. Even the door hinges were expertly made not to squeak. It was a masterpiece of architecture and craftsmanship. They walked—or in his case, was dragged—through the encampment of Altujan hovels and buildings that made up the colony. Elegant stone structures rose around them, none ever more than two stories, in triangular-shaped groups. The ones with the best craftsmanship often faced the center plaza, while the shoddier structures were placed outward.

All Altujan walking about were dressed in rust and black-checked garb, whether it was in the form of loose shirts, coats, or pants. Blood red hair weaved and parted as if it were a river.

Grotesque statues of Altujan defeating humans, and even Chosen, in battle stood in prominent places around the colony. He watched other prisoners and slaves in sackwear, eyes glazed over with sap-induced delirium, as they hauled stone across town to supply their captors with material for challenges or general building. Altujan children in checkered rags feasted on a barely-cooked slab near him, peering in curiosity over their greasy hands at him. He tried hard not to think of who that banquet may have been.

"Those dragons you and your allies killed have been doing wonders to feed our colony. Suppose we should be thanking you," Mastreh said. She snarled at James's quizzical glance. "The humans called us flesh eaters centuries ago, made it easier to go along with wiping us out. What's ironic is that we only ate human when we were exiled, starving. Sometimes they would stumble across us in a year of need. Human? Not my favorite, if I'm honest. We have everything we need here." He felt her grip tighten on his chains. "Our kind has had to rebuild, but we've become something greater, something worthy of the Elders' respect. We will have our vengeance on your kind. Mark my promise on that."

James caught many nods of respect cast in Mastreh's direction from the red-clad Altujan. She was the embodiment of every horror story the Temple had used to scare him and Gemmi into obedience as children: strong, cruel, and starving for vengeance. And her fellow colony members showed that they held these traits in the highest esteem.

They came to a magnificently built structure near the edge of the high-rank buildings. The beams, support, and furnishings were all expertly chiseled out of stone. Where did they get all of it? An awning of bumpy, molted dragon skin stretched over the supports, casting a green hue over the Altujan high-bloods standing beside a map. Zatran was among them. He looked up at Mastreh strolling up the steps to the meeting platform, painfully bumping James's toes against the steps as she pulled him along.

"What are you doing with this one?" Zatran frowned. He obviously was not overjoyed to see Mastreh here.

"He's been lying to us. Vayne isn't with him." Mastreh crossed her arms, still holding the end of James's chains.

Zatran shut his eyes tightly as if suffering from a headache and took two steps, crossing the distance between him and James with surprising swiftness. The Altujan stood less than an inch from James's face. Violet eyes blazed, black teeth ground in barely controlled rage.

"You don't hold Vayne, do you?"

James shrugged, feigning confidence. "Maybe it was just indigestion. Could have sworn I felt sick." The look on Zatran's face was enough to grant him a fleeting moment of satisfaction before the blow struck his face. James fell, weighed down by his chains and the force of the open palm. Mastreh didn't attempt to pick him back up.

Kicking James with each word, Zatran slowly began to lose his temper, "You *insufferable, miserable, wretch*!" He waved a dismissal to Mastreh. "Take him back to the troughs. We'll reserve some bloodbreathing for him." Smiling, he bared his teeth at James. "Just for fun."

Honest

Metal bit into the tip of Ariel's finger again, causing her to swear sharply. "Etah lash me," Ariel said. Samira and Leonard raised their eyebrows in surprise. Curses were not something that came out of her mouth often, or ever. Well, they would have to get used to it today, because a long time had passed since she could remember being this anxious or *angry*. Samira had harbored all of this resentment at her and Leonard for leaving? It was the least funny joke she had ever heard after Samira's confession. Working on the Champion of Astus's stone gauntlets, Ariel couldn't even look at her.

The restraints were beautifully crafted. Memories from the dusty book she had read at the refuge flooded back to her as she worked. Altujan were sorted into different factions of the colony: builders, smiths, warriors, and hunters. How good you were with your craft within your faction determined your social status, meaning a builder of exceptional station had labored to keep Samira restrained. No need for farmers, they never grew anything, just hunted or kept livestock.

A quiet click sounded, and Ariel felt the slight movement of the locking mechanism at the base of the gauntlet. For a scary moment, she feared that she had broken her metal shard, but closer inspection calmed her nerves. She quickly pulled the stone bracer off of Samira's left hand and moved to the other one.

Leonard paced outside the cage, stroking the stubble on his face, more of a full beard now since their journey had begun. "So what do we do? There are still around..." He counted mentally. "...*seven or eight* glaives and swords out there, at least. We don't have our weapons." He shuffled uncomfortably. Ariel was well aware that his inability to manipulate much earth without his mace was a source of considerable embarrassment.

Another muffled click and Samira's other hand was free. Ariel heaved herself into a standing position, her knees popping, and threw down the shard. It chimed against the stone floor. "No need, Leonard. *We're* the weapons." She wiped her bloody fingers on her sackwear. "Use your muscles for fighting and not courting for once."

Leonard nodded quickly, the corner of his mouth twitching upward.

Samira stood uneasily, rubbing her temple with her thumb, a habit she would never give up, it appeared. "I'll take care of the guards. You two need to find James, Roy, and the others. If I make noise and bring others to my location, it leaves you free to get everyone to safety."

Ariel rolled her eyes at Samira taking point but could find no holes in her logic. As long as Samira could hold off the guards outside, that would give her a chance to find the others. "Leonard, you find your soldiers. It's possible that some of them are still alive, and we'll need all the help we can get if we find a ship to steal." She hoped there would be a ship at least. The book she had read had mentioned nothing about Altujan sailing anywhere. *But they had to have gotten to the Tarsals somehow, right? Even if it was centuries ago.*

They gathered near the door to the chamber, huddled together, steeling themselves for the fight ahead. Metallic blood-scent lingered from Ariel's bleeding hand when she breathed in deeply through her nose, extending her senses outward and feeding oxygen into her body. Air moved from the corners of the chamber and converged on her position. Opening her eyes and nodding to Leonard, she thrust her hands out toward the solid wooden door, hurling a torrent of wind. It punched against the wood and shattered it outward with the pieces hailing on an unlucky guard standing just outside.

Shouts of confusion chattered in the open air outside the chamber. Their prison had been a lowly-built structure at the lower point of a triangle formation. The other buildings making the triangle were inferred to be prisons as well.

As Ariel stepped into the white-blue sunlight, her eyes burned, and she felt the urge to sneeze. She fought these distractions and ducked, narrowly missing a swinging polearm. It screeched against the brick wall behind her. Ariel grabbed the wooden shaft and kicked out hard, catching the guard that was holding it in the shoulder. With enough leverage to wrestle it away from him, she spun quickly. The glaive twirled and smacked the Altujan in the side of the head with the butt of the weapon. He slumped immediately to the ground. She glanced to the side and saw Leonard deliver a blistering punch to a guard on her left. He glanced in her direction.

"Go!" he hollered and sprinted off toward the other prison structures. Muffled shouting sounded within them, dozens of voices crying to be let out.

Ariel frantically looked around. Several sentries were left, and they circled around. Her eyes landed on Samira, who emerged from the barrack, left hand held outward, electricity popping in her eyes.

"You heard him. Go," she said firmly.

Dashing away, Ariel fought the urge to turn around. Even in the daylight, blinding flashes lit up the area as Samira engaged the remaining Altujan. She was a liar, but Samira could handle this. Ariel had no doubt of that.

Tropical trees with green and purple fronds peppered the Altujan colony, not doing much to shade the slate-gray buildings but providing the monsters with that sap they loved to use. Several of them had spiles jutting from the bark, dripping with the blue substance. The roads and grounds around the buildings were made of dirt and sand, like dark-golden sugar.

Where are they keeping them? She searched for a building that might resemble the chamber that they had just left. While some varied in size and integrity, none looked different enough to be suspect. She hid behind a masonry wall and crouched. Did she dare climb one of these buildings to get a better look? It could at least help her get her bearings.

Several panicked shouts moved behind her in the direction of where Samira fought. She was a Dragoneater. She could buy them some more time. Ariel's anger at the woman didn't change the fact that she didn't want her to die. Ariel's Spiathi values would compel her to lend aid if needed. She had to find the others fast. Hopefully Leonard was having better luck.

She came to a narrow, two-story building with shoddy cobbling. It's V-pattern resembled more of a U due to a sad-looking sag in the middle. Careful to avoid the sag, she gripped bricks toward the corner of the structure and began to climb. Her cut fingers stung with the pressure, but she ignored that for now. She reached the apex of the building and scampered across the roof. Maintaining a low profile would be the only way to not get caught.

Ariel noticed a group of soldiers quickly making their way back in the direction she had come. Sharp bursts of lightning continued to flash to her flank, distracting the rest of the colony. It was a relief that the sap they had been most recently injected with had worn off before they attempted this. Perhaps with Ariel and Leonard having weaker power and Samira being effectively restrained, the enemy had not entertained enough suspicion. Either way, it was their mistake.

Ariel continued to survey the colony in front of her. Hundreds of domiciles stretched across the island in triangular formations around a single point, an awning that looked to be made of dragon skin that covered something. An altar? It was possible. They did worship Elders, as they had called them. Could they be keeping Roy or James there?

More shouts echoed from behind her, heading toward where Samira fought. She had to hurry.

The wind carried much toward her, too much to decipher all at once. Sounds, smells, even some feelings floated along the air currents. She extended her senses outward, feeling for anything that could give her a clue. There had to be something. There had to be.

"*Tah, you have your orders.*" No, that wasn't it.

The smell of burning roots. Not it, either.

"*They've escaped? How? Who let this happen?*" Getting warmer.

The sounds and smells blew past her rapidly from one to the next. Ariel flitted through each one, concentrating hard until a voice she recognized hit her ears.

"*Please.*"

She started. It was him. This was very, very bad. More than that. Roy was pleading, begging. She followed the current to the source, a low but very wide structure at the opposite edge of the awning. Of course. Activity was heavy toward the center of the settlement, but she would be damned if she didn't get there in time.

An arrow zipped past her head, actually catching a few strands of hair as it sped by. She rolled to her left, off the edge of the roof and toward the ground. Rolling again as her feet hit to mitigate the force, she came up sprinting around the circular pattern of the inner streets. Another arrow narrowly missed her, slamming into a wall and shattering on impact. A quick glance at the wood from the arrow shaft was enough to confirm that someone was using *her* bow, or at least just the arrows she had made. The anger pushed her limbs to move even faster. Where were the arrows coming from?

She deflected the next one with a short burst of breath, changing the air around her to push the projectile to the side. It veered off course and stuck into the rough soil. Where the source was and who was firing were still mysteries. The trajectory suggested somewhere to her right flank, but she wasn't completely sure. Ariel continued on. This wasn't the highest priority. She had to get to Roy and James.

The arrows clacked off the brick walls around her, narrowly snagging her patterned calf. She grunted and slapped a hand to her leg. It wasn't serious, just a scratch. Her sackwear flapped as she ran. At least she could move in it, but it wasn't terribly comfortable. Very itchy.

Yet another projectile sped toward her, directly from the front this time. Ariel dropped to the ground and slid through the pebbles beneath her. It tore at her legs and her side. She grit her teeth and ignored the sting, looking ahead. Just fifty feet in front of her stood a short, bullish Altujan archer, nocking an arrow. He was using her bow, *her bow*. The pudgy fingers of her attacker gripped the sturdy wood of the weapon. From a distance, she could still see his shiny black grimace. Frustration. His prey was eluding his grasp.

This must be a hunter. Time to test his skills.

Ariel ran straight at the hunter, zigzagging to confuse him. The Altujan held steady and followed her leisurely with the bow. Releasing the arrow, he fired straight at her heart. She darted to the right suddenly. The arrow missed by a handwidth or two. He nocked another quickly. This one did have some skill.

She had to get close enough to ruin his accuracy. If she could get within reach, she would have him. Ariel drew in oxygen in a deep breath and held it, waiting for the enemy to loose the arrow, watching intently. As the next arrow flew, she pushed downward with both hands and exhaled all her breath in a sharp puff. A Dreadfront-strength wind left her and struck the ground, kicking up gold dirt, launching her into the air. *The third form.* Ariel sailed upward in an arc. Twisting madly in the air, she held onto her direction.

The hunter gasped and shielded his eyes. He looked up, the sun blinding him.

A sharp cry left the Altujan as Ariel crashed down upon him. He was knocked to the ground with a forceful thump, his arms limply slapping the soil. Already dazed, he looked up at Ariel just in time to see her fist rushing toward him. The force of the punch threatened to break her hand, but it held firm, knocking the archer out cold.

Huffing angrily, Ariel climbed off the Altujan and ripped the bow from his grasp. The feeling of the wood in her hand was like the embrace of an old friend, and she relished it. She took back her arrows and quiver.

Without pausing to catch her breath, she took off in the direction of Roy's voice on the wind, praying that she wasn't too late.

***

James sat in the spotless bloodbreathing chamber, arms strung up over his head this time. The chains pulled against the tops of his wrist, and there was an obstruction to any feeling in his hands now because of it. Zatran busied himself near the tanks of fluid he had siphoned from the trees, soaking rags in the substance. The sunlight from above was starting to burn James's skin, something he hadn't thought possible after nineteen years in the desert. Well, this had been a time of firsts.

This was definitely a first for lying to be voluntarily tortured and then tortured for lying. There was some irony in that, though not much he could appreciate. Those troughs less than twelve feet from him filled him with a sense of drowning even with air rushing in and out of his chest.

"You've wasted much of my time, godspawn," Zatran growled from across the room. "Lying was a terrible mistake. But now, instead of unknowingly wasting my time, I've decided to spend some precious minutes *intentionally* wasting my time. We're going to become best of friends, you and I. Well, until I decide we aren't."

James shook, trying desperately not to look at that foul, dark mouth, but found himself unable to look away. This was what he got for trusting others. This was what happened when—

The door burst inward, sunlight framing Mastreh's imposing figure. Her hair was wild, no longer combed to one side neatly. Disheveled leather armor covered her body, a tattered fencing shirt and trousers underneath it. A saber, jagged and cruel, hung at her belt. Her violet eyes glowed with anger but also with a strange eagerness. Zatran rolled his eyes.

"What?" he said.

"They've wriggled free," Mastreh spat. A bloodthirsty grin sprouted on her face.

Zatran had no words, but James watched his pale face grow uncommonly dark. A wide range of emotions passed over the Blood Herald's face before it settled on rage. "We need to contain this, *now*. But we need to do this ourselves. Worst case, we could call the other colonies, get them all here. But we wait until it's the last resort."

"Already done. The blue-clad are on their way," Mastreh said.

Zatran stopped, a controlled yet furious tone inflecting his voice, "You what?"

"I called them," Mastreh said slowly, condescendingly, "so that they can help us *contain* the supernaturally powered prisoners who have escaped on *our* watch. We could kill this whole uprising before it starts if we remove the Chosen from the game."

Tense silence fell over the room. James looked back and forth between the Blood Herald and his second in command. He held his breath, as if even the act of breathing could send them both into a fury and lash out at him. Zatran glared at his subordinate, keeping a firm grip on his knife, the other hand on his hip, patting softly.

"The day you second-guess my orders is the day you find yourself in the sea without limbs, Mastreh. We had an understanding."

"I don't understand weakness. Neither do the Elders, or the colony." Mastreh sneered.

Zatran glowered and placed his other hand on the handle of his other knife. His white knuckles whitened further as he gripped the blades fiercely.

Mastreh rolled her head around as if to crack her neck, but it made no sound, as if she had already cracked it recently. "After you then. Lead the colony. Let the Chosen kill you before I do, or maybe you'll survive and we'll spend another thousand years cowering in the shadows."

They left the room, posting a guard out front. James's breath left him in a panicked croak, followed by several more breaths. After spending time among these monsters and watching them interact, he understood why the room around him, and most others he saw, were impossibly clean. Shiny clean exteriors hid the savagery and violence underneath.

The troughs of blood sap still sat at the edge of the chamber, taunting him. His nostrils recoiled and simultaneously craned forward at the metallic smell. Trying and failing to slow his breathing, James blinked through blurred vision. Blurred by his shock and by his tears. This wasn't fair. None of this was fair. Why couldn't the world have just left him alone to be some poor bastard in the middle of the desert? He could curse a god, he could blame a deity, but what was he supposed to do when all of this had happened for *no reason*.

He tried again and again to melt his restraints, to feel heat within him and transfer it to the chains, but he could feel nothing. His heart rate refused to slow, and all he could feel was numbing defeat. There was some movement outside, a shout, muffled by the sound of his own breath in his throat. The sap had worn off, but James still felt nothing. He was nothing, had nothing. All this power that he had attained for no other reason than chaotic luck, and he was nothing. The Temple had robbed his childhood from him, saddling him with a name that wasn't his and killing his brother. And the only people he had ever considered friends were no better. Even his vengeance against the Temple would go undealt.

"James?"

He looked up. Several figures crowded the doorway, one of them a bit taller and bulkier than the rest.

He felt a hand on his shoulder, a face hovering in front of him. "James, we're getting out of here," Leonard said, shaking him softly.

Blinking slowly, James looked around him. He was surrounded by other prisoners in sackwear. Malnourished, filthy, barely able to stand up straight. None of them were people he recognized, except for a few standing behind Leonard. A ginger crescent, shaped like the moon, hovered over one shoulder, and wide green eyes peered over the other.

"Dathos drown me, son. You look terrible," Joskine said.

Leonard shot him a look. "Don't tell him that. He can't see what he looks like."

"Pretty sure he feels worse, Len."

"*Do not* call me that."

"Too late. You're Len now."

James tuned out their bickering. He was tired of it, acting like he was happy to see them when they were just going to lie to him some more. Badlai peered at him with concern, her expressive eyes trying to get an answer from him.

Leonard shook him again, nodding at Joskine to remove the chains. "Come on. We have to go."

"...lied to me," James muttered.

"What?" Leonard craned in.

"*You lied to me!*" James barked. "I trusted you, and none of you told me there was an Elder hiding among us in plain sight. All of you, the Temple, the Elders, the Altujan. You all use your power and the people around you to get what you want. *All of you are the problem!*"

Straightening up, Leonard bit his lip. There were words there. James could see them, could see the words ready to fly from Raslena's—or whatever's—Chosen. He saw guilt, he saw shame, he saw urgency, and he saw anger.

"You're right. We did lie to you. We said that we wouldn't, and we did anyway," Leonard said, brown eyes pleading. "We've all lied, and it's pretty obvious that we've come to sow what we've reaped, James. I'm sorry."

James turned his head, not interested in an apology. He felt his chains rustle, Joskine tugging at them.

"I ran away from Charodon, Roy nearly killed me, and it turns out that Samira was responsible for all of it. Raslena crush me, I don't even want to *know* what I'll find out tomorrow. But they're all I have. They're all that *you* have. We aren't the gods. We are terrible people. People like us don't deserve the power that we have.

I don't even know how we can wake up each morning and face each other, but I think you do."

James squinted, confused.

"We didn't have you before. You can keep us honest, James. The life you've had until this point gives you the ability to tell us when we're wrong. We've known this power and have been shaped by it for most of our lives. It's corrupted us, but you can make us better. I know it doesn't seem like it, but you already have. I've seen it, even if you haven't." Leonard caught James as Joskine finally undid the clasps around his wrists.

James's arms spasmed in protest. Wheezing against Leonard's shoulder, he waited for his breath to deepen, normalize.

Leonard spoke into his ear, calming him, "We've spent our entire lives just going through the motions of being Chosen. The empire and the Temple have gone through the motions of being altruistic. But you, you may be able to help us do it for real. You can do what the Temple never could. You can help others to be *better*."

A minute passed. Leonard looked over his shoulder nervously. They had been standing here for much longer than was safe to do so.

James's anger still clung to the front of his mind, but he understood that he still needed the others to get out alive. He understood that they had come back for him. And he understood that Leonard may be right. "Where to?" James sighed.

Leonard's expression hardened as Joskine clapped him on the muscular back. "To help Sam and then get out. The woman infuriates me, but we can't leave her behind."

Not sure how to feel, James nodded. Joskine pressed something into his hand. It was a sword. Not his, but it was enough. James tightened his grip around the rough leather wrap of the sword's hilt and gritted his teeth.

It was time to go.

Crimson and Violet

Samira lashed out, pummeling an Altujan with the butt of a stolen glaive. He stumbled backward and left an opening for her to slash. The long blade of the glaive carved a deep canyon in his chest, violet, jagged. Falling among the rest of the slain soldiers, his leather armor squelched loudly. She doubled over briefly, leaning on the weapon, and panted.

Blood leisurely trickled from her forehead where a sword had nicked her, and her left hand was already spasming from the electric current flowing through her fingertips. Letting loose too early had been a mistake. Strike her, she would only be able to do something significant once, maybe twice more.

More than a dozen bodies were strewn around her in the shape of what loosely resembled a ragged star. Black scorch marks dotted the dark-golden dirt around her, and more than a few trees no longer had fronds. Violet blood soaked into the earth, reflecting the off-blue sunlight. She hadn't had a fight like that in years, hadn't *killed* like that in years. That seemed to be all she was good for, either killing directly or getting others killed.

Running in the direction that Ariel had gone, Samira snapped the polearm of the glaive against some toppled rock, leaving her with a three-foot blade with a handle of similar length. Even though there was a lull in attackers, she could clearly hear the sounds of mobilization in the distance. She could lead them in a chase around the compound and give her friends—well, probably not friends anymore—a chance to escape.

What about James? Did anyone find him? Her feet smacked against the soil as she followed Ariel's bare footprints. It wasn't like there were any flesh eaters not wearing shoes. She winced, feeling an upturned thorn enter her foot. *Ignore it, strike you.*

The tracks that Ariel's light feet made in the dirt began to shuffle, with indents and strange patterns marking the sides of a street. A fight had taken place here. Samira surveyed the area; a plump imprint of a body was outlined in the space between two buildings nearby. A few drops of purple blood accompanied it. Ariel looked like she had walked away the victor. Following the tracks that led onward, Samira inhaled in short bursts.

The improvised sword in her hand sang, slicing through the air. Ariel had most likely gone in the direction of Roy, or at least wherever she assumed he was. It made sense, since he was the top priority. Secure him and their chances of survival went up tenfold. Despite this, she felt her already racing heart scream at her. There was no telling how Roy would react to the truth. The man she had considered to be her best friend would likely now want to see her dead.

"There she is!" a gruff voice called from her left.

Samira turned frantically, narrowly missing the whistling blade of a sword. It gleamed at her with a blackened, serrated edge. Why did these monsters have these edges to all their weapons?

Pulling backward and leaning against a nearby structure, she made out four soldiers, all armored in leather with red-checkered fencing shirts underneath. Each one brandished one of those strange, toothed blades along with black and white snarls.

Samira growled, sidestepping one attack and bringing her blade down with the force of a lightning strike. It sank into the shoulder of the next soldier, splitting her armor and collarbone. Wrenching her sword free, Samira batted aside a blow from another Altujan. A boot collided with her stomach and sent her back, gasping.

She barely had time to duck before the next blade flashed near her head. They were surrounding her, pinning her against the wall. Her right arm groaned in protest as she swung outward in an arc while ducking, blade biting in the leather breastplate of a male Altujan. It connected, but it didn't do enough damage to be fatal. He roared and attempted to stab downward straight into her glaring eyes.

Grunting, Samira yanked the blade free of the leather and flicked her wrist upward at the male's forearm. The edge caught him just enough to falter his thrust, drawing dark ichor and making him recoil slightly. She lunged forward and tackled the soldier. Samira cried out as the metal teeth of his blade ripped through her sackwear, dragging against her shoulder blade. A warm trickle immediately bloomed from her back. The blood stuck her shirt to her skin.

Samira rolled off the sentry and thrust a hand directly at the two remaining enemies. Lightning rushed from her fingertips and hurled one of them, a male, backward through the wall. The mortar connecting the stones crumbled and fell inward on top of him. She spied the last one, a female, and approached slowly. The last soldier's maroon eyes were wide with horror, and they darted nervously to Samira's hands, one holding a blade, the other crackling with blue lightning. Thunder rumbled inside her chest.

"Your armor, *now*," Samira growled.

The woman nodded, raising her hands and looking to Samira's left.

Samira raised her shard of metal to the left on instinct, blocking a swipe from the one she had tackled. From the corner of her vision, she saw the other one rush toward her, weapon held aloft. Yelling wordlessly, Samira swept her blade in a wide arc. The steel caught one in the throat and the one she had tackled in the same spot as before. This time, the weapon bit clean through the breastplate and smashed through his ribs.

They fell as one, leaving Samira again panting and swearing under her breath. Her whole back was now slick with warm red. She tried raising her left arm, navel height, chest height, shoulder height...

"Strike me!" she cursed. That was only going to get worse. The only way to heal it would be to bandage it and rest, and neither of those were possible right now.

She set to removing the dead female's armor, throwing it on hastily, not even doing all of the straps. Careful armoring was not needed. Buckling the breastplate on, she jogged after Ariel's tracks, still visible in the soil. Her back throbbed in protest, but she grit her teeth. This was going to get striking annoying.

Shouts of confusion, anger, and flat-out panic sounded throughout the colony as Samira carefully made her way toward where Ariel had headed. Smoke rolled over the roofs. While merciless and sadistic, the colony proved to be woefully unprepared for an uprising. Zatran may have kept up a facade of a tightly-run operation to them while they were in captivity, but it was clear that they were not ready for a threat like all of the Chosen running amok. At least most of them were. Roy and James were still a mystery.

She came to a lowly-built stone building that stretched for three times the length of any other building in the colony. Its masonry was more advanced than any imperial structure she had seen thus far. Whoever had taken the time to construct this had been careful indeed, making a bunker strong enough to withstand Kostran-made catapults. The door was already off its hinges, an unconscious guard slumped near it. His armor had been removed, and his sword taken. Hearing strained voices inside the structure, Samira ducked through the door and into the building.

Roy sat huddled and delirious on the floor, dried sap—and some that looked fresh—covering every inch of his head and shoulders. Orange glowed around him. His ramblings bounced back and forth across the walls. They passed through bars and reverberated down the corridor-like structure. But when they came back, they came back as laughter. Uneven cackles that made her striking skin want to find a new home. Ariel knelt over Roy, sweating and aiming a wobbly arrow into the cage. She wasn't aiming at anything in particular as far as Samira could judge. The darkness inside the pen was too vacuous to see any potential target clearly enough. Ariel's composure was breaking.

"Roy, wake up! You have to fight it!" she urged. "Please wake up. Please wake up."

Another wave of demented laughter rolled from inside the cage.

"*Shut up!*" Ariel screamed at the blackness. She loosed an arrow between the bars, launching it into nothingness. Only a timid clatter sounded in response. More laughter followed.

Samira approached, warily glancing at the chortling cell. Turning to look at Roy's shivering body, she saw a new wave of convulsions take over with every new burst of cackling. "We have to get him out of here. Whatever is in there is making things worse." She leaned down to haul him upward.

"Don't touch him! This is *your* fault!" Ariel roared, outrage lighting her sapphire eyes.

"You're right. It *is* my fault. But I don't want him to die any more than you do, so let me help you. He *needs to get out of this room*," Samira said.

Angrily shouldering her bow, Ariel scooped up Roy and draped his arm over her shoulder. Her other hand clutched the toothed saber she had taken from the guard. If Roy came back to his senses, he would need a weapon. The laughter grew louder as they left the building, blinking at the sunlight.

Roy heaved, retched while he subconsciously fought against the Eye of Nature, babbling incoherently.

The guard Ariel had knocked out blinked and rested a hand on the wall he sat against. His pale face attempted to frown, eyes still hazy, head trickling blood.

Samira knelt in front of him and placed her broken glaive-sword at his throat. "Where are the docks?"

"Dock?" he mumbled, dazed.

"*Ships! Where are the striking ships!*" she screamed.

The sentry mumbled some more.

"Speak up!" Samira snarled.

"Northern perimeter.."

They didn't wait for him to finish the thought. Ariel didn't object to Samira taking Roy's other arm, instead glaring ahead toward the sounds of a fight.

I'm so sorry, Roy. Samira blinked through tears and pain, preparing herself for what was next. The blood spread along her sackwear against her back. *Fight just a little longer. Just a little longer, and I'll make this right. I promise.*

***

Motion was a blur around James. Sackwear and checkered garments clashed in a ferocious, furious tidal wave of violence. Freed prisoners in rags, some missing limbs, rushed their Altujan captors. Through the haze of his eyesight, through the trauma, James gazed in awe as the captives attacked with everything they had. Some of them did so literally, picking up rocks. One of them, a man missing an arm with gaunt features, fought alongside Joskine against a pair of soldiers. It was obvious that the man had once been a soldier or perhaps a mercenary.

"Iarus! For Etah! Dathos protect me! Astus!" shouts and cries from the Sackwearers swirled around them, creating a disturbing whirlwind of prayers.

Bodies clashed and fell as James waded shakily through the carnage. They passed the dragon skin awning, now swarming with battle. Leonard stalked protectively in front of him, his stolen sword, and his power shielding him from the chaos. Altujan fell to wide slashes of Leonard's blade. Stone walls and other structures fell as Leonard kicked against them. Shards of polished stone pelted enemy soldiers, and the ground rumbled with the steps of the burly Chosen. This power oozed from Leonard in a steady stream, but James's spine tingled.

He's using too much strength at once. Already, he could see Leonard's movements begin to slow. Not enough to impede him in battle but just enough to notice. It wouldn't be long before Leonard was dragged down completely, unable to move, unable to fight.

From behind him came a yell as a red-clad screamed in attack, serrated sword stabbing at James's gut. James ducked quickly, making way for Leonard to twist and arc his blade across his body. It plunged into the chest of the monster.

"Now isn't the time to become a pacifist, James," Leonard grunted. "Although I support your choices *after* we get out of here." A glaive flashed and cut through the sackwear above his collarbone. He shouted and pounded the hilt of his weapon against the leather cap of the assailant that wounded him, denting it and the Altujan's head with a jolting crack. "Raslena crush me, that stings."

It was as if he were back in the storm, tossing in a sea of writhing bodies, all fighting for control of the swell's direction. James was tossed between two opposing forces. His sight began to darken, his senses dulling. He barely could feel the muted heat of the people and creatures around him. There was something else he could sense though.

Lighting shot from outside his vision and pelted the awning with an enormous, bright, crash. The stretched and lacquered dragon skin burst alight, flames devouring the material greedily. A bright spot burned in James's consciousness now. It was a path, clearing the way through his clouded shock.

Between the gaps in the fighting, he saw Ariel and Samira walking, dragging Roy with them, headed in their direction. Samira appeared to be hurt but pounced into the battle, ripping through the already distracted Altujan, screaming a challenge. Ariel leaned Roy against a secluded wall and unshouldered her bow. Roy looked as if he were still fighting, comatose, unable to move. A pang of guilt ran through James. What he had said to Roy may have been the last thing that Roy heard before defeat at the hands of Charodon.

The flames gobbling the awning were dwindling, and they were using the fuel at an alarming rate.

"James!" Leonard bellowed.

He thrust his hand outward, extending his soul and grasping the flames before hurling them down at the battlefield. The sparse grass bloomed in fire, rocketing the temperature of the square to twice what it was. Orange and yellow light engulfed the entire area. Smoke billowed upward. Feeling the comfort of the scorching heat growing around him, James felt new clarity behind his eyes. Clarity, focus, yes.

And rage.

He channeled the heat into himself and rushed the enemy alongside Leonard. Hatred inside his chest, he pushed onward through the blaze around him. Smooth strokes of his sword, like Roy had taught, took over. He danced as if the blade were a flame of its own. James sliced down an Altujan, rending his armor completely in two. Leonard stomped frantically into the earth and kicked up a wall of rubble that pounded against an incoming polearm.

A bright light trailed from James's sword as he swung. Flames had somehow engulfed the blade itself. Escaped prisoners and red-clad continued to scrabble around them.

"Teach me to do that!" Leonard yelled.

"I don't know what this is!"

"You never like to make things *simple*, do you, James?"

The sword felt hot in his hand, scalding even, but it was a comfortable burn. That was the only way he could describe it. Delicate yet powerful. Using the first and second form in tandem, he maintained the flames around him and controlled them. Spinning, slashing, he had become a firestorm. Altujan shied away from his attacks, blocking the light from their eyes, hissing at the burn. Their sallow faces were illuminated, looking even more sickly, their black teeth seeming to absorb the light. From inside his chest, the billowing rage seethed. These monsters would feel the fear they had subjected him to, the pain, the terror, everything.

A yelp sounded next to him. He glanced over at Leonard, who was frantically patting flames from his sackwear. The fires around them had doubled in height, trapping the Altujan and prisoners alike. Sweat poured down James's face. Was this him? Heart rate pounding, he turned his attention back to the enemy, and a familiar pair of cruel violet eyes emerged and made contact with his.

A single pair of boots crunched along the now dry and brittle soil toward him, "I must say, a level fight isn't my preference," Zatran taunted. "But this is perhaps a nobler death for you than bloodbreathing." He slid two long hunting knives from his belt, both glistening with that translucent blue sap. The Blood Herald's eyes flicked toward the rising flames. They showed concern for only a moment before turning back to James with a considerable level of contempt.

"You're a monster, Zatran," James spat, the hot coals in his stomach blazing. "I'll make you breathe your *own* blood. For myself and everyone here."

"My, how confident. It's a shame that you were lying. You would have made a *wonderful* host for an Elder, you know. Such a strong fighting spirit! Do you know how lucky you are to be able to host? We can't do it! It's simply awful."

Leonard stepped beside James. "Careful, you'll burn yourself out if you don't calm down."

James glanced down at himself. His sackwear was charred and hanging from him loosely. Pink burns had begun to spread up and down his arms, numbed by his adrenaline and anger. He may not be able to feel them now, but he could get seriously hurt if he ignored them.

"Scorch me."

"Exactly my point," Leonard said. "We'll take him together. Let Sam and Ariel sort out the rest of this lot. Mastreh is still out here somewhere. Can't forget about her."

"What about Roy?"

Leonard grimaced. "Let's hope he can hold on."

James looked forward toward Zatran. The monster threw off his checkered jacket, exposing scarred, pale, yet lean arms. The scars stretched horizontally across his biceps and forearms, obviously the result of testing the paralytic sap on himself.

Nodding to each other, James and Leonard charged.

***

All this chaos was *very* exciting.

Rhaiga couldn't remember the last time she'd had this much interest invested in an event at all. Many paths intersecting, so many of them ending. Blood, both red and maroon, wetted the ground around her. Her bare feet squelched in it. The moistened dirt seeped between her toes. She had discarded her boots not long into her voyage, tossing them overboard. The garments felt odd to her after not using them for centuries, though she was now just remembering what *feeling* was like.

Sounds of death sang to her, like that thing her host had liked. Music, that was it. There was no rhythm to a pathway ending, but the melody was exquisite.

She crossed the Altujan colony toward the Vaecus paddock. There was always one where Altujan lived. Though the laughter of the creatures was faint, she could still hear them. Vayne had never been fond of them, but she and Dhorh found great use for them during the times before. They had been good companions. Before the War of Lost Faith, when the Chosen had cast the Elders out.

A spark of a forgotten emotion fluttered through her, the pit opening in her chest, the desire for murder. She wasn't sure what this feeling was and didn't quite know if she liked it or not yet.

When she made her way up to the paddock, a squat, well-built structure with tremendous width, it became clear to her that the calls she had been hearing had just come from one creature. Just *one*? A litter could number up to twelve if she remembered correctly. How had these bumbling Altujan managed to kill—at the very most—eleven of the sacred beasts of the Elders? She stepped inside, and the cackling stopped. Even the echo of the creature's chortles was silenced immediately, an eerie quirk that she enjoyed. Sturdy cage bars contained her new pet, still sulking somewhere in the darkness. Rhaiga shed the skin of the veiled woman.

In her true, pale form, she wrenched the door to the cage free, feeling strange. Was that exhilaration?

"Your cage is gone, friend," she called in a singsong voice. This really was turning into a pleasant day.

The sound of soft padding progressed through the darkness toward her.

Her three eyes glowed. "There you are."

What walked on all fours out of the cage made her pale face crinkle in some semblance of happiness. It was so *beautiful*.

Fifteen feet from head to tail, a long, feline body lumbered across the polished stone, claws scraping. Wings, supple and leathery, stretched outward in a display of dominance.

The skin of the thing had the same leathery, dry complexion. Washed-out black in color, it shifted in and out of sight, even as it stalked right toward her. Though it had no eyes, she knew it could tell she was there. The mane of sensory whips on the back of its head, a nest of two-foot-long appendages that resembled taut ropes, writhed like sentient tentacles. They tasted the air, determining where she was and what she was. Vaeci were incredibly intelligent creatures after reaching maturity, but it appeared that so few did. It took decades even though they grew quickly in size.

"Never thought I'd see one of you again," she mused. The creature bristled as she reached toward it with a scraggly hand. It snarled and bared its jagged teeth. The Elder did not flinch. The room was silent. Neither of them moved.

Rhaiga tilted her head and waited.

The creature's sensory whips rolled before going limp. A curt hiss escaped its mouth as it bowed its head, deferring to her, now its master. Rhaiga blinked in satisfaction as the creature submitted. This made things so much more interesting.

Flight

Roy's body had drifted away from him, and his soul was under attack. Now trapped in his mind, pain rumbled through his consciousness in wave after wave, a sea of swords ramming into his skull. It threatened to split his very sanity apart. Whatever that creature in the cage had done with its laughter, it had done its job of unhinging his mind.

Roy saw flashes. Orange, blue, yellow, gray, orange, orange, orange. The bright, cold savagery paralyzed him. Charodon couldn't be allowed to break through. He would kill the Altujan, kill James, Leonard, Samira, Ariel. The waterscowls that had once called him slayer, but now called him friend, would die. Without someone to battle over control, to distract him, the Eye of Nature would rip through them all.

Hatred for Leonard coursed through him. The bastard would finally see the fruit of his cowardice. Roy would die, and nothing would protect anyone from what was coming. What James said fueled the hatred further. He had lied to *protect* him! Hadn't he?

And Samira, her mission was held paramount over her friends. The only reason she gave any drowning attention to Roy's impending death was because the Elders were involved. Her quest to prove herself to that zealot of a father had been her focus over him, her best friend. Even Ariel had left him. She had come back just in time to watch him die after two years of not even *trying* to search for him!

Charodon roared over his thoughts, making Roy answer him in return with a roar of his own. Anger rolled within him, boiled, thrashed. The ice that normally took over his body and mind was now a frothing river, steaming, ready to blow at any moment. They had never cared about him. He was their freak, their pet.

"You finally see, don't you?" Charodon howled. *"I'm the only one, the ONLY one who sees you."*

"No." He choked. Charodon's very presence was strangling him.

"The Scaleslayer is us. We exist because of them! They did this to you! Let me loose, and vengeance will be ours on whomever we choose."

He yelled in frustration as the hate, the despair, washed him away.

And he slammed into something. A wall, no, an *army*. Thousands of people stood, floated, at the corner of his mental battlefield. The dark, shapeless specter of Charodon loomed over him, casting a shadow through the flashing, disorienting chasm that was his mind.

The people standing behind him were familiar. They had been there during the first bloodbreathing, his fatigued brain grasped the memory. Faces blurred as they went farther out, but ones closest to him became incredibly clear. A woman in a black veil leaned over him, her mouth speaking words he couldn't hear, words he didn't know.

An old man, flickers of light washing over his pockmarked face, mouthed the same words. The young boy silently said the words, his bald head shining as bright as the rest of this torturous mindscape. An army of specters spoke to him soundlessly, eerily trying to tell him something that he couldn't hear.

"I can't hear you!" he screamed, distraught. The pain threatened to rip his mind in half. The pain, the pain...

"Let go."

"What?" he croaked.

"Of your hatred." The voices faded into focus. *"Let go."*

Roy somehow stood up. His subconscious still roared. Charodon still roared. The voices, the bellowing, the blinking light, his loathing, they whirled around him in a dizzying hurricane."

"Stop! Stop it!" Roy screamed into the typhoon. "I said stop!"

"If you do not let this anger go, you will become nothing," the old man insisted. His voice was wavering but deliberate. His blind gray eyes stared ahead into nothingness. *"You will become one of us."*

The storm of senses still whipped about him, tearing at his thoughts, his humanity, prodding him into rage like an animal.

"Forgive them."

"I can't," he mumbled.

"Forgive them," the specters commanded.

***

Ariel shot down another Altujan, catching him with an arrow under the knee. The flesh eater squirmed as he went down, screeching. She was backed against a challenge wall, firing into the battle. There was so much movement that it was hard to find an opening. Sackwear and the enemy's checkered garb stormed the clearing, blocking her path to the northern perimeter and to the ships. She shot another one in the wrist before they had the chance to club Samira with a glaive pole. Ariel had to remind herself that she needed the woman, as disgusted as she was with her.

James and Leonard had made it to the center of the pavilion ahead of her, near the now-burning awning. Samira was at the outskirts of the battle, too cautious with her lightning to just blast her way through friends and foes to get to the middle. For all they knew, the whole colony was now here, engaging their prisoners in a brawl. And they needed each and every one of the captives that Leonard had freed.

Born for the infantry, Leonard had rounded up these sick, dejected men and women and turned them into fighters within the span of a few minutes. The promise of freedom went a long way, and the sackwearers hungrily clutched that promise close to their hearts. They attacked the red-clad with fierce defiance, beating down those who had tortured them and in some cases perhaps *eaten* them. Keeping up that intensity would be difficult, for the prisoners would only tire faster, and the flesh eaters would recover from their surprise. A lone red-clad soldier charged at James from behind, barreling toward his unprotected back. Leaving no time to think, no time to contemplate, Ariel leveled her bow.

Before she realized where she had been aiming, she loosed the arrow shot through the enemy's neck. He went down just a few feet from where James fought. A wave of sickness slithered over her for a moment before she shut it down. *We have to set such things aside. It's kill or be killed now. They look human, but they will kill you and all of your friends.*

Roy sat slumped against the wall behind her. She could have sworn that mist was already starting to curl off of him, like moisture before a storm. His mumbling had stopped, giving way to a silence that was much more coldly terrifying. She had seen the orange glow creeping across his eyes. It was taking him over. Not only could she lose him right here, but she would also be the first to be eaten by Charodon, no longer leashed by his host. The acrid, earthy smell of burning dragon skin wafted by on the air, accompanied by thick black smoke. She let out a breath, banishing it to another part of the battlefield.

There was something wrong about this fight. All of the major pieces were here, but there was something she couldn't place.

Mastreh. She was nowhere to be seen.

Ariel swept her gaze over the fighting, to the north, the east, seeing nothing of that sauntering bitch. Wherever Mastreh was, it was in anticipation to strike,

Ariel was sure of it. The Altujan woman was a snake, and her venom could be a death knell for their little escape attempt.

Flames licked the sky where Leonard and James fought. James was going to burn himself out soon if he wasn't careful, and Leonard didn't have the strength to soldier on after using too much power. She had been there for more than a few fights where they had to stay in place for hours before he was able to move again.

Movement, subtle and quiet, caught her attention to the side. It was close, way too close.

She dropped her bow and snatched an arrow from her quiver, holding the shaft like a spear. They were too close for her to shoot, much less defend against with her bow in the way. It was Mastreh. She had snuck behind them, around the colony, with what looked like a small army of Altujan in *blue*.

It was another colony. Mastreh had gone and brought reinforcements. The Vice Herald's black teeth bared in a smirk before she rushed Ariel, pouncing, her bloody maroon hair flying. Mastreh's eyes were beaming with glee.

The flash of a blade replaced that bloodlust with shock and a healthy mix of terror. A serrated saber cut through the side of her neck, narrowly missing a major vein—assuming that Altujan had the same veins as humans. Dark purple liquid spurted from the wound, spraying outward. Ariel looked to see who had swung the sword and gasped with relief and surprise to see Roy panting, clutching the sword she had stolen.

He looked terrible. His whole right eye was completely orange, and he was breathing heavily, clearly exhausted, eyes sunken and dark. She was three months older than him, but in this moment he looked ancient. Something had happened to him while in that trance, and she wasn't sure if she wanted to know what it was.

Mastreh clapped her hands over the V on her neck and pressed down against the wound, gasping at the pain. Thick blood began to paint her lips, turning them from an off-white to a sickly purple. Her eyes glared at Roy, unforgiving, furious, and afraid. The Vice Herald sank to her knees, her hands and armor growing slick with violet.

"Breathe that," Roy spat. He wobbled as if his own weight was something he was still getting control over.

Following Mastreh, the soldiers of the neighboring colony charged, taking Roy's counter as an invitation to attack. Their blue and gray checkered garments were in stark contrast to their dark red hair. The same black teeth and white lips grimaced, the same burgundy eyes blazed. There must have been a hundred or more as they came surging through the alleys toward Ariel and Roy. Weaving between walls and squeezing between buildings, they were slowed down enough to buy them a few seconds.

Wrapping one tattooed arm around Roy, Ariel turned toward the battle. She had only done this once, not even twenty minutes ago, and only just carrying herself. Roy's eyes were still swimming with orange, struggling to focus on her. Wind intensified, buffeting them as she extended her consciousness outward.

"What are you doing?" he panted.

"Hold on tight." Ariel gritted her teeth. He didn't attempt to ask why, wrapping his lean arm around her shoulder weakly. She drew in another breath, as deep as she could go.

Behind them, the shouts of the Altujan were getting closer through the trees, walls, and buildings. Mastreh gurgled through her own blood in a drowning scream, still kneeling, refusing to fall.

Ariel blew out her breath sharply, releasing a torrent of wind from her own lungs toward the ground. The force of the wind against the dirt launched them up and over the battle as if from a catapult. Roy's grip across her shoulder tightened in incredulity.

Screams of the blue-clad were drowned out behind them as the air pounded against her ears. Mastreh and the newcomers were out of reach, out of mind, for the time being. Ariel and Roy went up, twenty, forty, fifty feet into the air, soaring and holding each other all the while. Wind rushed past them and drowned out

Ariel's other senses. Hearing, smell, touch, they were all gone. For a short-lived moment, Ariel felt the sensation of flight, the wind catching under her and holding her and Roy aloft. Her adrenaline surged.

All she could register was the sight of the battle passing under them, and the ground rushing to meet them as they reached the peak in her trajectory. The edge of the battle to the north, the way toward the ships.

The way toward escape.

Prophecy

James danced backward, narrowly escaping a poisonous cut from Zatran's knife. The Altujan's assertion of disliking a fair fight appeared unwarranted, for he was incredibly nimble. He flitted from Leonard to James in a heartbeat, slashing, rolling, snarling. A feral animal, masquerading as something humanlike. The glow and trailing flame from James's sword had gone, and the burns that covered his arms had moved from a pink warning to an angry red. Now the stinging was starting to give way to bright pain.

Leonard slammed his blade into the crunchy dirt beneath them, willing the earth to shake. A miniature earthquake rumbled through the battle, tripping Altujan and sackwearers alike. Leonard winced. His ribs likely never had a chance to set and heal after the dragons.

James took the opportunity to stab at the Blood Herald but barely missed as Zatran rolled away.

Sackwear and checkered coats were still much too intermixed. There was no way that he could make a sweeping attack. This also meant that Samira, with all her power, wouldn't be able to do much without frying any friendlies. Roy was indisposed, leaving only two of them capable of clearing the battlefield enough to finish Zatran.

James called to Leonard frantically, sidestepping Zatran's thrust, "Clear everyone out!"

Leonard took the opportunity to swing at Zatran's neck, missing by inches. The Blood Herald skittered away. "Where do you expect me to send them?" Leonard asked, huffing.

From the very edge of his vision, a dark shape moved across the sky, heading toward the north. Squinting to focus, he finally made out a twisting shape of gold and black. Gold hair and skin with swirling black tattoos, clutching a mass of black hair and ragged sackwear. Were they scorching *flying*?

James pointed up with his sword. "With them!"

Zatran rushed James again, holding his knife in a reverse grip. "No one is leaving, not while I have you in my sights," he said. James could *hear* his black teeth grinding.

He parried a swipe from the Blood Herald, wincing as his burns protested. Starting to lose his composure, Zatran abandoned Leonard completely, seeking James's death fervently. There was something in James's deception that the enemy Herald despised.

Leonard was shouting something indistinguishable to the sackwearers, trying to get them to move to the north. James didn't hear any of it, focusing solely on the fight in front of him.

He held his sword in the space between him and Zatran. He kept his distance, made the enemy attack first. It was remarkable how Roy's teachings came to him without having to think too hard. Regardless of how James felt about Roy, the sparring had saved his life enough times to remember the lessons. He glared into Zatran's purple eyes, seeing the hatred, the desperation.

They circled each other, the battle around them was no longer a concern. The world was just them.

"You wanted Vayne to be back so badly, didn't you?" James said.

"Quiet," Zatran stiffened.

There it was, the edge he needed. Strength starting to ebb away, James noticed that the flames around the battlefield—the ones he had maintained—were now winding down to kindling. He smirked and continued to pace. "You didn't have a scorching care in the world about Charodon. You just wanted Vayne, the master of the Elders, to tell you what a good dog you are. Because if he did, you wouldn't have to worry about Mastreh. The others wouldn't *dare* contest someone backed by an Elder. Everyone in your colony knows that she is the stronger by far."

"I said quiet!"

James was laughing now, chuckling at the madman that had tortured him. "But now, you found out that Vayne isn't coming to praise you. How long before Mastreh just gets it over with and dumps your limbless body into the sea? My wager is any day." He shouted loud enough for any other Altujan listening. Glancing around, he could see that they *were* listening.

Taking this distraction, Leonard had led a large portion of the sackwearers toward the north to safety.

"Because you're nothing, Zatran. You barely had the colony running *before* we started causing problems. Now you have to call in other colonies, ceding ground? Mastreh won't like that. Leonard is usually better at jokes than me, but I think this one takes the pot."

Zatran struggled to respond, his protests escaping his mouth in incoherent roars.

"The Altujan survived for centuries, endured, exemplified strength and cunning, only to put *you* in charge!"

That hit the red-clad Blood Herald exactly where he wanted. The torture, the beatings, the cruelty, had been out of cowardice, desperation, and insecurity. Zatran had gambled on a boon from what he had thought was his god come to save him, and he had lost. Red hair disheveled, left eye twitching, Zatran screamed and charged James, waving both knives savagely.

Drawing in the remaining heat from the flames around him, James grasped the fire and hurled it straight at Zatran. The ball of bright yellow flames struck the Altujan in the chest, taking him off his feet and sending him crashing to the dirt with a loud crunch. Several red-clad soldiers ran to his aid as James hurdled the bodies in the square. He dashed toward Leonard and the sackwearers.

Samira had joined them in the pandemonium. She stood, bleeding in several places, eyeing the Altujan reinforcements that lined the opposite edge of the square. Her braid hung mangled down the middle of her back.

Zatran swatted away the soldiers attempting to pick him up, taking one of their glaives, "Pursue! They can't escape the island!"

The company in blue at the edge of the battlefield raised their weapons obediently—after a nod from what looked like their commanding officer—and advanced across the ruins of the awning, now burned completely. These soldiers were fresh, and their eyes gleamed expectantly for a fight.

"Leonard," Samira said.

Leonard yelled and thrust his steel downward, muscles bulging. With another scream that contained a lot of pain from his broken ribs, he twisted the sword to the left.

Zatran stepped forward and hurled the glaive as the earth began to shake violently.

James's teeth rattled from the force of earth ripping itself apart between the humans and Altujan. Rending in two, a rift over twenty feet in width yawned in front of Leonard. Golden dirt sprung into the air, and Altujan buildings and walls of poor caliber disintegrated from the force of the earthquake. James held his hand up, wincing at the hot pain of his burned arms, to shield his eyes.

The Chosen of Raslena had done it. A chasm spanned the length of the battlefield, blocking their pursuers and giving them time to escape. James turned to congratulate Leonard until he saw where Zatran's polearm had landed.

Half of the blade was embedded in Leonard's gut, the point slightly poking out through his back. His sackwear was already drenched in red. Spiky hair still bobbing, Leonard's head drooped. Dull shock glazed over his eyes, and his breathing was already thin.

Across the chasm, Zatran shrieked orders to his soldiers. The rift that Leonard had made would only be a temporary setback. Already, soldiers in blue-checkered uniforms were scrambling to find materials to use as bridges.

Samira and Ariel rushed to Leonard. Roy stood back, a confused, vacant stare painting his face.

Reaching him first, Ariel tore a strip of cloth from her shirt and pressed it to Leonard's abdomen. It was immediately soaked in blood. She whipped her head desperately to Roy. "Help me!"

Shaking his head violently to refocus, Roy shakily ran to Ariel, shedding his sackwear shirt and folding it into a pad. Scars from where Charodon's teeth had punctured his skin undulated as he handed the pad to her. She pressured the makeshift bandage to the wound. Leonard's hazel eyes were unresponsive, staring straight ahead. Those terrible, thin, wheezing breaths still passed his lips.

Roy's lip carried a barely perceptible tremble.

This wasn't happening. Leonard was a scorching ox. He'd been fighting through broken ribs for the last week! James trembled, the reality hitting him through the initial shock. Could this actually be it? They had survived so much up to now, but Zatran's glaive had just shattered this luck. He expected Leonard to make some kind of joke, to brush it off, to scoff at the blade, but he just puffed out those weak breaths. Leonard was dying. Had he not been standing there, protecting James and the rest of them, James would have been the one impaled.

It turned out James could get people killed too.

"James, come on," Samira pleaded. She stood by Leonard, leaning over him and trying to get him up. Blood dripped from a deep wound in her back, hindering the movement of her arm. Sackwearers that stood nearby jumped as she called to them, "Get to the ships. Northern perimeter. Get us ready to sail, *now*." They scrambled away, catching the tone in her voice.

"Wh...what do we do?" James stammered.

"We have to go. Help us with him," Samira said quickly.

Leonard couldn't walk; he had lost too much blood. Roy and Samira had to carry him if they were to keep moving. As they shuffled away, holding Leonard, James looked back across the chasm toward the enemy. The Altujan were tearing the whole settlement apart to find means of pursuit. Zatran screamed at his soldiers, his face curdling blue.

Behind them all, atop a building, was a nightmare.

Rhaiga's three eyes bore into him. Her pale, gaunt figure crouched atop a squat structure, accompanied by a dark, formless shape. She had *followed* them.

"We need to move faster," he yelled.

The others didn't ask what he meant. Roy and Samira, still slowed by Leonard, were only able to do a meager jog. Even that was pushing it. Ariel had been extremely clear that they couldn't remove the glaive from Leonard's torso here. It would kill him on the spot.

Ariel tore ahead after the mass of sackwearers approaching what appeared to be the northern edge of the island. A swarm of gray crabs, scrabbling over each other to get to safety.

Every step felt too slow, his feet—bare and bloody—felt heavier in the dirt than before, and his eyes were drooping. The only thing keeping him up was the pain of his burns. Adrenaline from the fight fading, he realized that they hurt more than he had previously thought. Like a thousand hot nails, he felt it just under his skin.

Screams from the Altujan had faded, but they had not gone away. They stayed at a constant warble, a siren, at the edge of his perception. Faint but still there. Twelve more minutes passed, the three of them panting, doing their best to keep up with Ariel and the now-liberated sackwearers.

Ariel kept them all pointed in a single direction, but it got more and more difficult as the outskirts of the colony approached. Tight spaces from walls and shoddy buildings suddenly gave way to a sprawling shipyard. Packed with vessels, the docks spanned around the northern curve of the island. There must have been over a hundred, maybe even more that they couldn't see. He found it odd that the Altujan would have wooden ships and docks. All of their previous architecture had indicated a fondness of stone. But some things—especially ships—were not meant for those materials. Wind buffeted the checkered sails of the warships docked near the uncharacteristically rocky shore. Several colors spanned the coast: red, blue, green.

Samira gasped as she saw the ships, her eyes open in horror. She had come to the same conclusion that he had.

The vessels weren't here for petty piracy or misadventure. This was an *invasion* in the making. Those ships could not leave this island.

The sackwearers had chosen a ship with the checkered red sails of Zatran's colony, swarming the gangplank and up the hull in some cases. Ariel leapt aboard, bare feet slapping against the wood, and shouted orders to prepare the rigging, sounding as if she were doing it while still trying to conserve her breath. If she could give them a good enough boost to speed away, it would be a head start that might give them a chance.

Without even a glance at each other, Samira and Roy hauled Leonard onto the ship. Roy immediately sprinted across the deck, shoving over passengers, desperately searching for bandages and anything he could use. Samira went through storage bins, searching for supplies. She nervously glanced at the other ships, ready to set sail. This was bad, so much worse than they had thought. Zatran's troops may have been uncoordinated, but the blue-clad had seemed formidable, disciplined, ruthless. Having not even met the other clans, James wondered if it could get even worse.

James set to untying the ship from the thick, wooden post at the edge of the dock. The rope wouldn't budge. The vessel had been docked for long enough that the rope had all but fused to the post, tied too tight. Trying to calm his thoughts, James attempted to heat the rope and burn through it. Scorch it, nothing happened. He should have known that he wouldn't be able to use the third form in that capacity yet.

"Ariel! Help me with this," James grunted as he tried to budge the rope.

Ariel, standing above him at the stern of the ship, stayed frozen. He flicked his gaze over to her in exasperation to see that Ariel was not looking at him. Her bow was drawn and her terrified eyes stared straight back toward the settlement. Her arms tensed as she drew an arrow back all the way to her cheek.

James whirled around to get a glimpse of what she was aiming at. He spied the collapsed roof of a squat watchtower. He saw the Eye of Death crouching on top of one of the few still standing walls. It was Rhaiga. The abomination's colorless skin glowed under the sapphire sun behind her. The horned head faced James and Ariel, its three eyes gazing intently. She had spanned the gap, seemingly with no effort, and was taunting them.

"James, come on!" Samira bellowed at him, sprinting up the pier. James came back into reality and drew his stolen sword. They had to leave, immediately. He raised the sword above his head and brought it down on the rope with everything, anything that he had left. The rope split in two, and James's sword bit into the thick wood of the pier, lodging soundly. He looked over at Ariel.

"Get us out of here!" he screamed. She glanced once more at Rhaiga before rushing to the main mast. James tugged once, twice, and a third time before his sword jerked free of the wood planks. Samira began pushing the ship away from the dock. James rushed to help her, joined by a handful of sackwearers. The others poured across the deck, fighting for position to put the vessel as far away from this haunted island as possible. The ship groaned as they strained against the wooden hull, splinters of wood digging into their hands.

Roy, covered in blood and exhausted, rushed to the starboard rail where James and Samira were shoving off. He held out a hand, and James gripped it weakly. Roy tightened his grasp and hauled James over the side of the ship, hot blood running from his hand down James's arm. He looked back at Samira. She stood at the end of the dock, bleeding, now slowly being left behind by the ship as Ariel breathed wind into the sails. The force of Ariel's wind caused the vessel to lurch outward violently. James could tell Ariel wasn't prepared for it, and she barely held to the ropes that were wrapped around her hands

"Sam!" Roy yelled.

Samira looked to him quickly and nodded before turning and hurling lightning at the war vessel to her left, splintering the hull with a shattering flash. The wood scorched immediately then sizzled as it was overtaken by the waves. She threw lightning again, hitting the next warship down. It sank too. She was staying behind. James could see dark lifeblood staining the back of her sackwear.

"Sam, don't!" Roy screamed.

"Let her do it," Ariel called, blanching as the rigging gouged her hands.

Samira sank another three ships before looking back. Her withered braid still whipped around with that same defiance, and her amber eyes—for just a moment—glowed brighter than the sun overhead. Shaking her head slightly, she raised her powerful left hand over her head and pelted the docks with lightning. The blast splintered two ships at once, forcefully enough to vibrate James's teeth on the escaping ship. They were over eighty feet away now. Samira was shaking, and her left arm spasmed violently. She stumbled and fell to one knee.

Feet pounded the deck near James, and he saw Joskine struggling to hold Badlai from the rail. She bucked wildly against her fellow sailor, trying to reach the hurdle, eyes wide in anguish.

"We have to go back." James shook his head.

Ariel cursed, seeing that Roy clearly wouldn't leave without Samira. "Turn around." She said to a nearby sackwearer that held the aura of authority.

The man Leonard had freed first, the one with one tattooed arm, blinked quizzically at her.

Ariel turned and shouted, "Turn the ship around before I change my mind! She may be a liar, but we can't leave." Ariel's convictions had overridden her personal feelings. She wasn't happy about it, but she wouldn't let a person that she knew—a person who was still close to her—die to a clan of monsters.

Before they could plan any further, water suddenly erupted in a splash directly below the stern of the ship. Ariel's cry of surprise reached James's ears as his eyes registered Roy in the water, blood that wasn't his—and some that was—drifting into the surf around him. That scorching man. What was he doing? He was barely able to walk a minute ago.

Roy struggled for a moment before gaining a loose grip on the water around him. The red-tinted water glistened off his skin, and his mop of hair now hung in his eyes. Even though the water was more than thirty feet deep by James's estimation, Roy began to slog toward shore as if he were walking through a shallow pond.

"Go back!" Samira roared angrily. Her next strike landed in the water, just narrowly missing the next available ship.

Roy said nothing, still pushing through the waves.

Samira growled in frustration, no doubt up to her limit with Roy's stubbornness. "Just let me do this! Let me do one thing right! I've messed everything up, *everything*! I lied to you, Roy. I knew we were hunting Charodon that day. All of this is *my fault*! You placed your faith in me, and I killed it, so just let me go!"

The shock and hurt was so abrupt that they didn't have to see Roy's face. It hit his entire body, rolling through him and, for a scary moment, looking like it would sink him beneath the waves. For that instant, the sounds of battle, men tromping across the deck, Badlai fighting against Joskine, and even the sounds of the shrieking Altujan faded, replaced only by the rushing of the water and Roy's stunned silence.

Samira tearfully nodded to her best friend, confirming the truth.

James watched in absolute incredulity as Roy straightened himself and forded on toward the beach, refusing to leave his friend to a horrific death.

"You don't get to do this noble sacrifice that you want so badly, Sam. As if that's going to make up for it," Ariel yelled. "You're coming back home to make this *right*." Ariel's hands visibly shook in the rigging, not just from pain. Etah's Chosen glowered toward the shore.

James turned back to the beach. His gaze briefly registered a white blur charging toward Samira.

"Rhaiga!" James screamed.

Samira instinctively dodged to the right as the pale, nimble ghoul lunged for her. The Eye of Death fixed all three eyes on Samira, brandishing spindly fingers, each longer than dragon's teeth. James had no idea what Rhaiga could do, but he could only assume how most of her interactions with living things ended.

In the water, Roy bellowed for his friend, redoubling his effort to force his way through the surf.

All shouts to change course were severed by a gargantuan crack, and a bright glare of light seared James's eyes. The blue-white blaze of the sun was momentarily lost, replaced by a radiance unparalleled. It came from the island, from Samira.

The lightning explosion subsided, torching an afterimage into James's vision, making no difference between when he blinked and when he stared ahead. Through the clearing dust and displaced surf, James could distinctly see an ugly, brutish scorch mark covering a large portion of the shore. Samira was gone, nowhere to be seen. Altujan warships were aflame—those that hadn't been vaporized. There was no way that anything should have walked away from that.

And yet there Rhaiga stood, her pale body reverse-silhouetted against the scorched shore. No one on the ship moved, save for Joskine, hurling a rope down to Roy.

Roy slumped in disbelief, sinking below the surface for half a moment.

Samira, Chosen of Astus, had fought an Elder in accordance with her prophecy. And it appeared that the prophecy had come to an end.

Part III

A Brighter Path

Deathless

Rhaiga strolled through the burning Altujan colony. *These* were the followers that had nearly led her and the Elders to victory all those centuries ago? They all crouched, timid before her now, as if she were some prized artifact that was too valuable to even look at. All maroon eyes were averted in different directions, so long as they didn't meet hers. Pathetic.

She came to a stop near the center of the square after casually leaping the crevasse the Chosen had created. Her Vaecus waited dutifully for her, its sensory whips writhing in anticipation. She could have sent it after the Chosen, she guessed, but there was much work to be done here. Dozens of blue-clad and red-clad shrank before her. It was times like these that the pit in her chest deepened greatly, and dealing death became her burning desire.

"Look at me," she said tersely.

Every gaze snapped to her form, though most still didn't meet her eyes. Most focused on her height, some on her fingers. All of them were unsettled by her, making it obvious that they had expected Vayne himself—if any of the Elders were to show up. Well, too bad for them. They had her to deal with, and for the first time in centuries she was *unhappy*.

It was an exhilarating feeling. To be, well, *feeling*. The sight and serenade of death, seeing another Chosen up close, and experiencing the burn of that magnificent lightning power had rejuvenated her thirst for this grand undertaking of Vayne's. Perhaps it was time to take a new host. That LightningChosen would have been a prime candidate, but when the surge of light and electricity had faded, the woman had been nowhere to be seen. Annihilated by her own blast, most likely, or blown into the sea. Even though her last few hosts had disliked bloodshed and avoided it, there came times where she *needed* it, and those times had become more frequent of late.

Rhaiga looked toward the now kneeling—it had taken them long enough—Altujan. They needed to be disciplined, made an example of, before the next phase of Vayne's plan could be enacted.

She called outward, using a louder voice than she had in as long as she could remember, "Who among you is in command?"

A red-clad male stepped forward, clothes singed, no doubt from the Fire-Chosen. He regarded her warily, violet eyes shifting back and forth between her eyes and her hands, which she kept at her sides, idle. Nonetheless, he stood straight-backed and spoke clearly.

"Zatran is my name, Great Eye. I serve you enth—"

Rhaiga ripped out his throat with the swiftest of motions. Her bony white fingers were now a dark purple, glistening like a shimmering glove. Soldiers around them gasped and flinched but didn't dare move away. One or two whimpered quietly. Zatran face-planted into the gold dirt, gurgling, twitching. Rhaiga felt the pit in her chest close ever so slightly.

"Your forces will be reorganized going forward, and weak leadership will not be tolerated," she announced to the throngs of kneeling blue-clad and red-clad Altujan. "You are burdened with divine purpose in service to us, and I won't see you burdened further by incompetence. Who was his Vice? I would speak with them."

Several red-clad pointed shaky, cowering fingers toward the opposite end of the square, near a particularly dense section of walls. Why would the Vice Blood Herald be hiding in the back of the force? Perhaps one neck would not be enough today.

She patted the back of her Vaecus's head, and it cackled obediently, a dry sound that elicited a cringe from all who heard it that rippled through the battalion as if a disturbance from a stone plopped into water.

Rhaiga and her pet strode through the crowd, white and black parting a sea of red and blue.

The Vaecus padded along, wings folded along its back. With the feline body and wings, many mistook the ancient creatures for some kind of dragon, but this was not the case. The leathery skin and sensory whips gave it away. Dragons were too primal, had no impulse control. The great beasts would tear through anything and everything on their base instincts. No, Vaeci were much different. Smaller, yes. More vulnerable to blades, yes. But they were a hundred times smarter.

A crowded group of Altujan huddled around something. Parting for her, they revealed a kneeling red-clad female covered in her own ichor. It stained her checkered coat black, still gushing—albeit weakly, now—from a gash in her neck. The Vice Herald's hands pressed firmly against her own throat, limiting oxygen in order to staunch the blood flow. This one was remarkably tough. Her dimming eyes glanced upward at Rhaiga. Dim but *burning*. Yes, this one would do nicely.

Rhaiga crouched in front of the kneeling female, still towering over her. "It appears that they have escaped. A pity isn't it?" She held up a hand, blinking all three eyes at once. She had to do it consciously, otherwise they would all blink at separate times. "No need to answer, because we both know that it *is* a pity. It's a pity that the Chosen escaped, right under your Blood Herald's nose, no less. It's a pity that he waited to call in reinforcements."

The Vice was still listening, the only one of the followers to look her in the eyes, to look *death* in the eyes, without blanching. Her breathing was controlled if not very weak.

"We don't have to worry about him anymore," Rhaiga gestured with her purple-covered hands. "But it appears that your promotion will be short-lived. You won't get to exact the punishment that they deserve. The one they deserve for what the humans have done to your kind. And *that*, I think, is the greatest pity of them all." She motioned to the Vice's bloodstained garb.

Altujan around her murmured, hushed voices contemplating who would take command after this one—Mastreh, some called her—finally succumbed.

Mastreh herself still knelt, hands clamped on her own neck, wheezing.

Rhaiga cocked her head. This presented another opportunity. This one could be used. Vayne and Dhorh had their own strengths, to give and take disease or memory. Well, she could do something similar, yet better.

Cupping her hand over Mastreh's mouth and nose, Rhaiga pressed downward, stifling the Altujan's breathing completely. The newly promoted Blood Herald could do nothing, as she still held the last of her lifeblood inside her neck with her own hands. Red-clad and blue-clad alike stood motionless and watched, not daring to interfere with Rhaiga's actions lest they wind up without a throat like Zatran. Mastreh's frantic, gurgling attempts at breathing pushed against Rhaiga's hands, but Rhaiga kept her elongated palms clamped over the Vice's face.

The breathing stopped, and Rhaiga leaned Mastreh against the wall. Mastreh's bloody hands slid away from her neck and fell loosely to her sides.

"It is one of the greatest injustices of nature that we cannot take your species as hosts," Rhaiga said, looking over Mastreh's body. "I cannot use your bloodlust for myself, but *you* must now use it for *me*. Your path does not end today. I deny you your death. We will pursue these Chosen, and in so doing will launch a campaign not seen in this world for over a thousand years. Vayne has seen this, and I will give my whole power to see it done. Mastreh, take up the mantle of Blood Herald and lead your people to victory."

The terrified Altujan onlookers tore their gaze away from Rhaiga to look at Mastreh, slumped against the wall, covered in her own dark ichor. Mastreh no longer breathed and had no more blood to bleed.

But she was not dead. Not at all.

Not Worth It

The polished deck of the ship was swarming with activity. The sails flapped and cracked like whips under the pressure of the stiff breeze, and James sat at the stern of the vessel, gazing back at the world behind them, a small flame in his hand. He'd taken it from a torch they'd found in the ship's hold. The heat relaxed him.

After everything that had happened, it felt as if the world had stripped away the promise of this same moment over a month ago. Or perhaps it had replaced any promise of things getting better with *reality*. The promises of tension, death, uncertainty. Those were certainly present now. When he had watched Epot Detharn dwindle in the distance, leaving behind the place where his brother had died, he thought that there might be some hope for the future, to bring the oppression of the Temple to a crumbling ruin.

But what he hadn't expected was to become someone like the Temple, like the Elders, or the Altujan. Distrusting, bitter, indignant. Perhaps he had been this way for a long time. The Elders and Altujan sought vengeance against the Chosen and humanity. The Temple had enacted vengeance against Gemmi for thieving their wares. James had let this indignation and fury cloud his judgment, even against the people, the friends, who had saved him multiple times. Yes, they had lied to him, but their hearts had been in the right place, and he'd treated them like scum.

From what Ariel had said, Leonard wouldn't last much longer unless they got him to an actual surgeon, not someone like her who had only a rudimentary knowledge of field medicine. Their vessel was in good shape, but it was meant for transporting a large amount of people, not for making long distances quickly. James felt a swell of sadness when thinking about Leonard. He had his flaws like the other Chosen, but he had sacrificed himself for James, as had Samira. That was something that James would likely never be able to thank them for.

The Tarsals were no longer visible after escaping. It had been a few days now, maybe four. Luckily, there were some former sailors among the sackwearers, and of course Joskine and Badlai. The other sailors who had been with them, including poor Amry, had been killed. There was a particularly heavy spot in James's heart for Amry. The boy hadn't deserved to die at the hands of those ghouls.

Badlai had been quieter than normal after Samira's death—if that were even possible. Joskine was as loud and as hearty as ever, trying to keep morale up among the recently freed prisoners. In some respects, it was easy for him to do. People who were recently freed from being scorching livestock and slaves probably had cause to be more cheerful. Joskine had worked with a one-armed sackwearer, Hadsen, to form a crew that ran the ship relatively smoothly, given the circumstances. Among the many supplies aboard the warship, they'd found a map plotting a course to Collis. Greade Harbor, to be exact. They would be able to find plenty of help there.

No help would be available from Ariel's side. When using her own power to propel the ship forward, Ariel had inadvertently torn much of the skin from her palms and wrists while holding the rigging. She was lucky that she still had fingers. James had seen what her hands had looked like under the bandages, a ruffled coating of skin akin to torn paper. She had wept upon seeing her forearms, not because of the pain but because the glyphs on her wrists—family and friends—had been disfigured beyond recognition.

And James still hadn't seen Roy. The man had shut himself inside the lone cabin toward the stern, sitting in the dark with no company but Leonard's soon-to-be corpse. Ariel went to check on them periodically, but she always left the cabin—shutting the door gingerly with her bandaged hands—looking more defeated than she had when going in.

Their ship was too slow, their crew was exhausted, and they had only a vague notion where they were. Not to mention a likely impending Altujan invasion, spearheaded by the Eye of Death herself. Could they just have one catastrophe to deal with at a time? Was that too much to ask for?

Adding to the madness—or hopelessness, whichever one would call it—was what James had divulged to everyone during the day previous: his revelation from Vayne. He hadn't been sure how many would react. Roy, of course, had already heard this from him. Ariel was more disturbed, pressing him. Could they *really* trust the word of an Elder? But James was telling the truth. He knew he was.

James didn't know if he could find the strength to go to the empire without Leonard. He would only have Roy around for a bit longer before Charodon broke out. And if Ariel went back to Spiath, maybe he'd strike out on his own, make his future what *he* wanted.

But what *did* he want?

"*What do you want?*" Roy's voice echoed. "*With your life. What do you want?*"

"*I think you keep us honest, James.*" Leonard's voice followed.

The bloodbreathing, the death, and the *hopelessness* had seemingly washed away the desire for anything he had wanted before. James still hated the Temple, but the last few days had more than soured his taste for retribution. It was turning him into something that he didn't want to be, hollow, hateful.

James sighed and leaned against the railing, taking some strange comfort in the rocking of the ship. He never thought that the swell of the ocean would put him at ease, but it had been a very tumultuous journey. More unexpected things had happened.

He turned at the sound of heavy boots—the one thing everyone had been thankful to find in the supply hold was boots—pounding against the deck toward him. He really wasn't in the mood for Ariel to deliver more bad news.

"You've been here for the whole day, lad," Joskine said. He slapped a hand down on the rail next to James. "Some of us are starting to get worried." Crescent-Beard gave an optimistic smile, showing a new hole in his smirk where he had lost a tooth during the fight. It was a new grin from the sailor, something that James hadn't seen before now, but it suited the man. It showed a softer edge. Bruises on his face were starting to heal, but several cuts he'd been given should have been treated with stitches.

"I'm thinking," James said quietly, looking back out to the sea. The azure rays of the sun were starting to fade, turning the water a darker, more shimmering blue. "Joskine, what are you going to do once we make it? *If* we make it."

"Hadn't thought that far ahead," Joskine mused. "Didn't think we would make it out of there alive. Maybe I'll go back to Scourge Atoll, but I don't know. It doesn't feel right to go back after what's happened. Vilch is dead, that won't be a surprise to anyone. People from our homeland die on jobs all the time. But something's different now. The way I saw things isn't the same anymore."

James raised an eyebrow, puzzled by this new, reflective Joskine. "What do you mean?"

"Well, pardon me for saying this to you, lad, but I couldn't have given a drowning thought to you youngsters when we left the port. I thought Lady Ariel and Leonard were snobs. I didn't think much better of the rest of you either. But after Lady Ariel saved me, it got more difficult to ignore you. Dathos drown me, I've got two nephews at the Atoll who aren't much older than you lot." Joskine snorted fondly and shook his head. "I think there's a reason I met all you Chosen, a bigger reason than I can explain. That probably sounds right foolish, doesn't it?"

"It does," James couldn't help saying. "Divine reason isn't a thing, Joskine. You say 'Dathos drown me' like it means something. Dathos is fiction. Or at least he's fiction based off a person or a lie."

"I never said that Dathos or any of the others were the divine reason." Joskine stroked his beard. "I think it's the lot of you. Have to say, I never really believed in Dathos, but I believe in this." He nodded to the flame still crackling in James's hand. "I believe in all of you." Joskine shrugged and moved away from the railing. His feet plunked across the deck.

Turning incredulously, James watched Joskine stomp confidently to starboard, imagining the thoughtful look on the man's face while he discussed the heading with Hadsen. Why in all the scorching world would Joskine believe in them? The Chosen were just people, extremely flawed people, and he was not exempt. They were no better than the fable that was the gods, least of all himself. He'd let his bitterness toward the world and his outrage at his friends cloud his mind. Now three of them were almost gone before he'd realized what was important.

The flame grew slightly in his hand before he extinguished it completely, looking back out to sea. James was no god. He was just a man, and he wasn't worth it.

Ships Carrying Monsters

Roy and Ariel sat by Leonard's side in the tight cabin of the ship. The warship had been sailing for about five days now, and the exhaustion that had blanketed everyone on this vessel hadn't gotten any better. It was a kind of shock, purified trauma. Every sackwearer on the ship had experienced horrible pain at the hands of the Altujan. The effects of the bloodbreathing on Roy and James were not easily dismissed either. Both repeatedly had recoiled at the sight, or even the *smell* of blood. The sap those monsters had used had warped their very senses.

Ariel's shoulders throbbed as she crossed her arms. Everyday tasks were now quite infuriating to complete, adding to her hopelessness as even the few things she could control dwindled. She even needed Badlai's help to *dress* herself after finding clothing to replace their sackwear. Embarrassing. Especially since Badlai became too preoccupied with trying to read the glyphs on Ariel's skin to remember that Ariel's arms didn't work. That one had become too distant, too unresponsive since Samira had died.

The sailors had found the crates with Altujan textiles, allowing most of them to shed their oppressive sackwear and feel like human beings again. The shirts were a bit too loose on everyone, but they were a welcome change. Ariel and a few of the other Spiathi prisoners had immediately cut the sleeves from their shirts and jackets. The checkers on her jacket reminded her of the Altujan she had shot down.

In the time since they had escaped Zatran's colony, Leonard had not woken up, and it didn't look like he was going to. The wound was a deep one, tearing through quite a bit of muscle tissue along with an unquantifiable amount of internal bleeding. She and a sailor with a steady hand had been able to remove the blade from Leonard's stomach, but a lot of the most significant damage was already done. She had done all she could, bandaged the wound, and used antiseptic they had found to keep rot away.

They had been lucky to find that much, as the Altujan warship was stocked with mainly tools of invasion. Was it the life of the Chosen to face constant death? She had thought that there was something else to being given this power, something that would let her help her people without bloodshed, but it didn't seem like that life had any basis in the real world anymore. It made her heart wilt to give up on that particular dream.

The lantern in the corner of the cabin had grown dim. Even though she was right next to him, Ariel couldn't see Roy's face. She could tell he was upset, and she had known him long enough to see when he was hiding it. He did look much different without his black cloak, dressed in Altujan red and gray checkers. That stupid cloak had survived every single fight without fail until now.

Still keeping her arms crossed, she nudged Roy with her shoulder. "You should get some sleep."

Roy shook his head.

Ariel sighed in annoyance but not surprise. She sometimes forgot how stubborn he could be. "Roy, you aren't in any condition to be up and about. You're hurt and spent," she said.

"He tried to apologize," Roy croaked, "and I threw it in his face." The man he had threatened to kill numerous times was dying, and now Roy couldn't do anything to stop it.

Ariel ignored the pain in her hand and grabbed his wrist, her bandaged fingers only able to grasp him feebly. "You've been sitting here since you woke up. You haven't even cleaned the blood off of yourself, and you're clearly hurt." He started to protest, but she cut him off, "You can't do anything else for him right now. The best thing that you can do is sleep and regain your strength."

Roy looked over at Ariel's face with a hollow expression. He sighed.

"He's going to die," Roy said. It wasn't a question, and there was a sense of...loss. And shock.

She nodded, resting her head on his shoulder.

"It's all my fault," he whispered.

Ariel removed her head from his shoulder and glanced at him, not understanding.

Roy saw her inquisitive gaze and bowed his head. "He needed me, and I was too weak."

She gingerly turned him to face her, shaking her head forcefully and ignoring the screaming of her hands. "No, of course it isn't your fault. Sam lied to you. She's the reason why you're—"

"Why I'm a monster," Roy finished.

She struck him impulsively on the shoulder. Ariel immediately sucked a breath inward and regretted the decision. Damn that *hurt*. "Don't say that, ever."

"It's the truth, Ariel. He's a part of me now, and he's a part that I'm too weak to stop," Roy said quietly, matter-of-factly. "It wasn't *just* Charodon that killed those villagers. It was him using *my* weakness. Every time Charodon has killed, I'm to blame for letting him off the leash. I almost let him kill you."

Ariel turned away from him, looking instead at Leonard's pale yet peaceful face. Etah lash the man, if he were awake he could help her talk some sense into Roy. Instead it was just her. "And I forgave you the next day, Roy. I should have gone back immediately, but I thought you were dead. Every time I heard a rumor of Charodon's wrath on the continent, I thought that it was him, wreaking carnage in the husk of your body. I was weak too."

Roy didn't answer her right away, tracing his finger along the scar on his face. "It would have been better if Leonard's knife had killed me." He was serious, convinced.

She whirled on him. "Take it back." Ariel waited for him to recant, to apologize, but no sound left his lips whatsoever. She searched his face for fresh tears but found none. They had all dried. She looked desperately for anything but found nothing.

This was all wrong. Charodon had taken Roy's whole life away, made him a depressed husk, a ghost. He had forgiven Leonard, it appeared, but what about himself? Something had happened to him on the battlefield with the Altujan, when he was fighting for control against his passenger. She wanted to embrace him, to wrap her arms around him, tell him that she loved him. That he wasn't the monster the world told him he was, that he told himself he was.

But would he even listen?

Roy refused to speak further, just looked down at Leonard's listless body, his face a mask. It normally was a mask, but she was always able to read his eyes. The smallest glint in his cold, turquoise eyes could tell her so much. But now the eyes said nothing. This was the Roy she feared. Not for herself but for him. This emotionless Roy was one who had given up, the one who had lost his fight. It was one she couldn't bear.

Ariel stood, wincing a bit from her arms, and pushed the door to the cabin open with her shoulder. It still pained her to do so, but that wasn't the worst pain she felt at the moment, not by far.

"I'll bring water," she muttered.

Roy didn't respond.

***

Vayne and Dhorh's were the only feet that left the ship once it landed. Of course, there was another passenger that would leave the vessel shortly, the Mangler. All of the survivors of the Epot Detharn razing had succumbed three—no, four—days ago. Remarkable.

What Vayne still couldn't place was where exactly they were. Time and lack of sight had jumbled his sense of direction, and what he could still remember was too fuzzy or outdated. The ship had reached Collis, the upper continent. Of that he was sure, but the exact placement of their landfall could at best be an educated guess. Dhorh's stolen memories of a sailor indicated they had landed somewhere on the Spiathi coast. The moderate ship had run aground, quite forcefully so. Vayne and Dhorh had been thrown to the deck when the bow had collided with the shore.

His bare feet crunched against crumbling, rocky sand. At least, that was how it *sounded*. He could hear Dhorh's quick footsteps beside him, and he could sense that the Eye of Memory wanted to say something.

"Speak, Dhorh," he said calmly.

Dhorh paused, his footsteps subsiding before moving forward again. "I'm just not clear, Vayne. Rhaiga has her task of getting the Altujan in shape to launch an invasion. We sail to Collis before her to do what exactly?"

"Do you know what my favorite thing in all of creation is, Dhorh?" Vayne asked. His voice whistled a bit as he breathed in. He didn't have to see to know that his fellow Elder was shaking his head. Thousands of years, and Dhorh still only half listened to his anecdotes. Vayne leered briefly. "The spider."

"They're nature's perfect creation," Dhorh recited, though Vayne could have done without the exasperated tone.

So he *could* listen.

"They are tiny yet can bring down the biggest of prey. They know when to lay a trap, know when to strike, and have the potency to make a single blow fatal," Dhorh grumbled.

"Exactly," Vayne said passionately. "And we, as superior beings, can emulate the spider in pursuit of victory. I have thought long about this in the years we have been in exile. With the balance shifted from us to the humans, we no longer possess the raw strength we once did. In a sense, we have become smaller."

Dhorh sounded like he was starting to understand. "So we lay a trap like a spider, and we strike in the right place."

Vayne nodded, continuing to shuffle forward. Pride swelled in his chest, another feeling that he had forgotten. Exile had been a curious thing for all of them. Regular emotions had seemed to leave the three of them, favoring a singular state of mind over the years. Now that they had returned, would *all* their emotions begin to come back? He wasn't sure if he liked this. The resentment—and yes, perhaps fear—that he had felt over the years in the dunes had fueled him to create this work of genius.

Although he could admit that Rhaiga and Dhorh had not benefited as much as he. The character traits of the hosts that they inhabited had started to become the default as time had worn on in the Dunes. Vayne—who inhabited a man who had been near death and afraid—had been able to harness that fear and plan for their return. But Rhaiga especially had taken to the confusion and rage of the woman she had fused to, a lonely priestess who had known no friendship or enjoyment, only duty. He wondered what Rhaiga would be like inside the body of a hero or zealot.

Dhorh was much easier to maniipulate. Since he only cared about his memories, Vayne could simply make his orders as if he were directing Dhorh to keep the recollections safe.

He felt Dhorh stiffen next to him. "There's someone here," Dhorh said.

Vayne continued his slow gait. "Then let us meet."

The sound of a singular pair of boots greeted them, fading into Vayne's peripheral. They sounded purposeful, strong. Whoever was approaching them, there was an official air to them.

The voice that spoke was even more so, "Sir, are you in need of assistance? I noticed your vessel seems to have run aground. Are there any injured aboard?"

Vayne, pretending to be delirious, wobbled a little extra. "Yes. Please, help us. Everyone on our ship is ill. There was no one to steer."

"I can go and fetch others to help," the stern man said.

Dhorh, catching on, interrupted, "There's no time! Mama is on the ship, and she's barely breathing anymore. Don't leave us!" Vayne heard a slight smack as Dhorh grabbed the man's wrist and started towing him to where their ship more-or-less rested on the pebbly beach.

Vayne walked behind them, letting Dhorh's distraction lead the man farther away from the mainland. This man would have to do, though he wished they could bait him into accepting his presence. They couldn't always afford to do what Charodon did, for taking hosts by force would wear out their durability. Unfortunately, he didn't have much choice, as this old and withered body had outlived its usefulness.

The man turned toward Vayne, apparently still being led along by Dhorh. "What is your name? Where are you coming from?"

Vayne struggled to remember the name he had used at Epot Detharn. "Yomon. We were traveling to escape Boane. The city has collapsed into chaos, and my grandson and I were some of the only survivors. The rest of us fell ill during the journey, and I fear that many won't make it."

"You have my word that we will do our very best to help them," the man promised. "I'm Gaunt, Dragoneater and Lord of Companies of the Collisun Empire, Ambassador for Spiath. I am sorry to hear of your troubles. Boane always was a hastily built tower, ready to fall under pressure."

Hardly believing his luck at the person they had found, Vayne decided to keep him talking as they neared the ship. The sound of rushing waves became louder.

"Collisun? Is that where we are now? Apologies, Lord. I am without sight and am not entirely sure where it is we have landed."

Gaunt stammered out an apology, "You're in Spiath, my friend. Just a few miles south of the Basalt Watchtower. I'm here on Imperial business. My company is about half a mile away."

They reached the ship, firmly lodged into the shore despite the rising tide. It lapped at their feet hungrily. Gaunt stepped around them and squinted upward at the deck. Or at least, that was what it sounded like he was doing.

"How many are you with?" Gaunt asked, his voice taking a solemn tone.

"Enough," Vayne said. Cutting off the man's confused response, Vayne lithely lashed outward at Gaunt with his hand, placing his flat palm against the man's sternum. He heard Gaunt's short gasp, *felt* the man's soul flutter. Vayne felt as if he were being sucked through a tube. He had often forgotten the sensation of taking a new host, and it was not always a pleasant one, particularly if the host resisted.

Vayne's essence poured into Gaunt's body, pumping thousands of years of bitterness, cunning, and knowledge into a sack of organs and bones yet to pass fifty-two. It was cramped, with Vayne's consciousness pushing against the man's. The sensation wasn't unlike pouring oil into a brimming goblet of water. They wrestled and kicked, but Vayne's consciousness won out, brutally subduing Gaunt's and pushing him into the corner. A passenger.

"*What is this?*" Gaunt's voice sounded in his head. "*What is this? Where am I?*"

"You have become a stepping stone to a greater path," Vayne said, his voice suddenly sounding deeper. Gaunt's frightened questions were stuffed in a dark crevice within Vayne's new body. Hopefully this one would not take too long to break. He didn't have time or energy to devote to consuming an ornery host. But this was the best option. The old husk was becoming an encumbrance, and he would need every advantage in the trials ahead.

Vayne opened his eyes, and he could see. *He could see!* Colors danced before his eyes, clear and crisp. The vivacity pulsed around him in everything. The reflections of the incoming water that washed over his feet, the grass that swayed and dipped in the wind. He could see each individual pore on his now muscular, suntanned, tattooed arm. Before him rested a withered corpse, the shell of the body he had cast aside. Its blank eyes stared up at him, unseeing, as they had been for centuries. That host had served him well, had given himself to Vayne willingly, but the time had come to move on, forge ahead. Even if this host would not last as long, it was necessary. Vayne could always just take another one.

Using Gaunt's body, he knelt beside his old host. By the Eyes! His knees actually bent! He placed a hand over the eyes of the man whose soul he had claimed over three thousand years ago, a man whose name had suddenly come back to him. "Thank you, Klaern. I will remember you fondly."

Voices reached the edge of his hearing, much farther than his previous ears would have been able to detect. He looked inward from the shore to see several men running to his position, led by a tall man with dark Kostran skin. A single braid whipped across his back as he ran.

"Gaunt! What is it?" the Kostran shouted.

Holding his hand up to halt them, Vayne glanced at Dhorh. The two shared a glance—something actually possible now—and Dhorh's childish grin flashed for just a moment before he sobbed with artificial anguish.

"Stay back!" Vayne called, holding a hand up to his face. "It appears a sickness has struck this vessel. The boy was the only one left alive, and his grandfather succumbed on the shore."

"Understood." The Kostran nodded. "We will pull together an apothecary and supplies to aid the boy. We must get the king away from this settlement and back to Takhral."

Vayne looked at Dhorh and gave an encouraging smile. To the Kostran, it appeared that he was comforting a scared child. "Understood," Vayne said. This turn of events benefitted them nicely. Rhaiga had her job of leading the Altujan into Greade Harbor to cut off supply routes. Here, Vayne and Dhorh would sow the seeds of chaos within the empire's most vulnerable member country. It was so clear now, with fresh eyes. This was where the real work began.

***

Roy sat in the darkness of the cabin, soothed by the slight rocking of the ship. His head still felt sharp stabs of pain, but they were getting to be less frequent. He had dozed off at some point. Still able to see vague shapes in the cabin, he could see the edge of the makeshift bed that Leonard was resting on, the outline of the cabin door.

As more things started to come into focus, his eyes rested on a cup in front of him. Roy felt the contents of the container slosh back and forth as he picked it up. Its coolness dripped over his hand and wrist. Ariel had left him water.

He drank greedily, gulping down the water with no hesitation. It soothed his skin as he wiped the drops from his mouth and leaned back against the cabin wall. The splintering wood prickled at his back while he stared straight ahead. The pain from the splinters didn't feel good, but they helped to keep him focused and climb out of the grogginess he felt. Silence reigned supreme over the cabin, and that silence made him uncomfortable. Leonard would have come up with a joke or something to ease the tension. Samira probably would have just prayed, and that was only slightly less annoying.

Dathos—or whatever—drown that woman. She'd lied to him for all these years, but he missed her. Anger and hurt couldn't replace that. Roy swished the cup around some more before realizing he had drunk all of it too quickly.

"A blow to the head will make you thirsty," Roy said aloud. The cabin answered with silence. Leonard wouldn't have responded to that even if he was awake, but Roy found the lack of response strangely insulting. "You know I can't make jokes," he said defensively.

Roy looked at the shape of Leonard in the dark. The rising and falling of his chest was barely perceptible in the gloom, or was it the motion of the ship? Roy looked between his feet. He knew that Leonard couldn't hear him, but he was still struggling to speak. This would be the only time he could make things right. Some part of him still desperately clung to the hatred of his former friend, needing to keep the hatred going. It would be so much easier to hate Leonard, to cheer at his death.

But those specters in his most recent vision, there had been something familiar about them, some connection that had tethered him to them. When James had told them all of his vision with Vayne, he had been startled to hear descriptions of the same blind man and young boy as he had seen. Were these visions of the other Elders?

Part of him didn't believe that, even if James's description did fit. They had been urgent, like they genuinely wanted to help him, but why?

"He deserves it," a raspy, deep voice spoke in his head. *"You've said it yourself for years. It's all his fault."*

Roy shook his head. He wasn't interested in listening to Charodon.

The voice spoke again, *"You're a monster because of him."*

"You're the monster," Roy shot back. "I'm just too weak to control you."

"Uh huh," Charodon snickered. The sound rang in Roy's mind like breaking glass. *"All the same to someone on the outside."*

He tuned the voice out, wringing his hands and ignoring the welling anger he felt freezing in his stomach, a more constant feeling these days. This wasn't going to be the day he lost control; he had gotten too close last time. Charodon would have to wait. But he did have a point. The only reason that Charodon had broken out and killed people was because of Roy's weakness, his inability to put a clamp on the monster's impulses. He could make all of the excuses he wanted, but in the end Charodon was right that no one looking from the outside would care.

Roy inhaled deeply, the sound of his breathing swirling through the cabin. He looked again toward Leonard, still motionless, still waiting for death. For years, it had been all he wanted to hear: Leonard apologizing for his suffering then moving on out of his life. It had been a lingering craving that never went away. Every time he had eaten and Samira muttered an offering to the gods, he had prayed for revenge. He would wake in the middle of the night and swear retribution over and over again.

But it had been a waste. Leonard was dying, and it didn't make anything better. Roy was still miserable, and he knew who the fault truly belonged with. He shuffled on his knees toward Leonard and knelt by his side.

"I'm sorry," he said finally. The silence of the room was ear-splitting. "You were afraid, and I was looking for someone to blame. And Samira, she was just doing what we all do, trying to do something good with her life." He waited for a response from Leonard, knowing he wouldn't get one. "It was no one's fault that it happened. It was just bad luck." Tears traced down the length of Roy's scar, only coming from the full-turquoise eye. He nodded and gripped Leonard's arm.

Finally, after three years, he could see it clearly. The mistakes that Leonard and Samira had made, they were only mistakes, nothing more. They were, and always had been, his friends. Roy becoming possessed by Charodon had been a freak accident, and no one was to blame.

"*And after?*" Charodon's voice resurfaced. "*I suppose it was bad luck that you killed those villagers? It was all thanks to your cooperation.*"

"You killed them," Roy whispered. "I would never help you."

"*You see, that's where your mortal brain becomes too narrow. You help me by being weak. You always have been, and that weakness lets me have all the fun I want. So thank you, boy. For your help.*"

Roy shook his head vigorously. Bile threatened to rise up in his throat as a result. Still refuting Charodon vehemently, he positioned himself into the corner of the cabin, using the connecting walls to prop him up. It was a useless gesture, but he would try to sleep anyway.

Charodon was silent now, uncharacteristically so. Ever since he had made a permanent place in Roy's mind, all he had done was talk. It was exhausting. But those last words had been all Charodon needed. Now Roy was left in silence in his own thoughts. It was in these thoughts that he came to a painful, irrefutable conclusion.

Leonard and Samira were innocent. The reason the Scaleslayer existed was because of him, but it didn't have to be. He couldn't rid himself of the Elder, but there was a way to stop it, to rid the world of Charodon completely.

Roy would have to die, he *needed* to die.

✦

A Talk About Dreams

The world was a shaky place, covered in shadows that weren't completely natural. They were pointed every which way with no sign of a light source, as if they existed of their own will. Unable to close her eyes as the shadows began to move faster, Samira was helpless, watching as the darkness folded on itself over and over until she was in a place that was familiar but just off.

"Well, what do you think?" a snickering voice asked her.

Samira whirled around and lifted her left hand in the direction of the words. Dhorh, the Eye of Memory, stood before her. The devil was against a tree, dressed in trousers and a jacket. Dhorh wore no shirt underneath, and Samira could see each individual rib poking through the skin. The blue sunlight streaming through the thick foliage above them hit his horns in such a way that Dhorh's appendages looked sickly purple. Even though she had been "unthreaded" for most of their interaction, she had heard James's description of this bastard and knew who he was. James had also said that he was a striking smug prick.

"What do you want?" Samira snapped.

Dhorh held up his hands and smirked, his perfectly white teeth glinting, "I'm not here to hurt you this time. Vayne doesn't know I'm doing this, and I'd prefer to keep it that way."

Samira pondered the Elder's eyeless simpering and straightened, kicking at a rock next to her foot. The rock rolled away, as if it were real. If she could kick a rock in here...

"I hope you aren't thinking of doing anything heroic or stupid," Dhorh said, his voice oozing condescension. "You kicked that pebble because I *allowed* you to. If you want to attack me, better do it when you're awake. Now sit."

Without a second's pause, Samira was seated. Instantaneously. There was no motion that brought her to the ground. She simply *was* sitting. She glared at Dhorh as the moss tickled her bare feet.

The devil grinned again and crouched in front of her.

Dhorh flicked Samira's forehead. "I find that letting you interact with the memory best helps the *illusion*. But if you can't behave, I'll just have to keep you here." His empty sockets crinkled, as if squinting at Samira's face. It was a profoundly disturbing expression.

Samira nodded slowly. The next instant, she was standing beside Dhorh—he was quite a bit shorter than her, she noticed—looking out over a mossy bog. The swamp was densely packed, with a green-gray smattering of color that made her sick to look at. Her memory came back to her in an instant. So Dhorh was as sadistic a devil as James had described.

"We're at the Draypond Marshes."

"Precisely," Dhorh chirped. "I wanted to visit the place where your prophecy went wrong. Vayne speaks of prophecies too, but not the kind where you Chosen are the heroes. You and your friends are the worst symptoms of a disease that is killing the natural order of things. Humans aren't meant to be in control of the world, of the future. They're brutal, disorganized, and profoundly selfish beings that prioritize the advancement of themselves above order. That isn't how things are supposed to be."

"And what is Vayne's solution to this perceived problem? Kill us all, I suppose?" Samira asked, voice saturated in sarcasm. This tirade had been relayed to her by James. She knew Vayne's convictions already.

"Oh, don't be dramatic. Even Vayne knows that this isn't possible. Humans are a part of the world now, whether we like it or not. And seeing as we need human hosts to live now, eliminating all of you seems like a bit much. You simply need to be put in your place, scattered too thin to rebuild after we've torn down this mess you call civilization, especially after banishing us for nearly twelve hundred years. That made Vayne particularly annoyed," Dhorh said.

Samira rubbed her temple with her thumb and squinted at Dhorh. "What's the point of all this? So we're the problem, the gods are the problem. Why are you here, and why aren't you telling Vayne about it?" She kicked a pebble into the bog before her, scattering the tadpoles with the miniature splash.

Dhorh turned his back to Samira and stalked toward a mossy glade a few feet away. "All that time in the dunes gives you time to think. Or doubt, I guess. I trust Vayne, but this vision makes me wonder. You see, my brother Charodon isn't like the other Elders. He never bought into the grand vision for the world that Vayne described. He didn't see a world that had a past, present, and future—only a world where nature ruled. A world where he ruled. He didn't need convictions. He simply was."

"It sounds like you admire him." Samira rolled her eyes.

Dhorh grimaced. "I'm starting to wonder what a world that simply *is* would be like. Charodon craves only his destruction and blood. But Vayne wants something completely different, something that might not even exist anymore. And even if it isn't a world where destruction and blood rule, what would a world left to itself look like? I hold on to the memories that I unthread, keep them safe. And a world of order that Vayne wants would be what protects them, wouldn't it? But what if a world left to its own devices did the same?"

Samira was beginning to lose her patience. "What is it that you want from me exactly? I have a fight with Rhaiga to win."

"Ha! Quite a bold statement from a dead woman," Dhorh exclaimed. "Well, *nearly* dead. That blast of yours was quite impressive. I suspect you've blown yourself almost into the exact middle of the sea, from what Rhaiga said." He watched—or pretended to—the fading ripples on a pond in front of him. Tadpoles and other creatures circled beneath the shimmering green surface. "I see your memories, your mistakes, your regrets. In a way, I know you better than anyone now. More than a best friend, even a lover." He grinned as she shuddered. "I know that your prophecy is a sham, known it for centuries actually, since I am a *real* god. But you've recently accepted that. I need to know when a dream is worth giving up on, if Vayne's dream is worth giving up on, for the sake of my threads."

"Don't you already know *striking* everything?" Samira interjected. "Isn't that what you always gloat about?"

"I hold the collective memories of everything I unthread. That being said, I don't have much agency when it comes to the future." Dhorh shrugged. "This bog we're standing in is what you remember of it. I couldn't tell you what it looks like now or even ten minutes from now."

Samira had begun to tune him out. The green-gray haze of the marshes steeped her eyesight, making her sick. A familiar feeling of sickness she had felt three years ago. This place haunted her memories often, and no amount of sleep or drink could ever take her mind off the horrible mistake she had made. It had taken her best friend and made him into a wild animal, thrashing against his own impulses. Roy's sullen depression was the result of her own negligence and ego. And that ego had been boosted by the man that raised her.

"My father is like you," she whispered.

Leaning against another tree and casually scratching his left horn against the bark, Dhorh frowned. "Ah yes, Namon. The proud father. I see many memories of him. I certainly don't see any resemblance though."

"He's a fool." Samira gazed at the foggy, drooping trees around her. "All he ever believed in was a lie. The Temple fed him a story that he became obsessed with during my childhood. And when I grew up, he passed it on to me." She snorted a bit at her memories. All the while, feeling Dhorh's eyeless sockets boring into her. "Everything the Temple told him was accepted with no second thought, that a Chosen of Astus would be the one to kill the Alderaye. Men would live without the threat of the old world, all the things that make people feel good when they hear it." She sighed. "And I believed him, just like you believe Vayne."

"And you're saying I'm a fool, like your dear zealot father." Dhorh said, head still resting against the tree. "Can't believe it took you this long to lose your friends." Something behind him croaked, and he turned his head slightly.

"You want to know when a dream is worth giving up on?" Samira barked. "It's when following that dream destroys what you care about, all right? My father's dream—my dream—pushed my friends away. It killed Talia, and it's going to kill Roy too now. And now I have to live with it, give it up. So just go away and let me!"

The cracked grin on the Eye of Memory's face split even further as he pushed himself off the tree and put his face close to hers. Samira refused to look away from the disturbingly perfect smile.

"Thank you, Samira. This chat has been *very* productive. We should do this more often." Dhorh reached forward and placed a clammy finger on her forehead.

Samira's entire body went cold as she awoke to find herself floating on a half-submerged mass of flotsam. Blue sunlight scorched her eyes, and she clapped a hand to her face to block the stabbing rays. How long had she been afloat like this? Parting her fingers ever so slightly, Samira peered through the haze. Blue was all she could see. Strike her, what did she even *do* back there? All she could remember was Rhaiga's eyes drilling into her. The fear of that moment touched her mind and made the water around her slightly colder. In that instant, her feelings had taken over and released a lightning strike that had blown her far into the sea, probably destroying most of the island. Her skin stung from the sun, and her left arm throbbed.

Looking down at herself, Samira saw that her sackwear had been nearly shredded, marked with numerous holes and burn marks. A lacework of fresh scarring angrily wove across her left bicep. She could feel the pulsing pain, like a lit candle just under her skin. The power from the last blast clearly had slipped from her grasp for only a second. But she had learned years ago that a second was more than enough time to do horrific damage.

"Strike me." She noticed her dry lips. The salt on the air provoked nipping pain as it hit her dehydrated and itchy face. Rubbing her eyes, she surveyed the swelling horizon. If only she knew how long she had been out here. From the state of how hungry she was, she wouldn't be surprised if it had been twelve striking years.

A speck no larger than her thumbnail was drifting across the horizon. Swearing again, Samira stood and shakily balanced on the unstable debris beneath her.

"*Hey!*" she screamed hoarsely. Blood trickled from the corner of her dried lips. Waving her quivering arms above her head and throwing off her balance, she prayed—to Astus, anyone—that it was a ship. "*Help!*" she continued "*Please hear me! Please* striking *hear me!*" Panic briefly shot through her as she fell backward onto the flotsam—already exhausted—and it wobbled. It was a miracle she hadn't slipped off. This debris was much flimsier and more waterlogged than she had originally thought.

The spec steadily grew into the form of a dingy ship, likely a fishing vessel. Relief washed over her as she saw that the sails were not Altujan colors. Now to figure out where she was. As the vessel grew closer and closer, Samira forced herself to her feet and stood to greet her rescuers. Figure out where she was first, and then figure out what to do next.

An hour later, she was aboard the ship, draining a water skin. The water was a bit stale, but at that moment it was the most delicious substance that Samira had ever tasted.

She drank greedily, incomprehensibly parched. How long had she been adrift? The burns from the sun—and from her own doing—felt as if they had been there for ages but also felt incredibly fresh and painful. She was slumped against the mast of a cargo vessel, Kostran make by the look of it, called the *Storm Tower*. Never had she seen such a lazily named ship in all of her life. She saw several of her people marching purposefully across the deck, silver earrings indicating their trade as merchants. Her own white earrings were gone, either torn off by the blast or washed away in the sea. She ran her fingers over her bloody earlobes absentmindedly. None of these sailors looked particularly friendly, but she had barely traded more than a few words with any of them as of yet. An officer's coat was draped over her shoulders, covering the tattered sackwear she still wore.

A pair of squared black boots planted themselves in front of her. Samira looked up to see a tall Kostran man with a gray braid. The sea had not been kind to this man, and the weathering of his face made him appear far older than he probably was. He crossed his arms and raised an eyebrow, as if waiting for her to speak.

Samira just looked back down, not interested in a conversation.

Getting impatient, the man knelt and took the empty water flagon from Samira's hand. "Have you gotten enough water?"

Samira gave a quiet nod. "Thank you."

"Finally, we're getting somewhere," the man said, sighing. "I'm the captain of this ship."

Samira looked up quizzically at the patch on his right sleeve. All Kostran merchant captains were required to have their name and title on their sleeve for easy identification at market. Stitched lettering labeled the man *Captain Moron*. Samira squinted harder; that couldn't be right.

Moron rolled his eyes. "It's pronounced '*Muh-Roan*'. Astus strike my father. Thought he was being funny."

"Fathers can cause a lot of grief." Samira looked down at her hands. "I'm Samira."

"Named after that Chosen, huh. You want to tell me how you got all the way out here on a slab of wood in those clothes?"

Samira rubbed her temple. The knuckle at the base of her thumb popped. "I fought a devil and blew myself up."

Moron shrugged. "If you don't want to tell me, it's your business. You're lucky we saw you. Just about hit the winds that would take us back up north. Were headed back to Collis from Bo'Shyk." His tired eyes glanced up to the bow of the ship. "Where are you headed?"

A moment passed before Samira made a decision. "Thesera. I'm going back to Kostra." It was time to go back home, give up on this fool's dream of hers before anyone else was hurt.

"Just so happens I know a man who's headed that way too." Moron scratched his clean-shaven chin. "Meeting up with him when we make landfall." The captain stood and started walking toward the bow. "We can give you a hammock to sleep in if you're willing to help keep the ship afloat. Keep the coat too. Doubt the smell will come out now."

A quick whiff of herself made Samira wish she had drowned. The ocean mixed with sulfur and smoke. Striking perfect. "Landfall where?" she called.

The exhausted captain called back over his slumped shoulder, "Greade."

Samira sighed. Of course they were going to that striking harbor. The thought of going to Leonard's hometown filled her with dread, reminding her of the friends she had betrayed. She wasn't even positive if they had made it. Not even a fraction of those ships had been destroyed. Deciding to keep her mind on other things, she held out her left palm and focused on her energy. Her senses went quiet except for the beating of her own heart. Only when she could hear nothing else could she create lightning. That space between heartbeats—it was when she felt the surge, the life, the power.

Only this time, the familiar crackle of electricity across her hand didn't come. She grimaced and concentrated harder, waiting for the telltale pop. Nothing happened. For hours she tried, but no electricity formed. The still-fresh scars on her bicep throbbed. A cold, calloused hand closed around her chest, freezing her lungs. She'd felt this before after she'd killed Talia and damaged her right arm. The fight against the Altujan and Rhaiga had overextended the limits of her power. Astus's gift, her power, was fading.

Greade

James stood at the starboard rail of the ship beside Joskine and Hadsen. This wasn't ideal, according to Ariel, sailing into Greade Harbor on a foreign ship without Leonard to smooth over any unavoidably ruffled feathers. But Ariel was a Chosen, and that was still worth something. Apparently, some had been kings or even emperors in the past, but the last few centuries had seen them more as military generals. It was a considerable political power, but not enough in some cases.

James tried to look inconspicuous as the ship listed toward Greade Harbor. The pride of the empire's trade economy covered a great deal of the visible coast and the surrounding countryside. Impressive, densely packed cobblestone buildings provided a shield from the fierce wind of the coast, and even from a short distance James could see the famous high grasses of Collisun. It danced and bobbed as vigorously as Leonard's hair. James couldn't imagine growing up in a place so bizarre. He squinted against the wind. Glowing in the sun was a magnificent white spire that disappeared into the heavens. It presented itself as a beacon to any that approached the city.

"Is that the Marble Watchtower?" James whispered to Hadsen.

The sailor nodded. Spiathi by James's estimation, the man sported an impressive amount of glyphs on his remaining arm, including one on his hand. Multiple glyphs curled around the base of his neck, and his thick black mustache was the only hair remaining on his head. Despite his decidedly non-Spiathi hair color, diamond eyes spoke the truth about his homeland.

Hadsen and Joskine shuffled nervously beside him as the ship coasted into the harbor. Here, the trading appeared incredibly regimented, with none of the charm of Epot Detharn. James could see trading company symbols fighting for space among the marketplace at the opening of the shipyard.

James profusely hoped the checkpoint would be swift. With Leonard dying in the cabin of their ship, they didn't have the time to waste breath with the Harbormaster.

James couldn't decide if it were fortunate or unfortunate that he could see no man who matched Ariel's description of the Harbormaster waiting for them at the docks. Instead, a group of smartly-dressed dignitaries stood expectantly. At the forefront of the group stood a man and a woman in slim black coats with bronze buttons. They looked to be identical siblings in their forties. Dark-brown hair tied back, the two gazed upon the stolen ship with disdain visible to a blind man.

James noted that Ariel didn't look pleased in the slightest to be met with these two. The ship listed up to the dock, and several sackwearers rushed to tie off the mooring. The sibling dignitaries stepped back in disgust, their gray eyes scrunching up. Their bony cheeks were frozen in pompous disinterest.

One of them, the woman, called in a velvet voice across the pier toward the deck of the ship, "Who among you commands this ship? State your business in Greade Harbor."

Ariel cleared her throat, causing the siblings to whip their heads in her direction. "This ship is under my command. I am Ariel, Chosen of Etah, returning from a mission on the orders of Emperor Alaric Treft. This is my ship and crew, and we are in dire need of medical attention and supplies."

"Ah, Ariel! So good to see you alive," the man drawled.

"Lucian." Ariel said, looking like she needed to spit after saying his name.

James immediately disliked this man. Every detail of the man's hawkish, smug face made his skin bristle.

Ariel clasped her hands behind her back. "Where is the harbormaster? We need to speak with Rollo."

Both twins smirked at once, which made James incredibly squeamish. The sister leaned forward and leered. "Severin Rollo is ill, and as such we are serving as harbormasters in his place. We might as well, since we are already here on orders from the emperor himself."

"And what might those orders be?" Ariel frowned.

"That's irrelevant to your situation, which from the looks of it is on an unidentified ship filled with—what should I call them—*unfortunates*?" Lucian tilted his head. "What is the meaning of this?"

James crossed his arms, anxiety welling in his ribcage. This was already off to a worrisome start.

Ariel sighed. "We came back from the emperor's mission but ran into trouble along the way. And it's likely that the trouble will follow us here. Lucian, Petra, we *have* to evacuate the city. Altujan and far worse have resurfaced, and they're probably going to come here first."

Petra snorted. Her astoundingly long lashes fluttered over predatory gray eyes. "Please spare us the tall tales, Chosen. Altujan were of a world long ago. Why the emperor sent you and Leonard off to that sandpile is something I will never understand. I also don't understand why Leonard thinks he could have *you* meet us in his stead."

"Leonard is gravely injured. He needs a surgeon immediately," Ariel growled. "Send for Rossel. *Now.*" A sharp breeze zipped through the harbor, ruffling the smart black jackets of the siblings. Allowing nervousness to overtake their sneering demeanor for just a moment, they resumed their posturing.

No order was given, and it was clear that they felt safe with the number of spearmen surrounding the dock. The soldiers in form-fitting gray gambesons stood in a loose formation that would still be enough to shame the whole of Boane's Garrison. It looked like the local Seaguard had been tasked with protecting these snobs.

Lucian gave Ariel an annoyed glance. "Now what was this about evacuating? I don't see any reason why we should believe you without any hard evidence of these *Altujan* you claimed to see."

"Is this scorching ship and the recently freed prisoners on it not enough for you?" James called from the rail. People like this reminded James of the clerics he'd grown up with, wielding their positions of power and hiding behind their guards. Leonard's life was at stake, and James wouldn't sit patiently while his friend bled out. The heads of the twins swung in James's direction, and he could feel their cold, silver gazes slide onto him like slime as they did it.

Petra sniffed. "And who do you think you are to address Trade Visors for the empire in that way?"

"We found him," Ariel said. "He's the one the emperor sent us to find. The Chosen of Iarus."

"Oh, so you've found the savior, have you?" Lucian rolled his eyes. "Prove it."

James eyed his surroundings, extending his senses, searching in vain for the smallest spark that he could take hold of. The voyage had left him feeling hopeless and with enough frustration that he would have been happy to rid the man of his eyebrows. But in the middle of the cloudy afternoon, with no lamps alight, he could do nothing but stand there like an irked child. Without control of the final form, James felt no more a Chosen than the wooden rail next to him. He glared through the spotty sunlight at the siblings and said nothing.

Lucian nodded in mock astonishment. "Impressive. Now, to address your request, we will do no such evacuation of the harbor. Greade Harbor is an important bastion of trade for the empire. Evacuation would result in a complete halt of business, meaning the empire ceases to generate revenue, and instability reigns." He leered at Ariel, eyes traveling across her shoulders. "Without sufficient evidence to back up your claims, we can't in good faith jeopardize the financial stability of the empire or Greade Harbor."

"This is about more than just your business interests, Lucian." Ariel sighed. "People's lives are at stake. We can't waste any time. You *need* to announce an evacuation."

"I would entertain the idea," Lucian gave a rotten grin. "for the price of a drink."

James thought he could see Ariel suppress a shiver

Ariel set her jaw. "I don't dabble in swill."

James smirked as she drew a pink flush from Lucian's face.

"Careful, Chosen. You'll find that crossing the line won't go well for you. Divine power and the Temple can't protect you from everything," Petra threatened.

Without missing a beat, Ariel sprung across the gap of water and onto the pier, inches from the siblings. Diplomacy wouldn't work here. They controlled diplomacy too comfortably. Petra and Lucian squeaked before backing away sharply. The sound of their polished shoes squealed like rats against the worn wood of the dock.

Snakes they were not, James realized. They were worms.

Ariel stood inches from the Trade Visors. "That line?" She pointed back at the edge of the dock. The sea breeze that whistled through the harbor began to swirl and dive in every direction.

A creaking door drew James's gaze toward the cabin where Leonard had been resting. Straining with Leonard in his arms, Roy shambled from the shadows of the compartment. James felt a slight shock at how terrible he looked. Roy's unkempt hair and beard were matted, and crusted blood flaked from the side of his head. One orange eye and one turquoise eye battled over what to focus on. James couldn't tell if it was due to Charodon's influence or not. In his arms, Leonard's limp, pale body elicited shallow, wheezing breaths. Despite his visible shock, James forced his legs to move him across the deck. There, he took one of

Leonard's arms, assisting Roy with carrying Leonard off the ship. Joskine rushed over to help.

"Is that...the *Scaleslayer*?" Lucian whimpered.

"I'm your biggest concern here, not them," Ariel said softly. "Because if you don't send someone to get Rossel *right now*, I will fling you so high into the air that you will die of old age before you hit the ground."

"We aren't evacuating the city over a rumor. Chosen or not, you don't have the emergency powers. Only the emperor himself can override our judgment," Petra insisted. James couldn't imagine that many people spoke to the twins like Ariel just had.

"Then I guess we'll have to protect these people from the Altujan *and* from you," Ariel growled.

James panted as he, Roy, and Joskine hauled Leonard's body up the gangway in as gentle a manner as they could muster. Several seaguardsmen sprinted away into the city, and Ariel stood, arms crossed, staring down the siblings until they retreated from the docks.

***

Rhaiga's human form was somewhat of a mystery to her at times. The stringy mass of thread that sprouted from the back of her husk's head—whatever it was called—was constantly tossed about in the sea wind. Her host had been obsessed with it, she remembered, always fussing over the way it was contorted. Hair. That was it.

Altujan feet thudded against the deck on all sides of her, giving her a decidedly wide berth as they propelled the ship forward. Memories that Dhorh had given her from the sailor allowed her to inspect the work that the red-clad and blue-clad carried out on the ship. Several dozen more ships sliced through the water around them. If only they had more time to prepare, things would be running smoother, but the Chosen had forced their hand.

She looked to the side and snapped her fingers at the Vaecus prowling at her side, as if inspecting the ship with her. Its sleek, leathery body circled the deck like an imperator circled floundering prey, its wings folded tightly against its back. Soon, her attack dog would be able to use them. Memories surrounding her pets of the past gleamed in her subconscious. Before the banishment, she often played with them where they were bred at Altujan colonies, pups and adults. This one was hardened, a hunter, no doubt the result of a strict and harsh upbringing. Good, it was what she needed. No room for soft pups this time.

A familiar set of footsteps clonked behind her, and Rhaiga turned to face Mastreh. The newly-minted Blood Herald was at face level with Rhaiga's human form, which was definitely not preferable. In truth, Rhaiga didn't even understand what she had done to Mastreh, not fully. Thousands of years, and the Eye of Death didn't know *how* she imprinted deathlessness on mortal beings, only that, like Dhorh and Vayne with their powers, she could deal death and take it away. The creature had to be near death, and the subject would remain the same being they were. Hence, Rhaiga only imparted this gift—or curse—on beings that were loyal.

"May I ask a question, My Eye?" Mastreh tilted her head.

The shallow pit in Rhaiga's chest began to cave inward. "I suppose I can't stop you from asking, can I?" she said without emotion.

"What is my purpose, now that you have spared me? Am I to lead my people as something new? I feel...strange. Angry. Do I still serve my people as Blood Herald?"

"You are my instrument," Rhaiga replied curtly. The hole in her chest deepened whenever Mastreh spoke. She should have taken away the Altujan's tongue first. "Your purpose is to be a hero for your people, lead them to victory. That is your path."

"I—" Mastreh started.

Rhaiga cut her off with a shush. She put her finger to her lips. "We all walk the path. It is all we can do. Vayne has given us the path of sacking Greade Harbor, cutting it off from the rest of the empire, a first step to realizing the world he envisions. Greade is a massive human trade port, necessary to keep currency and supplies pouring into the empire. We snatch this from them, and they are left with significantly fewer options."

Mastreh tried to interject, ask more questions.

"You are a weapon," Rhaiga hissed, "and you are *only* a weapon, a weapon that the Altujan surely need to take back what once belonged to you. One Elder can't take a city on their own as we once could, so an army is necessary. When the Elders take back what was *ours*, you will also get back what was once *yours*, the land of Spiath." She waited for a response from the Blood Herald, but none came. "Go straighten out the rigging out there. It's too loose."

The Vaecus chirped as Mastreh stomped away.

—◦—

A Tale of the Chosen

James, Roy, and Ariel stood around Rossel the surgeon's table as the surgeon and his wife—an apothecary—tended to Leonard's wounds. The glaive that had pierced Leonard's gut had miraculously missed his bowels and only grazed his kidney, leaving a minimal amount of internal bleeding. It was scaring away the infection that was the issue, as the flesh around the wound had become a furious red. Leonard's normally bronze skin had become paler than even Roy's, and the spiky hair that normally had a life of its own had begun to droop. His eyes flickered beneath his eyelids, and sweat poured from his strong brow.

The stony slab of a table he lied on was slightly too small for him, as his feet hung off the edge. James found it strangely funny despite the dire circumstances. Scorch him, Leonard would probably have complained had he been awake enough. The ramshackle medical cottage they stood in was extremely cramped, a hastily built addition to the shack that Rossel and his wife lived in. Sagging rock made up the majority of the walls, save for a brick hearth in the corner that they used to boil water. Countless cobwebs spanned the ceiling, and the floor was a thick, grainy sand. Numerous candles populated every flat surface in the undersized space, casting a light that washed away any shadows that could obstruct the surgery.

Theos—the apothecary—leaned over Leonard's stomach and dabbed with a wet cloth around the wound. She was Kostran, like her husband, with a long braid of dark hair down her back and red piercings in her ears and nose. Samira had worn jewelry that was white. Was there a difference in color of piercings based on profession? Theos had a habit of raising one of her thin eyebrows when she worked, as if she were skeptical of something. It made James nervous. Rossel worked beside her, handing her different oils and medicines. He simultaneously cleaned his tools to patch Leonard back up in surgery. Ariel had mentioned that Kostran scholars often worked as both married couples and business partners.

"Will he live?" Roy asked hoarsely.

"He's lost enough blood to make it very touchy," Rossel said, "and the infection certainly isn't helping. If we can keep him alive through the night, then we should be able to have him stay that way. At least until he's stabbed again."

Theos nodded with concern. "But he won't be in any condition to be doing much of anything. Chosen or not, he's a man who needs to heal."

"How do you know that Leonard is a Chosen?" James scrunched his brow.

"We moved here from Kostra shortly before he was born. Everyone here knows of the Harbor's Divine Son, the pride and joy of this city," Theos replied. "We were there on the day he left his mother's house, about to bring over something to their neighbor."

"That couldn't have been terribly pleasant to have witnessed," Roy muttered. He scratched his head against the wooden doorframe.

"We come across much more queasy subject material in our line of work. But yes, it was quite awkward. We've looked after him periodically since then," Rossel said, washing his hands in a basin.

Rossel and Theos focused on their work. Neither of them showed interest in continuing the conversation while working.

Ariel walked carefully to Roy and placed a bandaged hand on his shoulder. "I need a drink," she said, nodding toward the city outside. Looking at him hopefully, she smiled earnestly as Roy reluctantly nodded, grabbed his arm, and looked toward James expectantly.

James shook his head slowly, gesturing that he wanted to stay with Leonard. He was guessing that those two needed some time to themselves. Plus, Leonard would need someone here if he woke up. If and when the man ever woke, James needed someone to settle this conflict he had been feeling. His heart seemed to violently shift between an intense vengeful hunger against the Temple and a deep-seated hollowness. The indigo of the sunset covered what little he could see of the city outside as Ariel and Roy left the cottage.

Theos placed a stool near the wall for James. Nodding thanks, he took his seat and sat silently as the two worked. Their craft was too complicated for James to comprehend. Rossel muttered the names of tools, each more confusing than the last, which Theos handed to him. Their hands worked steadily, fluidly, like moving statues.

"I've heard of Kostran scholars before, but I always thought that they lived in libraries, surrounded by books instead of people," he said, watching the surgery with slight repulsion and a great deal of fascination.

Rossel gave a slight chuckle. "That's true for a lot of scholars. But surgeons and apothecaries are a different kind of scholar. We spend a lot of time with books, it's true, but we also are around people."

"We study books, study religion, but then we have to put what we have learned into action. The faith and the knowledge that we cultivate is to be used for people's betterment. You can't do that unless you have a balance of both knowledge and experience," Theos said.

James pondered this. He guessed that was correct. What was the point of learning the sword if you never used it? Or learning to read and then never picking up a tome? Kostrans used a blend of faith *and* science, a union that was decried as heresy in Boane. "You said that you use faith and study to learn your profession?" he asked.

Rossel glanced up from his work before continuing. He had finished whatever he had been doing with the scalpel and was now cleaning the wound again. Theos was carefully threading a needle to sew up the incision. "Of course," Rossel said. "How can we carry out the will of the gods to help those in need if we don't study their teachings? Additionally, we cannot provide the help to those in need if we aren't studying the science."

"But what if the gods didn't exist? What if their teachings were a fiction?" James asked.

Theos frowned before beginning to sew up Leonard's stomach. "You are saying the gods are not real?"

Yes. "If they weren't, what would you do?"

She shrugged. "The gods don't decide everything. I may use the teachings of Etah to help people I wish to see safe, so she guides my desire to help. But my desire is already there." She raised her eyebrow, but this time it was at him instead of her work. "Rossel and I, we help people who are hurt, who are sick. That is the path we chose. The gods can guide us along that path, but it is ours, just like a warrior can fight to protect his homeland or a merchant can sell to those who want food or goods."

"But what about a Chosen? What would a Chosen do if there were no gods?"

Rossel pondered this. "Then I guess the Chosen would do what they want. They would be the closest things to gods."

James shook his head. "Gods are supposed to be all-powerful, eternal. They're supposed to be strong and wise, right? Chosen are just people. That would be impossible."

Theos took a short knife and cut the thread she had been using. Leonard's wound was now sewn up, a jagged red checkmark on Leonard's taut stomach. "In our studies," she said, "we've read many stories about the Chosen. Most of the Chosen in recorded Temple history actually. They may not be depicted the same way where you come from, but on this continent, the gods' champions are known for their power and deeds. Many of them were heroic, many were flawed, some truly despicable, but there were some who stood out, who were different."

Sitting forward on his stool, James gestured for her to continue. Rossel unrolled a dressing cloth and began to place it over Leonard's sewn-up wound to keep it dry.

"This Chosen was one of...Dathos was it?" Theos glanced at Rossel.

"Raslena," Rossel murmured.

"Yes, that's right," Theos said. "He was a hero who was said to roam this very land. His power was legendary, as were his kindness and his wisdom."

"This sounds very generic for a Temple story," James said.

"So far, it does," Theos said. "But stories also have a *middle* and an *end* to them. This Chosen was like the others in many ways. He fought against horrors that most humans couldn't. He saved entire villages and turned down rewards that he was offered. Everyone on the upper continent knew of this man, not only because he was a Chosen but because he was a heretic."

James perked up. That couldn't have been right. "He was a what?"

"You heard me. He was a heretic. He believed that the gods didn't exist, much like you do."

"I never said that—" James began.

"Hush, boy. We know more about people than you think," Rossel said. He looked at Theos. "Continue, dear."

"This Chosen claimed that the gods had only ever been stories from the Temple, and that the world was as it was. He asserted that the Chosen were the *actual* gods of the new age. The people were aghast, decrying him and asking how he could be so blasphemous. They spurned him, called him a traitor to the human race. He lived his whole life as a nomad, traveling from place to place, and was increasingly shunned everywhere he went." Theos kept speaking, passion flowing into her storytelling. Her tan eyes were alight, glowing with the excitement of the story, "As an old man, he was approached by a young girl, a child who was a fervent believer at the Frostspring Honor Refuge. As a test from her teachers at the Refuge, she was told to convert him."

"And did she?" James asked. He leaned forward on his stool almost to the point of falling off.

"I'm getting to that," Theos said, waving her hand excitedly. "She told him again and again that the gods were just, that they gave Chosen their powers to carry out their will on earth, that humans were too untrustworthy to be given these powers and needed gods for guidance. The man could not be swayed. The girl finally threw up her hands in disgust. 'You're a fool, old man!' she said. 'If this were true, we would all be doomed, for Chosen know nothing about being gods!' The old man looked at her and said, 'You are right, child. Chosen don't know how to be gods, not yet. But what do gods know of what it is like to be *human*, to be alive?'"

James cocked his head, confused. "I don't get it. Isn't being human much less *enviable* to being a god?"

Rossel looked at his wife, not wanting to interrupt her. Theos, however, gestured it was fine and smiled at him. They clearly both enjoyed this story. Rossel took a deep breath. "This Chosen believed that by understanding what it means to be human, they could be better than gods. They could understand what it is like to experience happiness, love, anger, regret, despair, and to *manage* all of those things. He theorized that the Chosen could understand people more than gods could and shared a collective desire with humanity to preserve life and free will. They could bear the example for the rest of humanity to follow."

"So you're saying that this man thought that the Chosen could be an ideal for people to strive toward and be an example that was more concrete than a god?" James asked.

"A man may make mistakes. He may stumble or fall, but in the end he can be a just man, a godly man," Rossel said.

"*I believe in the lot of you.*" Was this what the Crescent-Beard had been trying to tell him?

"What was this Chosen's name?" he asked.

"His name," Theos said, "was Gemmi the Chasmwalker."

The widest grin in years overtook James's face, bringing a stinging tear to his eye. Even in death, his brother was showing him the way, lighting the path.

Scaleslayer

Roy sat in the shadowed corner of the tavern, lest he be recognized. It wasn't a huge danger, but around this part of the continent many knew of the telltale scar that marked the Scaleslayer, even though the Scaleslayer had been reportedly "killed" about two years ago according to the empire.

Sounds of cards hissing across wooden surfaces, shadows performing on the walls, red faces, light music, all things Roy had loved before. Now he hated being in such a crowded space. He felt so out of *place*. Not long ago, nothing would have been more desirable than to sit down in a well-lit inn and strike up a conversation with a local, play cards with Leonard, or get into a drinking contest with Ariel and Samira. Granted, the last one was always fun in the moment but never in the morning. Ariel always won them anyway.

What made him feel so out of place wasn't the bright lanterns or the loud screeching of chairs or even the shouting of drunkards back and forth. What really made him uncomfortable was the laughter, the happiness. It was something he'd felt excluded from since that day three years ago. Everyone in the place was blissfully enjoying their lives, not a care about Elders or demons. He was the only one to sit at a bar and order a drink to take away the fear that if the wrong circumstances happened he would risk killing everyone crowded around him. The world was drinking and laughing, having fun and relishing. And they all did it without him, *despite* him. He couldn't be one of them anymore, even though he desperately wanted to.

"*They all look tasty,*" Charodon rumbled

Some in the tavern glanced at him with narrow suspicion, others with a hint of nervousness that went away after a few more sips. Many eyes were instead drawn to the one other stranger in the tavern, stupefying the barkeep with a tall order.

Roy smiled briefly.

"One bottle of Pallet Gin please," Ariel said playfully. The portly barkeep tiptoed to the shelf behind him to gingerly remove a dusty, completely full bottle from the very top. Poor man was just out of reach but managed to keep from flopping to the ground so he could nudge the gin with his fingers until it toppled into his hand. He looked quite proud of himself until Ariel cocked her head to the side and politely asked for another. "And also, you should leave the city come morning."

She had the habit of making a room already so full of light become absolutely brilliant. It wasn't as if she did anything special either, she was just being *Ariel*. Sometimes, it just didn't seem fair. But you could never resent her for long.

"*Forget the girl, forget everything. Let me out.*"

Ariel fluidly weaved through the packed tables and brought her radiance into the shadows with him. Her smile faded a bit, not going away completely but perhaps becoming more genuine. Dathos—or whatever—drown him, she was beautiful.

Ariel set a bottle of the stuff before him with a dusty *clunk*. She then sat across from him, uncorking her own bottle. The thing must have held enough Pallet Gin to kill three men. The taste of the stuff alone was enough to kill five.

"Drink," she commanded warmly. "I paid good money for that."

Roy shifted in his seat. "Look, I...wait a minute. No, you didn't." He distinctly didn't recall her putting any money of *any* national origin on that counter.

She grinned. "No place that has this stuff is sad to be rid of it."

"You know why, don't you? It's disgusting."

Ariel shook her head, pale gold hair washing over her tattooed shoulders. "To you, maybe. It reminds me of home."

Roy glanced around behind her and caught some not-so-subtle looks from other patrons at the tavern. He could see a question on everyone's face, the same that he felt in his mind whenever he was near Ariel: why is she here with *that* wretch? Never able to find an answer, he shrugged it off and popped the cork from his bottle.

A crocodile's territorial hiss came from inside his consciousness. Charodon did not like Ariel, as he seemed to find it more difficult to isolate Roy when she was around.

They clinked the bottles together and took a swig. Roy choked down the bitter, piney liquid. Made by using the Pallet Fruit native to Spiath, the gin was normally considered an acquired taste, as the fruit itself tasted like soapy dirt. But Spiathi swore by—and drank in gallons—the gin exclusively. Roy himself often favored Kostran red wine instead. He pointedly noticed that she set her bottle down long after he did.

"What are we doing here?" he asked.

"I'm worried about you," she replied, "and this isn't a place where you can just shut down and ignore me." She looked sternly at the bottle in his hand, and he obligingly took another sip.

The gin shocked his mouth, all the while going down smoothly. He couldn't fathom how she could drink this stuff and still have a clear head.

He set it down. "Don't be worried."

"I am though. You've gotten even quieter than usual since the islands. And there's what you said in Leonard's cabin."

"I was tired. I was worried about him and wasn't thinking straight," Roy said quickly. "I didn't mean it."

"We both know that you did." She swatted away his excuses.

He sighed. Her interrogation was working just like she had intended. "Okay, I did. So what?"

Ariel set down her bottle and placed a bandaged hand over his. "You don't have to be alone against this, Roy."

"That's the problem though, isn't it?" he said, tapping his head with his pinky finger. "I'm not alone. He's constantly up here, making a mess of the place."

"It's mine now. You haven't had the sense to get used to it yet."

Ariel must have seen him wince, because the bandaged hand over his squeezed. She peered at him, watching the orange of his corrupted eye as it swirled in his pupil. In that moment, she wasn't looking at him anymore, he realized. She was looking through him, at his enemy.

"You can hear me, can't you?" she said firmly. "I'm going to toss you out of Roy like a tavern drunk. And then you're mine, do you hear me?"

Roy felt Charodon flare inside his veins. *"Try it, and I will kill you both."*

He pushed Charodon downward, drowning out the hissing of the demon by focusing on the warmth of her hand. The bandages had started to unravel, revealing still-healing skin. Roy swallowed the involuntary flash of anger and gripped his bottle. Ariel's gaze had shifted from one of threats to one of concern.

"He didn't like that," Roy panted.

"He's gotten far too comfortable in there," she said. "I want to help you, Roy. We all want to help you."

"And what if I don't deserve help?" he mumbled. "If you knew what he's made me think, what he's made me *do*." Roy looked down at the table. The noise of the bar had suddenly grown with the lack of Charodon whispering to him. He could hear the low voices, the dawning suspicions.

"...looks familiar."

"...that scar..."

"...those eyes..."

Roy shrank into the shadows behind him. How many of the people in here had known someone he'd killed or terrorized? He was never sure what happened when

Charodon took over, and there was never much time to run away from people before he lost control. Even when he managed to get away, Charodon would often seek out others to torment. His eyes flitted to the back exit, no more than ten feet to their left.

Ariel followed his gaze and nodded solemnly. "This was a bad idea. Let's go." Her once sincere comfort had died, replaced by a dejected grimace.

He wanted to apologize to her, to say he was sorry for ruining the one chance they'd had in weeks to relax, but her covered hand grasped his tightly as she stood to leave. Her other hand still gripped her bottle. Roy left his drink at the table and followed her quickly. Conversation in the tavern slowed as the patrons watched the two strangers leave, becoming quiet but not silent enough for Roy and Ariel to miss some more conspiratorial remarks.

"Enjoy your drinks," Ariel called into the quieted alehouse, "and then leave the city."

The moon was already up as they opened the door, and their skin became washed in a dark red hue.

Still holding his hand, Ariel led him through Greade Harbor. The port city was the exact opposite of Epot Detharn. Rocky grass populated every square inch of the ground, growing over the attempt of a road as they walked. The overgrown streets twisted up and down the hilly terrain. Wooden buildings populated the very center of the city where the richer residents lived.

There wasn't a tree for miles, allowing Ariel and Roy to see for ages despite some of the structures. Farther out, stone buildings became the custom, indicating a lack of funding to import trees from Spiath or Kostra. All of the buildings were coated with a thick lacquer to keep the persistent winds from penetrating the homes.

Gray gambesons strolled past them. Seaguard soldiers, while seeming to be in great numbers earlier, turned out to only have a great concentration around the markets as well-armed security. Once they had seen the full force, it was a measly three thousand. Not even half what they would need to actually hold the city, and no Arochs to be found. The Twins' mismanagement was on full display. Despite being such a large city, Greade never faced threats bigger than the odd pirate fleet. Not for much longer, though.

Ariel leaned in and spoke into his ear, "Follow me."

He shivered as her lip brushed his ear, "Where?"

She tugged his hand and led him past a few more wooden buildings, including the lavish one where the harborlord lived and where Petra and Lucian were undoubtedly staying during their business occupation. Just beyond the splendid and excessive home towered the structure that was the highlight of the area, the place people came from all over the continent to pay their respects.

"The Marble Watchtower," he whispered. Roy had seen it before only once when they came to see Leonard after he had been discharged from the Infantry. Before they had all left together as a family. The meager gin in his system distorted his vision slightly, making it seem like the white spire was leaning over him. He leaned backward to look up at it out of habit. It towered even taller than the Basalt watchtower, which had been slightly over three hundred feet tall. It was said that the Watchtowers had been the birthplace of each of the gods, structures that had existed for hundreds of years before the empire or any kingdoms. Looking at it now, there could be no other explanation in his mind even though he believed James's claims deep down. What else could have created this brilliant obelisk?

The beautifully patterned marble swirled around the wide base and became lighter as it ascended into the heavens. Unlike the Basalt or Shale watchtowers, this structure had stairs that spiraled all the way to the top. Without even conferring with each other, Roy and Ariel approached the steps and began the climb. Wind swirled around them in a cautious tenderness. Exaggeratedly careful, Roy placed his foot on each step while holding Ariel's hand.

They finally graced the top, puffing from the climb and immediately sitting in the cool marble center of the platform that sat at the apex. It was roughly thirty feet in diameter, a circular shape. The north stretched in front of them. Rocky grassland waved and shimmered like an ocean in the burgundy moonlight.

However, the actual sea shone red behind them in a splendid, beautiful, sparkling radiance. Ariel turned around and gasped slightly at the view. Wood and stone houses the size of matchboxes were scattered in slightly rectangular patterns around the base of the tower, spiraling outward toward the shore. A few ships listed lazily over the bay.

Ariel scooted next to him and leaned her head on his shoulder. "Remember the time we climbed the Basalt Watchtower?"

"I was just thinking of that myself," he said.

She chuckled. "I'd say that this view may top the one we had from that night."

Roy agreed, thinking fondly of that evening. So much had changed since then. It was saddening to think that it had been almost four years since that night, and even more saddening to think of how much was different now. "I was so sure, so terrified that if I ever saw you again you would have a glyph on your hand," he said.

"Never," she said, smirking. She pulled away to look at him, holding his gaze.

He nodded, his dry mouth twitching upward for a moment, "I always knew that you wanted to get away from all this, that it takes a toll. I thought that maybe after what happened, you would leave and settle down." The thought had scared him almost as much as Charodon did, the thought that she would leave and he'd never see her again. Or worse, that he would see her again but she would bear a glyph on her hand, the mark of Spiathi marriage. Despite his repeated attempts to tell himself that she wouldn't want to see him after Charodon had attacked her, he'd always held some foolish hope.

"Then again," she said, teasing, "why were you so afraid of that happening?"

Drown him, was he actually going to say it? The words flowed freely in his mind, but his drowning mouth could never muster them. She looked at him expectantly.

Charodon resurfaced. *"You know why you can't say them. Deep down, everyone knows you're a monster. And who could love that? I'm all you've got."*

Roy shook his head slightly, trying to shove the demon down again. Ariel noticed. Her brow creased with worry.

"Roy?" she grabbed his shoulder with a covered hand.

He collapsed and sprawled backward as Charodon lunged for control yet again. Struggling to keep a grip on his own body, Roy grunted as the monster clawed for purchase. The flashes of blue and orange took over his vision once more, and he saw the spectral image of the Eye of Nature towering over him. It was clearer this time, with the vague shape of the scaly head still blurred but distinguishable.

Barely hearing Ariel's panicked voice through the roar of his conscious battlefield, Roy shouted at Charodon, "Get out! I'm in control, and you just live here."

The specter blurred as it shook its crocodilian head. "*This control you seem to leverage, how long do you intend to keep it? You can't even hold on for more than a few days now.*" The devil was uncommonly civil. This was the eye of a hurricane, a means to spare him from the tumult of the storm long enough to convince him to give up.

"I'll hold on as long as I have to," Roy panted. "Or I could fling myself from this tower right now."

"*Don't bluff with me, boy. I would have control long before you meet the ground, and you know it.*"

Roy's breath caught in his throat.

"*You don't have to do this, you know.*" Charodon sighed. "*A Chosen and an Elder binding has only ever happened once before you and me, and it brought power undreamt of. It nearly remade the world, conquered it. You wouldn't have to hide what you are.*"

"No." Roy shook his head. "I don't believe you."

Orange and blue separated into a thousand colors, ones that Roy had never even imagined. They swirled around him and the blurry phantasm of Charodon's consciousness.

"*I'm giving you a choice, Roy!*" It was the first time that Roy could remember the Elder using his name. "*You can throw away the title of 'Monster' and become a great and terrible god. You don't have to be ashamed of what you and I have done. In a world where we work together, what we've done will be seen as strength."*

The swirling colors parted behind Charodon to show images, memories of pure carnage. The villagers from the Marshes torn apart, the citizens from the fishing town drowning in their sunken homes, Leonard's face beaten until it was unrecognizable, Ariel's hardened expression as she leveled a bow directly at him. Samira, poor Sam, with a look of horror as she viewed the destruction Roy had wrought.

"Sooner or later, they will all abandon you. Because you are a monster. That's why I understand you, why I want you to reach your potential."

"Don't show me this." Roy turned away. "I'm not interested in your corrupted dream. I know I'm a monster, but I'll die before I become what you want."

"So be it." Charodon snarled. The blurry image of him became jagged, hostile.

"You will retreat, demon," an old voice croaked from somewhere behind Roy.

Roy didn't really turn to see the old man from before. In this flashing, tumultuous mindscape, the space around him morphed until the withered ghost stood between him and Charodon. Others stood beside him: the bald child, the woman with the veil, and still more that weren't as distinct. These were the people who James had described when meeting Vayne in his visions. These couldn't be the Elders. They were something different.

The solidifying shape of Charodon snarled at the other specters standing between him and Roy. "You're in my way, spirit. This matter doesn't concern you."

His milky eyes looking sternly at the Eye of Nature, the old man stood firm. "This body and mind still belong to the boy."

"Not for long," Charodon leered. "When he is consumed, I will reach heights that even gods dream of." A pocket opened in the blinding swirls of light to show the night sky, the sky that Roy's real eyes stared at. It looked like a dark maroon pit compared to the strobing effect of his cognitive battlescape. In the center of the pocket, a face looked down at him with worry and despair, her metallic blue eyes somehow connecting with his despite his inability to hear her words.

"Ariel," Roy gasped.

Charodon's shape began to harden, becoming more vivid. The other ghosts shrank back. "Rhaiga and her court of Altujan are nearly here. This conversation of ours seems to be an inconvenience for the girl."

If Charodon was telling the truth, then the people of the city were in danger. Ariel could fight the Altujan or challenge Charodon, but not in tandem. The only way for her to get the people out safely was if she left him. Either leave and give the people a chance before Charodon and Rhaiga clashed or stay and be torn apart by both.

The sand in Roy's hourglass was spent. There were no more ways out. All he could control was *when*.

The old man glanced at Roy, and even with his blind eyes, he seemed to know what Roy was thinking. "Don't do this, Roy. You have to forgive."

"I've already forgiven them. There's nothing more I can do." Roy said quietly. He turned to Charodon, now a pristine image, "Let me talk to her, tell her to go. Do this, and I'll give you what you want. I'll give up."

Charodon cocked his scaly head. His orange eyes blinked slowly, and the already toothy false grin on his reptilian face grew sharper. The demon sensed victory, "It's a deal."

Someone Like Gemmi

Leonard didn't remember the exact moment that he woke up.

For a moment, he thought he was dead. This blurry, out of focus place didn't look familiar to him. He was on a stone table that was too short, his legs dangling off the edge. Raslena crush him, maybe he *was* dead, damned to an eternity of objects too small for him. Words from someone he thought he knew rang through his head.

"It was nobody's fault that it happened. It was just bad luck."

He raised a hand and ran it through his spiky hair, still somehow bobbing up and down, impossibly standing up. Leonard immediately regretted the action, his stomach exploding in a ball of pain. Gasping, he weakly dropped his arm, letting it hang off the table.

A person he couldn't see spoke from just outside his vision. "Rest, boy. You are safe here." Their voice sounded familiar, and the accent was quite obviously Kostran. His vision started to clear, letting him catch dilapidated masonry above his head.

"What—" He couldn't say any more. Leonard's tongue betrayed him, too parched to utter any more syllables than that. All he could do was squirm with this stupid hole in his gut. Trying to calm himself down, Leonard reached outward with his thoughts, feeling for the sturdiness of the earth. His consciousness hit bitter rock far beneath him. It couldn't be. Of all places he could have woken up, it was here. The crumbling rock mixed with dense soil gave it away.

He was home. He tried to raise his head and look around.

"I said *rest*, Astus strike you. But what do I know? I only patched up the giant striking hole in your gut." The voice, belonging to a man, rounded the side of the table and stopped to his right. Through the blurring of his sight, Leonard saw Rossel's analytical eyes look him up and down, as if disapproving of the state that he was in. *But he was the one who patched me up! The stern idiot.*

If Rossel was here, that must mean that Theos was nearby too. Leonard smiled slightly. The apothecary had often checked on him when his mother had shut herself away. In a way, the Kostran woman had been more of a mother than Lydia had ever been.

Rossel caught Leonard's smirk and called to the next and only other room in the shack, "Theos! The son you adopted is awake."

The sound of feet hurriedly shuffling through sand announced Theos as she rounded the table. Her luminous amber eyes beamed at him, and her closed-mouth smile spread across her face like a warm fire. "Big as an ox, and yet you show up on our doorstep stuck like a pig," she teased.

Leonard chuckled before realizing that was a bad idea. Pain flared up inside his extremely tender gut. His insides felt like watery soil, held together by a few strips of gauze. It didn't help that his broken ribs had never healed right. He supposed that Rossel probably had to re-break some of them during the surgery.

A cacophony of noise sounded from beyond the cottage, growing louder until the door burst inward. James backed into the room, trying and failing to keep Joskine from shouting and causing a scene. The Crescent-Beard's face held a stony look of concern, and he leveled an irritated glare at James.

"I will throw you aside, boy. I don't care if you fry me alive with a side of scythefish. Let me *see* him, drown you!" Joskine said through clenched teeth.

"They said no other visitors until the morning, Joskine," James yelped.

"We make exceptions in rare cases, James," Theos said from beside Leonard. "Especially when they are this insistent."

Joskine shoved past James and stomped to the table, glancing at Leonard's face. Leonard had to stifle a laugh at the comically shocked expression Joskine wore.

The sailor threw his head backward in a bellowing guffaw. "Guess Hadsen will have to pay up now that you're awake, Len. I *told* him that you would make it!"

Leonard groaned. "I have half a mind to die right here and make you pay him if you call me Len one more time."

Smiling slightly, James stepped forward so he was beside the Crescent-Beard. "I kind of like the name. Maybe I'll call you Len from now on too."

Looking at Rossel, Leonard pleaded. "Please tell me that you messed up the surgery."

"Sadly, you are going to be all right, son," Rossel said, suppressing a laugh of his own. "You were unconscious for short of a dozen days, and the worst of the infection has gone. However, there is absolutely no striking way that you can be doing any of your normal Chosen shenanigans. That hole in your gut is going to take a long time to heal, as are those ribs."

Leonard rested his head back against the cloth Theos and Rossel had placed at the head of the table. Just the simple movement of raising his head had cost a significant amount of strength, as if he were an infant again. Theos brought a cup of water to him and tilted it to his dry lips. Leonard slurped it down immediately.

"Maybe now that he's awake he can convince people to leave this place," James said solemnly.

Joskine saw the quizzical look in Leonard's eyes and sighed. "Things have taken a bit of a turn, Len. And not in the right direction."

"I suppose that Sam has a plan to barely get us out, no matter what it is. Raslena crush that lying woman." Leonard rolled his eyes.

Everyone standing around him shuffled uncomfortably, suddenly having a keen interest in the sandy floor. James's face was especially conflicted. What had Samira done now? Leonard still had a lot of things to say to that woman about what she had done, and with quite a few choice words. He wrinkled his brow.

"Leonard, Sam is dead," James said.

It was as if he had been stabbed again. Leonard's anger melted away immediately, forced out of him by heavy, molten grief. *Dead?* They must be joking with him, some macabre prank on the man who just came back from death. But James, always terrible at hiding his emotions, was telling the truth. Black dread—numb and somehow excruciatingly painful at the same time—welled up in his throat. Despite having just wet his lips, Leonard's mouth was too dry to speak again. "How?" he rasped.

"We stole a ship from the flesh eaters' harbor. They're planning a full invasion of the continent, Leonard. There were *hundreds* of ships, and the blue-clad ones were right behind us. Sam stayed behind to destroy the remaining ships and give us a chance," James said. "And Rhaiga…"

Leonard closed his eyes. Raslena crush him, it couldn't be possible. Samira had been the strongest of any of the Chosen. Even with one hand, she had possessed enough power to blow up a small castle. Some of the last feelings he'd experienced around her had been that of white-hot fury, but now the loss felt worse than any wound he bore. His throat burned. He wanted to scream.

Instead, he cleared his throat with some difficulty. "And Roy? What of Ariel?"

Before anyone had the chance to answer him, a heavy gong ripped apart the tranquil night. Seeing Leonard's muscles tense before Leonard even felt them, Rossel pressed down firmly on Leonard's shoulder, keeping him on the table. Samira had bought them even less time than they had thought.

Rhaiga and the Altujan had arrived.

Joskine flinched and put a hand to the sword at his waist. "We have to find those two."

"Ariel said they were going for a drink," James said. "I'll go to the tavern."

Leonard shook his head and struggled to sit up. He bucked against Rossel's hands, shirking off the restraint. The crater in his belly screamed at him, impossible to ignore, but Leonard sat up anyway. It took an agonizingly long time, but he finally sat. Sweating and panting, he shook his head again. Ariel would try to get Roy into a public place to open up. But when that didn't work, they'd go somewhere else.

"They won't be there," he said, steadying himself on Rossel's shoulder. "I know where they'll be. Whenever those two are alone..." Leonard grunted in pain.

Rossel vehemently shook his head. "What did I just tell you? You *can't* just get up and walk around! Your stitches are going to tear."

"Begging your pardon, sir, but he can't very well stay here." Joskine growled, looking toward the door. For all they knew the Altujan could have landed already. The bells were still tolling, blasting the air with their dreaded gongs.

James moved to help Leonard up. Leonard looked into the young man's eyes and saw something new there. "Where are they?" James asked.

Leonard smirked and held his stomach as James draped one of Leonard's arms over his shoulder. "They'll be at the highest point around. Luckily, I think we all happen to know where that is." He groaned as he attempted to get up once more, but couldn't heave himself from the table.

James stiffened and pulled a finger to his lips. Joskine began to ask what was wrong, but James shook his head vigorously. The bells forced the silence out of the cabin, but the slightest pause in the deafening sound gave way to a split second of terror. Leonard then heard what came for them between the frantic clanging of the alarm.

Mad laughter, slightly inhuman, creeping around them from outside.

***

Ariel shook Roy's limp body, screaming into his blank, staring eyes. "Give him back! Give him back, you *bastard!*" The orange swirled around the blue of his irises, trying to force the blue out like a predator trying to flush a smaller animal. Etah lash her, how could another attack this bad be happening so *soon*? Without even realizing it, her screams carried wind with them, tossing Roy's black hair and scrambling her own. Ariel's hands throbbed with pain, but she held tightly to him anyway.

Low groans left Roy's lips. Even in the moon's red glow, she could see him start to turn blue. Charodon was choking him. Already, his skin began to slowly molt and split apart, exposing sickly scales underneath. She was powerless. She couldn't stop it.

Haunting, deep chimes of the harbor bells tolled with each tear of Roy's skin. They beat to the sound of her shouting, to the ragged breaths of the monster.

Ariel turned to look hurriedly at the harbor with tears streaming down her face. There, she saw what must have been well over a hundred ships, packed to the rails with Altujan. Seaguardsmen—not nearly enough—scrambled toward the docks in a flimsy perimeter like gray ants. And over the bells, over Roy's breathing, over everything...

She could hear the cackling.

That creature had followed them there, probably brought along by Rhaiga as a pet. That monster had done enough damage already.

"No," she said. "No, no, no, no."

Those foolish twin ghouls hadn't taken their advice or evacuated the city. Everyone who lived here was about to be slaughtered. She had to get them all out, but what about Roy? If she left to give the people a chance, she'd risk letting him die. Ariel would have to leave *again*.

But she couldn't, not this time. The bells and insane laughter needled at her eardrums, taunting her.

Ariel thought back to what she had told Samira all those weeks ago when she had saved Joskine. *"He is important to* someone, *and if I can keep him alive, then I will. No life is worth taking away."* The people of Greade Harbor all had families, friends, people they loved too. Was it selfish to leave them all and try to help him? That was assuming she even *could* help Roy.

The bells blared into her ears still, insisting that time was up.

***

James slowly pulled his new short sword—taken from the seaguard—from its sheath. It was a simple weapon but much nicer than the one he had owned before. Its blade was honed steel, sharpened and polished until he could not only see his own reflection but the reflections of the cobwebs in the ceiling.

Between each strike of the bells, he heard the insane cackling of Rhaiga's pet monster. It was circling them, getting closer each time. Though the stones and porous bricks of the shack were lacquered to keep the wind out, the sound of the creature permeated every square inch of the inside space, stinging his bones. It made it hard to breathe. Every round of laughter brought flashes of blue. The sap. Drowning. Bloodbreathing.

Across the room, James caught a glimpse of Joskine carefully drawing his sword. Rossel and Theos swiftly scooped up scalpels from the surgery table. Leonard looked around wildly for a weapon, not that he could reach any at the moment.

Knuckles popping as he gripped the leather handle of his sword, James held up his other hand in a gesture to stay put. It was pure luck that he had heard the creature over the sound of the bells. He hadn't even been listening for it.

Scorch him, Samira would have heard it coming from miles away. She probably would have even noticed the ships coming before the lookouts did. That thing outside was moving at Rhaiga's direction. He'd forgotten that the scorching thing had *wings*. Suddenly, he was back in the cathedral, surrounded by towering offerings to the Temple of Iarus. Young and helpless, scared and shaking. They were coming for him again, coming to kill him.

The cackling came from the exterior of the shack mere feet from him, and his throat bulged with bile. They had no idea what the thing could do, or even if it knew they were in there. Heavy scraping of the creature's claws—a sound that closely resembled a screaming whine—raked against the stone wall.

Okay, so it definitely knows we're here. James glanced at Joskine, who had crossed to Leonard's table as quietly as possible. Theos and Rossel clutched each other in the corner. They huddled near stacks of bandages and other supplies, trying to lose themselves in it. He'd been here before, in this terror, this hopeless situation.

The door—even though it was firmly shut—would not hold the monstrous dark thing from bursting in. It would tear the room to shreds, then it would go looking for Roy to finish him off. Rhaiga had thought of everything, and now the people of Greade Harbor were going to be slaughtered because they put too much faith toward the twins. Staked their lives on it.

"I believe in the lot of you."

James looked back at Joskine's face. It was creased with worry and shining with sweat. The man's entire patchy beard stood on end. Shaking his head in disbelief of what he was about to do, James took a step toward the door. Why was it Joskine of all people who said the one thing to change his mind?

Scraping claws screeched against the stone outside, sounding as if the monster was *burrowing* into the shack. Its laughter became focused, more determined somehow. Leonard's eyes grew wide as he saw James shuffle to the only thing keeping the creature outside.

"James, if you're about to do something stupid..." Leonard hissed.

He turned back and looked at the four ragged, distraught people huddled toward the back of the surgeon's shed. Terror plainly painted their faces, immobilizing them. The same terror wobbled through him. His legs shook but still took another step. James was right in front of the door now. Short, panicked breaths escaped him as he gripped his sword in one hand and the door handle in the other. It was unlocked. Trying to calm himself down, he extended his consciousness around the room, feeling the comfort of the candles. The needles of heat soothed his nerves slightly and cleared his head.

The creature's laughter had begun to get even louder, becoming a howl that threatened to shake the cottage off its rigid stone foundation. It found a way to seep into his bones, but he did his best to ignore it. He would protect them. Yes, they had lied to him. But they had also bled for him, encouraged him, and cared about him more than anyone since Gemmi. That was enough for him to let the lies go.

And now today, he was going to do for them what Gemmi had done: give them a chance. The world was a brutal place, and James had seen the brunt of it his whole life. Who knew what had made him Chosen? He simply was, and he could either sulk down the path of vengeance and hate he had been on his entire life since his brother's death, or he could start a new one. Right now. If he took it upon himself to be someone worth following, he could be someone good. Someone like Gemmi.

"Leonard, you said that I can keep you all honest, that we can be better," James said, looking sincerely at his friend's terrified brown eyes. "Thank you for believing that." He rested a hand against the door, ready to shove it open. The rough wood prickled his palm. "It's time for me to be better." The Temple had taken his brother from him, but with that loss James had the chance to make himself an ideal to strive toward. Rather than tearing things down, he could build a greater future, one that shone beyond anything the Temple could corrupt.

Ignoring Leonard and Joskine's whispering pleas, James mustered all the strength and courage that he could find within himself. Without even thinking, he drew the firelight of the candles to himself and pounded the door open, his fist engulfed in flame.

The cackling abruptly vanished and was replaced with a deep, catlike hiss. He had its attention. The tall grass was stained black with the blood of seaguardsmen, several bodies strewn silently outside the cottage. James looked into the gloomy shadows outside of the cabin and settled his eyes on the creature for just a moment. In the dark, its shape registered as formless, but the flickering rays of his handlight reflected off the dull, leathery skin of its snout. Below the snout was a jagged grin of slippery, slimy, pink-from-blood teeth. James couldn't actually tell how big it was. The night swallowed the rest of it, making it seem like it was everywhere.

While it stood pondering him, James darted into the night, holding his flame out in front of him to see where he was going. *I need it to follow the light. If I can draw it away, that leaves Leonard and the rest of them a chance to escape. I just hope they actually do the smart thing and get out of here.*

Wait, what was that? It sounded like thunderclaps in his ear. The air cracked—a sound that mimicked a massive whip catching flesh—just behind him. Daring to glance behind him as he ran, James failed to suppress a bleat of terror. He had forgotten once again that the monster could fly! It bore down on him from behind and above. The ragged claws on all too humanlike paws stretched outward to grasp him. They were no less than forty feet from Rossel's cabin. He could sense the monster's aura, nothing but icy blackness. It made the fire in his hand falter, numbing his mind. What *was* this thing?

Ducking to avoid the claws, he rolled to the left. Talons skewered the air where his neck and shoulders had just been. He heard the determined chortle of Rhaiga's pet as it passed over him. It wasn't going to be fazed easily. The monster twisted in midair with surprising agility and landed facing him. Tendrils at the base of its skull writhed like snakes, reaching out and waving, trying to touch the world around it. They spasmed with each clang of the bells.

That must be how it knows where it's going. Even though the dark red moonlight made the creature hard to see, James's fire clearly showed that it had no eyes. Those whips on its head could probably sense every move he made. Meanwhile, he could just barely see where he was going. It would be able to pick him out of a field like those creatures Samira had once told him about. Bats. Or a snake.

James barely had time to roll left again. Rhaiga's pet lunged for him once more, this time clipping his calf with a claw. He felt the slick pain as the knifelike talon—naturally spiny—easily cut through his pant leg and skin. It had been *expecting* him to go left again. James stumbled and nearly fell as he got up out of the roll. He couldn't feel much now because of his adrenaline, but that wound would eventually become a problem if this went on too long. He had to lead it away toward the outskirts of the city. If he could do that, it was possible that it would end up downing only him. Him and no one else.

Chirping in a childlike laugh, it bared its maw, extending its teeth forward and reaching toward him. Drawing courage from the flame in his hand—slightly diminished now—he rushed away in the direction of the east. The closest city was west, Theos had said. So that meant east was the direction people would be running away from. He could already hear them. Screams harmonized with the chiming alarm bells as townspeople sprinted from their homes. While the twins hadn't taken their warning seriously, there had obviously been some citizens who listened to Ariel. Even if it was a little late, it was better than nothing.

James panted, pounding his feet against the rockbed beneath the high grass. It was taller now, up to his calves. The paralyzing crack of the monster's wings echoed near his head again. Sensing another lunge from behind, James gripped the fire he held onto. Tensing, he dropped to the ground and hurled the fire into the beast's face as it snapped at him. Flames washed over its head and crackled as it hit the sensory whips. For a moment, the thing wobbled in the air and landed shakily. It skidded against the rocky grass ungracefully before righting itself and turning back to James.

He willed the flame in his hand to grow slightly larger. He needed more firepower without wasting everything he had in his hand. *Still have to be careful, otherwise I could burn myself up too quickly without realizing it. Watch my heart rate, control my breathing, keep my eye on the beast.* He glanced through the buildings toward the harbor. Several dozen shadowy boats were rowing toward the shoreline. How many Altujan had made for land?

A clawed paw shredded the oxygen he had exhaled moments ago. Scorch him, he had to stay focused. That thing would tear him to pieces if he didn't pay attention. Its teeth shone in the light of the fire. A slight leer—or at least the shadows made it appear that way—distorted the leathery snout, singed a bit by James's attack.

Shouting came from back near the area where he had run from. Still too close! Everyone was still in danger. He stepped forward and got ready to run again. Immediately sensing his intentions, the creature crouched, ready to pounce after him.

To The End

The world rushed back to Roy, disorienting him with the sudden darkness. Even with the bells clanging at the base of the tower below and the sounds of the approaching invaders, the world stood eerily still compared to where his mind had just been. His numbed skin felt the pins and needles sensation of reforming over scales, but only marginally.

He glanced upward at where Ariel stood. She was looking out over the shoreline, watching the Altujan ships that were just a few hundred yards out. They sped ever closer with each passing second. Her covered hands twitched, instinctively reaching for her bow at the thought of the intruders. Roy sat up, and her metallic eyes glanced back at him. They widened as she saw that he was awake.

"Thank Etah." She gasped and stumbled to him. Ariel knelt and embraced him. Drown him, he wished he could stay here forever, thinking of nothing but her warmth. Something was different about all this, but he couldn't place it. A finality, a knowledge that this was it? Charodon had given him this small mercy out of impatience, and Roy knew that it would be best not to waste it. This would spare him the last few hours of agony and fighting. He closed his eyes and stayed motionless, determined not to forget this. He *would* remember life.

He reluctantly pulled away and looked solemnly into her hopeful face. "You have to go." He winced as he watched the light in her expression die. "I think this time is it."

Her brow hardened, and her mouth drew into a line. "Don't give me that."

"He's giving me a chance to let you go if I give up." Roy stood up.

She growled. "I don't want to hear another word. You can't give up."

Roy rubbed his temple with his thumb, just the way Samira used to. "It's the only—"

Ariel rounded on him and jammed a bandaged finger into his chest, grimacing slightly but still holding an expression of frustrated rage. "In all the time I've known you, you've always refused to let anyone or anything tell you what to do. The empire tried to make a pawn of you, and you shrugged them off. Charodon bit you, and you didn't give up hope for *years*. No matter what the world seemed to be screaming at you, it wouldn't change the man you are. A man who wants to do what's right."

Roy struggled to stammer out an argument. He needed desperately for her to get out of here. How could she not see that?

"This isn't a choice that just affects you. This affects me, *and* Leonard, *and* James. Etah lash me, it even affects Sam! She died so that we could make it to the empire alive, and you want to just spit on that sacrifice too?" Ariel shouted. Her blue eyes were glowing with hurt.

"I have to do the same. I have to give myself up like she did, make up for what I've done and give you all a chance." Roy shook his head. The creeping cold of Charodon's presence was starting to slip tendrils back into his mind, about to rip him back from the windy apex of the tower to the flashing prison that Roy would die in.

A voice on the wind reached his ears, cutting through the clamoring bells. "She did what she did as penance for her mistakes. Mistakes that she made all on her own, Roy. None of this was your fault."

Roy and Ariel spun around to see Leonard and Joskine struggling toward them up the tower steps. Leonard—leaning on Joskine and bleeding from freshly torn stitches in his stomach—was pale, shaking in the cold, but his face had a stronger expression than Roy had ever seen. The man's hair was as drowning lively as ever, bouncing and dancing in the wind like it always did. Joskine tried to ignore how much Leonard was bleeding on him and gingerly guided the Earth's Chosen across the polished marble. Their steps clicked in tandem with the still urgent ringing of the bells.

Roy felt Charodon pause in disbelief as Leonard stumbled on bare feet toward him, leaving Joskine's support and resting a hand on his friend's shoulder.

Tears, hot and blustery, poured from Roy's swirling eyes. Why? Why, of all *drowning* people, was Leonard here? "It was all my fault. I was too weak to stop him, too weak to see that you were just scared. I could have killed you! I nearly killed both of you! Why don't you *hate me*? This would make it easier, would make this all easier, if you hated me."

Leonard pulled Roy into an embrace, letting Roy sob into his shoulder. Ariel rushed to them and wrapped her arms around them both. Roy could feel Charodon's patience run thin. The icy-hot knives began to stab behind his eyelids again. Indistinguishable from his tears, the knives stung. His head felt like it was breaking apart. Still, he couldn't move, would not move out of the warmth, the comfort of Leonard and Ariel.

Finally, the words from Leonard—the man he had vowed to kill for three years—unshackled him. "You are the strongest person I know, Roy. A lesser man would have given in to that monster immediately to stop the pain. But you, you endured it for years in an effort to save those who would have been destroyed. You fought back every step of the way, but you shouldn't have had to bear this burden alone. The villagers that day, everyone since then, *were never your fault*. It was *him*. You've never been weak, and we're not going anywhere this time. We're with you. To the end."

Charodon bellowed wordlessly through Roy's eardrums, making him cringe. But Leonard and Ariel hugged him tighter. With each moment that passed, Roy felt the ice within him slowly melt away. Colors began to flash around his eyes as Charodon lunged for him, trying to pull him back into his mind. He could see the specter right over Ariel's tattooed shoulder. The other ghosts stood around him as well, shielding him from the demon. They seemed as if made of mist, like fog being chased off by the sunrise. The old man's wispy form smiled.

Barely able to see, Roy separated from them both and took a deep breath. The air felt clearer than before. The world around the faces of his friends blurred and he exhaled, preparing for what happened next. When he looked into their eyes, the world wasn't complicated anymore. They wouldn't abandon him, nor would he abandon them.

Tuning out the cackling of the creature, the haunting chorus of bells below, and the Eye of Nature's threats, Roy wiped the tears from his eyes. "Go on then. I'll handle this." He gestured toward his brow.

Leonard and Ariel began to protest.

"Did you not listen to a word I just said?" Leonard groaned.

"Every word." Roy smiled. A genuine smile.

Ariel shook her head "I don't know what—"

Roy pulled her in and stopped her mouth with a kiss. Energy surged through his mind, forcing Charodon further outward.

Finally pulling away, she cocked her head to the side, an optimistic look on her face but worry in her eyes and voice. "What are you going to do?"

"He's not breaking out tonight," Roy said, confidence crashing through him like waves. "Tonight, I break him. You and Joskine go and help the city. I assume James is already doing something stupid."

"He's hunting that laughing bastard down there!" Joskine yelled over the wind. His crescent-shaped beard flapped at a ninety-degree angle. "Buying you some time, the lad is. I think he changed his mind after that right fine speech I said to him."

Roy shook his head. Who would have thought? He glanced at Leonard, who was starting to look a bit woozy from the height and thinning amount of blood. That wasn't good—actually, none of this was good. James fighting whatever that monstrosity was, Leonard about to pass out, Altujan ready to tear the city apart, and the Eye of Death on the loose. Lovely.

The only thing he was sure of was that if he died tonight, Charodon's hand wouldn't be the one to kill him.

"How do you know?" Ariel gazed at him. "How do you know that..." The wind swirled her hair in a halo, tickling his face. "You said you can't be rid of him."

"No," Roy said, "I don't know. But I might as well figure it out." The flashing of his vision was starting to grow stronger, the blinding colors returning to full strength. Not even able to see her face, he grinned. "I love you. Now go save them."

***

Samira bounded to the bow of the ship, squinting at the steadily growing Marble Watchtower. Something was deeply wrong. The alarm bells were blaring, and there was *some* activity in the city, but there was no effective defensive force. The impotent Seaguard and nothing more, barely three thousand men. Astus strike that fool of a harbormaster, did he send away *all* of the city's defenses?

She growled and turned to Moron, who stood just behind her, rubbing his eyes. "We need to get closer. Fast."

Captain Moron's eyes flitted around with concern. "Those bells have a very specific protocol, Samira. No ships in or out of the Harbor during an emergency. I could lose my whole cargo if I break that law, not to mention a stint in the harbor cells."

Samira pointed indignantly toward the shore. "There is a striking *armada* of Altujan out there about to destroy the place. Do you think your cargo is going to matter then?" The moon made the enemy ships even more eerie, as if they were floating on a sea of blood. Over one hundred of them hovered just outside the harbor. They held the city hostage just by being there.

Her borrowed coat fluttered a bit from the force of her pivot. She stomped down to the main deck. Even from this far away, she could hear it. It was proof that her friends still lived, that they were in grave danger.

Cackling in the dark. And if Rhaiga's pet was here, it meant that it would be going after Roy.

Moron's square boots followed behind her. His fatigued voice getting more annoying by the second, "What can we even do? It's not like a bunch of *sailors* are going to be of any use."

"A bunch of sailors once helped me kill a dragon, Moron. I wouldn't use your profession as an excuse," Samira snapped. She stalked over to the shoreboats, chose the sturdiest one, and kicked it over the rail. "I need a sword! There's something in that city that will massacre every living thing for a hundred miles if we don't do something. This is my chance to do something *right*, and I'm not going to let a ship full of cowards slow me down!"

Flame Itself

This was a bad idea. This was a bad idea. This was a *scorching* bad idea.

James rounded the corner of another building, narrowly missing the monster's teeth. They weaved through the jumble of stone structures at the outskirts of Greade Harbor. He was a rat running through a maze, but there was no exit. No other objective but survival. The flame in his hand was now betraying him, the heat showing the beast exactly where he was going, but he didn't dare extinguish it. It was only by the light of this miniscule fire that he could even see where he was going. The moon had sulked behind thick clouds, and he thought he heard thunder rumbling. Not that much could be heard over those scorching bells. His pursuant was above him, hopping nimbly from rooftop to rooftop, waiting to ambush him.

Bellowing a deeper, more haunting laugh than before, the abomination dropped to the ground directly in front of him. It spread its powerful wings to the side in an attempt to block his escape. His only route cut off, James brandished his sword and slashed at the creature with a wild yell. The whips on its head twitched, and the lean arm of the beast lashed outward.

Hardened claws batted aside James's blade. Before he could react, its muscled tail whipped at him as Rhaiga's attack dog turned. The appendage collided with him forcefully, catching him in the stomach and slamming him against the exterior of a house next to him. Oxygen was purged from his lungs, and James slumped to the ground, gasping. The tail, thick as a young tree and with the feel of coiled rope, flipped around and crushed against his stomach. James's eyes bulged and he gasped, pain shooting through his abdomen. His intestines felt as if they were being pushed up into his ribcage.

Pinned, gasping for air, and his sword being flung somewhere he couldn't see, James grasped at the creature's tail, trying to lift it. The beast yowled and snarled but still kept his body pressed against the earth. He could barely see anything with the tall grass shooting up around him.

Then a flicker—orange and calming, like sunlight of a different color—took hold near his left side. Bright orange flames devoured the windswept grass, illuminating the face of the monster, just a foot from his own. Its sensory whips twitched at the perception of the fire, but the face, the salivating maw, was trained directly on him. This thing was death, it was hunger, it was deceit. Everything that James despised, the culmination of his cynicism lived in that false grin.

"What do you want? With your life, what do you want?"

James felt the warmth continue to trickle across his shoulders and back, licking at his face. The palm where he had cupped that candle's worth of fire had touched the dying grass, setting it alight. What was once just a prick of heat had now become a blooming garden of dancing brilliance. He felt it caress him, and the warmth he felt spreading across him intensified as he drank it in. If he hadn't known how to harness this power, he would have felt as if he had swallowed the sun. But now the blaze pulsed through him with his heartbeat. He was one with it. He *was* the heat.

A smell of singeing flesh reached his nostrils. Quickly trying to get ahold of his breathing, James tried to quell the flames a bit. But it wasn't his skin that was burning.

Growling in increasingly pained yelps, the monster holding him down stayed put. Its toothy smirk still frozen, as if daring him to increase the intensity. It could still sense him, still knew he was there.

Taking his hand off its tail, James reached toward the fire to his left, closing his fingers around the warmth he felt. It tickled the inside of his palm, and he felt his arm pulsing with strength. He looked back into the leering, eyeless face above him.

"I want to light a path for people away from harm." He gritted his teeth. "From dishonesty and danger, from the Temple. Away. From. *You*." Gripping the flames near him and slamming them against the creature's head, James tugged and rolled as much as he could muster. He felt the immense weight of the tail give way as a ragged yelp-laugh bounced off the labyrinth of stone buildings around them.

Wheezing and standing cautiously among the rapidly spreading inferno, James wobbled to his feet, fists clenched tightly. He glared at his opponent. The beast, shaking its head and warbling, stomped its front paws and shrieked a challenge.

"So you don't like a little heat? Get used to it!" James taunted.

Still bellowing, Rhaiga's pet leapt up to its hind legs and flared its wings outward. Blotting out a startling amount of the sky behind it, the wings of the beast pumped in a dominant blast of air. In an instant, James was plunged back into darkness, surrounded by smoke and his own disbelief. It had put out his flames. Not even the candle in his palm remained.

Through the thick smoke, his adversary grimaced, smoke rolling in and out of its mouth as it chortled in triumphant puffs.

"Scorch me," James cursed, coughing. He turned and ran.

James managed to hit the eastern edge of the city before Rhaiga's pet caught him. An all-too-familiar crack of artificial thunder bounded across the now suddenly flat expanse of waving grass. It was now tall enough to reach his hips, and it scratched at his legs, holding them up as he tried to pump them harder.

The boom of the creature's wings whooshed like one of Ariel's gusts of wind. He screamed in desperation to get away—a guttural cry that he had never heard from his own throat—until that scream was replaced by one of incredible agony. Hungry claws sank into the flesh of his left shoulder, attempting to carry him off like a field mouse. James's shoulder was already slick with blood. It looked black in the night as it spilled down his arm.

His sword still somewhere back inside the city and his flames gone, James beat against the creature's tough hide with his right fist. It felt as if he were punching a wall draped in a tapestry. He punched at the leg that held him. Nothing. Stomach lurching as he realized that his feet were no longer on the ground, James panicked, thrashing back and forth against the momentum of the creature.

They wobbled in the air, but the beast held firm, shrieking at him as they flew. The shore grew closer and closer, and James could see boats of the Altujan knifing through the waves. There must have been over eight thousand—a lesser number than he had originally thought, but more than enough to cause significant damage to the city.

The monster dropped him to the ground, sprawling him on his stomach and chasing the air from his chest. James gasped and choked, rolled over, disoriented by the grass. Nothing was in view, and he heard the crunching of the monster prowling through the shrubs to his left. More crunching approached him from the direction of the shore.

"You're an interesting lot to follow." A woman's voice floated over the swaying field. It was a smooth voice, calming. Just the sound of it made him feel eerily tranquil despite his bleeding shoulder and crippling terror. He looked upward through the grass and saw a woman with tan skin—much like his own—leaning over him. A black veil covered her face, only showing a mouth with a near-imperceptible smile.

James panted, terrified. This woman was eerily familiar, exuding a presence he had felt once before, on the night he had left Boane.

"Rhaiga," he breathed.

The knowing smile on the woman's face grew wider. "Glad my Vaecus could bring you to me for a proper introduction." She gestured toward where the creature paced outside of James's vision. "Vayne told me your name, but I'm embarrassed to say that I've forgotten it. Not much point in learning the name of a person already walking the path. Although I do faintly remember that burn you gave me at the Sandstone Watchtower."

Outside his field of vision, the winged monster chortled as if in agreement.

She knelt beside him, her face slowly blocking out any light from the world outside his grassy cocoon, like death slowly smothering his senses. "It was never easy to learn the names of Chosen. They never lived long enough to tell me."

A swell of oxygen finally made its way into his lungs, and James retched, coughing and sucking in air. "You're a monster. You brought the Altujan here to kill all of these innocent people."

Rhaiga shook her head. She was wearing a black coat with matching trousers. No weapon hung at her narrow belt. "Everyone is following their path, Chosen. I do not deal death indiscriminately. I merely see them to the end of their journey. I observe Vayne's will carried out upon this wayward world." Her smile revealed white teeth as she said it, but the expression had a strained edge to it, a furious hunger.

James could hear the lie rolling from her tongue. "You don't believe that." He glared up at her face and watched the certainty falter. "You enjoy killing, the chaos. You need it, but that's not what you tell yourself. This nonsense about the path is a way for you to justify it and call it order, because it's the word that Vayne uses."

Her mouth twitched, anger overtaking her expression for a moment. Rhaiga straightened up and leered again as her skin rippled and bled into white. Like when Dhorh transformed, her bones and the sinew over them tore and re-fused together into something inhuman. "You're not wrong, boy. But we are not mindless animals like Charodon. We understand our tasks for what they are, our duties. This world has lost its way, and we—the first gods—have returned to guide it back into the age where we had dominion." The trousers and coat stretched and ripped at the seams, hanging off Rhaiga's gaunt body loosely in rags that floated like smoke. She shrugged, and her sickly, translucent skin stretched over her collarbones like it might split. "You could have walked a different path, you know. The Chosen never started as our enemy."

Staring in horror at the Eye of Death, James sputtered a curse. The sight of Rhaiga's true form would never be something he could fully comprehend. Her three eyes glowed in the night, staring at him intently.

"Though I will say that sometimes work and pleasure can go together. Dealing death after such a long banishment has been *so* refreshing." Rhaiga blinked all her eyes at once. Standing up straight and sauntering off, she called backward to where James shivered. "It's a pity that the path you walk ends here, Chosen, but it won't end by my hand. Not when Charodon's host still lives. Goodbye, Chosen. Best start walking."

Without another sound, she was gone. James's breath caught in his throat as the sounds of the bells in the distance continued. Outside the edge of the city, it could be a peaceful thing, to lie there and look up through the grass.

His ears twitched at the sound of crunching grass to his left, and before he could blink the toothy, singed face of the creature was there. Its slimy, jagged fangs loomed over him. Even with the burned state of his skin, the cool, dripping saliva of the creature made him wince. It had caught him, his sword gone. James reached up and touched the snout of the monster shakily. Cackling in some animalistic curiosity, it let him. The faint memory of the beach found its way to him, along with Samira's words.

"If I were to catch a lightning strike and throw it back, I would feel as if I were holding an entire storm in my hand."

James remembered the flames that he had used to burn the Vaecus just minutes ago in the city. He imagined the heat pumping through his muscles, energizing his breathing. It felt as if the sun were in his belly. He would not let them die. He was going to be better, a light to illuminate the path forward.

"But now that I've mastered the final form..."

The creature chirped in discomfort as James laid his whole palm against its muzzle. His hand began to glow. Brighter, hotter.

"I have become a storm myself."

An explosion, larger and hotter than dragonfire, erupted from his hand. The dark red of the field suddenly became brighter than daylight, a miniature sun that had not risen but instead suddenly *was*. James channeled the force of the blast, flinging both him and the Vaecus backward in opposite directions. Somehow maneuvering himself in the air, James landed on his feet and rolled to mitigate the impact.

He came to a stop more than sixty feet from where the fireball had started. The grass around the area was incinerated. A dark cavity in the earth—ringed by a steadily growing circle of flame—smoldered where he and the creature had grappled. Beyond the hole, the monster shrieked and writhed in the grass like a fish strung up on land. It thrashed wildly, as if unsure of where it was before righting itself and roaring a challenge. The scorched and scarred sensory whips on its head flailed in rage, and the Vaecus flared its wings outward.

That was it. The secret to beating it was using intense heat to disorient it. If the sensory whips on its head were overwhelmed with heat, it couldn't sense him.

"Good for me, I figured it out. Now how am I supposed to scorching kill it?" James muttered. While the heat definitely hurt it, the beast was still standing in one piece, and it looked more furious than wounded. He doubted that he could muster enough heat to burn it up without cremating himself. It was a problem that he would have to solve on the fly. Rhaiga was nowhere to be found, meaning she must have made it inside the city by now.

James watched as the Vaecus barked another challenge to him. He felt the warmth rise up within him again as he scowled and lit a fire in his hand. "You're in my way, bastard."

***

The wind roared in Ariel's ears, not quite drowning out the sound of Joskine's screaming. If he held on to her any more tightly, she wouldn't have enough air in her lungs to safely land. To be fair to the Crescent-Beard, she hadn't given him much warning before leaping from the top of the tower, taking him with her. The stairs would have taken too long, and this *was* the fastest way to get to the ground. It whooshed upward to greet them as they fell.

Even though the air streaming around her stung her eyes, Ariel could clearly see Altujan dismounting from their boats and slogging through the knee-deep water to the shore. Some leapt from their boats to the docks and ran along the piers toward the first of the buildings. Seaguardsmen, shaking and holding wobbling spears toward the water, provided a quavery first line of defense. Some retreated back into the city.

Still ringing, the bells were now accompanied by panicked screams. Townspeople rushed away from the docks as pale monsters in rust and blue charged toward them, slamming into the Seaguard's line. The black teeth of the Altujan clacked menacingly, intending to lay siege to each and every person here. But they would never get the chance.

"I love you. Now go save them."

She would stop them. No innocents were dying tonight. Everyone's lives would remain whole. Most of the people had made it to the tower and were fleeing to the western edge of the city. They wouldn't get far with the flesh eaters pursuing them. Ariel decided she had better put a stop to that.

Drawing as much breath as her lungs would allow, Ariel let all of her air loose from her mouth in a scream that stopped the advancing enemy cold. The blast of wind that came from Ariel blew through the twisting streets toward the shore. Carts were overturned as the air tunnels that were created by the buildings allowed the wind to triple in force. Ariel's air current smashed into the Altujan weaving their way between the structures, sending them tumbling backward into each other.

The force of her exhalation halted her and Joskine's descent completely, and they stopped falling just feet from the ground. Solid earth greeted her boots and she stumbled. Apparently, landing still required some work even though she had been able to use the final form of her gift.

Joskine slipped and fell to his knees, trying to keep down the food he had eaten earlier that day.

"Your warning was quite vague before you jumped off a *drowning Watchtower*!" Joskine gasped. He shakily stood and drew his sword. The man's eyes were incredibly wide with disbelief and still-receding fear.

"I told you to stay close to me. Sorry that I didn't have time to go through the details," she said, still looking ahead to the streets.

An orange glow had begun to seep into the deep red of the night to the west. Dawn was still hours away, and the light was the wrong color.

"They're going to burn the city to the ground! Joskine, I need you to find some people to go and keep that blaze away from the west side of town! If we can contain the Altujan to this side of Greade, we can give everyone enough time to escape."

"Leave that to us, my Lady!" A slim voice called. Hadsen appeared beside her swiftly, as if he had been riding the winds himself.

Badlai stood silently behind him with her jaw set. The ones behind Samira's death were here, and Badlai held a sword, more than willing to fight back.

"We fight with you. None of us are going back to these bastards. We'll keep that blaze away from the cityfolk. Half of us will stay with you and the Crescent-Beard!" Hadsen said. His black stubble and golden skin were slick with sweat. He had obviously been running around to rouse the rest of the sackwearers from around the city.

Ariel nodded. "Go on then. You're a good man, Hadsen."

The one-armed sackwearer saluted her—it was a salute she had never seen before—before tearing off in the direction of the flames, trying to skirt to the side so as not to run into the enemy head-on. Badlai followed him, her auburn hair streaming behind her. About fifty sackwearers stayed behind and brandished weapons. A small band of townsfolk joined them, determined to defend their city along with the eight hundred or so remaining seaguardsmen.

Ariel turned back to Joskine as she unshouldered her bow. Just the motion of moving her arms and wrists sent a spike of pain through her torn flesh. The sailor glanced at her with concern, but she shook her head. "We're doing this, Joskine. You and me. We have to give everyone a chance."

"What about James?" Joskine shouted over the approaching cries of the Altujan. Their shouts echoed through the alleyways and swaying grass.

"We have to hope that he's found a way to beat the creature. It has to have *some* weakness," she said, drawing an arrow. Her teeth about cracked as she clenched them together.

"And Len? Roy?"

She shook her head as her mind raced. "Leonard's already made fools of us in thinking him dead once." Her voice softened. "And Roy will be fine. I know he will." He had finally said it! Years of dancing around her feelings and the excruciating inner rending that it had caused had been healed in an instant with those words. She trusted him with her life, and even though things looked dire she knew that Roy was not dying tonight. Charodon was *not* breaking free. She almost felt pity for the devil.

This was a battlefield—no time to think about that. Ariel shook her head. What could they do? She looked at the roads that led to the square she and Joskine guarded at the base of the Watchtower. There were three of them, with two opening up on either flank. If the Altujan attacked from three sides, they would be pinned against the back end of the square and up against the tower. Ariel felt the tall grass scratch at her leg. Damn this flat wasteland! If she were home in Spiath, it would be so much easier to get a better vantage point. Collisun's lack of trees and abundant swaying grasses did little to tilt the playing field in her favor.

Another gong of the bells pierced her eardrums. They had been loud before, but here at the wide base of the tower the instruments, bigger than carriages and right behind them, were deafening, close to drowning out the clash of the Altujan with the Seaguard. Swearing she could feel blood trickling from her left ear, Ariel glanced at the bronze monstrosities. Both of the ancient alarm bells looked heavy enough to pin a dragon. Skillfully smithed, the gigantic instruments that once were a shining metallic masterpiece were old and somewhat deteriorated. Immediately, a plan began to form under her knitted brow.

"Joskine, bring those down!" she pointed at the bells. A relieved yet confused Joskine nodded. He seemed about as happy as she was to finally have those dreadful things cut down and no longer making noise, but she would make them even more useful.

The Siege of Greade Harbor

R oy could feel, kind of.

He felt the oppressive presence of Charodon lunge for his mind again, felt the swirling torrent of colors around him like a vibrant blizzard. The cold was still there, but it wasn't as overwhelming as before. Beside him sat the old man, the boy, and the veiled woman. Others, blurred and unfocused, remained behind him.

Charodon's shadow, an image that fazed around the reptilian face, loomed across the mindscape from him. It had blurred, but was still very much there. Leonard and Ariel's words still repeated, echoing throughout the swirling battlefield.

"You are the strongest person I know, Roy. It was never your fault. It was him."

"I forgave them for their mistakes," Roy said. "But I never forgave myself."

The old man nodded knowlingly, wrinkled jowls trembling. "Yes. You had to let go of your hatred, but the strongest hatred to let go of is often for yourself."

Roy stood. "You're the people who the Elders took as hosts, aren't you? The bodies that they took over."

The bald child spoke. "My name was Detres. I once hosted Dhorh."

"My name was Stoya. Rhaiga lives in what is left of my body," the woman wearing the veil said.

"My name is Klaern, and we are the Consumed," the old man moaned, "those who were used by the Elders, or as some call them, the Alderaye. After they devour our souls, we are cast out but remain for all eternity. Some of us chose to take the Elders for passengers, but we eventually were consumed. I once hosted Vayne, the Eye of Disease, because I didn't want to die. I was a coward, and now my soul has been cast aside."

"Is this what I'll turn into?" Roy asked. Even though he knew this was a dream, his mouth felt dry. "Is that why I can see you?"

Klaern sighed sadly. "The process has already started. When an Elder is consuming, it is easier to do so if they break the mind. That is why they often try to coerce us or trick us. But Charodon takes his hosts by force. He has been trying—and succeeding—to break your mind. But if you deny him that, you deny him the easy route. If the mind will not break, he will take a long time to break the body. You can live a life. A short one, but a life nonetheless."

Roy breathed sharply. "So I'll never be rid of him. There's no way to cast him out?"

"None that I know, dear boy." Klaern said. "It's possible that one before you managed it, but I know not how they did it."

Roy's mind began working. He hadn't expected to hear anything promising, but there now was a lingering, flickering hope. He'd been convinced that in the end Charodon would always be there, but if one had done it before him, he would find it. Drown everything else. The Eye of Nature would never have control of him again. For the sake of the innocents, his friends, for Ariel.

He turned from the Consumed, bowing his head and taking a step toward the blurry image of Charodon. "Thank you, Klaern. I may be able to talk to you, but

I won't join you. Not yet. I'll keep looking. One way or another, I'll be rid of Charodon someday. Even if it takes me the rest of my days. I've never been alone in this. I've just failed to see it."

Charodon's voice boomed through the flashing maelstrom, clear as day. *"I don't have to consume you."* The glow of his orange eyes pierced everything, creating miniature suns in the blurring storm of colors. *"We can work together. I've been around for thousands of years, boy. This world has never changed from what it once was: clay. For all this time, it's been waiting for someone to mold it. That fool Vayne is too weak to do it, the humans fumble with it, no one has been able to do it."*

"And you think that if I join you we can mold it?" Roy glared.

"We will rip the clay to shreds. Throw down the pieces and stand atop the pile. The future, eternity, will be ours."

The brightness of the spinning colors around them had faded. Dark crimson bled into the bright mental battlefield that Roy and Charodon stood on. Roy took another step toward the Eye of Nature. "Never."

The night sky slowly melted into place around him. Charodon roared and hissed, leaping for him. Closing his eyes and breathing deeply, Roy imagined he was back atop the Basalt Watchtower. Ariel was with him, and so were Samira, Leonard, and even James. Tears welled up in the corners of his eyes as he saw them smiling, happy, and safe. This was what he wanted, what he *needed*. And he would do whatever it took to make it happen. Samira was gone now, true, but this was what she had fought for. She had just gotten distracted like so many had before.

He opened his eyes and looked back up to the demon's specter that taunted him. It was gone, replaced by a single man with black hair, two turquoise eyes, and a scarless face.

It looked just like him. It *was* him. The part of him that he had lost that day—a man who had loved the world, one who had known how to forgive.

One with hope.

"Let's go." He smiled with a narrow mouth. "They need us."

Even in his head, Roy could feel tears travel down the path of his scar. The screams of Charodon began to fade gradually. The shadows, the flashing, all of it began to dissolve. Pain eased away, and soft light overtook the shadows as he reached for Past-Roy's hand. Fading, standing just behind Past-Roy, Klaern beamed proudly.

"This won't get rid of him," Roy said softly. He grasped the hand, letting himself be hauled up.

"No," Past-Roy confirmed, "but it will give us back today, and that's enough."

Frigid coastal air stung his face, and Roy's eyes ripped open. He was back atop the tower. Well, he supposed that he had never left. Ariel and Joskine were gone, but Roy spied the spiky-haired shape of the Earth's Chosen.

Breathing deeply as he hauled himself up, he stepped with certainty, more than he'd had in years, toward his friend.

Sensing someone behind him, Leonard turned and yelped, "Crush me, Roy! Couldn't give me any kind of warning you were awake?" He peered at Roy, and a relieved tremble bloomed across his features. "It's really you, isn't it? You did it."

"For now." Roy grinned.

The city below teemed with the sights and sounds of battle. Altujan poured through the grassy streets like ants. It seemed that whatever meager line the Seaguard had mustered was no more. Greade Harbor's alarm bells normally would have been ringing incessantly in a time like this, but closer inspection revealed that they had been cut down and used as barricades to plug the entrances to the square below them. Steady columns of smoke rose from the east and the west, but the west had been recently put out, as the smog was of a whiter hue. The smoke from the east was still fresh.

"Why is the field to the east burning?" Roy shouted over the wind.

"Some kind of blast out that way. Can still crushing see it every time I blink," Leonard said. "James ran out that way, and the cackling stopped since it happened. Willing to bet that it was his doing."

"The final form." Roy shook his head. "Sam would be proud."

Neither of them could say anything more. Nothing could hide the fact that they missed her despite her mistakes, and it pained Roy to think that Samira would never see what her teachings had done for James.

Roy ran a hand through his hair. "What of Ariel?"

"See for yourself." Leonard pointed downward.

Eyes straining to focus on the square directly below, Roy picked out a crowd of people, the size of ants, scurrying from barricade to barricade. They pushed defenses into place to fight the intruders. He couldn't see her now, but Roy knew that Ariel would be where the danger was thickest. He could see the Altujan swarming toward them, spilling through the streets like red and blue beetles.

"I'm going down there," he said. "You stay up here."

"Fine by me." Leonard scoffed. Blood, some dripping through Leonard's fingers, speckled the white stone beneath him. "I have work to do up here. Those bells aren't sturdy enough to repel an attack for long. They're good improvised barricades, but we need something stronger. I'm going to bring it down."

Roy tensed, stepping to the very edge of the marble. The ground waited, eager to rush up and meet him. "What? The Watchtower?" Roy gaped.

Leonard nodded, setting his jaw. "Those people down there don't need a stone tower right now. They need something between them and the enemy. And I can give that to them."

Nodding, Roy drew the serrated Altujan saber he'd taken from the islands. The blade dripped with sea water as he used the third form, conjuring the spray of the ocean around him. The battle loomed beneath them, calling them to fight, to protect, to save. Roy had another chance to do that.

And drown him, he would.

***

Ariel sat down hard, dizzy and gasping for breath. The final form was a useful tool, but the heat of preparations had made her forget the consequences of using it. Her lungs felt on the verge of collapse, quivering within her chest. Never had she tried to move something that heavy before, but it had paid off.

Once the alarm bells had shaken the ground with their fall, Ariel had forcibly moved them to block the street entrances on either side of the tower. With nowhere else to go, the enemy would be funneled straight toward them.

A hastily built barricade of carriages, debris, and crates blocked the last opening to the square. Grass and rocky soil were strewn all over the space, having been ripped up by the massive bronze bells. Residual wind from Ariel's power still swirled through the makeshift battle station. It carried the smell of smoke that wafted over from the fires that Hadsen and his men were fighting, it carried the now near-deafening cries of the enemy as they piled into the remaining open street, and it carried the feeling of unease before a fight.

Ariel shakily climbed to the roof of a building adjacent to the barricade and quickly unwrapped the bandages around her hands. The skin was still sensitive, but she ignored the stinging. She needed these hands, and it was time to get them dirty. The shouting Altujan were bearing down on the barrier. From this vantage point, she could pick them off from above. Drawing her bow quickly, she nocked an arrow and waited. The enemy thundered closer.

She loosed a shaft into the advancing horde, sensing it connect with a target. The unlucky Altujan fell and was immediately swallowed by the stampede.

Altujan slammed against the barricade, toppling some of the wooden crates from the top. *Leonard should be the one doing this. He's the expert with this commanding stuff.* Baring their black teeth, the flesh eaters began to scrabble over the splintery barricade like crabs, some taking arrows from sackwearers. Shivering as she remembered the glowing fish that beset their ship, Ariel loosed another arrow at the advancing enemy.

"Len's Aroch! To me!" Joskine screamed. Leading a group of sackwearers, Seaguard, and townspeople, the Crescent-Beard charged to the barricade with a spear. His feet slid in the loose dirt, but his momentum carried him forward into battle. Ferocity only matched by a dragon, the man engaged an emerging enemy soldier. The men and women following him took on the other Altujan that hurdled the barricade.

Ariel exhaled slowly and fired another arrow, pinning a blue-clad to the cart behind him, dead. Behind the barrier, hundreds of Altujan plunged into the chokehold. There was no end to them.

Mustering another deep breath, Ariel loosed a torrent of wind down the bottleneck. Altujan went sprawling backward and tumbled over each other, thrashing and scrambling to try and keep their balance. The oxygen around her was wearing thin, or at least her lungs were telling her it was. Her power was starting to get overwhelmed by having to use the final form over and over again. Stumbling forward and almost falling from the roof, Ariel got a hand on another arrow from her quiver. They were starting to run out. She ignored her screaming hands and fired another shot toward another enemy leading the charge. The Altujan ducked but was still caught just above the collarbone.

Several arrows whizzed past her head. Ariel fell flat on her back against the slanted roof to miss the incoming shafts. Determining where the arrows came from, she fired another two at the Altujan archers from her recline.

Ariel looked back at the chokehold to see the barrier breaking down. The sheer force of the enemy pushing against it had finally broken through. Unimpeded Altujan roared and charged, their feet thundering against the torn grass and dirt. Wielding a knife in one pained hand and her bow in another, Ariel rolled from the roof and landed not far from Joskine. She weaved through a blizzard of steel toward her friend, swatted aside a blade with her knife and clubbed the Altujan in the back of the head with her Oreleaf bow. The assailant went down, skull cracked. Joskine and several dozen other sackwearers pushed through the charging flesh eaters, trying to hold them back, but they were forced to give up ground.

Ariel glanced backward to see that the base of the Watchtower was getting closer. She hoped at least that she had given the city folk enough time to escape, but it didn't look like she was going anywhere.

Joskine called her name, and she exasperatedly looked up from an invader she had just defeated. She had only looked away for a second before another Altujan took his place and thrust at her with a blackened sword. Ariel felt a bright, keen sting in her side and grunted angrily, spinning through most of the attack and slamming the blade of her knife into the foe's chest. The Altujan gurgled and fell.

"*What?*" she snarled.

"Should we be concerned?" The sea rat was bloodied from a blow to the head. He pointed upward with his finger hastily before bellowing and parrying a swipe from another Altujan.

Ariel followed his gaze and focused on something rocketing toward them from up above. A wave of excitement rushed through her as she steeled her lungs yet again and exhaled forcefully, slowing the momentum of the falling anomaly. Her breath was cut off as a new enemy swung at her with a patterned glaive.

Roy hit the ground with the force of a tidal wave, bringing down thousands of gallons of water upon the attacking regiment. Altujan clambered in an attempt to dodge before they were washed off their feet. Roy rested on one knee and thrust his hands outward, pushing the water back through the street that the assault had come from. He was trying to send them backward toward the sea, but even the amount of water he had conjured was not enough. It had disoriented the enemy however, and they could use that. Roy charged the confused and waterlogged Altujan with his stolen saber at the ready. He slammed into their haphazard line and cut through them like paper. Slashing, spinning, he flowed like water from one opponent to the next.

Ariel rushed to his side and protected his back, engaging an Altujan that had gotten enough of her wits about her to try an ambush. Water misted everything, and Ariel's feet sloshed in the mud, but she planted herself between the attacker and Roy, batting the flesh eater's blade aside and shoving them backward. Joskine cut the Altujan down before she could charge Ariel again.

The three waded through the sea of rust and blue, pushing them back slightly and giving the sackwearers and townspeople room to breathe. It wouldn't be long until the enemy regrouped. Roy's appearance had set them back, but this didn't make a significant enough change.

Something appeared to be charging through the ranks of the enemy—or at least, the enemy appeared to be parting for something—at an inhuman speed. Roy quickly rested a hand on Ariel's shoulder, signaling to be ready. Altujan before them stopped and stood their ground.

Ariel tensed. They were all but pushed back. What would the enemy stop advancing for?

The throng of invaders parted to reveal a woman sauntering through the mud, a saber at her side and a familiar black cloak draped around her shoulders. Her dark-red hair wreathed the bloodlust in her violet eyes, and a black collar buttoned up to her chin covered the spot on her throat that Roy had opened.

Ariel's throat constricted as if by a noose. This wasn't possible.

"As you can see, Host of Charodon," Mastreh sneered, "I'm still breathing."

***

The Vaecus whipped its tail downward, slamming the ground just to the side of James. He felt his jaw rattle from the force of the blow. That could have broken him completely if it had hit. It was clear to him now that the creature was no longer playing with its food but was carrying out a vendetta. He was a threat now, and the beast knew it. James sprung upward as the tail swept to the side, trying to take his feet out from under him. From the air, James belted another burst of flame toward the creature's face. The flames, producing daylight clarity, washed over the sensory whips and sent them into a frenzy. Disoriented. Unsure. Blind.

As the creature shook its head, James charged inward. He saw the sensory whips snap to attention. No more than a few seconds—that was all a single hit would give him. It would have to be enough. A deadly, razored paw came downward at him, and James fired a quick burst into the beast's face, throwing off its aim. Claws sheared through his sleeve and shaved the thinnest bit of skin from his good arm. The claw marks in his left shoulder still gushed blood, and his shirt was now sticky with it. Grunting with the sting, James swung and felt his fist connect with the monster's snout. Swelling heat flared within him, and his fist flashed brightly. A blistering wave of fire washed over him and the Vaecus. The smell of searing flesh pummeled his nostrils, but not just of the creature.

Screams, both James's and the beast's, echoed across the engulfed grassland around them. White hot pain covered his arm, and he dropped to the ground next to the beast. Beside him, he could hear a mournful snicker escape the monster's leathery mouth—still alive. Even in the light of the crimson moon, James could see his right arm covered in an angry red. Sore, pronounced, and stinging blisters had sprouted from his skin, making his arm seem like some otherworldly appendage that had just been grafted onto his body.

Another croaking chuckle came from the monster's cracked grin. The sensory whips fluttered limply against its neck.

James groaned as he sat up gingerly, slowly building up to a yell from the flaring pain in his arm. "*Scorch* me!" he swore.

Well, that was precisely what he had done. He hissed through his teeth and maneuvered his way to a kneeling position. The sprawled-out creature beside him was hardly moving, its limbs—including the wings and tail—twitching and steaming. Some of the leather membrane in the wings had cracked or torn from the heat. The rough dirt ground against his knees while he shuffled toward its head.

He stopped just behind its head and panted as if he had just lied against the Sandstone Watchtower in the sun for weeks. A persistent, pulsing, dull pain had sprung up just behind his eyebrows, and he took a moment to focus. "I feel sorry for you," he said softly.

The creature's whips perked at his voice.

"You were strung along like I was. We didn't know any better, but we should have. We have to be our own gods, and we have to live up to that. I won't let either of us be used."

The creature's wings lifted ever so slightly.

James rested his left hand on the Vaecus's head, ready to summon enough heat to put it down. Even if it blistered his other arm, he would do it to keep this monster away from his friends. He furrowed his brow, ignoring the now vision-blurring headache.

The creature shot upward, beating its wings downward hard. In trying to catch his balance, James grabbed the only thing near him with his blistered right hand—the beast's sensory whips. He screamed, flying upward, hanging from the creature, soaring toward the heavens.

Watchtower

Roy glared at Mastreh through the seawater dripping from his disheveled hair.

The Blood Herald walked leisurely toward him with a jaunt in her step. Her white-painted smirk exuded malice, and her hand gripped the hilt of a sword—his own. She wore *his* sword and *his* cloak! Murderer, thief, invader, monster.

Joskine and Ariel stood closely by him, frozen just as he was.

How was she even alive? Despite his weary state during their escape from the Tarsals, he knew for a fact that he had cut her throat. She *should* be dead.

"Disappointed to see me, Chosen?" Mastreh taunted. She wore red and blue painted leather armor underneath the black cloak. Wreathed by her maroon hair, her triangular face glared at him. "Your bloodbreathing isn't finished. Tonight, you're going to *drown in it*!" She leveled the sword with the flat of the blade facing up and pointed it at him. Altujan around her followed her lead, ready to charge.

Roy glanced to his side at Ariel. Mud and blood speckled her face and glyphed arms, and her unwrapped hands clearly bothered her, but the look in her eye told him immediately that she wasn't going anywhere. "You ready?" he whispered.

"Always," she whispered back.

"Get around her flank. Try to cut off any chance to dodge attacks." Roy tightened his hold on the stolen Altujan saber. His eyes were firmly on Mastreh. "Joskine, you're there to make obstacles. Swing in a frenzy so she can't predict your target. Maintain distance, both of you. We win this by—"

Mastreh's sword flashed, and she was suddenly in front of him in an inhuman burst of speed. He barely slapped away a savage swipe before she switched her sword hand from right to left and stabbed at his shoulder. Roy rolled his shoulder out of the way but was too slow. Sharp pain flared in his chest as the tip of the blade hit his collarbone. A red stain appeared on Roy's shirt—already growing larger.

Ariel batted the sword away with her knife just in time to duck. Mastreh's sword glided over her head.

Mastreh skirted backward as Joskine jabbed toward her ribcage with his spear. Already, the other flesh eaters had charged, engaging the rest of the humans.

Roy drove forward, slashing toward Mastreh while she was distracted. Even in the relatively sheltered middle of the city, the wind screamed past his ears. Mastreh easily blocked each of his attacks and cut toward Ariel's already wounded abdomen, barely missing as Ariel rolled away.

She's good, Roy thought as Mastreh whirled and kicked Joskine's spear away. *Better than any of us*. The Altujan brought her sword down in a blur and chopped through the shaft of Joskine's spear.

The Crescent-Beard grunted and fell backward, just evading a thrust from Mastreh.

She turned back to Roy and Ariel, smiling ferociously. "That failure Zatran isn't here to stop me from killing you now, Chosen," she said, hacking at Ariel and taking off a tuft of gold hair. "Rhaiga and the Elders don't *need* Charodon, which means you're all mine if he doesn't come out to play!"

Roy yelled and attacked in a blinding hailstorm of strikes. "I. Don't. Need. Him. *Either!*" He landed a cut on Mastreh's bicep, but not a deep enough one to stop her. The Blood Herald took no notice and swung in a wide arc. Roy barely brought up his saber in time.

Seeing her chance, Ariel lunged into Mastreh's blind spot and ran her knife through the armor into the dead warrior's ribs.

Roy felt relieved as Ariel yanked her knife back, but no spurt of violet blood followed. No gasp of pain emerged from the Blood Herald's white lips.

Mastreh grinned her dead smile and kicked Ariel away.

Raging, Roy brought his sword down, intending to cleave into the Altujan's body. Charodon stirred within him—he exhaled forcefully, dispelling the thoughts of the devil.

Mastreh met his sword with hers and pulled her collar down with her other hand. The sight of the smooth gap in her neck, just across the dark V where Roy's sword had cut it, was disgusting. No blood dripped from the wound, nor did it seem to pain her. It was unnatural, unbelievable, and it was *terrifying*.

Gold hair flew behind Mastreh, and the tip of a long knife suddenly protruded from her chest. Ariel pushed the knife in further and growled.

"Oh, but what of your *convictions*, Chosen?" Mastreh cried in fake astonishment. Her insane laughter somehow echoed through the battlefield despite the din.

"I don't kill people," Ariel spat. "But there's *nothing* human about you."

"Clever, aren't we!" Mastreh roared. Twisting and bringing both arms around in an arc, she threw Ariel and Roy backward. Roy stumbled precariously in the mud, his eyes wild. Drown him, what in the world *was* she?

Ariel leaned on his shoulder and breathed heavily. It was obvious that the cut to her side pained her. His senses of the water around him were a bit blurry.

Fury, glee, and hunger all fighting for space in Mastreh's gleaming eyes, the Blood Herald charged again.

***

Her boat hadn't even reached throwing distance to land before she had leapt out.

Samira had never run faster. Her legs—while greatly malnourished—refused to stop pounding through the grass streets. The boots Moron had given her were heavy but sturdy enough for her to blow through tangled patches of rock or debris. Clashing metal and battle screams rolled over the port toward her. It all led to the Marble Watchtower. Whatever her friends were doing, that was where they had chosen to make their stand.

Panting and holding her sword in a reverse grip, Samira hurdled a fallen pillar and continued forward. She listened for the bells. Nothing. She listened for the cackling. Nothing. All she could hear was...

Screaming. Awful and inhuman. They felt like knives to her eardrums. Not even Charodon made such a sound. Altujan skittered around the city, standing between her and her friends. She snarled and prepared for the deadly slog toward the city center. Suddenly, something caught her gaze.

It was coming from off to the east. Samira followed the sound and squinted through the darkness before having to shield her eyes. A screaming, blazing comet hurtled across the sky, bringing a false dawn to the dead of night.

"Strike me." Samira's face lit up in awe.

***

Roaring and darkness were all that James could decipher up in the air, and his blistered arm felt as though it were being threaded by hundreds of searing needles. The world made no sense up here, perilous and tumultuous. Still, he kept his grip on the creature's sense whip.

The Vaecus could feel him hanging on. It shrieked in anger, flipping, tumbling, rolling, doing anything it could to be rid of him. James could guess that it was going to try and shake him off at a height that wouldn't allow him to get back up once he fell. His legs flailed back and forth as he was whipped asunder by the creature. The blisters on his arm had all burst, exposing his scorched skin to the air. They screamed in unison—one in pain and the other in frustration. Blurred flashes of the town below caught James's vision. It was bringing him back toward the fight. If it got back into the city, it would make a straight path toward Roy and Charodon. That *could not happen.*

His hair stinging his eyes, James grunted and closed his fist. Heat built up in his body. He willed it to go hotter and allowed it to boil over until his left hand became wreathed in flame. Thrusting his left hand forward, he hurled flame at the creature's head. A splitting shriek left the monster's maw as the flames saturated its senses, and it lost direction. It flapped its wings, changing its course so forcefully that something in James's right shoulder popped. He hit it again, and the Vaecus flew faster, higher.

James repeatedly washed flames over the creature's head until it moved erratically, panicking as he took away its senses. It was overloaded with heat and had no notion of even which way was up. James still didn't let up. He gnashed his teeth tight enough to crack and struck again with a blow that flashed white. Something *ripped* in his hand from the unbridled heat, and he cried out. The Vaecus screeched from agony, its sensory whips now alight.

They streaked across the sky. Shapes passed by with the clarity of sand in the wind. James looked at where the monster—no longer able to tell direction—was going. A massive white shape loomed.

***

They were headed straight for the tower, Samira realized. Whatever James was doing to the beast was working, but perhaps too well. If they hit the tower, they both would splatter.

"Pull up." She breathed, sprinting toward the Watchtower. "Pull *up,* strike you!" Samira swore as her overlarge boot clipped a jutting rock, and she tumbled into the grass. The course, wavy turf scratched at her as she struggled to rise. Strike her, she wasn't going to make it. No matter what she did, nothing ever helped. She was doomed to watch all of her friends die. Mistakes, pride, negligence, all of them were hers to claim.

Cries of the Altujan echoed off the stone buildings that surrounded her, sounding like they were closing on her location. She struggled to her feet and looked desperately to the streaking ball of flame above her. Altujan screams were definitely getting closer. Breathing deeply, Samira tuned out the din of the world, raised a shaky left hand, and waited for the space between heartbeats.

And felt nothing.

Samira snarled at her hands. These striking things were excellent at causing pain, but what else were they *good* for?

James and the creature flashed white, still rocketing toward the tower.

Again, Samira willed her heartbeat to drown out the world, extended both hands, and threw them down.

***

The gigantic white shape rushed forward to meet them, like one of the Khavanh whales that Joskine had boasted about seeing. Through the numb pain that clouded his mind, James felt his brain click. *It's the tower!*

He was still holding on to the creature's whip! Terrified, he tried to let go but couldn't, the unfathomable heat from his attacks had fused his hand to the creature's appendage. Wind needled his eyes. His vision went dark as he attempted to wrench his right arm free. Sounds of metal on metal and screams on the wind reached his ears as the sensory whip came free of the creature's head, and then he could feel the world reel.

With no clue where he was, James thrashed in the air and was blinded by an overwhelming radiance.

A thunderous boom whited out everything, but a glimpse of the creature burned into his retina before the Vaecus was vaporized by the light. Lightning coursed through the already scorched beast, and it exploded into ash. The lightning strike rushed downward still and struck the Marble Watchtower. A chorus of ruptures sounded from the tower. Crack after crack hit James's ears, but he fell too fast to cover them. The tower groaned and swayed like an ancient tree, leaning farther to the left.

A hand closed around James's left wrist and gripped him like tempered steel. His arm screamed in protest as his momentum was stopped immediately. For a moment, he was certain that he would continue downward but was incredulous to find himself suspended some hundred feet above the ground. His wrist—already starting to bruise—was firmly in the grip of a large, muscled man with impossibly spiky brown hair.

"What was I going to say...about you doing something stupid?" Leonard gasped. The man looked incredibly pale, paler than the marble he rested against. Even Leonard's eye color was drained.

His vision adjusting to the darkness after the lightning strike, James could clearly see that Leonard's wound was bleeding again.

"How are you even—"

A deafening crack silenced James, and a whoosh sucked the wind away from them both. The Marble Watchtower, a symbol of the gods and their immovable strength, was falling at the place where the lightning had cracked it. A heavenly marble tree that had been met with a celestial axe.

Leonard heaved James up onto what was now the top of the Watchtower. They watched, dumbfounded as the broad structure hung in the air for a tranquil moment before slamming into the ground below, crushing buildings and shaking the continent. James and Leonard clutched each other to keep from falling. Soil, rocks, water, and grass sprung into the air. Mist hung in the air, as if a storm had come through.

"Thank you," James whispered.

"No," Leonard said, "thank you, James. For making us better."

Storms

Roy collapsed to the ground when the tower crashed to the earth, suddenly blinded by the mud and debris that scattered in every direction. Drown him, Leonard had done it!

"Ariel!" he called.

There was no response.

An unseen boot collided with his torso, followed by the swipe of a blade, drawing a thick line of blood. His upper stomach screamed in protest.

"*Get up!* I want you on your feet when I kill you." Mastreh threw him to his feet, snarling, covered in silt.

He swept his left hand forward, and the muddy water around his feet catapulted upward, flying into the Blood Herald's eyes.

She shrieked as the salt and gritty mud covered her vision, seemingly more from frustration rather than pain.

Mastreh backed away into Ariel's waiting strike. Ariel's knife went through the back of Mastreh's knee, taking her down to a kneeling position but causing no pain. Sliding forward in the mud, Roy brought his sword across in an attempt to score a hit on her neck that would—he hoped—kill her for good. She pulled her arm up and took the blow across the forearm. The blade bit deep but brought forth no Altujan blood.

"You've already seen all the blood you're going to get from me!" Mastreh frothed. "Rhaiga chose me to end the Chosen. Your kind will know your place again!" She grasped the blade and yanked her arm toward her chest. The hilt came free of Roy's grip, and he was suddenly weaponless.

Mastreh wrestled to her feet and pounced on Roy, sword held high and ready to plunge into his chest. They hit the ground, and Roy felt the air chased from his throat as the mud fastened on his limbs.

Before the tip of the blade could pierce his flesh, a Dreadfront-force squall hurled Mastreh more than twenty feet to the right. The wind passed right over Roy like a river. He felt Ariel pick him up, her archer's hands firmly standing him on his feet. Mastreh rolled through the mud, her armor smacking wetly against the silty ground.

Sackwearers fought fiercely around them, but the Altujan had pushed them back too far. They were getting surrounded.

A pure, exuberant note blasted above the din of battle. Roy jerked his head toward the sound. Where had he heard that sound before?

The sound was joined by dozens, *hundreds* of voices, perhaps more, all roaring for battle. From behind the Altujan lines sprung figures in armor of vibrant blue that washed away the faded tones of the flesh eaters. They sliced down the Altujan and pushed into the clearing. An Aroch, the elites of the empire, had stumbled across the city under attack.

"Remember when Vilch attacked us in that meadow?" Ariel huffed. Roy nodded quickly. He had no idea how they were both standing. They had both been repeatedly cut by the seemingly unkillable Altujan leader.

"Can we pull it off?" he groaned.

"Maybe not, but we aren't exactly winning here."

Across the clearing, Mastreh staggered to her feet, wielding both Roy's blue saber and the serrated Altujan blade. She had mud smeared across her face, and the colored varnish on her armor had started to bleed and drip. Violet eyes ablaze, she stalked toward the Chosen.

Roy bellowed and thrust his hands forward. As if a well had opened in front of him, roaring water sprung from his palms. The smell of salt flourished. He kept a hold on his senses, feeling as though he were floating, imagining the endless, drifting space of the ocean. He envisioned that ocean living, swelling in his own body. Roy was not a man and was not Charodon; he was the sea. Frothing and green, the water flowed across the already damp and muddy square. Grass drowned beneath the reservoir that Roy created.

Beside him, Ariel breathed in deeply and shot a hand to the side. She appeared to be snatching the wind and throwing it in a different direction. It swirled and spun around them, growing in size and velocity. The water—Roy could feel it rising in his chest, spilling into his lungs—lapped at their knees before being swept into the air by the gale that Ariel created.

Mastreh shielded her eyes from the artificial rain as she ran at them, but the wind again took her off her feet.

Roy and Ariel stood in the middle of their own personal Dreadfront. The wind and water spun faster, faster, until the typhoon was ripping grass from the dirt by their sturdy roots. Armies were not enough, nature was not enough, the Blood Herald was not enough to quell the storm. It thrashed Mastreh through the air again and again. Deathless, the Altujan could do nothing as she was humiliated and tossed by a force she couldn't hope to counter. Aroch and Seaguard soldiers, sackwearers, townspeople, and Altujan alike clung desperately to their surroundings to avoid being swept into the squall.

Water was fully present in Roy's lungs. He could feel a steady stream now pooling in his chest. Doing his best not to breathe, he continued to pump water into the storm. Mastreh couldn't be given even a second to get up. They just had to keep this going long enough to figure out how to restrain or kill her for good.

He glanced in Ariel's direction and saw that her normally bright face had become a disturbing shade of bluish-gray. She was asphyxiating. Neither of them would be able to keep this up for much longer. Water began spilling out from between Roy's lips and out his nose, and he gagged on the salt. He was drowning from the inside out. He took a shaky step forward, trying to bring the storm crashing down on Mastreh.

The Blood Herald saw her chance in that moment. As the wind whipped her around in an arc, she hurled the swords just as Roy brought his right arm down with the dead weight of thousands of gallons of water. Ariel screamed out the last of her oxygen and propelled the winds into impossible speeds. Before the swords could even reach Roy, they were crumpled to a horseshoe size with a muted creak—just as if it were at the bottom of the ocean.

Roy lost control of the storm and dropped to his knees, retching as water flowed from his mouth, ears and nose. Salt stung his nostrils and eyes. Conjured rain pattered against his head and shoulders. Air finally graced his windpipe, and he inhaled greedily. The wind had stopped, and he could hear gasping and coughing behind him as Ariel regained her breath, albeit sluggishly. He looked up from the ground and squinted through the rain toward the tower. A ragged, jumbled fissure had sprung up toward the middle of the obelisk's length.

Roy's gaze snapped to something just in front of him, catching movement. A trio of glowing eyes peered at him through the mist. Rhaiga shifted in and out of focus, clutching the somehow motionless body of Mastreh. Roy couldn't move, not with half a lake's worth of water spilling out of him. His eyes connected with the Eye of Death, and he saw curiosity, possibly recognition.

And rage.

Rhaiga's three eyes burned as deeply as the roots of Charodon's hatred, still buried deep in Roy's soul. He knew that feeling, and he knew that the Eye of Death was no longer a disinterested watcher. She was in this war now, fully. Killing Samira had been a sport for her—a fun game, but the fun was over.

As seamlessly as she had appeared, Rhaiga backed into the fog and was gone. He stared blankly ahead into the rubble and destruction that the Elder had brought to Leonard's home. His black cloak, the drowning thing, sat in a waterlogged heap. He sighed. The world wasn't done with him yet.

He felt a hand lightly touch his shoulder. Ariel, still breathing a bit shakily, stood beside him. She said nothing, simply absorbing the knowledge that they'd made it. Fatigue bloomed throughout Roy's whole body as if on a delay, and he leaned his head against her hip. But what about that flash of light? That hadn't looked like James's power. What was a drowning Aroch doing around here without telling the twins first?

"Shh."

"I didn't say anything," Roy said.

"You're still worrying. You don't hide it."

Groans and the creaks of plate armor started cropping up around the clearing. Whole buildings had been decimated by the storm and the falling tower. The debris would require hours of sifting through. The Aroch soldiers—like true professionals—were already up and about, tending to the wounded and restraining any Altujan who were unfortunate enough to be taken captive.

"We have to go talk to them." Roy sighed.

"In a minute," Ariel said contentedly. "Let's just rest here for a minute." And Roy couldn't help but agree.

***

Samira collapsed to the ground, spasming, limbs fighting her commands after destroying the Watchtower. She hoped that Astus would forgive her for bringing down the symbol to the gods, but it was an unfortunate casualty in her attempt to save her friends.

She hid in the shadow of a collapsed tavern, no doubt filled with people just a few hours before, but luckily empty when it had fallen. Day would be in full effect before too long. She would have to decide what her next move would be before she was found. Nothing tugged at her more than the desire to walk out into the light, to see them, to beg for their forgiveness and move forward.

It was just too farfetched of a dream to come true.

"I thought I was raising a hero."

It turned out her father had been half right. She had done good in her life, but there was so much she had done wrong. Perhaps this suffering gnawing at her limbs now was justice. If her gifts from Astus really were fading, it would be for the best.

The Altujan had been driven back by an Aroch, of all the possible miracles. Blue plate armor and swift decision making had overtaken the chaos of the city, restoring peace for now. Striking good timing too. If they hadn't shown up when they did, Samira would have been helpless against the invaders approaching her. Luckily, the arrival of the Sapphire Aroch had been a brilliant distraction.

Some time passed—she didn't know how much. Groaning with exhaustion, she tried and failed a few times to heave herself up before making it to her feet, shaking the whole way up. It would be a long walk back to the *Storm Tower*. She just hoped that Moron hadn't sailed off without her. Wouldn't that be a striking dilemma.

Not even two steps toward the shore, she heard a flat voice softly call out to her.

"Sam."

Badlai stood amid the rubble outside the ruined tavern. Her clothing was torn and stained with violet, and she was bleeding slowly from a gash above her eyebrow. It gave her brow an angry, accusatory expression, but her eyes showed nothing but bewilderment and relief. Badlai ran and caught Samira before she could say anything, arms enveloping Samira in the midst of her electric spasms. The sailor set her down gently, checking her for wounds. When she only found scars from the most recent fight with Rhaiga, Badlai sighed with slight repose.

"How?" she asked. Her voice was quiet, no emotion, but her expression said all it needed to.

"I guess Astus wasn't done with me yet," Samira said, looking down at her hands. She could still see the skin involuntarily twitching, left and right arms now equally numb. This wasn't what Samira wanted, to run into anyone. It made this decision so much harder. And Badlai had been nothing but good to her from the first moment. She was wonderful, more than that.

Which meant that Samira had to stay away from her, had to stay away from everyone.

Badlai placed a hand on Samira's arm, eyes asking questions. *What's wrong*?

"I have to go," Samira said.

The hurt in Badlai's face brought a wave of guilt over her. She wanted desperately to take the words back or say she didn't mean it.

Samira stifled tears and pulled herself up to one knee. "This is for the best."

"No."

"It is," Samira urged.

"*No.*"

With a shaking hand, Samira massaged her temple with her thumb. "*Please* listen. I can't go back to them. They won't take me, and I would find new ways to get them into trouble even if they did. Storms do nothing but destroy. It's all I've done for my whole life. I've made everything worse by being in this fight, and the only way to give the rest of you a chance is to step away. The only sure way that everyone survives is if they never see me again. I can't always go blasting my way through life. But you know what? That's all I know how to do."

Eyes misting over, Badlai took Samira's shaking hand and squeezed it. "Don't."

Samira threw the hand away and stood up, trying, failing, to keep tears back. "I knew someone like you once, Badlai. She was kind and beautiful, but she was a fool because she didn't have the good sense to stay away from me. She's *dead*. I got her killed, and I was too stupid to see it before it was too late." Samira glared into those transfixing green eyes. "I won't let anyone else die that way."

Badlai stood up and watched Samira limp away toward the shore, suddenly angry. It was an expression that Samira had never expected to see from the sailor.

"It's for the best," Samira assured.

"For everyone, or for you?"

Samira turned at the sudden, accusatory question. Who was Badlai to think that she knew better? This woman, who had seen everything fall to ruin at Samira's hands. She scowled, "You took an oath of silence, didn't you? Long before you became a sailor."

"I did."

"Then stop talking," Samira hissed, shakily moving her foot toward shore. It would take her hours to get back on her own, but that was how the Chosen of Astus would do things from now on, for the greater good. She glanced backward to see Badlai still there, hands angrily clenched at her sides, looking like she had a few more choice words with which to break her oath.

Samira stopped and sighed heavily, not looking back. "Just go away." She shuffled away without another word.

The Sapphire Aroch

Leonard had collapsed by the time they had come down from the tower, weighed down by his injury as well as his power. James helped to lay his friend—pale and shivering, but still happily chattering—on a stretcher supplied by the Aroch fighters. They wore blue plate armor that dazzled in the light of the slowly rising sun, and three of them began attending to Leonard's reopened wound.

The remains of the Marble Watchtower stretched across the decimated city, having broken in several places when it fell. The lightning strike that brought it down had come at just the right time, killing the Vaecus and cutting off the escape for most of the invaders in one blow. Some of the enemy still lived, having sailed away before the rest of the Sapphire Aroch could apprehend them. Rhaiga was most surely among them. Without her pet, she would be at a disadvantage, but James worried about what other resources she and Vayne had access to. The worry diminished at the sight of a burly man with a patchy red beard.

"So you made it, eh? I knew you would be since you were so moved by my speech, but it's nice to know for sure." Joskine pounded James on the shoulder in a gesture that angered his already seething burn, but James grinned anyway. The Crescent-Beard's face was swollen from a blow he had taken during the battle, but the smile didn't waver an inch.

"I tried reciting your speech to the creature to see if that would work, but I guess it didn't appreciate genius, Joskine," James quipped.

Leonard shook his head as the sailor belched out a wheezing chuckle.

"What happened down here?" James asked. From the corner of his eye, he spied Badlai sulking near the edge of the square, eyes looking miserable.

"We held them as best we could here, Lady Ariel, Roy, and I. Things looked like they would be all right until that Mastreh woman showed up. Ain't natural, that one. Lucky that these soldiers showed up when they did or we would have been in trouble, Dathos drown me." Joskine scratched the bald part of his chin and slumped down beside where Leonard lay. "You should have seen Roy and Lady Ariel, Len. They were incredible. Would have thought that I was in the middle of a Dreadfront if I didn't know any better, and I think they might've even summoned lightning?"

Leonard rolled his eyes at the familiar nickname but let it go. "That's impossible. Neither of them can do that, even working together." Sweating a bit from the exertion, Leonard sat up despite repeated attempts by the Aroch surgeon telling him to lie flat. "Where are they now?"

"Catching their breath. I'd say they've earned a rest for a few minutes," the sailor replied.

Leonard finally relented to the surgeon telling him to relax. A troubled expression crossed his brow, but it melted away as the surgeon started stitching him up.

James sat in the mud and grass, too exhausted to care. He would find a bath sometime soon, but for now he needed to get off his feet. One of the surgeons left Leonard's side and produced a swath of bandages. Commanding James to hold out his arms, they wrapped his limbs tightly to hold in any remaining blood.

He hadn't noticed, but the heat from his fight with the Vaecus had thoroughly cauterized the claw marks in his left shoulder. The skin was burned and scarred, but the wound was mostly closed. Lathering a strange, wispy-smelling substance on his right arm for the burn, they wrapped it in a softer cloth and left to tend to others.

Sunlight had now cast away all but the deepest shadows. It made the armor of the Sapphire Aroch blaze as if the light were being reflected off a hoard of diamonds. A commotion sounded near to the left.

"You *stupid* boy! Why won't you ever listen?" Theos rushed to Leonard's side, followed closely by Rossel. An Aroch soldier—a commander, possibly—in dark-blue splint armor accompanied them.

James smothered a smile, or at least tried, because Leonard glared at him when he saw his face.

The apothecary and surgeon knelt beside their surrogate son and began asking his condition from the Aroch surgeons. They immediately scolded Leonard when the caregivers relayed that Leonard had been uncooperative with their commands.

"Trust me, this one won't listen to surgeons," Rossel said, a fair amount of resignation in his voice.

"Seriously, Leonard," Theos chided.

"Then perhaps he would listen to someone in command," the Aroch officer said. She looked to be a few years past Leonard's age with black hair that had been messily tied into a bun at the back of her head. She squinted at Leonard with cold green eyes in a familiar way. Perhaps there was a history. Blue sunlight reflected off her pale skin and highlighted a raised scar that wove around her jaw to the corner of her mouth. "Leonard, you are to follow every order from these surgeons as if it came from myself. You will heal, and you will do it *right* so that you may continue to be of service to the empire. Do you understand?"

Rather than answer her directly, Leonard gestured to James. "James, let me introduce you to the Commander of the Sapphire Aroch and Dragoneater, Lady Rosamund Clane."

"Answer me," Clane said tersely. "Do you understand my order or not?"

"Fine, I understand, Clane." Leonard sighed. "But you may want to let Moss know that James here is the man the emperor is looking for. Dragoneater and Chosen of Iarus. We found him in Epot Detharn while he was fleeing from Boane, along with two other Chosen."

Clane raised an eyebrow at James. A Dragoneater, and she killed one without being a Chosen. James struggled to think of a greeting, but she had taken a step toward him before he could say even a simple hello.

"The Pathlighter's Champion? This one?" Clane asked. She clasped her hands behind her back as if performing an inspection.

This was what Leonard had promised them, the foreign champion of a god that no longer existed. Would it be better to play along with the charade instead of blowing up the empire's expectations, potentially making him a public enemy? His first few interactions with Collisun natives had told him that they didn't take kindly to outsiders. If he was going to make a good impression, he would have to go along with the lie.

But he knew what happened when one went along with it, when one bought into what the Temple had sold. Gemmi, Igard, Samira, they were all victims. He wouldn't let that happen again.

"Iarus is dead, but I do have his gift," James said, trying not to look away from those merciless green eyes. He raised a bandaged hand and channeled his senses through his body. Mustering what little heat he could, James conjured a small flame in his hand that burned away the bandaging. It looked transparent and ghostly in the streaming sunlight. "I guess that makes me the Pathlighter now."

Several Aroch surgeons and soldiers gasped. Whispers floated around them. Clane's eyebrow raised even further, and her scar gave her the impression of smirking even though her mouth gave no indication of emotion.

James met her gaze, waiting for her to decry him a heretic.

"It's no concern of mine or of the Sapphire Aroch what beliefs you carry. If you plan to help Collisun, the emperor will accept your help," Clane said with a pragmatic tone. The commander turned to Leonard, who was still being fussed over by Theos and Rossel. "You've done what the emperor tasked you with, and he rewards greatly for services done in his name. You've expressed in the past that you desire your own Aroch."

Leonard nodded.

"I'll see that you get it," Clane said.

Several soldiers near them flinched toward their weapons as Joskine howled triumphantly.

"I guess that makes me your first volunteer, Len!" Joskine whooped. A few Aroch soldiers offered their hearty congratulations. Leonard must have been more popular in the empire than he and Ariel had let on. Clane strode forward and shook James's hand with a professionally firm grip.

"We will leave at first light tomorrow." She was an inch or so taller than he was but stood as if she had several more feet to her height, the seal of a Jackal stamped into her collar. "We could use your help with search and rescue of any civilians who were caught up in this. Greade is a major trade center, and this attack will cause problems all over the empire. I'll leave the bulk of my Aroch here and escort you back to Triridge."

"Thank you, Lady Clane," James said. "Ariel and Roy will want to assist with the search and rescue as well, I'm guessing. I will find them and bring them here."

Clane's eyes narrowed, "Roy?" She spun on her heels to Joskine and Leonard. "Iarus scorch you, you told me that you and Ariel had *killed* the Scaleslayer."

"I'm happy to say that Roy is incredibly difficult to kill." Leonard winced as another stitch was threaded through his gut.

Roy and Ariel stepped into the bustling makeshift infirmary camp, "I've always thought that you were just terrible at trying to kill me, Leonard," Roy said.

He and Ariel walked in tandem, clearly sporting wounds that needed attention. Blood clumping her gold hair, Ariel held a cloth to a wound in her side, and Roy looked to have a nasty cut near his collarbone and another across his abdomen.

Leonard smirked at Roy's jest, but Clane and her soldiers didn't find Roy's presence funny. James felt his senses spike upward as every soldier drew their blades, pointing them at Ariel and Roy. Heat was beginning to rise off of every living thing here, he could feel it, and soon that heat was going to boil over.

"You've allowed this beast to endanger my soldiers and every citizen of this city?" Clane said coldly. A hand went to the longsword at her side.

"Watch what you call him, Jackal," Ariel threatened.

Roy calmly placed a hand on her shoulder to signify it was all right. Ariel bit her lip.

Walking on shaky legs and holding his hands above him in surrender, he came to a stop in front of James and Clane. "James." Roy looked at his wounds. "The cackler?"

James held up his burned right arm. "Ashes."

"Well done. I owe you." Roy smiled, and James failed to contain a grin himself.

James never got to see Gemmi grown up, never saw the kind of man that Gemmi would have been. But if he had, James was confident that his older brother would have been like Roy. His friend did what he could to help the people who needed it. James realized that whether it was from the Elders or from the Temple, he wanted to do the same.

Clane's hand had not left her sword. "You know this man, the Scaleslayer?"

"He's saved my life a dozen times to get me here." James gestured to Roy. "This man is no slayer. He's a good man, and I would be dead without him. He also has crucial information about the enemy, so I suggest you listen to him."

"Out of the question," Clane said, prompting a deathly stare from Ariel. "He's terrorized the empire for years, killed hundreds. Even if he did help you get here, we can't let him come with us, and we can't let him walk away." She slid the longsword from her belt.

"Charodon, the one that possesses me, has killed many. And I can't argue that he has caused terrible pain for the empire, maybe to some of the people here. But I'm doing what I can to keep that from happening," Roy said. "All he craves is destruction; he has told me as much many times. I'm the best chance we have of keeping him contained until we can find a way to kill him." Roy glanced back at Ariel. "But I can't say it will be without risk."

"And there lies the problem," Clane countered, making a point of keeping her sword leveled at him. "I won't take whatever it is you claim to house in your body back to Triridge and potentially kill thousands."

James crossed his arms. "Roy comes with us, or we don't go. You can tell your emperor that the Pathlighter doesn't work alone." He could see the anger flash in the Jackal's eyes as she looked between Roy and him. He knew that this threatened to upend the goals of the empire, not to mention make Clane the one to blame.

Clane looked back at Leonard to see the same resolve and growled. "Fine, but he will stay at the back of the march, *and* he will not step foot in the Sovereign Base. We will arrange for lodging at the edge of the city, where members of the Sapphire Aroch will keep him under guard at all times. If and when his services are needed as a swordsman and a mercenary—and *only* those two things—I will send for him personally. Is that understood?"

Roy bowed. "Thank you, Clane."

The commander and her soldiers sheathed their weapons, and Roy walked back to where Ariel stood. Ariel looked extremely unhappy with the deal that was struck but said nothing. They walked forward into the camp to Leonard, his sutures now completely finished. Ariel hugged James as he greeted them. They were all hurt, but would make it.

Clane stalked away toward the rubble that used to be the Harbormaster's home. "Make sure that Ariel and the Scaleslayer receive proper attention to their wounds. We leave on the morrow."

***

The throbbing in Samira's left arm pained her almost as much as her decision to leave.

Samira sat at the stern of the *Storm Tower*, sailing eastward and trying to think of anything else as Greade Harbor and the Sapphire Aroch shrank in the distance. She hugged the officer's coat—her coat now—tighter around herself. It shielded her from the wind along the coast, but not from the loneliness that gripped her heart. They were stepping into what would eventually become war, but she knew that they were better off without her. All she had ever done was cause problems. That would not happen again. She would continue on as she should have done from the start: alone. It was faster to travel to Kostra by land, but she'd convinced Moron to sail her there. Less chance of running into the others that way.

No one she cared about would get hurt. The best way to make sure of that was to stay away from them, take herself off of the board. She would find a new life and would striking find a way by herself. Samira cast the memories of the other Chosen out of her head, no use to think about them, but Astus strike her there was one who lingered for too long. Badlai's hurt gaze haunted Samira's vision whenever she closed her eyes. Better to have let that one go than end up with another tragedy like Talia, Samira tried to convince herself.

Reflected sunlight from the waves shone into her eyes, but she didn't attempt to shield them. Her left arm was still twitching from her use of power at Greade. She had been aiming for the creature and luckily had hit it, but in her frantic state it was a foolish thing to do. It had definitely been a beginner's mistake to use her power before her arm had a chance to recover from her fight with Rhaiga, but the situation hadn't left her much choice.

"We'll be reaching Kostran waters within the next few days, Chosen." Captain Moron clomped up to where she sat. The man yawned and massaged his neck, perpetually exhausted.

Samira nodded and slid down from her perch to the deck. "I appreciate your assistance, Captain."

"If you don't mind me asking, Chosen, I heard that others like you were in the city. There any reason you didn't go with them?" he asked.

"I'd slow them down," Samira said. "Just the way it is. I should go to Thesera. I have business at the Watchtower."

"I doubt they'd turn down a Watcher and a Chosen. Rest up and then watch the skies for us, yeah? Folk at Greade said that a storm was due to come through."

Moron walked away, leaving Samira alone, as she should be, to stare back at the shrinking coastline, hoping that she would never see the other Chosen again.

Death and Memory

Violet blood dripped across the planks of the battered ship, spreading slowly from the heap of corpses in front of her. It coated Rhaiga's arms up to her emaciated elbows. Altujan—all of them, useless—cowered against the rail of the ship. This feeling...what was this feeling? Rhaiga had forgotten this, and she hadn't a clue what to do about it.

Her pet, her beautifully subservient Vaecus, was cinders. That Chosen, the descendant of Iarus, *he* had done this. Not to mention her champion had been bested by a couple of upstart godspawn. This task had been Rhaiga's to complete, her victory to collect, her path to walk. And the path had been cut off, paved over by the Chosen. Vayne would not be forgiving.

Rhaiga didn't even feel the next Altujan she killed. Her vision was clouded with this strange emotion. Spilling his innards on the deck, he dropped from her grasp, and she moved as if in a daze to the next one. Time was slowed by this feeling, and as her hand closed around the throat of the next one, she felt the odd sensation grow. This one, she felt. Her skin tingled at the sensation of ripping flesh and the sudden silence of the being she held. Vision, starting to clear, Rhaiga stopped and blinked all three eyes at once.

Fury. It was the deepening of something in her chest. Locked away, danger-ous. Twelve-hundred years of nothing but sand, and she had become a husk, dormant. Her eyes burned with the emotion and shook. *Yes,* she thought. *This is fury, and killing makes it better.*

She came out of her revelation to see the Altujan scattering like sand before the wind. Extending an arm, she snatched one as it fled. Not even a full moment passed, and the soldier fell apart in Rhaiga's hands. A grotesque smack as the corpse hit the deck sent the rest of the soldiers into a frenzy. Mastreh slumped against the rail on the other side of the ship, using a cold sneer to mask her horror. Rhaiga ignored her champion. Mastreh would be dealt with. But first...

Several more Altujan were deconstructed at Rhaiga's spindly hands, screams silenced. The deck had been lacquered in glossy, thick blood. Each kill fed her rage, attempted to sate it, and failed. The deepening pit in her chest couldn't be filled, no matter how many of these bags of blood she took apart. They were no longer soldiers, Altujan, male or female. Nothing but clay to be pulled asunder. That Chosen in the field had been right. She *needed this.*

As soon as it began, the killing spree ended. Violet splattered the deck, the railings, even the *sails.* Now sated, the pit in Rhaiga's chest leisurely closed, and a feeling of calm put out the smelting remains of her rage, clearing her head for now.

A setback and nothing more. It was no concern of hers whether the harbor had been won. The seeds of what Vayne had ordered were planted, however small, and that was enough. Destroyed by the battle and seeing over half its population flee to Triridge, the port would be hobbled, sending the empire into disarray just long enough for their next move. Not what Vayne had hoped for, but it was good enough. He would just have to accept that. The Eye of Disease's expectations were getting on her nerves.

Her purpling knuckles popped as she flexed her hands and looked over the deck. A steaming stew of Altujan remains slipped back and forth with the swell of the waves.

"Thank you for your insight," she mused at her gruesome work. "You do seem to have talked some sense into me." Salt water sprayed over the deck and mixed with the blood, creating a transparent swirl.

Rhaiga stepped calmly through the roiling gore toward her subordinate. "I created you to end the Chosen."

"I apologize, my Eye." Mastreh bowed slightly, eyes widened in shock.

"I know, but as Vayne once said, that isn't what I want to hear coming out of your mouth." Rhaiga crouched in front of Mastreh, her joints crackling and skin stretching over her bones. "I thought you could be of use to me, but all that time in the Dunes must have withered my senses. I could give you the death that was withheld, but unfortunately for you I'm not feeling merciful. You'll simply have to wait until you deteriorate into nothing." Rhaiga tilted her head to gauge the Altujan's reaction, and she wasn't disappointed.

Mastreh's eyes had grown pale and distant, staring ahead like a corpse. The weight of what Rhaiga had turned her into had finally sunk in.

"My Eye—" Mastreh started.

Rhaiga snapped her head upright. "You are relieved from service, Mastreh. It appears that I can't use you, and neither can your people. A functioning tool would have done as I asked, but it appears that your functionality no longer fits the task at hand. You have exactly one minute to leave my sight." The Eye of Death stood and turned away.

Mastreh looked around shakily. The Altujan—if she could even be called that anymore—couldn't seem to find a rowboat, as they had all been torched by the humans. Mastreh's voice started the void in Rhaiga's chest again. The Eye of Death slowly turned and placed a hand on Mastreh's head, her hand covering all of her champion's face.

Mastreh whimpered, "My duty is to my people. To *you*."

"I. Said. *Go*." Rhaiga shoved the wretch overboard and watched with disinterest as the waves swallowed her. She would not drown; Rhaiga knew that much. Maybe Vayne could have made her useful, or perhaps the Altujan was always a crude utensil, not made of strong enough material. No matter, Mastreh would now wander the depths, likely forever. The thought closed the pit in Rhaiga's chest just a little.

The ship lagged behind the few vessels that still remained in the fleet. Even though the battle had not technically been a rout, her soldiers had still suffered heavy losses. Partly because of these new Chosen and also due to Charodon's inability to break his host. In all the time she had known him, the Eye of Nature had never failed to break the mind of a host.

These were strange times indeed.

It was back to the Tarsals now, per Vayne's instruction, but the pit in her chest widened a bit—it was a constant back and forth now—as she thought of the battle. Here she was going into what felt like exile all over again, all on Vayne's orders. Always on his orders. She pushed the thoughts away as a familiar pull at the base of her skull started pulsing, a different rhythm than the waves. Dhorh was calling.

Sitting down to avoid disorientation even though she had felt this thousands of times, Rhaiga crossed her legs and let her eyes close one at a time. When she opened them again, Vayne and Dhorh stood before her. This place seemed vaguely familiar to her. A large black obelisk of smoothed stone towered behind them, and the sun was crisp against the short grass—browning as the season came to a close. Dhorh was still inhabiting the child from before, but the Eye of Disease had taken the body of a younger man. This man was covered in glyphs, much like the Chosen who Rhaiga had seen at the harbor. A balding head of gold hair and a stern face protruded from the exterior, but she could still see the ambitious eyes of her fellow Elder underneath.

"Rhaiga," Vayne said in a deep voice that felt alien after centuries of the old man, "is it true that the harbor still stands?" Different host, but the same Vayne she knew. Calm and always to the point. It had always given her a sense of *something*. Perhaps unease.

"We accomplished what we set out to do." She shrugged. "The humans know that there is a threat. They'll be in a panic."

Vayne eyed her with an expression she couldn't place. "You failed to take the city. Where is the foothold you were sent to chisel into the empire's foundation for us? We have no leverage!"

Rhaiga felt the pit in her chest grow slightly. "We don't need the harbor," she scoffed. "The damage is done. All the humans need to know is that a profound and costly game is underway, but they won't know its scale or the players."

She saw Vayne's jaw set, sensed that he knew she was right.

"What did you do with this Champion of yours?" Dhorh said. "Did you toss away another broken tool?" He yawned and stretched his arms outward, seeming as if he were screaming at the sky in silence. The youthful and immature face really did match his personality, Rhaiga found. Twelve-hundred years in a desert with *that* had not been pleasant. But then again, she had been mentally locked away, as if she had intentionally blurred the years together.

Rhaiga frowned, puzzled by the thought. She *had* forgotten. Millennia stretched out in her mind where she could remember specific moments, whole epochs, but her time in the Dunes and leading up to it was foggy. Her anger spiked.

Vayne didn't seem to notice her musings. "We all use our power how we see fit."

Dhorh crossed his arms. "I'm not interested in sharing memories with another."

Vayne plucked a blade of grass from the still, windless glade they sat in and studied it. "You must gather the rest of the Altujan from the Tarsals, Rhaiga. Those who were not yet ready to sail for Greade will be ready when you return. Dhorh and I, as the spider, will poison the beast. But you, you are the predator that will drag the slowed animal to its death." The broad face of his new host glistened with sweat in the sunlight. "And then the pelt, the ruins of their empire, will be ours to mold and sew as we please."

***

Dhorh severed the connection from Rhaiga and Vayne, feeling more confident than he had in a while. Despite Samira's hostility, he had actually gotten some useful insight. The Eye of Memory knew that Vayne wouldn't return for another few hours. In a way, Dhorh felt jealous that Vayne had just *happened* upon a host with influence. Meanwhile, *he* had to play the part of a sick little boy while the Eye of Disease got direct access to the Spiathi king.

Doing what he normally did when he got bored, Dhorh sifted through memories. Some had been recently unthreaded and were fresh. Others were filmy or from someone with a slipping mind. While being able to see whatever someone else had seen, the memory was theirs first before it had become his. Some of his favorites were from creatures he didn't even remember unthreading.

A woman handing her daughter a cheaply made doll. Several men scooping up mud to construct a hut. A bird soaring over a wildfire. The sight of an imperator disinterestedly cruising by a fish less than a quarter of its size. A view of Triridge from the top of one of the peaks. A town excitedly rushing into the river to bathe.

They bled in and out of his vision as he let the outside world pass by. Calm. These memories reinforced his interpretation of what Samira had said. "*A dream is worth giving up when it hurts the ones you care about.*"

He loved these memories. Treasured them even. They were what he craved, and yet he already had them. Nothing would destroy them or take them away from him, except annihilation. And annihilation was coming. Vayne had seen this. Unless the Elders did something, they would die, would cease to be, just like the others, and the memories would disappear with them. He would do anything that Vayne asked him to if it would stop that, no matter how much it annoyed him.

A thin voice floated to him through the haze of dreams, "You're looking better today, boy." Dhorh opened his eyes to see a Spiathi apothecary wearing a cloth over her face. Her blue eyes sported a growing number of wrinkles at the edges. However, Dhorh found it odd that she would cover her face but not cover her arms. Some memories had recalled Spiathi as humans of strange dress, so he shrugged it off. The woman gestured for him to approach her. "Let's have a look at you, son."

He made a show of waddling over to her on small, lacerated feet. Vayne had told him to stay here and make it seem like he was getting worse. He wasn't sure if he actually *was* getting worse. His host body could catch a sickness, but illnesses had no effect that they could tell on Elders' true souls. He held out an arm to the Spiathi woman, and she placed a tiny, smooth leaf in his hand. Dhorh knew that he was meant to chew it, and he had never bothered to learn why.

She shook her head as she used a thin wooden tool to prod at his cuts, as they had spread to his arms and stomach. "Have you been chewing the medicine I give you?"

Dhorh nodded and popped the leaf in his mouth to avoid her questions. The flap of the tent opened to reveal Vayne—or at least his host's body. It was going to be a while before Dhorh got used to a form other than the old man. Vayne also wore a cloth over his face. It seemed to be protocol for the Spiathi. No doubt the Mangler had been doing what Vayne had created it to do, infecting scores already.

"No change then?" Vayne asked the apothecary.

"Worse," she shook her head. "I think it's spreading." Dhorh pretended to play with some of the wooden toys in the tent that had been left by a village member. One of them looked surprisingly like the doll from his memories.

"Thank you for checking on the boy. I feel responsible for him since I found him at such a horrible time." Vayne's sad tone was much more believable with the deep, mournful voice that he now used. "Can I please have a moment?" The woman packed her kit and slipped through the tent into the crisp day.

Dhorh set the toys down. "You don't seem to value how much patience I have to muster up to sit in this tent all day. What, are your new eyes proving as a distraction? Going to take up birdwatching?" Alone, he could drop all pretense and speak freely. No doubt the woman would have been taken aback by a child speaking in such a way.

"You'll wait in this tent until I tell you otherwise," Vayne said, swatting away Dhorh's attempt at banter. "We found my new host at a fantastic time, but the time is fleeting. I can feel the body burning away faster since I took it by force. I have to use it while I have it. *You*, on the other hand, don't have to do anything other than sit and play with your memories and your..." He eyed the wooden toys. "...playthings. We will be moving on soon."

Dhorh snorted and paced back and forth across the tent. He wanted to go out into the world and unthread, gain new memories. That couldn't happen if he was cooped up in here.

Vayne sensed that Dhorh wasn't paying attention. "You'll get what you want soon enough. In the meantime, I want you to pay visits to the Chosen. Each of them if you can."

"I can't visit all of their heads." Dhorh still paced. "Not the one Charodon lives in."

"He doesn't matter. Charodon will kill him sooner or later. Even if he is a Chosen, he can't withstand that beast."

Dhorh stopped. "Yes, but don't you think that poses a threat? Chosen and Elders bonding? What about—"

Vayne cut him off before he could say *last time*. "That's never happened before. And it appears there is no discernible difference."

Dhorh cocked his head at the Eye of Disease.

Vayne rolled his new eyes and left the tent. "Stay here until I say."

A feeling of strange numbness ran through Dhorh as he sat down. Didn't Vayne remember? It wasn't something that Dhorh mentioned because he knew that Yazdra and the others had been a subject that brought out Vayne's rare furious outbursts. But did Vayne not *remember*? Panicked breaths rushed in and out of his mouth as Dhorh realized he must have unthreaded Vayne, but why? Rushing, thrashing through the sea of memories that swelled within him, Dhorh searched for the memories but found nothing. He searched for memories of Yazdra and found only a single image.

"No one can remember, Dhorh," the girl's voice whispered in the aether.

Yazdra's true face, that of a slight female figure with light-gray skin, was frozen in front of him. Stars swirled in her features as if they were freckles on a human, and her pitch black hair spilled over her shoulder. But those eyes, starry eyes of every conceivable color, stared at him with a look of urgency.

"No one. Not even you."

He collapsed to the soft ground, falling and scraping an arm on the toys beside him. The quiet, smothering sounds of the Spiathi wild rushed back to him, and he stared at the canvas ceiling of the tent. Elders didn't breathe, didn't need to, but he still felt as though he were choking. Dhorh didn't know why or how...

But for some reason, he had unthreaded himself.

He couldn't remember anything from that time leading up to their banishment. In fact, banishment in the Dunes was a blur, just a rough slog of sorrow and losing himself in stolen memories. What happened that made him do this? He didn't even know it was *possible* to unthread himself. *What had he done?*

"Are you all right?" The apothecary's panicked voice snapped him into focus. His vision blurred before finally locking on the woman's crinkly eyes squinting at him with worry. Dhorh realized that actual tears had been wriggling free from his host eyes.

"I fell down," he lied.

Picking him up and scrutinizing his arm, she quickly took a ceramic jar and swiped a finger through it, picking up a milky paste on the tip of her finger. He said nothing while she spread the paste across the angry but shallow scrape along his elbow. "What happened?" she asked.

Dhorh clenched his fingers together into fists. He couldn't look at his hands, so he closed his eyes and continued trembling. "I don't know."

The End

To Be Continued

Rob Leigh is a native of central Iowa, and spent many of his early years in the summer reading program for his local library. Pivotal works of literature such as *The Odyssey, Percy Jackson & The Olympians,* and *Lord of the Rings* influenced his love of myths and adventure stories. The idea for *Pathlighter* started at that time and grew until the COVID-19 pandemic finally allowed the time to complete the story and spawn the idea for sequel novels. Rob now lives in Omaha, Nebraska and is planning outlines for the next installment of the *Pathlighter* series.